Mo Hayder has written some of the most terrifying crime thrillers you will ever read. Her first novel, *Birdman*, was hailed as a 'first-class shocker' by the *Guardian* and her follow-up, *The Treatment*, was voted by *The Times* one of 'the top ten most scary thrillers ever written'.

Mo's books are 100 per cent authentic, drawing on her long research association with several UK police forces and on her personal encounters with criminals and prostitutes. She left school at fifteen and has worked as a barmaid, security guard, English teacher, and even a hostess in a Tokyo club. She has an MA in film making from the American University in Washington DC and an MA in creative writing from Bath Spa University. She now lives in England's West Country and is a full-time writer.

www.**rbooks**.co.uk

Also by Mo Hayder

Birdman
The Treatment
Tokyo
Pig Island
Ritual
Skin

For more information on Mo Hayder and her books, see her
website at www.mohayder.net

GONE

MO HAYDER

BANTAM PRESS

LONDON • TORONTO • SYDNEY • AUCKLAND • JOHANNESBURG

TRANSWORLD PUBLISHERS
61–63 Uxbridge Road, London W5 5SA
A Random House Group Company
www.rbooks.co.uk

First published in Great Britain
in 2010 by Bantam Press
an imprint of Transworld Publishers

A CIP catalogue record for this book
is available from the British Library.

ISBNs 9780593063811 (cased)
9780593063828 (tpb)

Addresses for Random House Group Ltd companies outside the UK
can be found at: www.randomhouse.co.uk
The Random House Group Ltd Reg. No. 954009

The Random House Group Limited supports the Forest Stewardship
Council (FSC), the leading international forest-certification organization. All our
titles that are printed on Greenpeace-approved FSC-certified paper carry the FSC logo.
Our paper procurement policy can be found at
www.rbooks.co.uk/environment

Typeset in 11/14.5pt Sabon by
Falcon Oast Graphic Art Ltd.
Printed and bound in Great Britain by
CPI Mackays, Chatham, ME5 8TD

2 4 6 8 10 9 7 5 3 1

Mixed Sources
Product group from well-managed
forests and other controlled sources
www.fsc.org Cert no. TT-COC-2139
© 1996 Forest Stewardship Council
FSC

1

Detective Inspector Jack Caffery of Bristol's Major Crime Investigation Unit spent ten minutes in the centre of Frome looking at the crime scene. He walked past the road blocks, the flashing blue lights, the police tape, the onlookers gathered in huddles with their Saturday-afternoon shopping bags peering to catch a glimpse of the forensics guys with their brushes and bags, and stood for a long time where the whole thing had happened, among the oil leaks and abandoned shopping trolleys of the underground car park, trying to soak up the place and decide how anxious he should be. Then, already cold in spite of his overcoat, he went upstairs to the manager's tiny office where the local officers and the forensics guys were watching CCTV footage on a small colour monitor.

They stood in a semicircle, holding cups of machine coffee, some of them still in their Tyvek suits with the hoods down. Everyone glanced up as Caffery entered, but he shook his head, opened his hands to show he had no news, and they turned back to the TV, their expressions closed and serious.

The picture had the typical graininess of a low-end CCTV system, the camera trained on the entrance ramp of the car park. The opaque timecode graduated from black to white and back again. The screen showed cars ranked in painted bays, winter sunlight coming through the entrance ramp beyond them, bright as a floodlight. At the back of one of the vehicles – a Toyota Yaris – a woman stood with her back to the camera, loading groceries from a trolley. Jack Caffery was an inspector with eighteen years of the hardest policing in his pocket – Murder Squad, in some of the country's toughest inner-city forces. Even so, he couldn't fight the cold pinch of dread the image gave him, knowing what was going to happen next on the film.

From the statements taken by the local officers he knew a lot already: the woman's name was Rose Bradley. She was the wife of a C of E minister and she was in her late forties, though on screen she looked older. She was dressed in a short dark jacket made of something heavy – chenille maybe – with a calf-length tweed skirt and low pumps. Her hair was short and neat. She was the type who would be sensible enough to carry an umbrella or tie a scarf around her head if it was raining, but it was a clear, cold day and her head was bare. Rose had spent the afternoon browsing the clothes boutiques in the centre of Frome, and had finished the excursion with the family's weekly food shop in Somerfield. Before she'd begun loading the bags, she'd put her keys and the ticket to the car park on the front seat of the Yaris.

The sunlight behind her flickered and she lifted her head to see a man running fast down the ramp. He was tall and broad, in jeans and a Puffa jacket. Over his head he wore a rubber mask. A Santa Claus mask. To Caffery that was the creepiest part of it – the rubber mask bobbing along as the man raced towards Rose. The grin didn't change or fade as he got close to her.

'He said three words.' The local inspector – a tall, austere guy in uniform who must also have been standing outside in the cold, judging by his red nostrils – nodded at the monitor. 'Just here – as he comes up to her. He says, "Get down, bitch." She didn't recognize the voice and she's not sure if he had an accent or not because he was shouting.'

The man grabbed Rose's arm, cartwheeling her away from the car. Her right arm flew up, a piece of jewellery snapped and beads scattered, catching the light. Her hip slammed into the boot of the neighbouring car, catapulting her upper torso sideways over it, as if she was made of rubber. Her hair flew up from the scalp, her elbow made contact with the roof and she rebounded, whip-like, falling away from the car and landing on her knees. By now the man in the mask was in the driver's seat of the Yaris. Rose saw what he was doing and scrambled to her feet. She got to the car window and was tugging frantically at the door as the guy got the keys into the ignition. The car gave a small jolt as the handbrake came off, and shot backwards with a jerk. Rose staggered along next to it, half falling, half dragged, then the car braked abruptly, changed gear and skidded forwards. The movement loosened her grip and she fell away clumsily, rolling once, legs and arms in an ungainly crabbed position until she came to a halt. She recovered herself and raised her head just in time to see the car speed towards the exit.

'What next?' said Caffery.

'Not much. We pick him up on another camera.' The inspector aimed the remote control at the DVR box and shuffled through the different camera inputs. 'Here – leaving the car park. He uses her ticket to get out. But the picture's not so good on this feed.'

The screen showed the Yaris from behind. The brake lights came on as it slowed at the barrier. The driver's window opened and the man's hand came out, put the ticket into the slot. There was a pause and the barrier opened. The brake lights went off and the Yaris pulled away.

'No prints on the barrier,' said the inspector. 'He's wearing gloves. See them?'

'Freeze it there,' Caffery said.

The inspector paused the picture. Caffery bent closer to the screen, turning his head sideways to study the back window above the lit-up numberplate. When the case had been called in to MCIU, the unit superintendent, an unforgiving bastard who would screw an old woman to the floor if she had information that would improve his clear-up rates, told Caffery the first thing to check was whether or not the report was genuine. Caffery searched the shadows and reflective parts of the back windscreen. He could see something on the seat. Something pale and blurry.

'Is that her?'

'Yes.'

'You sure?'

The inspector turned and gave him a long look, as if he thought he was being tested. 'Yes,' he said slowly. 'Why?'

Caffery didn't answer. He wasn't going to say out loud that the superintendent was worried about all the dickheads out there who'd been known, in the past, to invent a child on the back seat when their car had been jacked, thinking they'd get a higher alert attached to the police hunt for the vehicle. These things happened. But it didn't look as if that was what Rose Bradley was up to.

'Let me see her. Earlier.'

The inspector aimed the remote control at the TV and flipped through the menu to the previous clip, to a point ninety seconds before the attack on Rose. The car park was empty. Just the sunlight in the entrance and the cars. As the time code flicked round to 4:31 the doors to the supermarket opened and Rose Bradley emerged, pushing the trolley. At her side came a small girl in a brown duffel coat. Pale, with blonde hair cut in a fringe, she wore pastel-coloured Mary Jane shoes, pink tights, and walked with her hands in her pockets. Rose unlocked the Yaris and the little girl opened the back door and crawled inside. Rose closed the door on her, put the keys and her car-park ticket on the front seat and went to the boot.

'OK. You can stop it there.'

The inspector clicked off the TV and straightened. 'Major Crime's here. Whose case does that make it? Yours? Mine?'

'No one's.' Caffery pulled his keys out of his pocket. 'Because it's never going to get that far.'

The inspector raised an eyebrow. 'Says who?'

'Says the statistics. He's made a mistake – didn't know she was in the car. He'll dump her first chance he has. He's probably already dropped her and the phone call's just working its way through the system.'

'It's been almost three hours.'

Caffery held his eyes. The inspector was right – those three hours were outside what the statistics said, and he disliked that.

But he'd been in the job long enough to expect the wide balls that came from time to time. The sudden swerves, the mould breakers. Yes, the three hours felt wrong, but there was probably a good reason. The guy might be trying to get a good distance. Find somewhere he was sure he wouldn't be seen to dump her.

'She'll be back. You have my word.'

'Really?'

'Really.'

Caffery buttoned his coat as he left the room, pulled his car keys out of his pocket. He'd been due to knock off work in half an hour. There were a couple of things he'd been considering doing with his evening – a Police Social Club pub quiz at the Staple Hill bar, a meat raffle at the Coach and Horses near the offices, or a night at home on his own. Dismal choices. But not as dismal as what he had to do now. What he had to do now was go and speak to the Bradley family. Find out if, apart from the statistical blip, there was any other reason their younger daughter, Martha, wasn't back yet.

2

It was six thirty when he arrived at the estate just outside the little Mendip village of Oakhill. It was a smartish executive development that must have been built about twenty years ago, with a wide no-through road and large laurel- and yew-bordered grounds sloping away down the side of the hill. The house wasn't what he would have expected of a vicarage. He'd imagined a detached place with wisteria and a garden and 'The Vicarage' carved into stone gate newels. Instead it was semi-detached, with a tar-and-chip driveway, *faux* chimneys and uPVC windows. He parked outside and switched off the car engine. This was the part of the job that froze him – facing the victims. For a moment he considered not walking up the front path. Not knocking on the door. He considered turning round and getting out of there.

The FLO, the family liaison officer assigned to the Bradley family, opened the door. She was a tall woman in her thirties with shining black hair cut in a bob and perhaps was self-conscious of her height: she wore flat shoes under the wide-legged trousers and stood with a permanent stoop as if the ceiling was too low.

'I've told them what unit you're from.' She stepped back to let him into the hallway. 'I didn't want to scare them but they had to know we're taking it seriously. And I've told them you haven't got any news. That you just want to ask some more questions.'

'How're they doing?'

'How do you think?'

He shrugged. 'Fair enough. Stupid question.'

She closed the door, then gave Caffery a long, appraising look. 'I've heard of you. I know about you.'

It was warm inside so Caffery took off his coat. He didn't ask the FLO what she knew about him, if it was good or bad. He was used to wariness from a certain type of woman. Somehow he'd dragged a reputation with him from his old position in London all the way out here to the West Country. It was part of what was keeping him lonely. Part of what was making him plan futile things with his evenings, like meat raffles and police pub quizzes.

'Where are they?'

'In the kitchen.' She kicked a draft excluder against the bottom of the door. It was cold outside. Freezing. 'But come through this way. I want to show you the photos first.'

The FLO took him into a side room where the curtains were half drawn. The furniture was good quality but shabby: a dark-wood upright piano pushed against one wall, a TV set in a marquetry cabinet, two battered sofas covered in what might pass for two old Navajo-weave blankets stitched together. Everything – the carpets, the walls, the furniture – was scruffy with years of kids and animals. On one of the sofas lay two dogs – a black and white collie and a spaniel. Both lifted their heads and watched Caffery. More scrutiny. More wanting to know what the hell he was going to do.

He stopped at a low table where twenty or so photos had been spread out. Torn out of an album – in the family's haste they'd pulled the sticky corners off the pages. Martha was small and pale with fine white hair cut in a fringe. A pair of glasses – the type that'd get a kid teased. In investigative circles conventional wisdom said one of the most important skills in finding a missing child was choosing the right photo to release to the public. It had to be representative for identification's sake, but it had to make the child appealing. He used his finger to move the pictures around. There were school shots, holiday shots, birthday-party shots. He stopped at one. Martha wore a melon-pink T-shirt, her hair tied in two plaits at either side of her face. Behind her the sky was blue and the distant hills were puffy with summer trees. From the view it must have been taken outside in the gardens of the estate. He turned it for the FLO to see. 'Is this the one you chose?'

She nodded. 'I emailed it to the press office. Is it the right one?'

'It's the one I'd have chosen.'

'Do you want to meet them now?'

He sighed. Eyed the door she was pointing to. He hated what he had to do now. For him it was like standing at the door to a lion's den. He just never knew with the victims how to get the right balance between the professional and the sympathetic. 'Come on, then. Let's get it over with.'

He walked into the kitchen, where the three members of the Bradley family immediately stopped what they were doing and lifted their faces to him expectantly. 'No news.' He held up his hands. 'I haven't got any news.'

They let out a collective breath, sank back into their miserable, stooped postures. He ticked them off in his head against the information the Frome police station had given him: that was the Reverend Jonathan Bradley over at the sink, mid-fifties, tall with dark blond hair growing thick and wavy from a high forehead and a wide, straight nose that would look as confident above a dog collar as it did above the grape-coloured sweatshirt and jeans he was wearing now. The word *Iona* was embroidered under a harp on the breast of the sweatshirt.

The Bradleys' elder daughter, Philippa, sat at the table. She was straight out of the rebellious-teen box with a ring in her nose and dyed black hair. In the real world she should be slouched on the sofa at the back of the room, one leg over the arm, finger in her mouth, staring blankly at the TV set. But she wasn't. She was sitting with her hands shoved between her knees, her shoulders hunched, a sick, terrified look on her face.

Then there was Rose, also sitting at the table. When she'd left the house this morning she must have looked like someone on their way to a church-council meeting with pearls and styled hair. But a face could change irrevocably in just a matter of hours, he knew from experience, and now Rose Bradley seemed halfway to the mad box in her shapeless cardigan and polyester dress. Her thinning blonde hair was smeared and plastered to her skull, there were inflamed bulges under her eyes and a hospital dressing on the side of her face. She was medicated too. He could see that from the unnatural droop to her mouth. Shame. He'd have liked her sharp.

'We're glad you're here.' Jonathan Bradley attempted a smile. He came forward and touched Caffery's arm. 'Sit down. I'll pour you tea – there's a pot ready.'

The kitchen was worn out and faded like the rest of the house, but it was warm. On the windowsill above the sink birthday cards had been lined up. A small shelf near the door was loaded with presents. A cake sat on a wire tray waiting to be iced. In the centre of the table there were three mobile phones – as if each member of the family had lined them up, expecting one to ring at any moment with news. Caffery noted the things, the places Martha seemed to be reaching into the room, but he didn't let the family see him focusing on them. He chose a chair opposite Rose, sat down and gave her a brief smile. She twitched her mouth back at him. Just for a moment. Her cheeks were spattered with broken veins from crying and her eyes were slack, the red rims sappy and loose against the whites – the way the eyes of head-injury victims sometimes went. He'd have to make a note to check with the FLO where the tranquillizers were coming from. Check there was a GP somewhere in the wings and Rose wasn't just raiding the emergency medicine cabinet.

'It's her birthday tomorrow,' she whispered. 'Are you going to get her back for her birthday?'

'Mrs Bradley,' he said, 'I want to explain why I'm here and I want to do it without alarming you. My firm belief is that from the moment the man who took your car realized his mistake – that Martha was in the back – he's been making plans to release her. Remember, he's scared too. He wanted the car, not a kidnap on top of a jacking charge. It happens in every case like this. I've got literature on it back at the office. I was reading it before I came over and I can get copies of it, if you'd like. On the other hand—'

'Yes? On the other hand?'

'My unit has to treat it as a kidnap because that's the responsible thing to do. It's completely normal, and it doesn't mean we're alarmed.' He could feel the FLO watching him as he spoke. He knew the FLOs attached red flags to some words when dealing with families affected by violent crime so he trod lightly on the word 'kidnap', said it in the light, barely there voice his parents' generation would have reserved for the word 'cancer'. 'We've got every ANPR team on alert. Those are the automatic numberplate recognition units – cameras watching all the major roads for your car. If he hits any of the major routes in the area we're going to pick him up. We've drafted in extra teams to do questioning. There's been a press release to the media so we're virtually guaranteed local and probably national coverage. In fact if you switch on the TV now you'll probably see it on the news bulletins. I've got someone from our technical department coming over. He's going to need access to your phones.'

'In case someone calls?' Rose looked at him desperately. 'Is that what you mean – that someone might call us? You're making it sound like you really think she's been kidnapped.'

'Please, Mrs Bradley, I meant what I said. This is all completely routine. Completely. Don't think there's anything sinister or that we have any theories yet because we really haven't. I don't believe for a minute the investigation is going to stay on the Major Crime Unit's books, because I think Martha will be back safe and sound for her birthday tomorrow. Still, I need to ask you some questions.' He fished a little MP3 recorder out from his inside pocket and placed it on the table next to the phones. The red light blinked. 'You're being recorded now. Just like you were earlier. Is that OK?'

'Yes. It's . . .' She trailed off. There was a pause, then she gave Caffery a flittering, apologetic smile, as if she'd already forgotten not only who he was but also why they were there, sitting around the table. 'I mean – yes. It's fine.'

Jonathan Bradley put a mug of tea in front of Caffery and sat down next to Rose. 'We've been talking, thinking, about why we haven't heard anything.'

14

'It's very early days.'

'But we've got a theory,' said Rose. 'Martha was kneeling up on the back seat when it happened.'

Jonathan nodded. 'We've lost count of the number of times we've told her not to but she always does it. The moment she gets into the car she leans over into the front seat and fiddles with the radio. Tries to tune it to something she likes. We're wondering if maybe when he took off in the car he was going so fast that she was thrown back – down into the footwell, maybe banged her head. Maybe he doesn't even know she's there – she could be unconscious, could be lying there, and he could still be driving. He could have abandoned the car already and she could be in there, still unconscious.'

'There's a full tank. I filled it up on my way into Bath. So, you see, he could be a long way away. An awfully long way.'

'I can't listen to this.' Philippa pushed her chair back, went to the sofa and began rummaging in the pockets of a denim jacket. 'Mum, Dad.' She pulled out a packet of Benson & Hedges, shook it at her parents. 'I know this isn't the time or the place, but I smoke. Have done for months. I'm sorry.'

Rose and Jonathan watched her go to the back door. Neither spoke as she threw it open and fumbled with a cigarette lighter. Her breath was white in the cold night air, and beyond her, clouds shattered and fragmented across the stars. Distant lights twinkled in the far valley. It was too cold for November, Caffery thought. Much too cold. He felt the frozen enormity of that countryside. The weight of a thousand lanes where Martha could have been abandoned. A Yaris was a smallish car with a relatively big petrol tank and a long range – maybe as much as five hundred miles – but Caffery didn't think the jacker would just have driven in one direction. He was local – he'd known exactly where the street CCTV cameras had been. He'd be too nervous to leave his patch. He'd still be somewhere quite close by, somewhere he knew. He was probably trying to find a place secluded enough to let her go. Caffery was sure that was what had happened, but the elapsed time was still knocking silently inside him. Three and a half hours. Nearly four now. He stirred his tea. Looked at the spoon rather than let the family see his eyes straying to the clock on the wall.

'So, Mr Bradley,' he said, 'I'm told you're the parish priest?'

'Yes. I used to be a headmaster but I was ordained three years ago.'

'You seem like a happy family.'

'We are.'

'You live within your means? If it's not a rude question.'

Jonathan gave a small, bleak smile. 'We do. Very well within our means, thank you. We have no debts. I'm not a secret gambler or a drug addict. And we haven't upset anyone. Is that your next question?'

'Dad,' Philippa muttered. 'Don't be such a rude shit.'

He didn't acknowledge his daughter. 'If that's what you're edging towards, Mr Caffery, I can promise you it's the wrong path. There's no reason for anyone to want to take her away from us. No reason at all. We're just not that sort of family.'

'I understand your frustration. I'm only wanting to get a clearer picture.'

'There is no picture. There is *no* picture. My daughter has been taken and we're waiting for you to do something about it—' He broke off as if he'd suddenly realized he was shouting. He sat back, breathing hard, his face a livid red. 'I'm sorry.' He pushed a hand through his hair. He looked tired. Beaten. 'I'm sorry – really sorry. I didn't mean to take it out on you. It's just you can't possibly imagine what this feels like.'

A few years ago, when he was young and hot-headed, a comment like that would have infuriated Caffery – this assumption that he couldn't know what it felt like – but with the benefit of age he could keep himself calm. Jonathan Bradley didn't know what he was saying, had no idea – how could he? – so Caffery put his hands on the table. Flat. To show how unruffled he was. How in control. 'Look, Mr Bradley, Mrs Bradley. No one can be a hundred per cent sure, and I can't predict the future, but I am prepared to go out on a limb and say I've got a feeling – a very strong feeling – there's going to be a happy ending to this.'

'Good God.' A tear ran down Rose's face. 'Do you mean that? Do you really mean that?'

'I really mean that. In fact . . .' He smiled reassuringly – and then said one of the stupidest things he'd uttered in his life. 'In fact I'm looking forward to the photo of Martha blowing out her candles. I'm hoping you'll be sending me a copy for my wall.'

3

The cement works in the Mendip Hills hadn't been used for sixteen years and the owners had installed a security gate to stop people coming in and joyriding round the flooded quarry. Flea Marley left her car about a hundred yards from the gates on the edge of the track among some gorse. She broke off a couple of branches from a nearby tree and placed them so that the car would be hidden from the main road. No one ever came down here but it didn't hurt to be cautious.

It had been cold all day. Grey clouds off the Atlantic blanketed the sky. It was windy too, so Flea wore a cagoule and a beanie. The chalk bag and the bundle of climber's cams, the knee and elbow pads were in the rucksack on her back. Her Boreal 'sticky' boots at a glance could look like hiking boots. If she encountered anyone she was a walker, strayed off the footpath.

She squeezed herself through a gap in the perimeter fence and went down the track. The weather was getting worse. By the time she got to the water's edge a squall had come up. Under the white cloud canopy, smaller, darker clouds stuttered along in regular squadrons: fast as flocks of birds. No one would be out on a day like this. She kept her head down anyway and walked fast.

The rock face was on the far side, out of sight of the quarry. She paused at the bottom and gave a last glance over her shoulder to check she was alone and ducked behind the rock. She found the place she wanted, dropped her rucksack and pulled out the few things she wanted. The key was speed and determination. Don't think, just do. Get it over with.

She rammed the first cam into the limestone. Her father, long dead now, had been an all-round adventurer. A *Boy's Own* hero – a diver, a caver, a climber. The adventure thing had rubbed off on her, but the climbing part had never come second nature. She wasn't like one of the climbing dudes who could do pull-ups on two fingers. This limestone was supposed to be easy to climb, with its vertical and horizontal cracks, but she found it a bastard – always got her hands in the wrong places – and now the crevices were full of the congealed chalk she'd used in the past. As she climbed she paused every few feet to rake the handfuls of white muck out of the fissures. Leaving tracks didn't work. Ever.

Flea was small, but she was as strong as a monkey. When you lived a life where you never knew what was coming round the corner at you, it paid to keep yourself hard so she worked out every day. At least two hours. Jogged, lifted weights. She was at her peak. In spite of her lousy climbing technique, the scramble up the rock took less than ten minutes. She wasn't even breathing hard when she reached the top.

This high up the wind howled around and flattened the cagoule against her frame. It whipped her hair into her eyes. She dug in her fingers, turned her head and looked back down into the rain-swept valley. Most of the rock was hidden except for this small section, which could, if her luck was really out, be seen by passing motorists. But the road was virtually empty: just one or two cars going by with their headlights and wipers on. Even so, she kept herself tight against the rock, making sure she presented less of a profile.

She dug her toes in, shifted her torso slightly to the left until she found the place, then gripped the scrappy roots of a gorse bush in both hands and wrenched them apart. She hesitated for a moment, not wanting to do it. Then she pushed her face in. Took a deep breath. Held it. Tasted it.

She let out the air with a long, hoarse cough, let go of the bushes, turned away and pressed the back of her hand to her nose, her chest heaving.

The corpse was still there. She could smell it. The bitter, gagging stench of decay told her all she needed to know. Overwhelming, but it was weaker than it had been. Fainter, which meant the body was doing what it should. During the summer the smell had been bad, really bad. There had been days she'd come up here and caught the odour down on the footpath, where even a casual passer-by could have smelt it. This level was better. Much better. It meant the woman's corpse was disintegrating.

The tiny gap Flea had put her nose to led to a crevice that snaked away back into the rock. Deep, deep down, almost eight metres below her, there was a cave. The cave had only one entrance and that was from under the water. The route was virtually impossible to find without specialist diving equipment and an encyclopedic knowledge of the quarry contours. She'd done it, dived down and entered the cave twice in the last six months that the body had been there, just to reassure herself that no one had found it. Now it was crammed into a hole in the floor, covered with rocks. No one would know it was there. The only clue to what Flea had done was the unmistakable stench working its way through the cave's natural ventilation system, through unseen fissures, to expel itself here, high up on the rock face.

A noise came from the other side of the quarry: the security gates were opening. She spread her arms and legs and let herself slither down fast, scraping her knees, getting a long orange line of soil on the front of her waterproofs. She ended up at the bottom in a crouch, hands out, ears trained on the quarry. In the wind and the rain it was hard to be sure, but she thought she could hear a car.

Stealthily, she crept to the edge of the rock. Poked her head round. Jerked it back again.

A car. Headlights on. Making its way leisurely down from the gates in the rain. And worse than that. She turned her head against the wet rock and peeped out again. Yes. It was a cop car.

Ho-ho. What now, smartarse?

Quickly she pulled off the knee pads, the chalk bag, the gloves. The cams higher up the rock face she couldn't get to – but the nearer ones she quickly released. She snapped them out and, with her discarded clothing, jammed them into a space under the gorse that grew at her feet. She dropped to her haunches and did a crab walk, out from the rock, shielded by the gorse bushes, until she reached another rock where she could straighten up and peer round.

The cop car had stopped at the far side of the quarry where all the discarded stripping material had been piled by the cement company. Its headlights were splashed with mud. Maybe he'd pulled in for a pee. Or to make a phone call. Or have a sandwich. He cut the engine and opened the window, put his head out and squinted up into the rain, then leaned over on to the passenger seat. Rummaged for something.

A sandwich? Make it a sandwich, for Christ's sake. A phone? No. It was a torch. Shit.

He opened the door. The rain and the clouds had dropped the daylight so much that the beam was strong enough to pick up the raindrops. It flashed off the car as he stood, pulling on a waterproof. It stuttered across the trees at the edge of the track. He slammed the door, went to the water's edge and shone the torch on to the surface of the quarry. Watched the water bounce and boil in the hammering rain. Beyond the gates, further up the track, one of the branches she'd used to conceal her car had been pulled away. The cop knew someone was in here.

That's you, then, she thought, knee deep in the proverbial.

He turned suddenly as if he'd heard a noise and aimed the torch at the place she stood. She shrank back into the lee of the rock, standing side on, the wind making her eyes water. Her heart was hammering. The cop took a few steps, his feet crunching on the gravel. One, two, three, four. Then more purposeful. Five, six, seven. Heading towards her.

She took a breath, pulled her hood off her head, stepped out into the beam. He stopped a few feet away, with the torch thrust out, rain dripping off the hood of his coat. 'Hello,' he said.

'Hello.'

He ran the torch up and down her. 'You know this is private property? Belongs to the cement company.'

'I do.'

'You a quarryman, are you?'

She gave him a half-smile. 'You've not been doing this long, have you? The police thing?'

'Tell me,' he said, 'what do the words "private property" mean to you? *Private property*?'

'Means I shouldn't be here? Not without authorization.'

He raised his eyebrows. 'Nice. You're getting the hang of this.' He shone the torch back up the track. 'Is that your car? Up there on the lane?'

'Yes.'

'You weren't trying to hide it, were you? Under the branches?'

She laughed. 'God. Of course not. Why would I do that?'

'You didn't put those branches in front of it?'

She held up her hand to shield her eyes from the rain and made a show of staring at the car. 'Wind must have blown all the stuff around it. Still, I see what you mean, what you're saying. It looks like someone's tried to hide it, doesn't it?'

The cop turned the torch on her again and studied her cagoule. If he noticed the sticky boots he didn't dwell on them. He came a couple of steps nearer her.

She reached into the inside pocket of her jacket. The cop's reaction was lightning fast: in under a second he had jammed the torch under his arm. He had his right hand on the radio, the left on the canister of CS gas in his holster.

'It's OK.' She lowered her hand, unzipped the jacket and opened it so he could see the lining. 'Here.' She pointed to the pocket inside. 'In here. My authority for being here. Can I show you?'

'Authority?' The cop didn't take his eyes off the pocket. 'What sort of authority is that?'

'Here.' She stepped forward and held the jacket out to him. 'You do it. If it makes you less nervous.'

The cop licked his lips. He took his hand off the radio and reached out. He rested his fingers on the edge of the pocket.

'There's nothing sharp in here, is there? Anything sharp I could cut myself on?'

'Nothing.'

'You'd better be telling the truth, young lady.'

'I am.'

He slowly slid his hand into the pocket, felt what was in there. He let his fingers run over it. A frown crossed his face. He pulled the object out and studied it.

A police warrant card. In a standard black leather wallet.

'A cop?' he said slowly. He opened it, read the name. 'Sergeant Marley? I've heard of you.'

'Uh-huh. I run the Underwater Search Unit.'

He handed her back the card. 'What the hell're you doing out here?'

'I'm thinking of running a training session in the quarry next week. This is a recce.' She looked up dubiously at the clouds. 'In this weather you may as well be freezing your arse off under water as top side.'

The cop switched off his torch, shrugged his coat a little closer round his shoulders. 'USU?' he said.

'That's the one. Underwater Search.'

'I hear a lot of things about your unit. It's been bad – hasn't it?'

She didn't answer but felt a hard, cold click in the back of her head at the mention of the unit's problems.

'Visits from the chief superintendent, I heard. Professional Standards starting an investigation, are they?'

Flea made her face go light. Pleasant. She folded the wallet and put it back in her pocket. 'Can't dwell on past mistakes. We've got a job to do. Just like you.'

The cop nodded. He seemed about to say something but must have changed his mind. He put a finger to his cap, turned and walked slowly back to the car. He got in and reversed about ten yards, did a sweeping three-point turn, and drove back up through the gates. The car slowed a little as he passed Flea's car, hidden in the bushes. He gave it a good look over, then put his foot down and was gone.

She stood, motionless, the rain pouring down on her.

I hear a lot of things about your unit . . . It's been bad – hasn't it?

She shivered, zipped up her jacket and looked around at the deserted quarry. The rain dripped down her cheeks like tears. No one had said anything about the unit to her face. Not so far. When she tested how it made her feel she was surprised to find the truth. It hurt that the team was in trouble. Something solid in her chest buckled a bit. Something that had been put there at the same time as she'd hidden the corpse in the cave. She took a breath, pulled the solid thing back together. Held it in tight. Kept breathing slow and sure until the feeling went away.

4

By eight thirty that evening there was still no sign of Martha. But the investigation already had some legs. A lead had come in. A woman in Frome had seen the local news bulletin about the carjacking and decided she had something to tell the police. She gave the statement to the local officers, who passed it on to MCIU.

Caffery drove there using the minor routes, the country lanes where he knew he could go fast and not get a tug from some bored traffic cop. It had stopped raining, but it was still blowing a gale. Every time it seemed the wind had died down to nothing it sprang out of nowhere and raced down the road, shaking raindrops from the trees, sending them arcing across his headlamps. The woman's house was centrally heated, but he couldn't get comfortable there. He declined tea, spoke to her for ten minutes, then went and got a takeaway cappuccino from a service station, took it back to her street and stood drinking it outside her house, coat buttoned against the wind. He wanted to get a feel for the road and the area.

This lunchtime, about an hour before Rose Bradley had been attacked, a man had pulled up here in a dark-blue car. The woman in the house had watched him from the window because he'd looked nervous. He had his collar turned up, so she never saw his face, but she was fairly sure he was white, with dark hair. He was wearing a black Puffa jacket and carrying, in his left hand, what she didn't recognize at the time but thought, in retrospect, might have been a rubber mask of some sort. She'd noticed him leave the car, but a phone call had diverted her attention and when she came back the street was empty. The car stayed there, though. All day. It was only when she saw the news bulletin and looked out of the window that she saw it had gone. It must have been collected at some point in the evening.

She was fairly sure the car had been a Vauxhall – she wasn't good at car marques but it had a dragon on it, she was sure – and when Caffery'd taken her outside and found a Vauxhall sitting under a streetlamp a few doors down she'd looked at the badge and nodded. Yes. In dark blue. Not very clean. And it may have had WW at the end of the numberplate, though she wouldn't swear to it. Apart from that she couldn't recall anything, much as she wanted to help.

Caffery stood at the place the car had been parked and tried to picture the scene, tried to work out who else might have seen it. At the very end of the dark, windswept street, a convenience store blasted light into the night: plastic shop sign above the window, offers posters pasted to the glass, a waste-paper bin with the local newspaper poster flapping under the chicken wire. He crossed the street, draining the last of the coffee, and dropped the cup into the bin as he entered the building.

'Hi,' he said, holding up his warrant card to the Asian woman behind the till. 'Manager in?'

'That's me.' She squinted at the card. 'What's your name?'

'Caffery – Jack, if you'd like first-name basis.'

'And what are you? A detective?'

'That's one word for it.' He nodded at the camera above the till. 'Is that thing loaded?'

She glanced up. 'Are you going to give me back my chip?'

'You what?'

'The robbery?'

'I don't know anything about a robbery. I'm a centralized unit. I wouldn't get that sort of information. What robbery?'

There was a line of customers waiting. The manageress gestured to a young man stacking shelves to take over from her.

She pulled her till fob out, hung it round her neck on a pink rubber spring, and motioned Caffery to follow her. They went past the lottery-ticket station, past two post-office booths, blinds down, and into a stock room at the back of the shop. They stood among the Walkers crisps boxes and unsold magazines that had been bundled up ready for return.

'Someone came in last week and pulled out a knife. A couple of boys, you know, hoodies. I wasn't here. They only got about forty pounds.'

'Boys, though. Not men?'

'No. I think I've got a good idea who they are. It's just a question of making the police believe me. They're still looking at the footage.'

In the corner a black-and-white TV monitor showed the back of the sales assistant's head as he cashed up a lottery ticket, beyond him the rows of sweets, and beyond that the street outside, litter blowing around in the dark. Caffery scrutinized the screen. In the bottom left-hand corner, past all the posters and magazines and parked cars, was the space where the woman had said the blue Vauxhall had been parked. 'There was a carjacking this morning.'

'I know.' The manageress shook her head. 'In town. That little girl. It's terrible. Just terrible. Everyone's talking about it. Is that why you're here?'

'Someone we'd like to speak to about it might have parked here.' He tapped the screen. 'The car was there all day. Can you pull up the footage?'

The woman unlocked a unit sunk into the wall using another key on the pink springy necklace. A door swung open to reveal a video recorder. She dropped the key and pressed a button. She frowned, pressed another button. A message appeared on screen: *Insert media card.* Swearing under her breath she hit another button. The screen cleared, for a second or two, then the message popped back up again. *Insert media card.* She was silent. She stood with her back to Caffery, not moving for several seconds. When she turned to him her face had changed.

'What?' he said. 'What's the matter?'

'It's not running.'

'What do you mean it's not running?'

'It's not switched on.'

'Why not?'

'I don't know. No.' She waved a hand, dismissing the words. 'That's a lie. I *do* know. When the police took the chip?'

'Yes?'

'They said they'd put another card in it and switched it back on. I didn't check. This card's completely empty. I'm the only one's got the keys so there's nothing on it since Monday when the police came for the pictures of the robbery.'

Caffery opened the door and stood looking through the shop, past the customers with their magazines and bottles of cheap wine to the road, to the cars parked in the pools of light dropped by the streetlamps.

'I can tell you one thing.' The manageress came and stood beside him, looking at the road. 'If he parked up there to walk into town he'd have been coming from Buckland.'

'Buckland? I'm new here. What direction's Buckland?'

'It's Radstock way. Midsomer Norton? You know?'

'Doesn't ring any bells.'

'Well, that's where he'd have been coming from. Radstock, Midsomer Norton.' She fiddled with the key fob on the spring around her neck. She smelt of a floral perfume – light and summery but cheap. The sort of thing you'd get from a corner chemist. Caffery's father had been a racist, in the sort of casual, everyday-pub-conversation way a lot of people had been back in those days. Lackadaisical and thoughtless. He'd told his sons that 'the Pakis' were OK and hard-working, but smelt of curry. Simple as that. Curry and onions. Now, in the back of his head, Caffery realized part of him still expected it to be true. And part of him was still surprised when it wasn't. That, he thought, showed how deep parenting could burrow. Showed how raw and skinless a child's mind was.

'Can I ask you something?' Her face pursed. It seemed to

close in at the mouth and the nose to a small point. 'Just one question?'

'Sure.'

'That little girl. Martha. What do you think he's going to do with her? What terrible thing is that man going to do to her?'

Caffery took a long, deep breath, stretched a good, calm smile across his face. 'Nothing. He's going to do nothing. He's going to drop her somewhere – somewhere safe where she can be found. And then he's going to run for the hills.'

5

Night had set in with a sort of vengeful permanence. Caffery decided he didn't need to pay the Bradleys another visit. There was nothing to tell them, and anyway, said the FLO, they were being swamped with well-wishers – neighbours and friends and members of the congregation bringing over flowers and cakes and bottles of wine to keep their spirits up. Caffery made sure the details of the Vauxhall were on the wire to all the ANPR points and then, because of the shitload of paperwork he had to catch up on, he drove back to the unit's offices, tucked behind a police station in Kingswood, on the north-easterly tip of the sprawling octopus that made up Bristol's suburbs.

He stopped the car at the electronic gate and got out in the full glare of the security lights, pulled back the sleeve of his shirt and studied the number scrawled in pen on his inner wrist. They'd had a theft from this car park three weeks ago – one of the unit cars had disappeared from right under their noses. Red faces all round and new access codes for everyone and he was still having problems remembering this one. He'd got half of the number on his wrist tapped in when he realized someone was watching him.

He paused, his hand on the pad, and turned. It was Sergeant Flea Marley. She was next to a car, holding the driver's door open. She slammed it and began to make her way towards him. The security light timed out and snapped off. He lowered his hand and pulled down his sleeve, feeling irrationally trapped by her.

Caffery was nearly forty, and for years he thought he'd known what he needed from women. Most of the time they half-broke his heart so he'd learned to be precise and utilitarian about it. But the woman coming across the street had started him wondering if it was less efficiency he was carrying around and more a ragged, hard ball of loneliness. Six months ago he'd been getting closer to doing something about that, until the moment everything he'd thought he'd known about her had had a bomb dropped on it when he'd seen her do something that meant she was nothing like the person he'd imagined. The chance discovery he'd made had gone through him like a storm, taken away everything he'd thought he felt about her, leaving him confused, puzzled and choked. Choked and disappointed in a way that was more like something from childhood than adulthood. From a time when Pakis smelt of curry and things went deep. Like being on the losing football team. Or not getting the bike he wanted for Christmas. Since then he'd bumped into Flea at work once or twice and knew he should tell her what he'd seen, but the words weren't there yet. Because he still hadn't worked out in his head why she'd done what she'd done.

She stopped a few yards away. She wore standard support-group winter kit – black cargoes, a sweatshirt and a waterproof. Her wild blonde hair, usually tied back, hung loose to her shoulders. Really and truly a support-group sergeant shouldn't look anything like she did. 'Jack,' she said.

He reached over and slammed the Mondeo door. Put some height and breadth into his shoulders. Made his face hard. His eyes ached from not looking too closely at her.

'Hi,' he said, as she got nearer. 'It's been a long time.'

6

Flea was still unnerved and on guard from what had happened at the quarry earlier. Then, this evening, the news about the car-jacking had trickled though the force, reaching her distant unit just before down-tools and giving her serious spikes in the head. Realistically there was only one person she could talk to about it. DI Caffery. At the end of her late shift she drove straight out to the MCIU offices in Kingswood.

He was at the gate near his car, surrounded by yellow pools of light that bounced out of the office windows behind him and reflected up from the puddles. He wore a heavy coat and was standing quite still watching her approach. He was dark-haired, medium height, lean under the coat and, even if you didn't know it from experience, which she did, you could tell from the way he stood that he knew how to look after himself. He was a good detective, a brilliant one, some would say, but everyone whispered about him. Because there was something a bit sideways about Caffery. Something a bit wild and alone. You could tell it from his eyes.

He didn't look pleased to see her. Not at all. She hesitated. Gave him an uncertain smile.

He took his hand down from the security pad he'd been jamming numbers into. 'How's it going?'

'Good.' She nodded, still a bit thrown by the expression. There had been a time, months ago, when he'd looked at her completely differently – looked at her in the way a man is supposed to look at a woman. Once or twice. He wasn't doing that now. Now he was regarding her as if she disappointed him. 'You?'

'Oh, you know – same shit, different day. I heard your unit's got some problems.'

News travelled fast around this force. USU had botched a few things lately – an operation over in Bridgewater when they'd been diving for a suicide victim in a river and had swum straight past the body. Plus the small matter of a grand's worth of diving equipment lost at the bottom of Bristol harbour. And other things – little mistakes and lapses that added up to the fat ugly truth of the Underwater Search Unit on its knees, performance targets missed, competency pay on hold, with only one person, the sergeant, to blame. This was the second time today someone'd thought to point it out.

'Getting tired of hearing it,' she said. 'We've had our problems, but we've turned the corner. I'm confident of that.'

He gave an unconvinced nod , and glanced up the road as if he was trying to see any good reason for them both still to be standing there. 'Well?' he said. 'What's on your mind, Sergeant Marley?'

She took a breath. Held it. For a moment she considered not telling him, just for the dull, unimpressed way he was communicating with her. It was like all the disappointment in the world was heaping out of him on to her shoulders. She exhaled. 'OK. I heard about the carjacker on the news.'

'And?'

'Thought you should know. He's done it before.'

'Done what?'

'The guy who's just taken that Yaris? He's done it before. And he's not just a carjacker.'

'What are you talking about?'

'A guy, yes? In a Santa mask? He snatched a car. There was a kid in it? Well, this is the third time.'

'Whoa, whoa, whoa. Hang on a second.'

'Look, I can't be the one who told you this. I got into shit over it the first time. I put my nose in it a bit too deep, eventually got a slap down from my inspector – told to lay off, stop hanging around the Bridewell station. No one got killed or anything so, really, I was wasting my time. None of this is coming from me. Right?'

'I'm hearing you loud and clear.'

'A couple of years ago, before you were transferred from London, there was a family down by the docks. Some guy jumps them, gets the keys and takes the car. Then again this spring. Do you remember I found that dead dog in the quarries up at Elf's Grotto? That woman's dog? The murder?'

'I remember.'

'But do you know why my unit was diving the quarry in the first place?'

'No. I don't think I ever even . . .' He trailed off. 'Yes, I do. It was a carjacking. You thought the guy had dumped the car in the quarry. Right?'

'We'd had a call from a payphone on the motorway. Witness reported seeing the car go in. It was a Lexus jacked from down near Bruton or somewhere. It turned out it wasn't a witness who made the call. It was the carjacker himself. There was no car in the quarry.'

Caffery was silent for a moment, his eyes not quite focused, as if he was rearranging it all in his head. 'And you think it was the same guy because . . .'

'Because there was a child in the back seat.'

'A child?'

'Yes. Both times when the jacker took the car he took a child with it. He got scared both times, dumped the kid. I knew it was the same guy because the children were about the same age. Both girls. Both under ten.'

'Martha is eleven,' he said distantly.

Flea felt suddenly heavy – heavy and cold. She half hated the idea she was about to bring to Caffery. She knew it would be like a slap to him. He had reason to care more than most about paedophiles. His own brother had been disappeared by a paedophile nearly thirty years ago. They'd never found the body.

'Well, then,' she said, her voice a bit softer, 'I guess that just about pulls it all together. It's not the car he wants, it's the girls. Young girls.'

Silence. Caffery didn't speak, didn't move, just looked at her, no expression. A car went past, lit up their faces. A few drops of rain fell.

'OK.' She held up a hand. 'I've said my piece. If you want to run with it, then that's up to you.'

She paused to see if he'd reply. He didn't, so she went back to her car and got in, sat for a while watching him, lit half by a streetlight, half by the car-park lights behind. Stony still. She thought about the way he'd looked her up and down. As if she'd somehow disappointed him. There was nothing left of the intent that had once been in his eyes. The thing that, six months ago, had half opened her heart and made her feel like dust and warmth at the same time.

Give it a day, she thought, starting the engine. If he hadn't done anything about the jacker by tomorrow night she'd be speaking to his superintendent.

7

That night there was an article about Martha on every news bulletin. Every hour, on the hour, all the way into the night. A network of people searching for her stretched across the county – across the country. Sleepless traffic cops sat on the ANPR points, eyes locked on their screens, checking every dark-blue Vauxhall that passed against the database. Other officers snatched a couple of hours here and there, their mobiles set to loud in case a call came through. Concerned citizens who'd heard the news put on coats and outdoor shoes to open their sheds, their garages. They checked the ditches that skirted their properties, the hard shoulders that ran near their houses. No one voiced their thoughts – that Martha could be dead already. On such a cold night. A little girl, in just a T-shirt, cardigan and raincoat. Shoes all wrong too. The force's photographic department had been distributing pictures of the pair she'd been wearing. Little printed ones with a strap and a buckle. Not meant for being outside on a freezing night in winter.

The hours went by without news. The night became dawn, the dawn became another day. A blustery, watery day. A Sunday. Martha Bradley wasn't going to be blowing out any candles today. In Oakhill Jonathan Bradley cancelled her party. He got a priest through the joint ministry to stand in for him at his services and the family stayed at home, in their kitchen, waiting for news. On the other side of Bristol, in the streets of Kingswood, a few people braved the weather to attend their local churches. They scurried past the MCIU offices, swaddled in scarves and hats, battling the arctic wind that hadn't let up all night.

Inside the building it was a different story. People went from office to office in shirtsleeves. The windows dripped with condensation. The place was heaving. Unarranged leave had been suspended and anyone under the rank of inspector was happily chalking up the overtime. The incident room was like a City trading floor, people making stand-up phone calls, shouting across the office. The jacker, in addition to all the other cases MCIU was fighting, had given them a migraine of biblical proportions and no one had slept much. In a series of emergency meetings that morning Caffery delegated responsibilities on the case. He had a goodish staffing quota, free rein to handpick his crew and he corralled a wish list: a pod of HOLMES indexers out of the computer room, and dibs on five assorted detectives. Then he chose a core team. Two men and a woman. They roughly spanned the skill sets he guessed he would need.

There was DC Prody. A big, neatly dressed thirty-something new guy who hadn't long come over to plainclothes. He'd done four years as a traffic cop in the Road Policing Unit and although no one would say it to his face this detail put him at the bottom of the food chain in the police cred hierarchy. Caffery was prepared to give him a chance, though. He had a feeling from first impressions that Prody might have the makings of a steady-hand cop. Plus he had background in Traffic. That ticked a couple of Caffery's boxes on a case involving cars. Next there was Detective Sergeant Paluzzi, who always said that if the guys in the team were going to call her Lollapalooza behind her back then she'd just as soon they cut to the chase and said it to her face. They did. Lollapalooza was a real number, with olive skin, sleepy eyes and an obsessive taste in high heels. Turned up at work each day in a lipstick-red Ka that she occasionally, cheekily, parked in the superintendent's unofficial bay just to get a rise out of him. Lollapalooza should by rights have been a disruption in the team but she was a solid worker and Caffery needed a woman if the case was going to take the paedophile turn Flea Marley had said it would.

Last on the list was DS Turner. An old hand, Turner was hit-and-miss as an investigator. He had two speeds – the 'interesting-job speed', which turned him into an up-all-night-living-on-his-nerves grafter, and the 'uninteresting-job speed', which made him a slothful bastard who had to be threatened with a disciplinary to get him out of bed. Turner was a father of two. On this case Caffery knew where his dial would be set. By ten o'clock that morning Turner was hard at it. He'd already rustled up two victims of the earlier carjackings and had brought them into the MCIU offices, where Caffery took them off his hands. The two should probably be interviewed separately, but Caffery was prepared to shove procedure if it meant he'd gain a few hours. He led them together to the only place he could find in the whole building with a modicum of sound insulation – a side room at the end of a corridor on the ground floor.

'I'm sorry about that.' He closed the door with his foot, shutting out the din, switched on the flickery fluorescents and put his pile of papers on the desk with his MP3 player. 'Take a seat. I know it's not glamorous.'

They each chose a chair.

'Damien?' Caffery held out his hand to the young black guy on the right. 'Thanks for making the time.'

'No worries.' He half rose and shook his hand. 'Hi there.'

Damien Graham was built like a professional footballer, wearing a magenta leather jacket and, on his massive legs, designer jeans. His credentials were all Jack-the-lad: you could tell just in the way he sat, his hand held casually with the sleeve up enough to display the heavy Rolex watch. He kept his knees open just the right distance to show he was in control. Sitting next to him, Simone Blunt was poles apart. White, mid-thirties, blonde and coolly elegant, dressed in top-drawer career-woman wardrobe: wide-collared shirt, killer legs in black nylons, and a suit cut short, crisp and not overtly sexy. Too professional to flirt.

'And Mrs Blunt.'

'Please – Simone.' She leaned forward to shake his hand. 'Good to meet you.'

'Hope you didn't mind not having Cleo here. Didn't think it was going to be appropriate. I'd like to speak to her later if that's OK?' Lollapalooza was babysitting Simone's ten-year-old daughter in another room. 'We're waiting for someone from CAPIT to come along and be with us. They'll know how to speak to her. CAPIT is the unit that—'

'I know CAPIT. They interviewed her when it first happened. Child Abuse and Protection something or other.'

'Protection Investigation Team. They're on their way.' Caffery swung a chair round and sat, elbows on the desk. 'Now, Mr Turner told you both why you're here?'

Damien nodded. 'It's that little girl last night.' The way he said girl – 'geh-awl' – pinned him as a Londoner. South London, Caffery guessed, maybe even from his old stamping ground, the south-east. 'Been on the news.'

'Martha Bradley,' said Simone. 'I take it you haven't found her.'

Caffery inclined his head a touch towards her. 'Not yet. And we don't know if it's connected with what happened to you both. But I'd like, if it's OK with you, to explore that eventuality a bit.' He switched on the MP3 player, then twisted it so the mic pointed to them. 'Damien. Do you want to start?'

Damien pushed his sleeves back. Uncomfortable in the police station with the posh totty next to him and determined he wasn't going to show it. 'Sure. I mean, it's going back a few years now.'

'2006.'

'Yeah – Alysha was only six at the time.'

'Did Turner say we'd like to arrange an interview with her when the time suits?'

'You'll have a job. I haven't seen her in two years.'

Caffery raised his eyebrows.

'She's gone. Gone back to the homeland, bruv. With her damn gully mother always running at the mouth. Sorry.' He made a show of correcting himself, smoothing his shirt and putting his head back, hands on his lapels, pinkies up. 'I do beg your pardon. I mean, my daughter is out of the country at the moment. I believe she might be in Jamaica. With her talkative mother.'

'You're separated?'

'Best thing I ever did.'

'Does Turner—' Caffery swivelled to the door, as if Turner might be standing there with a Moneypenny notepad, pen poised. He turned back. 'I'll tell Turner. If you could give us her number.'

'Don't know it. Haven't got a clue how to find her. Or my daughter. Lorna's . . .' he made inverted commas with his fore-fingers '. . . *finding* herself. With some wack person called Prince, runs a boat-rental place.' He cocked his head sideways, did his best Jamaican again. Probably for Simone's benefit. 'Him make him coil showing dem tourists da crocs. Know what I is sayin'?'

'She's got family here?' said Caffery.

'No. And good luck finding her is all I'm saying. And if you do, tell her I want a picture of my girl.'

'OK, OK. We'll come to that. Let's – let's think back to 2006. To what happened.'

Damien touched his fingers to his temples, then flicked them outwards as if the whole incident had scrambled his brains. 'It was a weird thing. A weird time, if I'm honest. We'd had a break-in, me and Lorna and Alysha, and that shook us up, plus we weren't seeing eye to eye, things were a bit rocky at work, get me? Everything's pretty fucked up anyway and suddenly *this* happens. We're in this car park—'

'Outside the theatre.'

'Yeah, the Hippodrome, and we're getting out the car and Alysha's bitch of a mother's out already, like she always was, doing some airhead thing with her makeup next to the car. But my little girl's still in the back, and I'm untangling the sat nav, like, and suddenly out of nowhere comes this – this *person*, all tooled up. When I look back I think it was the shock because it's not me to put up with crap – not in my nature, get me? But this time I'm like that. I just go rigid. And this person comes in and next I know I'm on the tarmac. See that?' He held up his hand for Simone to look at. Showed it to Caffery. 'Broke my damn wrist, damn *eediat*.'

'He took the car?'

'Takes the thing from under my nose. Think I'm so clever, don't I? But the man's fast – before I know it, it's all over and he's driving my car up into Clifton. He's only gone a bit and my kid's yelling at him in the back so much he loses it.'

'The files say half a mile away.'

'Yeah – up by the university.'

'He parked the car?'

'On the roadside. Burst a tyre on the pavement, like, but what's a new radial among friends? And then he's like that.' Damien pushed a hand towards the window. 'Legs it.'

'Leaves Alysha behind?'

'Yeah. But she's OK. I mean, she's a clever kid, you know? Got the smarts.' He tapped his forehead. 'So bright. She deals with it like it happens every day. Just climbs out the car and stands there looking at the crowd what's gathered and goes, "What you looking at? You going to get the police or what?" '

Simone gave a small smile. 'She sounds great.'

Damien nodded, smiled back. 'She's wicked. I swear.'

'Do you remember seeing a car?'

'What sort of car? I mean, there were cars everywhere. It was a car park.'

'A dark blue Vauxhall.'

'A Vauxhall.' He turned and raised his eyebrows questioningly at Simone, who shook her head and shrugged. Caffery noted it – this silent conferring. It meant that even if *he* hadn't decided it was the same person who had taken their cars, *they* had. Without knowing any of the details about what had happened to Rose Bradley they'd nailed their jacker as the same guy and had probably decided he'd taken Martha too. But Caffery had to keep an open mind. From a glance at Damien and Simone's original statements the attacks had had common denominators: the theft had been fast, with violence, and the jacker's clothing had been similar. A ski mask – not a Santa mask, but in both cases he'd been wearing a black jacket of some sort and low-slung jeans with loops and buckles. *Probably a fashion thing*, Simone had said in her statement. *But it made him look like he was planning to climb*

41

Everest, not steal a car. Rose Bradley's statement had said he was *wearing jeans with little pockets and straps.* Still, Caffery knew a handful of circumstantials like that didn't add up to a definitive.

'Damien? A dark-blue Vauxhall.'

'It's more than four years ago. Sorry. Not a Scooby.'

'Simone?'

'I'm sorry. There were cars everywhere. I really can't remember.'

Caffery nudged the MP3 player so its directional mic faced her. 'It was school drop-off time? In Bruton.'

She nodded and sat forward, eyes on the player. One arm she rested across her chest, hand placed lightly on her shoulder. The other she lowered to somewhere near her calf. 'That's right. I don't know how much you already know, but Cleo was nine then. She's turned ten since. It was two hours before I heard she was safe.' She gave Damien a small, sympathetic smile. 'The worst two hours of my life.'

Damien's mouth hung half open. '*Two hours?*' he said. 'I had no idea. I never heard about any of this. No *idea.*'

'It was in the local paper but it didn't get much further. I suppose when a child comes back safe and sound you don't hear about it. And, anyway, it was about the same time that footballer's wife went missing. Misty Kitson? Nobody was interested in what had happened to us.'

'Mrs Blunt?' Caffery cut across her quickly. He didn't want anyone veering off and talking about the Kitson case. He had his reasons. 'Who was in the car that morning?'

'Just me and Cleo.'

'Where was your husband?'

'Neil'd had an early meeting that day – he's at the Citizens Advice Bureau, advises on child custody matters, that sort of thing. I'm afraid I'm the breadwinner – still in the dog-eat-dog end of life. Raking in the filthy lucre.'

She was doing a good job of it, Caffery thought. Cleo had been at King's School in Bruton, the sort of education that'd put someone back a serious few bob.

'It happened outside the school?'

'Not right outside. Actually it was round the corner in the high street. I'd stopped to get something from the shop on my way into school. When I was walking to the car he just . . . *appeared*. Out of nowhere. Running.'

'Did he say anything? Anything you remember?'

'Yes. He said, "Get down, you bitch." '

Caffery stopped writing and looked up at her. 'I'm sorry?'

'He said, "Get down, you bitch." '

'The guy who did us said something like that,' Damien offered. 'Said, "Get down, you piece of shit," to me, called the missus a bitch. Told her to move her arse.'

'Why?' said Simone, wonderingly. 'Is it important?'

'I don't know.' Caffery kept his eyes on Simone's face. The same words the guy in Frome had said to Rose. He felt something start to tick deep in his thoughts. He cleared his throat, lowered his eyes and wrote 'Language' on his notepad. Question mark. Put a circle around it. Then he gave a confident smile. Damien and Simone looked back at him seriously.

'If it's the same guy,' Simone said, 'then isn't it a bit of a coincidence? Three different cars? Each with a different girl in it? I mean,' she lowered her voice, 'do you wonder if it isn't the cars he's after but the girls? Doesn't it make you wonder what he might have done to Martha?'

Caffery pretended he hadn't heard that. He let his smile broaden and encompass them in his absolute assertion that everything, everything, was going to be just fine. Fine as a fairy cake with a cherry on top. 'Thank you both for your time.' He switched off the MP3 player and gestured in the direction of the door. 'Shall we go and see if someone from CAPIT is here yet?'

8

Caffery's office was heated by a tiny groaning radiator in the corner, but the windows were soon steamed up with the four people that crammed into it to conduct the interview with Cleo Blunt. Caffery stood in the corner, arms crossed. A small woman in her fifties, dressed in a pale-blue sweater and skirt set, sat at his desk, with a list of questions in her hand. She was a sergeant from CAPIT. Opposite her, in swivel chairs, sat Simone and ten-year-old Cleo. Cleo wore a brown pullover and cord jeans, with pink Kickers, and her blonde hair in bunches. She was thoughtfully stirring the cup of hot chocolate Lollapalooza had rustled up from the kitchen. Caffery didn't need to see her sitting next to her rich mummy to grasp that this little character had private schools and Pony Club membership in her blood. You could tell it from the way she held herself. Still, she was sweet with it. Not obnoxious.

'Now,' the CAPIT sergeant began, 'we've told you why you're here, Cleo? Are you OK with that?'

Cleo nodded. 'I'm fine.'

'Right. Now, the man, the one who took Mum's car.'

'And never brought it back again.'

'And never brought it back. I know you've already had to talk about him once, and when I spoke to the police officer who asked you all the questions before, she was pretty impressed by you. She told me you were wicked at remembering things. That you thought about the questions, and that when you didn't know the answers, you didn't bother making it up. She said you were really honest.'

Cleo gave a small smile.

'But we're going to have to ask you a few more questions. Some will be the same questions all over again. It might seem kind of boring, but it is important.'

'I know it's important. He's got someone else, hasn't he? Another little girl.'

'We don't know. Maybe. So we've got to ask you to help us again. If it gets too much just tell me and I'll stop.'

The officer's finger rested on the list of questions Caffery had prepared. She'd been briefed with what he wanted and she knew he wanted it fast. 'You told the police officer before me that this man reminded you of someone. Someone out of a story?

'I didn't see his face. He had a mask on.'

'But you told us something about his voice. It was a bit like someone's . . . ?'

'Oh, I know what you mean.' Cleo half rolled her eyes, half smiled. Embarrassed by the words that had come out of her nine-year-old mouth just six months ago. 'I said he was like Argus Filch out of Harry Potter. The one who's got Mrs Norris. That's who he sounded like.'

'So shall we call him the Filch man?'

She shrugged. 'If you want, but he was worse than Argus Filch. I mean a lot worse.'

'OK. How about we call him the – I don't know – the care-taker? Argus Filch is the caretaker at Hogwarts, isn't he?' Caffery pushed himself away from the wall. He walked to the door, turned and walked back again. He knew the CAPIT officer had a protocol to follow but he wished she'd get a wriggle on. He turned at the window and crossed the room again. The CAPIT officer raised her chin and eyed him coolly, then went back to Cleo. 'Yes, I think we'll do that. We'll call him the "caretaker".'

'Cool. Whatevs.'

'Cleo, I want you do something for me. I want you to imagine that you're back in that car on that morning. The morning the caretaker got into your car. Now imagine it hasn't happened yet. All right? You're with Mum on the way to school. Can you picture that?'

'OK.' She half closed her eyes.

'What do you feel?'

'I feel happy. My first class is PE – it used to be my favourite – and I'm going to wear my new gym T-shirt.'

Caffery watched the CAPIT officer's face. He knew what she was doing. This was the cognitive interviewing technique a lot of the force was using these days. The interviewer took the subject back to the way they were feeling when the incident happened. It was supposed to open up the channels and let the facts flow.

'Great,' she said. 'So obviously you're not wearing the gym T-shirt yet?'

'No. I'm wearing my summer dress. With a cardie over it. My gym shirt was in the boot. We never got it back. Did we, Mum?'

'Never.'

'Cleo, this is difficult but imagine it's the "caretaker" driving now.'

Cleo took a breath. She screwed her eyes tighter shut and her hands came up to her chest. Rested there lightly.

'Good. Now, you remember his jeans. Mum says you especially remember his jeans – with loops on them. When he was driving could you see those jeans?'

'Not all of them. He was sitting down.'

'He was in the seat in front of you. Where Dad usually sits?'

'Yes. And if Dad's sitting there I can't see all his legs.'

'What about his hands? Could you see them?'

'Yes.'

'And what do you remember about them?'

'He had on them funny gloves.'

'*Those* funny gloves . . .' Simone corrected.

'Those funny gloves. Like at the dentist's.'

The CAPIT officer glanced up at Caffery, who was still pacing. He was thinking about gloves. The CSI's report on the Blunts' Yaris hadn't turned up any DNA at all. And the guy was wearing gloves in the CCTV footage at the exit barrier. Forensically aware, then. Bloody great.

'Anything else?' she asked. 'Were they big? Small?'

'Medium. Like Dad's.'

'And quite important now,' the officer continued slowly, 'can you remember where his hands were?'

'On the steering-wheel.'

'Always on the steering-wheel?'

'Yes.'

'They never came off it?'

'Umm . . .' Cleo opened her eyes. 'No. Not until he stopped and let me out.'

'He leaned past you and opened the door from the inside?'

'No. He tried to open it but Mum's child lock was on. He had to get out and come round. Like when Mum and Dad let me out of the car.'

'So he leaned across you once to try the door? Did he touch you when he did that?'

'Not really. Just brushed my arm.'

'And when he got out of the car did you see his jeans?'

Cleo gave the CAPIT woman a strange look. Then she glanced at her mother, as if to say, Are we going mad? I thought we'd gone through this already. 'Yes,' she said cautiously, as if this was another test of her memory. 'They were with loops. Climber's jeans.'

'And they looked normal? Not undone like he wanted the toilet or anything?'

She frowned, puzzled. 'No. We didn't stop at toilets.'

'So he came round, opened the door and let you out?'

'Yes. And then he drove off.'

The clock was ticking: the day was getting away from them. Caffery could feel every passing hour like a brick piled on his back. He moved to stand behind Cleo, caught the CAPIT officer's eye and made a circling motion with his finger. 'Move on,' he mouthed. 'Move on to the route he took.'

She raised her eyebrows coolly at him, gave him a polite smile, then calmly turned back to Cleo. 'Let's go back to when it first happened. Let's imagine you're in the car just after the caretaker's pushed Mummy away.'

Cleo closed her eyes again. Pressed her fingers to her forehead. 'OK.'

'You're wearing your summer dress because it's warm outside.'

'Hot.'

'The flowers are out. Can you see all the flowers?'

'Yes – in the fields. There are those red ones. What're they called, Mum?'

'Poppies?'

'Yes, poppies. And some white ones in the hedges. They're a bit puffy and stalky. Like a stalk with a puff of white on them. And the other white flowers like trumpets.'

'As you're driving along are there always flowers and hedges? Or do you go past anything else?'

'Umm . . .' Cleo wrinkled her forehead. 'Some houses. Some more fields, that deer thingy.'

'Deer thingy?'

'You know. Bambi.'

'What's Bambi?' said Caffery.

'The Bulmer's factory in Shepton Mallet,' Simone said. 'They've got the Babycham fawn out at the front. She loves it. A huge great fibreglass thing.'

The CAPIT officer said, 'What happened then?'

'Lots of roads. Lots of bends. Some more houses. And the pancake place he promised.'

There was a moment's silence. Then it sank in: she'd said something that hadn't been in her first interview. Everyone looked up at the same time.

'A pancake place?' Caffery said. 'You didn't mention that before.'

Cleo opened her eyes and saw them all looking at her. Her face fell. 'I *forgot*,' she said defensively. 'I forgot to say it, that's all.'

'It's OK,' he said, holding his hand up. 'It's all right. It's not a problem that you didn't say.'

'It was an *accident* that I didn't say it before.'

'Of course it was.' The CAPIT sergeant gave Caffery a steely smile. 'And aren't *you* the clever one for remembering now? I reckon you've got a much better memory than I have.'

'Have I?' she said uncertainly, her eyes flitting from her to Caffery and back again.

'*Yes!* Much, *much* better. A shame you didn't get the pancake. That's all I can say.'

'I know. He promised me one.'

Her eyes stopped on Caffery. Hostile. He folded his arms and forced a smile. He'd never been good with kids. He thought they saw through him most of the time. Saw the empty hole he was mostly able to keep hidden from adults.

'He wasn't very nice, then, was he, the caretaker?' said the CAPIT officer. 'Especially as he promised you a pancake. Where were you going to have the pancake?'

'At the Little Cook. He said there was a Little Cook up there. But when we got to it he just went straight past it.'

'Little Cook?' Caffery murmured.

'What did the Little Cook look like, Cleo?'

'Little Cook? He's red. And white. Holding a tray.'

'Little Chef,' said Caffery.

'That's what I meant. Little Chef.'

Simone frowned. 'There aren't any Little Chefs around here.'

'There are,' the CAPIT officer said. 'In Farrington Gurney.'

Caffery went to the desk, pulled the map over. Shepton Mallet. Farrington Gurney. Right in the heart of the Mendip Hills. From Bruton to Shepton Mallet wasn't a long way, but Cleo had been in the car forty minutes. The jacker had driven her in zigzags. He'd gone north, then hairpinned back south-west. And in doing that he'd gone past the road that led to Midsomer Norton. The place the convenience-store manager had mentioned. If they had nothing else for the jacker at least they could put a pin in the map on the Midsomer Norton and Radstock area. And focus on it.

'They do waffles there,' said the CAPIT woman, smiling at Cleo. 'I have my breakfast there sometimes.'

Caffery couldn't keep still. He pushed the map away and sat at the desk. 'Cleo, in all that time you were with the caretaker, did he talk to you? Did he say anything?'

'Yes. He kept asking about my mum and dad. Kept asking what their jobs were.'

'And what did you say?'

'I told him the truth. Mum's a financial analyst, she earns all the money, and Dad, well, he works to help little children when their mums and dads split up.'

'You sure there's nothing else he said? Nothing else you can remember?'

'I guess,' she said unconcernedly. 'I think he said, "It's not going to work."'

'It's not going to work?' Caffery stared at her. 'When did he say that?'

'Just before he stopped. He said, "It's not working, get out." So I got out and went to the side of the road. I thought he was going to give me my bag with my T-shirt in it but he didn't. Mum had to buy me a new one because we never got our car back, did we, Mum? We got the T-shirt at the school shop. It's got my initials and it's . . .'

Caffery had stopped paying attention. He was staring at a point in mid-air, thinking about the words: *It's not working.* Meaning it had gone wrong. He'd lost his nerve.

But if that was true for Cleo, it wasn't true for Martha. This time it was different. This time the jacker had kept his nerve. This time it was working.

9

By three o'clock the cloud cover had broken in places and the low sun shone obliquely across the fields in this corner of north Somerset. Flea wore the jacket with reflective strips for her afternoon jog. She'd got her dumb nickname as a child because people told her she never looked before she leaped. And because of her irritating, incurable energy. Her real name was Phoebe. Over the years she had tried systematically to iron the 'Flea' part out of her character, but still there were days when she thought her energy might burn a hole through the ground she stood on. On those days she had a trick to calm herself. She ran.

She used the lanes that laced through the countryside near her home. She'd run until sweat poured from her and there were blisters on her feet. Past stiles and half-dormant cows, past stone-built cottages and mansions, past the officers in uniform who poured out of the Ministry of Defence base near her house. Sometimes she'd run late into the night, until all her thoughts and apprehensions had shaken themselves loose and there was nothing left in her head save the desire for sleep.

Being physically in shape was one thing. Maintaining that fitness and control all the way through to the inside was another. As she turned the corner on the last leg of the run, she was picturing the Bradleys' Yaris screeching out of the car park in Frome. She kept thinking about Martha Bradley sitting in the back seat. Flea had got a friend from Frome station to read her Rose's statement. In it she'd said Martha had been leaning over from the back seat to tune in the radio when the car took off. So she wasn't strapped in. Had she been thrown around as the jacker sped away? He wouldn't have stopped to strap her in.

Nearly twenty hours had passed since Flea had spoken to Jack Caffery. It took time for the force grapevine to pass messages between distant units, but even so she thought she'd have heard by now if Caffery'd picked up her idea. What kept going through her head like a shriek was that there'd already been two chances for her to push her conviction that the attacks were connected. She imagined a world where she hadn't been intimidated by her inspector, a world where she'd followed her instincts, the jacker had been picked up months ago and Martha hadn't been abducted from the supermarket car park yesterday.

She let herself into the house from the garage, full of Dad and Mum's old diving and caving equipment. Stuff she would never move or chuck out. Upstairs she did her stretches and took a shower. The heating in the rambling old house was on, but outside it was seriously cold. What would Martha be thinking? At what point had she realized that the man wasn't going to stop the car and let her out? At what point had she realized she'd stepped full face into the world of adults? Did she cry? Beg for her mum? Would she be thinking now that she might never see her or her dad again? It wasn't right that any little girl should have to ask herself questions like that. Martha's head wasn't old enough to sort it all out. She hadn't had time to make safe places in her thoughts to hide, the way adults did. It wasn't fair.

When Flea was little she'd loved her parents more than anything. This creaky old house, four artisans' cottages knocked into one, had been her family home. She'd grown up there, and though there hadn't exactly been money coming out of their ears, they'd lived well, with long, untidy summer days playing football or hide-and-seek in the rambling garden that dropped in terraces away from the house.

Most of all she'd been loved. So very, very well loved. In those days it would have killed her to be separated from her family like Martha had been.

But that had been then and this was now and everything was different. Mum and Dad were dead, both of them, and Thom, her younger brother, had done something so unspeakable that she would never be able to find her way back to any relationship with him. Not in this lifetime. He'd killed a woman. A young woman. And pretty – pretty enough that she'd been famous for it. Not that her looks had done her much good. Now she was buried under a cairn in an inaccessible cave next to a disused quarry, put there by Flea in an idiot attempt to cover the whole thing up. Insanity, in hindsight. Not the way a person like her – a normal, salaried, mortgage-paying person – should have behaved. No surprise she was carrying this balled-up rage around. No surprise there was just deadness in her eyes these days.

By the time she was dressed it was almost sunset. Downstairs, she opened the fridge and stared at what was inside. Microwave meals. Meals for one. And a two-litre carton of milk that was past its sell-by date because there was only her to drink it, and if she did unexpected overtime it never got used. She closed the door and rested her head against it. How had it come to this – on her own, no kids, no animals, no friends any more? Living a spinster's life at twenty-nine.

There was a bottle of Tanqueray gin in the freezer, and a bag of lemon she'd sliced at the weekend. She made herself a tall tumbler, the way Dad would have done, with four precise slices of lemon, frozen hard, four cubes of ice and a splash of tonic. She put on a fleece and took the glass outside to the driveway. She liked to stand there and drink, watch the distant lights coming on in the old city of Bath in the valley, even when it was cold. You'd never take a Marley away from this place. Not without a fight.

The sun crept the last few degrees to the horizon, sent orange light streaming across the sky in huge shards. She put her hand over her eyes and squinted at it. There were three poplars on the edge of the garden to the west: one summer Dad had noticed something about them that had pleased him no end. On the solstices the sunset lined up exactly with one of the two outer ones, while on the equinoxes it set directly behind the middle one.

'Perfectly aligned. Someone must have planted them like that a century ago,' he'd said, laughing, surprised by the cleverness. 'Just the sort of thing the Victorians would have loved. You know, Brunel and all that malarkey.'

Now the sun stood exactly between the middle and the outer one. She looked at it for a long time. Then she checked her watch: 27 November. Exactly six months to the day since she'd hidden the corpse in the cave.

She thought of the disappointment in Caffery's face. The lightless reflection of his eyes last night. She drained her drink. Rubbed her arms to make the bumps go away. How long was it supposed to go on? When something so impossible and unimaginable had happened, just how long were you supposed to shut down for?

Six months. That was the answer. Six months was long enough. Too long. The time had come. The corpse wasn't going to be found. Not now. She'd have to pack the whole thing away in the back of her mind because it was time for other things. It was time to get the unit back on track. Time to prove she was the same sergeant she'd always been. She could do it. She was going to blot the disappointment out of everyone's eyes. Maybe then the walls in her own eyes would come down. Maybe the day would come when there weren't sour milk and meals for one in the freezer. And maybe, just maybe, the day would come when there'd be someone else standing on the gravel driveway with her, drinking Tanqueray and watching the night lower itself on to the lighted city.

10

Caffery's head felt full of lead. Like a cold, miserable ball with *It's not working* etched on it. He went down the corridor opening doors, delegating tasks. He gave Lollapalooza the job of tracking down known sex offenders in the Frome area, and told Turner to tickle up any more witnesses to either jacking. Turner looked a mess: unshaven, and he'd forgotten to take out the diamond stud earring he wore at weekends. The one that, with his spiky high-lighted hair, gave him the look of a devout clubber and sent the superintendent into paroxysms of abuse. Before he left the office Caffery pointed it out to him. Stood at the doorway, said, 'Uh, Turner?' and waggled his own ear up and down to give him the clue. Turner pulled it out hurriedly, pocketed it, and Caffery went on his way ruminating that no one in the unit seemed to give a damn about looking professional. There was Turner with his ear-ring, and Lollapalooza with her killer heels. Only the new guy, the traffic cop DC Prody, seemed to have checked in the mirror before he'd left home that morning.

He was sitting neatly at his desk when Caffery came in, lit only by a small lamp. He was shaking the mouse on the mouse mat and frowning at the screen. Behind him a workman, standing on a stepladder, was painstakingly removing the plastic cover from the fluorescent light fitting on the ceiling.

'I thought these computers were supposed to time out,' said Prody.

'They are.' Caffery pulled back a chair. 'After five minutes.'

'Mine's not. I leave the room, come back and it's still hot to trot.'

'The number for IT's on the wall.'

'*That's* where the extension list is.' Prody unpinned it and put it in front of him. Lined it up. Placed his hands on the desk and considered it carefully, as if its tidiness pleased him. He was such an orderly man compared to Turner and Lollapalooza. There was a dark-blue gym bag hanging on the wall and you could tell from Prody's physique that it got used. He was tall and broad and solid, with tightly trimmed hair that was just edging into grey at the sideburns. A big, handsome Kennedy jawline, slightly tanned. The only thing screwing up his appearance was the evidence of teenage acne. Looking at him Caffery saw, with a moment of surprise, that he was expecting good things from this guy. 'Every day's a little better. I'm not such a noob any more. They're even giving me leccy at last.' Prody nodded to the workman. 'They must like me.'

Caffery held up a hand to the workman. 'Mate? Can we have some space here? Just for ten.'

He got down the ladder without a word. He put his screwdriver into a toolbox, closed it and left the room. Caffery sat down. 'Anything new?'

'Nothing really. No bites from the ANPR points – not on the Yaris or the partial index on the Vauxhall in Frome.'

'It's definitely the same guy as the earlier two jackings. No getting away from it.' He put the Ordnance Survey map between them. 'You were in Traffic before you came over here.'

'For my sins.'

'Do you know Wells, Farrington Gurney, Radstock?'

'Farrington Gurney?' He laughed. 'Just a little. I mean, I lived there for ten years. Why?'

'The superintendent's muttering about bringing in a geographical profiler. Meanwhile I think someone who's spent enough time out on the roads knows more about the way the land lies than a psychologist.'

'And I get paid half as much, so I must be your man.' Prody

pulled the lamp towards himself and hunched over the map. 'What've we got?'

'What we've got is a fuck-awful situation, Paul, if you'll pardon my language. But let's suck that one up and think what to do about it. Look at this. The first jacking's over in minutes, but the second one, he took longer. And he went a weird route.'

'Weird how?'

'He came up the A37, going north, and kept going. Past Binegar, past Farrington Gurney. Then he turned back on himself.'

'He was lost?'

'No. Definitely not. He knew that road really well. He told the girl there was a Little Chef up the road a long time before they got to it. He knew where he was. And that's what I'm wondering. If he knew the area why did he take the route he did? Is there something along there he was attracted to?'

Prody ran his finger along A37, the road that came down from Bristol into the Mendips. He went down south, past Farrington Gurney, past the turn the jacker had taken. He stopped north of Shepton Mallet and was quiet for a moment or two, frowning.

'What?' Caffery said.

'Maybe he knew the road from north to south, but not from south to north. If he travelled it often in this direction he'd know this way to Wells, but he might not know it coming from the south. Which might mean that whatever he was using the road for – going to work or visiting friends or whatever – he only knew it up to this point. So he was stopping his route somewhere here, south of Farrington, north of Shepton. And yesterday's jacking was here. In Frome.'

'But I've got a witness who thinks the Vauxhall must have come through from Radstock, which is in the direction of Farrington. So let's just say this general area is important to him somehow.'

'We could put ANPR on these roads too. If they're not already over-committed around Frome.'

'Know anyone in the Tactical Traffic Unit?'

'Been trying to get away from the bastards for the last two years. Leave it to me.'

Caffery had noticed a file on the side unit. He stopped listening to Prody and stared at the name on the spine. After a moment he put his hands on the chair arms and pushed himself upright. Went across to the unit and glanced casually at it.

'The Misty Kitson case?'

'Yup.' Prody didn't lift his eyes from the map he was studying, trying to figure out a good place to position the ANPR units.

'Where'd you get the file?'

'The review team had it. Thought I'd give it a quick flick through.'

'Thought you'd "give it a quick flick through"?'

Prody stopped looking at the map and raised his eyes to Caffery. 'Yes. Just – you know, see if anything jumped out at me.'

'Why?'

'Why?' He said it cautiously, as if it was a trick question, as if Caffery had asked him something obvious, like *Hey, Paul, why do you breathe in and out?* 'Well – because it's fascinating? What happened to her? I mean a girl in the drying-out bin for a couple of days wanders out of the clinic one afternoon, and next you know, *ta-da*, she's gone. It's just . . .' He shrugged. Faintly embarrassed. 'Interesting.'

Caffery looked him up and down. Six months ago the Misty Kitson case had been a serious headache for the unit. At first there'd been a kind of excitement about it. She'd been a minor celebrity, a footballer's wife and very pretty. The media had fallen on it like hyenas. That had excited a lot of the cops in the team. But when, after three months, the unit had consistently come back empty-handed, the lustre began to tarnish. Humiliation had set in. Now the case had been back-burnered. The review team still had it, and they still chastised and sent periodic recommend-ations to MCIU over it. The press were still interested too, not to mention the occasional starstruck cop. But most of MCIU would have liked to forget they'd ever heard the name Misty Kitson. Caffery was surprised at this – Prody going to the review team off his own bat. Writing his own ticket like he'd been around the place for years and not just two weeks.

'Let's get this straight, Paul.' He picked up the file and felt its weight testing the bones in his fingers, trying to pull his hand down. 'You only still want to know what happened to Misty Kitson if you're in the media. Now, you're not in the media, are you?'

'I'm sorry?'

'I said, you're not in the media, are you?'

'No. I mean, I'm a—'

'You're a cop. Your official stance might be "We're still pursuing lines of enquiry," but the truth in here,' he tapped his temple, 'is you've moved on. The unit's screwed the lid on the Kitson case. It's over. Finished.'

'But—'

'But what?'

'Be honest. Aren't you intrigued?'

Caffery didn't need to be intrigued. He knew exactly where Misty Kitson was. He even knew roughly the route she'd taken out of the clinic's grounds because he'd walked it himself. He knew who had killed her too. And how. 'No,' he said levelly. 'Of course I'm not.'

'Not in the slightest?'

'Not in the slightest. I'm fighting one serious fire here with the jacker case. And I need all hands on deck. I don't need my men wandering into the review team and "having a flick through" old cases. Now.' He dropped the file on Prody's desk. 'Do you want to take it back or shall I?'

Prody was silent, looking at the file. There was a long pause, and Caffery sensed him struggling not to argue. In the end he swallowed it. 'Yeah, whatever. I'll do it.'

'Good.'

Caffery left the office, feeling irritated and jangled. He closed the door softly, not giving in to the urge to slam it. Turner was standing outside his room, waiting for Caffery as he came down the corridor. 'Boss?' He was holding a piece of paper in one hand.

Caffery stopped in his tracks, gave him a long look. 'From your face, Turner, I'd say I'm not going to like what you're going to tell me.'

'Probably not.'

He held out the paper. Caffery closed his thumb and forefinger on it. But something stopped him taking it from Turner's hand. 'Tell me.'

'We got a call from boys in Wiltshire. They found the Bradleys' Yaris.'

Caffery's grip on the paper tightened. Still he didn't pull. 'Where?'

'On some disused farmland.'

'And Martha's not in it. Is she?'

Turner didn't answer.

'If she's not in it,' Caffery's voice was calm, 'it doesn't mean she won't still turn up.'

Turner coughed, embarrassed. 'Uh – read it first, Boss. Wiltshire faxed it over. They're getting their own SOCOs to drive the original down to us personally.'

'What is it?'

'A letter. It was on the dashboard, rolled up inside some of her clothing.'

'What clothing?'

'Uh.' He gave a long sigh.

'What?'

'Her underwear, Boss.'

Caffery stared at the paper. His fingers were burning. 'And what does it say?'

'Oh, Christ. Like I said, Boss, maybe you should read it.'

11

The man crouched at the edge of the camp, the fire lighting his filthy face and beard red, making him look like something born not of woman but of a volcano. Caffery sat a few feet away, watching him in silence. It had been dark for four hours already, but the man was busy planting a bulb in the frozen earth. 'There was once a child,' he said, trowelling the earth away. 'A child called Crocus. Crocus was a girl child with golden hair. She loved to wear purple dresses and ribbons.'

Caffery listened in silence. In the short time he had known the vagrant, whom the locals called the Walking Man, he'd learned to listen and not to question. He'd learned that in this relationship he was the pupil and the Walking Man was the teacher – the one who chose most things about their encounters: what they talked about, where and when they met. It was six long months since they'd last sat together, but maybe the twentieth time Caffery had searched for him. Those hunts had been long lonely nights, driving lanes at five miles an hour, stretched up in the driver's seat, craning his neck to see over the hedgerows. Tonight, almost the moment he'd begun looking, the campfire had sprung up like a beacon in a field. As if the Walking Man had been there all along, watching Caffery's efforts with amusement. Waiting for the time to be right.

'One day,' the Walking Man continued, 'Crocus was taken by a witch and condemned to live trapped among the clouds where her parents could neither speak to her nor see her. They still don't know for sure if she's alive, but every spring, on her birthday, they turn their eyes to the sky and pray that this spring will be the one their child is returned.' He patted the ground around the bulb and dribbled some water on to it from a plastic bottle. 'It is an act of faith, to continue to believe their daughter is still there. An act of absolute faith. Can you imagine what it must have been like for them never to know for sure what had happened to their daughter? Never to know for sure if she was dead or alive?'

'Your daughter's body was never found,' Caffery said. 'You know how they felt.'

'And your brother's wasn't either. So that makes us twins.' He smiled. The moonlight caught his teeth, which were even, clean and healthy in his blackened face. 'Peas in a pod.'

Peas in a pod? Two men who couldn't have been more different. The insomniac lonely cop and the bedraggled homeless guy, who walked all day and never slept in the same place twice. But it was true they shared things in common. They had the same eyes. Astonishingly when Caffery looked at the Walking Man he saw his own blue eyes staring back at him. And, more importantly, they shared a story. Caffery had been eight when his older brother Ewan had disappeared from the family's back garden in London. The ageing paedophile Ivan Penderecki, who lived over the railway tracks, was to blame, Caffery had no doubt, but Penderecki had never been charged or convicted. The Walking Man's daughter had been raped five times before she was murdered by an itinerant offender on probation, Craig Evans.

Craig Evans hadn't been as lucky as Penderecki. The Walking Man, who in those days had been a successful businessman, had taken his revenge. Now Evans lived in a chair in a long-term care facility near his family home in Worcestershire. The Walking Man had been precise about the injuries he'd inflicted. Evans no longer had eyes to watch children nor a penis to rape them with.

'Is that what makes you different?' Caffery said. 'Is that what makes you able to see?'

'To see? What does that mean?'

'You know what I mean. You *see*. You see more than others see.'

'Supernatural powers, you mean.' The Walking Man snorted. 'Don't talk mumbo-jumbo. I live out here and off the ground, like an animal. I exist and I absorb. My eyes are open wider and more light gets into them. But it doesn't make me a seer.'

'You know things I don't.'

'So? What do you expect of yourself? Being a cop doesn't make you superhuman. No matter what you think.'

The Walking Man came back to the fire. He lifted some more wood on to it. His walking socks were spread out to dry on a stick shoved into the ground near the flames. They were good socks. The most expensive money could buy. Made from alpaca. The Walking Man could afford it. He had millions tucked away in a bank somewhere.

'Paedophiles.' Caffery sipped his cider. It stung the back of his throat and sat flat and cold in his stomach, but he knew he'd drink the whole mug and more before the night was finished. 'My specialist subject. Stranger kidnaps. The outcome is usually the same: if we're very lucky the child gets returned almost immediately after the assault, and if we're not, the child will be killed within the first twenty-four hours.' It was nearly thirty hours since Martha had gone. He lowered the mug. 'Or, now I think of it, maybe that's when we *are* lucky.'

'If the child is killed in the first twenty-four hours you're lucky? What's that? Police logic?'

'I mean that maybe it's a better outcome than those who are kept alive longer.'

The Walking Man didn't answer. The two men were silent for a long time, pondering that. Caffery raised his eyes to watch the clouds roll across the moon. He thought how lonely and majestic they were. He imagined a child with golden hair peeping down from them, watching for her parents. Somewhere in the woods a fox cub was calling. And Martha was somewhere out in the great spread of the night. Caffery reached inside his jacket pocket. He pulled out the photocopied letter that had been wrapped inside her underwear and held it out. The Walking Man grunted. Leaned over and took it. Opened it and began to read, tilting the paper forward so it caught the light from the fire. Caffery watched his face. A handwriting expert had already decided the jacker was trying to disguise his writing. While the Bradleys' car was being crawled over by the forensics guys, Caffery had spent a long time in his office, poring over the letter. Now he knew every word by heart.

Dear Mummy of Martha,

I am sure Martha would of wanted me to get in touch with you though it's not like she's said or anything. She's not very TALKATIVE at the moment. She has told me she likes BALLET DANCING and DOGS, but you and I know very well that girls of this age lie all the time. THEY ARE LIARS. See what I think is I think she likes other things. Not like she's going to admit that to you now, of course. She LOVED the things I did to her last night. I wish you could of seen her face.

But then she turns around and lies to me. You should see her face when she does that. Ugly don't even come near it. Luckily now I have REARRANGED things in that department. She looks much better now. But please, Martha's Mummy please can you find it in your heart to do me a kindly favour???? Pretty please? Can you tell the police cunts that they can't stop me now so don't bother. It's started now, hasn't it, and it ain't going to stop just sudden. Is it now?
Is it?

The Walking Man finished reading. He looked up.
'Well?'

'Take it away from me.' He thrust the letter at Caffery. His eyes had changed. They were bloodshot and dead.

Caffery returned it to his pocket. He repeated, 'Well?'

'If I was really a seer or a clairvoyant this would be the time I would tell you where that child is. I would tell you now and I would tell you to use whatever powers you have to get to her, whatever the cost to your life and profession, because that person,' he jabbed a finger towards the pocket where the letter was, 'is cleverer than any of the others you've brought to me.'

'Cleverer?'

'Yes. He's laughing at you. Laughing that you think you can outsmart him, you petty Bow Street Runners with your truncheons and your dunce's hats. He is so much more than he seems.'

'What does that mean?'

'I don't know.' He unfurled his bedroll and laid it out. He began to arrange the sleeping-bag. His face was hard. 'Don't ask me more – don't waste your time. For the love of God, I'm not a psychic. Just a man.'

Caffery took another swig of cider and wiped his mouth with the back of his hand. He studied the Walking Man's face as he got ready for bed. Cleverer than any of the others. He thought about what the jacker had said: *It's started now, hasn't it, and it ain't going to stop just sudden. Is it now?* He knew what the words meant: he was going to do it again. He was going to choose another car at random: any car, any driver. The only important thing would be the child in the back seat. A girl. Under twelve. He was going to steal her. And all Caffery had to go on was that it would, in all likelihood, happen within a radius of ten miles from Midsomer Norton.

After a long time of staring at the darkness on the edge of the firelight, Caffery picked up a foam mattress and unrolled it. He got out his sleeping-bag and settled on his back, the bag tucked around him to keep out the cold. The Walking Man grunted, and did the same. Caffery looked at him for a while. He knew he wouldn't speak again tonight: it was the end of the conversation and from that moment on not another word would be uttered. He was right: they lay in their respective sleeping-bags, looking at their own section of the sky, thinking about their own worlds and how they were going to battle through what life brought them in the next twenty-four hours.

The Walking Man slept first. Caffery stayed awake for several hours, listening to the night, wishing the Walking Man was wrong, that clairvoyance or a supernatural power did exist and that it was possible to divine, just from the noises out there, what had become of Martha Bradley.

12

When Caffery woke, aching and frozen, the Walking Man was gone. He must have got up and dressed in the dark, leaving nothing but the blackened fire and a plate with two bacon sandwiches on it next to Caffery's bedroll. It was a hazy day. Cold again. An arctic breath in the air. He waited a few minutes for his head to clear, then got up. He ate the sandwiches standing in the field, chewing thoughtfully and looking down at the patch of earth where the Walking Man had planted the bulb. He cleaned the plate with grass, packed up his bedroll and stood again with the things under his arm, studying the way the land lay: the fields stretching away, grey and dull at this time of year, bisected and criss-crossed with hedgerow. Although he knew little about the Walking Man's movements, he did know there was always a place near by, a protected place, that he could store a few things: things to be used the next time he passed. Sometimes that place was as far as half a mile from the camp.

The clue came from the grass: grey and stiff with frost. The Walking Man's footsteps were black, leading clearly away from the campsite. Caffery half smiled. If he hadn't been meant to follow them, those footsteps wouldn't be visible. The Walking Man never left anything to chance. Caffery set off, stepping carefully inside them, surprised to find his feet fitted exactly.

The footsteps stopped a third of a mile away at the far end of the next field and there, tucked secretly in the hedgerow, was the usual assortment of supplies covered with polythene: tinned food, a cooking pot, a flagon of scrumpy. Caffery tucked in the bedroll and the plate and secured the polythene around everything. When he straightened to leave he noticed something: about a yard along the hedgerow, tight under the hawthorn, a tiny patch of ground had been disturbed. When he crouched next to it and gently moved away the earth he found the bruised, tender tip of a crocus bulb.

Every person in the world had habits – Caffery thought later that morning as he pulled into a pub car park six miles away in Gloucestershire – from the obsessive compulsive who had to count every pea he ate, every light switch he touched, down to the drifter who seemed to have no aim and no direction yet could always find a good place to make camp and sleep. Everyone moved in patterns to some degree or another. Those patterns might be all but invisible, even to the persons themselves, but they were there, nonetheless. The Walking Man's patterns, the places he stopped, the places he planted crocuses, were slowly revealing themselves to Caffery. And the jacker? Caffery turned off the engine and opened the door, looked at the police vehicles: the forensics van, the four Sprinters belonging to the search units. Well, the jacker had patterns too. And they'd become clear. Given time.

'Sir?' The police search adviser – the POLSA – a small guy with neat John Lennon glasses, appeared next to the car. 'A word?'

Caffery followed him across the car park and through a low stone doorway into a room the landlord had set aside for the police to use. The games room, it smelt of stale beer and bleach. The pool table had been pushed to one side and replaced with a row of chairs; the dartboard was invisible behind a flip-chart stand where a series of photographs had been mounted.

'The briefing's in ten – and it's going to be a nightmare. This area the soil man's given us – it's massive.'

Every forensic test known to man had been thrown at the Bradleys' Yaris. There were signs of a struggle in the back seat – the upholstery had been torn and there were strands of Martha's pale blonde hair in a window seal, but the car hadn't yielded any fingerprints that didn't match a member of the Bradley family. The latex gloves, of course. No blood either and no semen. But there had been soil lodged in the treads of the tyres and an expert in forensic soil analysis had spent the night analysing the samples. He had put it together with how many miles the Bradleys estimated had gone on the clock, and decided there was only one place a car could have picked up a soil signature so unique: before the jacker had dumped it in Wiltshire he'd stopped somewhere out here in the Cotswolds, somewhere within a radius of about ten kilometres from this pub. Half the police force, it seemed, from the vehicles in the car park, had descended on the area.

'We knew it was going to be a wide net,' said Caffery. 'The soil man didn't have much time – we paid him to stay up all night.'

'With the area he gave me, I've identified about a hundred and fifty buildings that should be searched.'

'Shit. We'd need about six units to do that properly.'

'Gloucestershire's offering manpower. We're on their patch.'

'An interforce operation? I don't even know how you do that. I've never done a memorandum of understanding in my life, it's a logistical nightmare. We need to narrow it down.'

'That *is* narrowed down. Those hundred and fifty are just the buildings you could hide a car in. About thirty per cent of them are garages, mostly connected to private homes, so they're easy, but there are others you need Land Registry searches even to find out who owns them. And this is the Cotswolds, area of outstanding natural beauty. Half the places are second homes: Russians running some prostitute ring in London want to own a house next to Prince Charles but never bother to visit. It's either absentee rich bastards or bolshy farmers with single-bore shotguns. Think Tony Martin.' He tapped the back of his head. 'A round in the skull as you're running away. Welcome to rural bliss. Still, on a bright note, it rained yesterday. Perfect weather for it. If he parked out here the tracks will still be visible.'

Caffery wandered over to look at the photos on the board. A

series of tracks. Made last night in the lab using casts of the Yaris's tyres.

'There was something else in the soil, they told me. Wood chip?'

'Yes. So maybe a timber yard. Stainless-steel swarf, too, and flecks of titanium. The titanium's too small to say what process it came from so it's probably not relevant at this point, but the stainless steel means some kind of engineering plant. I've outlined seven in the area. And a couple of timber yards. I'm going to divvy up my team – half of them knocking on the buildings, the other half trying to find those tyre tracks.'

Caffery nodded. Tried to hide how despondent he felt. A radius of ten kilometres. A hundred and fifty buildings and Christ only knew how many driveways and lanes. It was going to be searching for a needle in a haystack. Even with extra units from Gloucestershire, with the warrants and the paperwork it was going to take for ever. And – the jacker's words came back to him: *It's started now, hasn't it, and it ain't going to stop just sudden –* time was the one thing they didn't have.

13

Flea's unit spent only 20 per cent of its time diving. During the rest they did other specialist operations, confined space and rope-access searches. On occasion they did general support-group work, including wide-range searches like this one in the Cotswolds.

They'd sat through the POLSA's briefing in the smelly games room. Her team was handed the job of hunting for tyre tracks. He'd given them a map with about six miles of road outlined in red and pointed them in the general direction, but when she came out of the briefing, got into the Sprinter van with the team and pulled out of the car park, instead of turning left to head out to the area, she turned right.

'Where are we going?' Wellard, her second-in-command, was sitting behind her. He leaned forward in the seat. 'It's the other way.'

She found a small passing space in the narrow lane, pulled the van over and cut the engine. She hooked her elbow over the back of the seat and gave the six men a long, serious look.

'What?' said one. 'What is it?'

'What is it?' she echoed. 'What is it? We've just sat through a ten-minute briefing. Short. Not long enough for anyone to fall asleep. Hurray. There's a little girl out there, eleven years old, and we've got a chance to find her. Now, there was a time when every one of you, to a man, would have come out of a briefing like that at a run. I'd have had to put muzzles on you all.'

They stared back at her, mouths half open, eyes dull and bovine. What had *happened* to them? Six months ago, when she'd last given it a thought, they'd been healthy young men, every one of them committed to and excited about his job. Now they had nothing: no spark, no enthusiasm. And one or two even looked like they were putting on weight. Getting flabby. How had this happened under her nose? How the hell had she not noticed?

'Look at you now. Not a flicker. That.' She held up her hand, rigid, horizontal. 'That is your brain-wave pattern. *Flat.* Not a spike. What the hell happened, guys?'

No one answered. One or two dropped their eyes. Wellard folded his arms and found something to gaze at out of the window. He pursed his lips as if he was going to—

'Whistle? Don't you dare *whistle*, Wellard. I'm not dense. I know what's going on.'

He turned back to her, raised his eyebrows. 'Do you?'

She sighed. Ran a hand through her hair. Sank back deflated in her seat and looked out of the windscreen at the brittle winter trees lining the road. 'Of course,' she muttered. 'I know what's going on. I know what you're saying.'

'It's like you're not here any more, Sarge,' he said. Some of the others murmured an agreement. 'It's that thousand-mile stare. Going through the motions. You say *we*'ve lost it, but if there's no one at home at the top of the pile then you might as well give up. And, not that it's all about the money, but it'll be the first year we won't be seeing our competency pay at Christmas.'

She turned again and eyed him steadily. She loved Wellard. He'd worked for her for years now and he was one of the best men she knew. She loved him more than she loved even her brother, Thom. A hundred times more than she loved Thom. Hearing Wellard speak the truth was hard.

'OK.' She knelt up and put her hands on the back of the seat. 'You're right. I haven't been at my best. But *you* –' she pointed a finger at them '– *you* guys haven't lost it. It's still there.'

'Eh?'

71

'OK. Think back to what the POLSA said. What was in the tyre treads?'

One shrugged. 'Wood chips. Titanium and stainless-steel swarf. Sounds like a manufacturing place.'

'Yes.' She nodded coaxingly. 'What about the titanium? Did that ring any bells?'

They stared back at her. Not getting it.

'Oh, come on,' she said impatiently. 'Think back. Four, five years? You were all on the unit then: you can't have forgotten. A water tank? Freezing day. A stabbing. You dived it, Wellard, and I was surface side. There was some dog kept coming out of the woods trying to mount my leg. You thought it was bloody hysterical. Don't you remember *that*?'

'Over near the Bathurst Estate?' Wellard was frowning at her. 'The guy chucked the weapon in the hatch? We found it in about ten minutes.'

'Yes. And?'

He shrugged.

She looked expectantly from face to face. 'Christ almighty. I've got to hand-feed you. Remember the place – decommissioned factory? It wasn't on this POLSA's map because it's closed down. But do you remember what it had been making when it was open?'

'Military gizmos,' said someone at the back of the Sprinter. 'Parts for Challenger tanks, that sort of thing.'

'See? The grey matter's starting to stir.'

'Which, I'm guessing, has some components made out of titanium? And stainless steel?'

'I'd bet my life on it. And do you happen to recall what we had to drive through to get to the damned water tank?'

'Christ on a bike,' Wellard said faintly, realization dawning on his face. 'A timber yard. And it's this direction – the way you're heading.'

'You see?' She started the engine, threw them a look in the rear-view. 'I said you hadn't lost it.'

14

Caffery stood alone on a small track that ran through pine forest, the air around him scented and muffled by the trees. A hundred yards to his right there was a decommissioned arms factory, and to his left a lumber-yard surrounded by worn, weatherboarded sheds. Sawdust, darkened to an apricot colour by the rain, was piled under a huge rusting hopper.

He kept his breathing slow and quiet, his hands slightly held out at his sides, his eyes focused on nothing. He was trying to get something elusive. Some kind of atmosphere. As if the trees could give up a memory. It was two in the afternoon. Four hours ago Sergeant Marley's team had ignored the POLSA's instructions and headed out here. They hadn't had to search long, just thirty minutes, before one of them had discovered a remarkably clear set of tyre tracks that exactly matched the Yaris's. Something had happened here last night. The jacker had been here and something important had happened.

Behind Caffery, further back up the track, the place was over-run with crime-scene investigators, search teams and dog handlers. An area had been taped out, fifty yards radius from the point of the clearest tyre marks. The teams had found footprints everywhere. Large deep marks made by a man's trainers. They should have been easy to cast for analysis but the jacker had studiously obliterated them, scoring the mud in criss-crosses with a long, sharp instrument. There were no child's shoes anywhere, but some of the man's prints, the CSI team had pointed out, were especially deep. Maybe the jacker had subdued or killed Martha in the car, then carried her away and dealt with her somewhere in the surrounding woods. Problem was, if he'd carried her, her scent wouldn't have touched the ground. And the weather was disastrous for the dog team – what scent line there might have been had been blown and rained away. The dogs had come in excited and salivating, straining at the leashes, then spent two hours chasing their tails, bumping into each other and running in circles. The lumber-yard and the derelict factory to Caffery's right had been searched. There, too, the teams turned up nothing – no clues that Martha had been anywhere near them. Even the disused water tank, now cracked and dry, hadn't got any clues to cough up.

He sighed, let his eyes come back into focus. The trees were giving him nothing either. As if they would. The site might as well be dead. From the direction of the lumber-yard, where they'd set up a work station, the crime-scene manager was wandering down the track. He wore his Andy Pandy forensics suit, the hood pulled down to his shoulders.

'Well?' said Caffery. 'Anything?'

'We've cast what he's left us of the prints. Do you want to see?'

'I guess.'

They walked back to the lumber-yard, their footprints and voices muffled by the trees.

'Seven different trails.' The CSM waved at the ground as they skirted the cordon. 'It looks like a jumble but there are actually seven distinct trails. They fan out in every direction and they all stop at the edge of the wood. No one can get anything after that. They could go anywhere – into the fields, through the plant and out on to the road. The teams are doing their best, but it's too big an area. He's tricking us. Clever little shit.'

Yeah, Caffery thought, peering into the woods as they walked, and he'll be liking how pissed off we are right now. He couldn't figure it out. Had this really been the place the jacker had taken Martha out of the car or had that happened somewhere else? Had he taken her miles away, knowing that the carousel of police expertise would descend on these woods and keep them occupied while he did his ugly business with her elsewhere? Not for the first time on this case Caffery had the feeling he was having his chain yanked.

Past the cordoned-off area, in the lumber-yard, teams were still working, moving around like ghosts in their forensics suits, the bitter smells of sap from the log sawmill hanging on the air. Next to a shed stacked with the stained dovecotes the yard produced, a temporary trestle table had been set up on which all the evidence the teams had gathered was being examined. The disused factory had been the worst to search – full of fly-tipped household waste: rotting old sofas and fridges, a child's tricycle, even a carrier bag of used nappies. The CSM and the exhibits officer had the job of deciding what to discard and what to tag and bag. They'd got the serious hump dealing with the nappies.

'I'm out of ideas on this.' The CSM took the plastic wrapping from a cast and placed it in front of Caffery. 'Can't work out what he's used here.'

A few people gathered round to look. Caffery got down on his haunches at eye level and stared at the cast. The bottom layer showed some traces of the footprints, but where the jacker had scored through them the plaster-of-paris had trickled deep into the holes made by the sharp instrument, creating spikes and peaks when the cast was reversed.

'Any idea what he used to make those gouges? Recognize that shape?'

The CSM shrugged. 'Your guess is as good as mine. Something sharp, but not with a blade. Something long, thin. Ten inches – a foot? Made a good job of it. We're not going to get any readable footprints.'

'Can I see?' Sergeant Flea Marley came forward from the group, holding a polystyrene cup of coffee. She was bedraggled from the search – her hair was a mess, her black coat unzipped to show her sweat-stained police T-shirt. Her face was different from the way she'd looked the other night outside the offices, he thought. A bit calmer. This morning her unit had fallen on its feet for a change and, really, he should be pleased for her. 'I'd like to look.'

The CSM held out some nitrile gloves. 'Want these?'

She put down the coffee, pulled on the gloves and tilted the cast to one side. Squinted at it.

'What?' said Caffery.

'Dunno,' she murmured. 'Dunno.' She turned it round and round. She rested her fingers thoughtfully on the tips of the spikes. 'Weird.' She handed the cast back to the CSM, turned away and wandered along the trestle table to where the exhibits officer was busily bagging and tagging the various bits and pieces they'd pulled out on the search to take to the forensics lab: tissues, Coke cans, syringes, a length of blue nylon rope. The place was obviously a hang-out for local glue huffers, the number of baggies they'd found. Most had been discarded in the field – along with more than a hundred plastic cider bottles. She stood, arms folded, and scanned the objects.

Caffery came up to her. 'See anything?'

She turned over a six-inch nail. An old plastic coat hanger. Put them back again. Bit her lip and looked back to where the CSM was wrapping the cast.

'What is it?'

'Nothing.' She shook her head. 'Thought the shape of those gouges reminded me of something. But it doesn't.'

'Boss?' DC Turner appeared from the direction of the main road, making his way between the parked cars. In a raincoat, with a little tartan scarf at the neck, he looked weirdly preppy.

'Turner? I thought you were on your way back to the office.'

'I know, I'm sorry, but I've just got off the phone to Prody. He's been trying to call – you must have been out of signal range. He's sent a PDF through to your BlackBerry.'

Caffery had a new phone and he could get email attachments wherever he was. The Walking Man would say it was typical of him to find more ways of never being absent from work. He fished in his pocket for the phone. The email icon was lit up.

'It arrived at the office an hour ago,' Turner said. 'Prody

scanned it and sent it straight over to you.' He gave an apologetic shrug, as if this whole thing was his fault. 'Another letter. Same as the one in the car. Same handwriting, same paper. Has a stamp on it but no postmark. Came through internal so we're trying to trace it back – but so far no one knows where it originated, how it got in the damned post.'

'OK, OK.' Caffery pulled out his phone. He could feel a vein pulsing in his temple. 'Get back to the office, Turner. I want you doing liaison for those search warrants the POLSA's after.'

He went further up the track to stand where he couldn't be seen, at the edge of the lumber-yard, behind an open-sided barn piled with the trunks of Norway spruces. He opened the attachment on the phone. It took a minute or two to download but when it came through he knew instantly it was from the jacker. Knew it wasn't a hoax.

Martha says hello. Martha says hello and says tell Mummy and daddy she's being really brave. But she doesn't like the cold very much does she. And she's not a big talker. Not any more. I've tried to have a conversation with her, but she won't speak a lot. Oh except for one thing: she's said a few times to let you know her mother's a cunt. Which maybe she's right about! Who knows! One thing's for sure: her mothers fat. Fat AND a cunt. Christ, life doesn't shine clean on some of us, does it? What a fat cunt she is. I look at someone like Martha and think that's the tragedy, isn't it, that she has to grow up and turn into a fat cunt like her mother? What does Mummy think about that? Does she think it's a shame her daughter has to grow up? Probably scared of what will happen when she leaves the house. I mean when Martha's gone who's Daddy going to diddle? Have to go back to having a ride on big tit Mama.

Caffery hadn't realized until now he'd been holding his breath. He let it out all at once. Scrolled up to the top of the letter and read it through again. Then, almost as if he might be caught reading a dirty mag or something, he shoved the phone in his pocket and looked around him. The vein in his temple was aching. On the other side of the yard Sergeant Marley had started the van and was reversing it back up the track. He pressed a finger to the vein, held it there for a count of ten. Then he made his way back to his car.

15

The Bradleys' was easy to spot as you drove on to the estate: there was a press pack camped opposite it, and in the front garden a pile of flowers and gifts that had been left by well-wishers. Caffery knew a private way in: he parked at the top of the estate and walked away into the grounds, wading through carpets of rustling leaves, looping round and coming at the house from the back. There was a door in the garden fence that the press hadn't found. The police and the Bradley family had reached an agreement: two or three times a day one of the family would show their face at the front door, just enough to keep the pack happy. The rest of the time they used the back entrance, coming through the garden. At three thirty p.m. it was almost dark, and Caffery slipped into the garden unnoticed.

On the back step there was a basket covered, like something out of a Delia Smith book, with a gingham cloth. When the family liaison officer opened the door Caffery pointed to it. She picked it up and beckoned him inside. 'The neighbour,' she whispered, closing the door behind him. 'She thinks they need feeding. We have to keep throwing stuff away – no one in this family's eating anything. Come on.'

The kitchen was warm and clean, despite its shabbiness. Caffery knew that for the Bradleys it was comforting – they looked as if they'd spent most of the last three days in there. A rickety portable TV had been brought in and stood on a table in the corner. It was showing the twenty-four-hour news channel.

Something about the economy and the Chinese government. Jonathan Bradley was at the sink, his back turned to the TV, his neck bent wearily. He was studiously washing a plate. He wore jeans and, Caffery noticed, mismatched slippers. Rose watched the TV from the kitchen table, dressed in a pink housecoat, an untouched cup of tea in front of her. She still looked medicated, her eyes glassy and unfocused. She was well built, Caffery thought, but not obviously obese and you wouldn't notice it if she was wearing an outdoor coat. Either the jacker was taking a shot in the dark, or it was just his own species of abuse. Or he'd seen her without a coat some time before the kidnap.

'Detective Caffery,' the FLO announced to the family, putting the basket on the table. 'I hope that's still OK.'

Only Jonathan responded. He stopped washing up and nodded. He got a tea-towel and wiped his hands. 'Of course it is.' He gave a tight smile and held out his hand. 'Hello, Mr Caffery.'

'Mr Bradley. Jonathan.'

They shook and Jonathan pulled a chair up to the table. 'Here. Have a seat. I'll make more tea.'

Caffery sat. It had been cold out in the lumberyard and his hands and feet felt hard and heavy. Finding the tracks should feel like an uptick in their box. Truth was, it hadn't moved them forward. The teams were still out there on the knock, rousing every householder and farmer. Caffery kept waiting for the POLSA's number to flash up on his phone screen. He wanted it to happen but, God, please don't let it happen now, he thought, not here in front of the family.

'You haven't finished your tea, darling.' Jonathan put his hands on his wife's shoulders and bent over to her. 'I'll make you a fresh one.' He took the cup and the basket from the table to the side. 'Look, Mrs Fosse's made us something to eat again.' His voice was unnaturally raised, as if this was an old people's home and Rose in the last stages of dementia. 'Nice of her. Need neighbours like that.' He pulled the linen cloth from the basket and sorted through the few things the woman had left. Some sandwiches, a pie and some fruit. A card, and a bottle of red wine with 'organic' printed on the label. Caffery kept his eye on the bottle. He didn't think he'd refuse if they offered. But the pie went into the microwave and the bottle stayed on the side, unopened, while Jonathan busied himself pouring hot water into a teapot.

'I'm sorry about this,' Caffery said, when they had cups of tea and slices of hot apple pie in front of them. Jonathan had seemed determined to keep up an illusion of normality, setting the table, serving food. 'Interrupting you like this.'

'It's OK.' Rose's voice was a monotone. She didn't look at him or the food, but kept her eyes on the TV set. 'I know you haven't found her. The lady told us.' She gestured at the FLO, who had settled at the other side of the table and was busy opening a huge file to take notes of the conversation. 'Told us nothing's happened. That's right, isn't it? Nothing's happened?'

'No.'

'They told us about the car. They said there was some clothing in it. Martha's. When you're ready we'll have it back, please.'

'Rose,' said the FLO, 'we've talked about this.'

'I'd like the clothing back, please.' Rose took her eyes off the TV and turned them to Caffery. They were swollen and red. 'That's all I'm asking. Just to have my daughter's property back now.'

'I'm sorry,' Caffery said. 'We can't do that. Not yet. It's evidence.'

'What do you need it for? Why do you have to hold on to it?'

The underwear was in the lab at HQ. They were desperately throwing test after test at it. So far no trace of the jacker's semen. Just like in the car. That made Caffery really uneasy, how controlled the guy was. 'I'm sorry, Rose. I really am. I know this is hard. But I have to ask you some more questions.'

'Don't be sorry.' Jonathan set a pot of cream on the table and distributed dessert spoons. 'It helps to talk. It's better to be able to talk about it than not. Isn't it, Rose?'

Rose nodded numbly. Her mouth fell open a little.

'She's seen all the papers, hasn't she?' Caffery asked the FLO. 'You showed her the one with Martha on the front page?'

The FLO got up, took a paper from a sideboard and put it on the table in front of him. It was the *Sun*. Someone in a women's clothing store the Bradleys had visited on the Saturday morning had sold the newspaper footage of Rose and Martha browsing near the window thirty minutes before the kidnapping. The newspaper had published a frame with a time stamp and the headline:

The last photo? Just half an hour before she is snatched by a monster eleven-year-old Martha shops happily with Mum.

Rose said, 'Why did they have to write that? Why did they say the last photo? It makes it sound as if . . .' She pushed the hair off her forehead. 'It makes it sounds as if – you know. As if it's all over.'

Caffery shook his head. 'It's not all over.'

'Isn't it?'

'No. We're doing absolutely everything we can to bring her home safely.'

'I've heard that before. You said it before. You said she'd be having her party.'

'Rose,' Jonathan said gently, 'Mr Caffery's only trying to help. Now, here.' He poured some cream on to her plate, then his own. He put a spoon into her hand and, taking his own, loaded it with apple pie and put it into his mouth, chewing carefully, his eyes on hers. He nodded significantly at her plate, trying to get her to copy him.

'She hasn't eaten a thing,' the FLO whispered. 'Not since it happened.'

'Typical you, Dad,' Philippa said from the sofa. 'Think food's going to cure everything.'

'She needs her strength. She really does.'

Caffery took the cream jug and poured it over his pie. He took a mouthful, and smiled encouragingly at Rose. She stared blankly at the newspaper on the table. 'Why did they have to write that?' she repeated.

'They'll say whatever sells papers,' Caffery said. 'There's not a lot we can do now. We did get the rest of the footage from the shop, though, and we've looked through it.'

'Why? Why did you need to do that?'

He arranged a chunk of pie on his spoon – did it carefully, taking his time. 'Rose, look. I know you've gone through it all before – I know it's painful, but I want to go back over that morning. I specifically want to talk to you about the shops you and Martha visited.'

'The shops we visited? Why?'

'You said you'd left the food shopping until last.'

'Yes.'

'I think you said you were looking for a cardigan? Was that for you or for Martha?'

'For me. Martha wanted tights. We went to Roundabout first and got her some. She wanted ones with hearts . . .' Rose paused. She pressed her fingers to her throat and struggled to maintain her composure. 'With hearts,' she continued, in a small voice. 'Red ones. And when we'd got those we went to Coco's. I saw a cardigan in there I liked.'

'Did you try it on?'

'Did she try it on?' said Jonathan. 'Does it matter if she tried a cardigan on? I'm sorry to sound rude, but what's that got to do with anything?'

'I'm just trying to establish a bit more about what that morning was like. Did you take your coat off and try the cardigan on?'

'You're not "trying to establish what the morning was like".' Philippa glared at him from the sofa. 'You're not doing that at all. I know why you're asking. It's because you think he was watching them. You think he was following them before they went anywhere near the car park, don't you?'

Caffery took another forkful of pie and chewed, holding Philippa's eyes.

'It's true, isn't it? I can see from your face. You think he was following them.'

'It's just one line in our enquiries. In my experience, random is rarely that random.'

'Does that mean you've got some more evidence?' asked Jonathan. 'Does that mean he's communicated with you again?'

There was something small and hard in the mouthful of pie. Caffery didn't answer while he worked it to the front of his mouth and pushed it with his tongue into the paper napkin. A piece of tooth, covered in pie. A broken tooth right in the middle of a case like this when he really didn't have time for a trip to the dentist.

'Mr Caffery? Has there been another communication?'

'I meant what I said. I'm trying to establish a little more of what . . .'

He trailed off, frowning at the napkin. It wasn't a *piece* of tooth at all. It was a whole tooth. But it hadn't come from him. He ran his tongue around his mouth. No gaps. And, anyway, it was too small. Much too small to have come from an adult.

'What is it?' Jonathan stared at the napkin in Caffery's hand. 'What've you got there?'

'I don't know.' Puzzled, Caffery wiped the tooth on the napkin and studied it closely. A tiny milk tooth.

'It's Martha's.' Rose was sitting bolt upright, her face absolutely white, her hands gripping the table. 'It is.' Her lips were pale. 'Look, Jonathan, it's her baby tooth. The one she used to keep in her locket.'

Philippa shot to her feet, strode to the table and bent over to peer at what Caffery was holding. 'Mum? Oh, God, Mum, it is. It's her tooth.'

'I'm sure.'

Very, very slowly Caffery put the tooth on the table about ten inches from his plate.

'How come it was in your mouth?' Next to him the FLO's voice was low and controlled.

Caffery looked down into his plate of apple pie and cream. The FLO looked at hers. They met each other's eyes and turned to Jonathan, who was staring at his own helping, his face ashen.

'Where did the pie come from?'

84

Jonathan's pupils were like pinpricks. 'From the neighbour,' he said faintly. 'Mrs Fosse.'

'She's been bringing food over since this started.' The FLO put her spoon down with a clatter. 'She's trying to help.'

Caffery pushed away his plate and felt automatically in his pocket for his mobile, not taking his eyes off the tooth. 'Where does she live? What number?'

Jonathan didn't answer. He bent over and spat a mouthful of pie into his bowl, then glanced apologetically at his wife, his eyes red, watery. He scraped his chair back as if he was going to get up. Instead he leaned over the plate again. This time when he opened his mouth vomit came out, splashing into the plate, little white trails of sputum and cream flecking the table.

Everyone stared at him as he mopped his mouth with a kitchen towel, dabbed at the mess. No one said a word. A long, cold silence spread around the kitchen as if no one had the confidence to speak. Even Caffery was silent, staring at the tooth, at Jonathan dejectedly cleaning the table. Then, as Caffery was about to stand, to do something constructive, get a cloth to help, Rose Bradley came to life. 'You pig!' She pushed her chair back with a loud scraping noise and jumped to her feet, pointing a finger at her husband. 'You absolute hateful pig, Jonathan. You think that if we just pretend everything's normal it'll all go away.' She reached across the table and in one move sent the plate flying off the table to crack into pieces against the cooker. 'You think *pie* and *tea* and mountains of bloody *cakes* are going to bring her back. You do. You really do.'

She snatched up the tooth and, ignoring the FLO who had half risen out of her chair, her hands up to calm the situation, left the room, slamming the door. A moment later, Philippa shot her father a filthy look and followed her mother, slamming the door again. Their footsteps sounded on the stairs, another door slammed. There was a thump, and then the sound of muffled sobbing.

In the kitchen no one spoke. Everyone sat in silence, staring at their feet.

16

Ten miles to the south in a street on the outskirts of the small town of Mere, Janice Costello, a thirty-six-year-old mother of one, parked her Audi and cut the engine. She turned to the back, where her four-year-old daughter was strapped into her car seat, ready for bed in pyjamas, Hello Kitty slippers and a hot-water bottle. She had a duvet tucked around her.

'Emily, sweetheart? You OK, poppet?'

Emily yawned and looked blearily out of the window. 'Where are we, Mummy?'

'Where are we? We're . . .' Janice bit her lip and ducked her head down to look out of the window. 'We're near the shops, darling. And Mummy's going to be just two minutes. Just two minutes, OK?'

'I've got Jasper.' She waggled her toy rabbit. 'We're having a cuddle.'

'Good girl.' Janice leaned over and tickled Emily under the chin, making her jam it down and wriggle gleefully.

'Stop it! Stop it!'

Janice smiled. 'That's a good girl. You keep Jasper warm, and I'll be straight back.'

She unbuckled and got out of the car, central-locking it. She gave Emily a last glance, straightened and stood under the streetlamp, looking anxiously up and down the road. She was lying to Emily. There weren't any shops round here. What was here, just around the corner, was an NHS clinic. It was playing host to a group counselling session. Three men and three women: they met every Monday and they'd be coming out – she checked her watch – any minute now. She went to the corner and stood with her back against the wall, craning her neck so she could see the building. The lights were on in the porch and in two of the front windows – maybe where the session was taking place – the blinds were drawn tight.

Janice Costello was about as certain as she could be that her husband was having an affair. Cory had been coming to this group-therapy session for three years, and she was pretty sure he'd developed a 'friendship' with one of the women. At first it had been just a nagging suspicion, just a sense that something wasn't right – a distance about him, not coming to bed when she did and long, unexplained absences when he took his car and claimed to have 'just been driving around thinking'. There were unexpected arguments over unimportant things – the way she answered the phone or put vegetables on the plate at dinner, even the mustard she chose. Mustard. How stupid was that? A stand-up screaming match over the fact he wanted grains because English mustard was 'so *parochial*. For Christ's sake, Janice, can't you see that?'

It was the casual mentions of 'Clare' that really tipped her off, though. Clare says this, Clare says the other. When Janice quizzed him he gave her a look as if he didn't know what she was talking about.

'Clare,' she repeated. 'You've just said her name about twenty times. Clare?'

'Oh, *Clare*. From Group, you mean. What about her?'

Janice didn't push it any further, but when she subtly slipped his phone out of his pocket later that night, when he'd fallen asleep in front of the TV, she found two calls from 'Clare P'. And now it had got to the point where she wanted to know. It should be easy. All she'd have to do was see him with the woman. She'd know instantly from his mannerisms.

The lights in the window went off and another came on in the hallway. The end of the session. Her heart began to pound.

Someone was going to come to the door any second. Her phone rang in her pocket. Shit, she'd forgotten to turn it off. She pulled it out, ready to kill it, but when she saw who was calling her finger came off the red button and she stared at it, not knowing what to do.

Cory. Cory was calling her. He was only ten yards away in the building and the moment the door opened he'd hear her phone ringing through the cold air. Her finger went back to the kill button, hesitated, then moved and hit the green.

'Hi.' Her voice was bright. She twisted back round the corner and stood facing the wall, one finger in her ear. 'How'd it go?'

'Yeah, you know.' Cory sounded tired, moody. 'Same old, same old. Where are you?'

'Where am I? I'm . . . I'm at home, of course. Why?'

'Home? I've just been calling you on the landline. Didn't you hear?'

'No – I mean, I was in the kitchen. Busy with dinner.'

There was a pause. 'Shall I call you on it now, save the bill?'

'No! No – that's . . . Don't, Cory. You'll wake Emily.'

'She's asleep? It's not even six o'clock yet.'

'Yeah, but you know – school tomorrow—' She broke off. Emily was in Reception: she was quite old enough to tell Cory they hadn't been at home tonight. She was getting into deep lies now. Deep trouble. She swallowed. 'Are you coming home?'

There was a long pause. Then he said, 'Janice? Are you sure you're at home? You sound like you're outside somewhere.'

'Of course I'm at home. Of course.' Her pulse was racing: she could feel the adrenalin making her fingers tingle. 'I've got to go, Cory. She's crying. I've got to go.'

She jammed her finger on the red button and dropped back against the wall, breathing hard. She was shaking. There was too much to think about. Too much. She'd have to make up a story about how she and Emily remembered they didn't have something – milk or coffee or something – and how they'd had to go out to the shops. Then she'd have to buy something to prove it. Or she'd have to say Emily wouldn't stop crying so she'd bundled her into the car and driven her around for a while hoping it would soothe her, the way it had when she was a colicky baby. She should go straight home and smooth it all out – make it fit the lie she was going to tell. But she'd come all this way and she couldn't just back off now. She had to see Clare.

Steeling herself she poked her head round the wall again. Jerked it straight back. The front door had opened. The bloody door had opened and there were people there, light spilling out on to the pavement, voices. She pulled the hood of her quilted jacket up, dragged it down low over her eyes and gingerly peered out again. A woman came out – an older woman with severely cut white hair and a long tartan coat – followed by another in a brown coat, belted. Janice didn't think either of them was Clare. They were too old. Too masculine-looking.

But then the door opened wider and Cory stepped out, zipping his jacket. He was walking half sideways, turning back to the building to say something to a tall thin woman with very pale straight hair. She was dressed in a long leather coat and high-heeled boots. She had a sharp, slightly bent nose, and was laughing at what he was saying. She stopped on the steps to the clinic and wrapped a scarf around her neck. Cory paused on the pavement and looked up at her. One or two people came out behind, filtered around them. The woman spoke and Cory shrugged. Rubbed his nose. Then he glanced thoughtfully up and down the street.

'What is it?' The woman's voice came through the air as clear as a bell. 'What's the matter?'

Cory shook his head. 'Nothing.' He looked up and down the street again, as if he was turning something over in his head. He went back up two steps, put his hand on the woman's elbow, dropped his face and murmured something to her.

She frowned, raised her eyes to him. He spoke again and she held up her hand, four fingers splayed. Then she turned them into a bright little wave. 'Whatever,' she said, with a smile. 'Whatever, Cory. See you next week.'

Cory stepped away, still checking cautiously over his shoulder.

He thrust his hand into his pocket, pulled out his car keys and began to walk purposefully away from the clinic. A bolt of panic went through Janice. Fumbling for her keys she trotted as fast as she could back to the Audi.

As she got nearer she could see something was wrong with the car. Her heart thudded, low and hard. The Audi sat about twenty yards away, under a streetlight. And Emily wasn't in it. 'Emily?' she murmured. '*Emily?*'

She broke into a run, not caring who saw her now. Her scarf unwound itself and flew off. She nearly dropped her keys. She got to the car, slammed her hands on the window, put her face to the glass.

Emily was crouched in the footwell under the back seat, surprised by her mother's horrified face. She'd unbuckled herself, crawled down there and was playing with Jasper. He was at arm's length, turned to face her as if they'd been having a conversation.

Janice dropped against the car, her hand over her heart.

'Mummy!' Emily shouted at the window-pane. She bounced up and down on the back seat. 'Mummy, guess what?'

Taking a deep breath Janice went round to the front, got in and turned to her little girl. 'What? What am I guessing, sweetheart?'

'Jasper's done a poo. In his pants. Did you get some nappies from the shop for him?'

'Shop's shut, sweetheart.' She forced a smile. 'Didn't get nappies. No shop, no nappies – I'm sorry. Get yourself strapped in, darling. We're going home.'

17

Caffery was glad he never got offered that glass of wine. If he'd had even a sniff of booze he'd have ballsed up the whole logistical nightmare that came after the tooth appeared in his mouth.

The neighbour, Mrs Fosse, a nosy, birdlike woman who wore slippers and two knitted sweaters, one over the other, had nothing to hide. He was confident of that after speaking to her for twenty minutes. She'd made the pie and put it on the doorstep with the other things at one o'clock. Hadn't liked to knock because she found it awkward, not knowing what to say: she hoped the little gifts expressed her feelings properly. Which meant the jacker had come into the garden and pressed the tooth into the pie some time in those two hours. He must have teased it down through the twin steam holes Mrs Fosse had made with a knife.

The Walking Man was right, Caffery thought: this man was cleverer than anyone he'd dealt with before. He decided to get the Bradleys the hell out of the vicarage as soon as possible.

'I hate you. I really, really *hate* you.' In the utility room Philippa was glaring at Caffery. Her face was white, her hands were in tight fists. The side door was open and an officer from the dog-handling unit waited on the doorstep, holding both of the family dogs on leashes and trying hard not to get sucked into this argument. 'I can't believe you're doing this.'

Caffery sighed. It had taken him more than two hours and ten different calls, first, to get permission for the move and, second, to find somewhere to take the family. In the end it meant that a team of senior investigating officers on an exchange exercise from Holland were turned out of the suites reserved for visiting police chiefs in the training block at HQ. Now the family were ready with their bags and their coats on. 'Philippa,' he said, 'I promise you – the dogs will be OK.'

'They can't be with someone they don't know.' She had tears in her eyes. 'Not at a time like this.'

'Listen,' he said carefully. He knew he had to be really cautious – the last thing he needed was a hysterical teenager upsetting this scenario. He'd called the two patrol cars that had been waiting just off the estate, out of the view of the press. They'd be rolling up any minute now, and when they did he wanted the whole family in and away before the reporters had time to wonder what the hell was going on. The head of Corporate Communications had been dragged out of a darts game in Brislington and was in hasty negotiations with some of the major newspapers. The jacker had tracked the Bradleys here from press photos of them coming and going from the house. It was a symbiotic relationship, and if the media wanted any more co-operation from the police they'd have to lay off any further coverage of the Bradleys.

'You can't take the dogs with you, Philippa. We can't have animals in the safe-house. They'll be looked after by the dog handlers. And you're going to have to understand how serious this is. You're going to have to understand that the man who did this to your sister is . . .'

'Is what?'

He rubbed a finger across his forehead. He wanted to say, Is cleverer than anyone I've dealt with? Cleverer and twice, no, three times, as weird?

'You can take one dog. *One.* The other'll have to go with the handler. OK? But you have to take this seriously, Philippa. Do I have your promise that you will? For your parents' sake. For Martha's sake.'

She looked at him sullenly, her dyed black hair flopping down over half of her face. Her bottom lip moved almost imperceptibly, and for a moment he thought she was going to scream. Or tear around the utility room kicking things. But she didn't. She muttered an almost inaudible 'S'pose.'

'Which one?'

She looked across at the dogs. They looked back at her. The spaniel tentatively banged its tail on the floor, wondering if this human discussion was an elaborate preamble to a walk. Seeing them together like this Caffery noticed just how old and infirm the collie was compared to the spaniel.

'Sophie.'

Hearing her name, the spaniel straightened eagerly, her tail metronoming side to side.

'The spaniel?'

'She's the best guard dog,' Philippa said defensively, taking the lead from the handler. 'She'll look after us best.'

The collie watched Sophie take her place next to Philippa.

'What're you going to do with the other one?' Caffery asked the handler.

'Probably ask around the force.' He looked down at the collie, which had put its head back and was looking up at him, as if it already knew he was the new person in charge. 'There's usually an idiot on some unit or other soft enough to be a foster-parent for a day or two. Until the whole thing blows over.'

Caffery sighed. 'Jesus.' He felt in his pocket for his car keys. 'Here.' He chucked the keys to the handler. 'Put it in my car.' The collie raised its eyes to him, dropped its head on one side. He sighed. 'Yeah, OK – don't make a big thing of it.'

He took Philippa and Sophie into the hallway, where her parents and the FLO were waiting among the hastily packed suitcases. He stood next to the window and peered out through the crack in the curtains. He'd told the cars not to use their blues and twos. Didn't want to stretch out the warning the reporters would get. 'Now, you know the deal. Our press office doesn't want you covering your faces when you go out there. The flashes will go off – just ignore them. Don't be baited. Just go about this business as quickly and calmly as you can. Pretend it's a fire drill. No panicking but just get everything moved along, OK?'

The family nodded. Caffery checked out of the window, looking along the silent estate. Still no cars. He was about to reach into his pocket for the phone when the door to the kitchen opened and one of the CSI officers who had turned up to forensicate the back garden, the basket and the pie dish appeared in the hallway.

'What?' Caffery turned from the window. 'What is it?'

The man, who seemed barely out of his teens and still had pimples on his chin, gave Rose Bradley an uncomfortable look. 'Mrs Bradley?'

Rose backed to the wall, her hands tucked tightly under her armpits.

'What is it?' Caffery said.

'I'm sorry, sir. It's the tooth you wanted to have tested.'

'You don't need it.' Tears welled in Rose's sore eyes. 'You don't need it.'

'We do need it, Rose,' the FLO said gently. 'Really. We do.'

'You don't. You can take my word for it. It's hers. The first tooth she lost and she never wanted to let go of it. We had it put into a locket for her. I promise – I'd know it anywhere.'

Outside, the cars were sweeping into the driveway. Caffery sighed. Great timing.

'Rose, please, give the gentleman the tooth.' He glanced out of the window. No time to head them off now. They'd have to start the whole exercise again. 'We can't help Martha unless you give it to him.'

'*No!* I won't. You have my word for it, it's her tooth.' The tears plopped out of her eyes. She lowered her chin and tried to wipe them on the shoulders of her blouse. 'It is her tooth. I promise it is.'

'We don't know that. It could be anyone's. It could be a hoax – it could be anything.'

'If you think it's a hoax, why are you moving us out? You believe me. So why do I have to give it up?'

'Jesus Christ,' he hissed impatiently. The whole exercise was falling apart at the seams. 'I have to tell your daughter to grow up and now I'm telling the mother to do the same.'

'That's not necessary,' said the FLO.

'Christ.' Caffery ran his hands through his hair. Outside, the cars had stopped. Their engines were running. 'Just – *please*, Rose. Please give the nice man the tooth.'

'Mum.' Philippa stepped up behind her mother, put her hands on her shoulders and held Caffery's eyes. There was no respect, just a look that said she and her mother were in this together and no one, *no one*, could understand what this whole thing meant. 'Mum, do what he says. I don't think he's going to give up.'

Rose was silent. Then she pushed her face into her elder daughter's neck. The sobs shook her body noiselessly. After a moment or two her right hand came out from her armpit and slowly unclenched. She held out the tooth on her open palm. With a quick glance at Caffery, the CSI man stepped forward and carefully took it from her.

'Good,' Caffery said, feeling a line of sweat break just under his hairline and trail slowly down into the back of his collar. He hadn't realized until now how tense he was. 'Now can we all get going?'

18

At six o'clock that afternoon the inspector came into the office, put a hand on Flea's desk and leaned over so that he was staring hard into her face.

She ducked out of his way. 'What? What is it?'

'Nothing. Just the superintendent likes you, apparently. I've had Professional Standards on the phone.'

'Yeah?'

'Yeah. That review of your competency pay? It's been suspended.'

'You mean they'll get their bonus?'

'Happy Christmas. Ching ching ching.'

When he'd gone she sat for a while in silence in her familiar office, surrounded by the things she'd got easy with over the years. The photos of the team on jobs pinned to the walls, the budget forecasts scribbled on the whiteboard. The stupid postcards stuck to the locker doors. One showed a man in snorkel and fins and read: *Steve had got all his diving gear, now all he needed was to find those elusive muffs his friends kept telling him about.* And a force poster on the wall about an anti-drugs operation: *Atrium: since 2001 we've arrested one person a day. Help us make that two.* One of the team had used a marker pen to delete '*a day*'. Flea would catch serious hell from the superintendents if they saw any of this, but she'd let the boys leave it all up. She liked their sense of humour. Liked the easy way they were around each other. They were going to get their money.

They could buy their Xboxes and their kids' Wiis and their alloy wheels and all the guy things that would make it a real Christmas for them.

The front door opened, wafting in a blast of cold air and petrol fumes from outside. Someone came down the corridor. Wellard, carrying a bag and heading for the decontamination room. She stopped him in the doorway. 'Hey.'

He put his head into the office. 'What?'

'You're going to get your pay. The inspector just told me.'

He inclined his head. A small, chivalrous bow. 'Well, thank you, kind lady. My poor disabled children will smile this Christmas for the first time in their sad, short lives. Oh, they will be content, kind miss. They will. It will be the best Christmas ever.'

'Make sure the one with the polio gets the iPod Touch.'

'You're not as nasty as you like to pretend, Boss. No, really, you're not.'

'Wellard?'

He paused, door half open. 'Uh-huh?'

'Seriously. This morning.'

'This morning?'

'You saw the cast the CSI made. You didn't recognize what the jacker used to score out his prints?'

'No. Why?'

'I don't know.' She felt something cold and half opaque patter across the back of her head. A shadowy picture of the forests they'd searched. The farmland stretching away to either side. During the search this morning there had been whispers about the things the jacker had said in the letter. No one outside MCIU was supposed to know but things got around the other units, and this morning all the officers had worked with their heads full of vague, unsettling notions about what the jacker might have done with Martha. 'Just a . . . feeling about that place. Something I can't quite put my finger on.'

'A hunch?'

She gave him a cold look. 'I'm learning to trust my "hunches",

Wellard. Learning I'm not as blonde as you think. And I feel like there's something in the . . .' she groped for the word '. . . the *environment* out there that was important. Does that mean anything to you?'

'You know me, Sarge, I'm a grunt. It's my stunning body I use to turn a dime. Not my loaf.' He winked and left the office, his footsteps fading down the corridor. She smiled bleakly and listened to him go. Outside, rain had begun to fall, so slow, fat and nebulous it could almost have been snow. Winter really was here.

19

At six fifteen a dark Audi S6 screamed through the small streets of Mere, gunning itself around the bends. Janice Costello was racing to get home before her husband, her hands gripping the wheel, sweat making her palms slick. The radio was on – a media psychiatrist giving his opinion on the carjacker who had kidnapped a little girl in Frome the other day: it was probably a white male in his thirties. Could be a husband, could even be a father. Janice shakily turned the radio off. Why hadn't she thought about that bastard before she'd left Emily on her own in the car? Frome wasn't that far from here. She was so, so lucky nothing had happened. She was losing her mind, taking a risk like that. Losing it.

Clare. It was all *her* fault. Clare, Clare, *Clare*. The name bothered Janice more than almost anything. If it had been *Mylene* or *Kylie* or *Kirsty*, any one of those young-girl names, she'd have found it easier. She could have pictured a big-breasted teenager with straightened blonde hair and 'BENCH' written on her bottom. But *Clare*? Clare sounded like someone Janice might have gone to school with. And the pale woman at the clinic wasn't sexy or brash or inexperienced. She looked like someone you could have a proper conversation with. She *looked* like a Clare.

It wasn't the first time Cory'd had an affair. That had happened six years ago. With a 'beauty therapist' whom Janice had never met but pictured as someone with a year-round suntan, expensive underwear and maybe a Brazilian bikini wax. When Janice had found out about it, the Costellos had gone into therapy together: Cory was so repentant, so mortified at the mistake he'd made, that for a while she almost forgave him. And then something else had entered the mix, something that changed her mind and convinced her to give him a second chance. She'd found she was pregnant.

Emily arrived in a rush in the winter and Janice was poleaxed with such unexpected love for her little girl that for years it didn't matter what was happening in the marriage. Cory was in therapy and had a new job in Bristol as a 'marketing consultant on sustainable product development' to a printing company. It made her laugh, that title, with the earnest way he disregarded his own carbon footprint. Still, he was earning enough money for Janice to stop work and take small freelance editing jobs, which paid a pittance but kept her skills sharp. For a while life had moved along serenely. Until now. Until Clare. And now everything had narrowed down to this obsession – nights lying awake, staring at the ceiling while Cory snored next to her. The secretive phone monitoring, the checking of pockets at the dry-cleaner's, the questioning. All leading to tonight – the darkened rush across town with poor Emily tucked up in the back of the car.

She lunged the Audi sideways, down the residential street. Screeched to a halt in the driveway of their Victorian semi. No Cory. When she turned round she saw that Emily, bless her – instead of sitting white-faced, terrified by the race home – really had fallen asleep, Jasper tucked between her chin and her shoulder like one of those neck pillows clutched by people trailing around in airports.

'Come on, sweetheart,' Janice whispered. 'Mummy's going to take you up to bed.'

She was able to bundle Emily out of the car and into her bunkbed without waking her. She rubbed toothpaste on a finger hurriedly round Emily's sleepy mouth – it would have to do for now – kissed the little girl on the forehead, tore off her own coat and shoes and threw them into the wardrobe. She was in the kitchen emptying the last of the milk into the sink when Cory's car pulled up outside. Quickly she rinsed the carton and carried it out to the front to put in the recycling bin.

Cory met her at the door, keys in his hand, suspicion on his face. 'Hello.' He looked her up and down, noting the outdoor shoes.

'Out of milk.' She rattled the empty carton at him. 'I went to try and get some more but the shop's run out.'

'You went out? What about Emily?'

'I left her, of course. I put her into a nice warm bath and gave her some razor blades to play with. For God's sake, Cory, what do you take me for? She came with me.'

'You said she was asleep.'

'I *said* she'd woken up. You don't listen.' She put the milk carton into the bin and stood, arms folded, studying him. He was good-looking, Cory. No getting away from that. But lately there was something soft about his jaw that made him seem almost feminine. And there was a bald spot starting on the top of his head. She'd noticed it in bed the other night. It didn't bother her, but she wondered what Clare would make of it. Was it worth saying something to him – just to puncture his ego? Or should she let Clare notice it?

'How was the session?'

'Told you. Same old, same old.'

'Clare?'

'Eh?'

'*Clare*. The one you were talking about the other day. Remember?'

'Why do you want to know about her?'

'Just showing an interest. Is she still fighting with her ex?'

'Her husband? Yes – the piece of shit. The things he did to her, to her kids, outrageous.'

There was a tinge of extra venom there. *Piece of shit*? She'd never heard him use that expression before. Maybe something he'd learned from Clare.

'Anyway – I'm thinking of stopping the group.' He pushed past her into the hallway, unbuttoning his coat. 'It's taking too much time. Things are changing at work – they want more hours out of me.'

Janice followed him into the kitchen and watched him open the fridge, hunt for a beer. 'More hours? That'll mean late nights, I suppose.'

'That's the one. Can't afford not to. Not with the world the way it is. The directors want me at a big meeting tomorrow afternoon. We're going to discuss it then. Four o'clock.'

Four. Like a slap, Clare's face came back to Janice, the way she was holding her hands up. Four fingers. They meant four o'clock. Cory and Clare were meeting at four. He wouldn't be answering any of Janice's calls because he'd be in a 'meeting'. And then, almost to confirm exactly what she'd suspected, he said conversationally, 'What are you doing tomorrow? Any plans?'

She didn't answer for a moment, just regarded him calmly, her heart racing. I don't love you, she thought. Cory, I really don't love you. And in a way that makes me very happy.

'What?' he said. 'Why are you looking at me like that?'

'Nothing,' she said lightly, then turned away and began unloading the dishwasher. It was supposed to be his job, but she always did it, so why should today be any different? 'Tomorrow? Oh, I think I'll pick up Emily from school and head over to Mum's.'

'That's an hour's drive.' He raised his eyebrows. 'I'm happy for you, Janice, that you've got the free time to do things like that. I really am.'

'I know.' She smiled. Cory was always pointing out how easy her life was, doing freelance stuff here and there, not a *proper* job like he did. But she wasn't rising to the bait. 'I finished the project for that website and I thought I'd take the time before I start the next job. I may stay at Mum's – maybe have dinner with her.' She paused and repeated herself very slowly, staring down at the handful of cutlery in which her face was blearily reflected. 'Yes. I won't be in town tomorrow, Cory. Not for the whole afternoon.'

20

By seven o'clock the world was so cold and dark it might have been midnight. There was no moon, no starlight, just the glow of the security lights in the lumber-yard at the end of the lane. Flea stopped her car and got out, shrugging on a fleece and a water-proof. She wore Thinsulate gloves and a wool beanie. Usually she was OK in the cold – she had to be in her job – but this autumn the weather had a hard, almost vindictive edge that seemed to affect everyone. She flashed her card at the soporific cop in the car that blocked the lane and clicked on her torch. The track through the pine forest was a pale, almost luminous yellow in the beam. The Yaris's tracks were surrounded by limp police tape, the ground covered in little forensics marker flags. She passed them and went through the pool of light cast by the yard's halogen lights, the conveyor-belts, sawmills and log splitters now silent and shadowy. She continued down the lane until she was in the grounds of the abandoned factory.

Flea had been home already. She'd jogged and showered and eaten and listened to the radio and read. She couldn't wind down. She couldn't stop wondering what it was about the search that wouldn't lie right at the back of her thoughts. If Dad had still been around he'd have said: *You've got a thorn in your head, girl. Better you take it out than leave it there and let it go to poison.*

Now she went to the tree-line, where the field began and where Wellard had been standing. She found the line of cleared land, the place that had been searched and the line of rubbish, like the boundary line of flotsam and jetsam a retreating tide had left. She twisted the beam to halfway between flood and spot. Shone it on the line of rubbish and tried to pull up images from this morning.

Whatever was bugging her had struck her after they'd searched the tank. She'd been standing over at the tank talking to one of the other team's sergeants about what time their shift finished and what staffing they'd have available if they had to go into over-time. The teams were still searching around them. Wellard had been over here at the edge of the field. She remembered watching him vaguely while she spoke. He'd found something in the grass and was talking to the crime-scene manager about it. Flea had been concentrating on what the sergeant next to her was saying and only half watching Wellard and the CSM, but now she could see the picture clearly. She could even see what he was holding out to the CSM. A piece of rope. Blue, nylon, about a foot long. The rope itself wasn't what she'd wanted – she'd seen it later on the exhibits table and it had been unremarkable in and of itself – but something about it had started up a particular thought process that she knew was important.

She went to the old water tank where she had been standing and switched off the torch. She waited for a few quiet moments, surrounded by the monster shapes of the winter trees, beyond them the ploughed fields stretching away, dull, immense and dead. From somewhere in the distance to her right came the giant sound of a train racing along the Great Western Union Railway, flying through the darkness. Flea had a desktop at home that drove her crazy by giving off a faint crackle moments before her phone rang. She knew what it was – electromagnetic currents try-ing to piggyback the speaker wires for antennae – but to her it always seemed as if the machine had prescience, a subtle inkling of the future. Wellard would laugh if she told him, but sometimes she imagined she had a similar electromagnetic warning system – a biological buzzer that sent the hairs up on her arms moments before a thought or an idea clicked into place. Now, standing in the frozen field, she felt it happen. A current racing across her skin. Just seconds before the knowledge fell neatly into her head.

Water. The rope had made her think of boats and marinas and *water*.

This morning the thought had gone as quickly as it had come – the other sergeant was talking to her and, anyway, there wasn't any water around here so she'd let it flit away. She'd dismissed it. But now she'd had time to think about it she realized she'd been wrong. There was water here. And not very far away.

She turned slowly and looked towards the west, to where the low cloud cover was up-lit a faint orange by a town or highway. She began to walk. Like a zombie, Sarge – Wellard would crack up to see her now. She cut straight across the field, frozen grass soaking her boots, hardly looking down as if something had a hook in her sternum and was slowly dragging her along. Through a small glade of crowded rustling trees, over two stiles on to a short gravelled lane, silver in the diffuse torchlight. After ten minutes she stopped.

The path she stood on was narrow. To her right the ground sloped upwards. To her left it ran steeply down to a tarry gully. A decommissioned canal. The Thames and Severn. An eighteenth-century engineering miracle, built to carry coal from the Severn estuary – when it had become redundant it had seen some service as a pleasure canal. Half dried out now, what water was left in the bottom had shrunk to a dark, poisonous-looking mulch. She knew this canal: knew its beginning and its end. To the east it extended twenty-six miles as far as Lechlade, to the west eight miles to Stroud. It was littered with the evidence of its former existence. The broken and rotting hulls of old coal and pleasure barges were dotted every few hundred yards. There were two in the short stretch she could see now.

She went a few yards along the towpath, sat down and swung her feet on to the deck of the nearest barge. The smells of decay and stagnant water were overpowering. Bacteria and moss. She put one hand on the deck and leaned over, shining the torch into the hull. This vessel wasn't like the old iron-built coal barges that had first used this waterway: it was newer, a timber-hulled Norfolk wherry, perhaps, with its masts removed and an engine fitted. Probably brought to this side of the country as a canal cruiser. The timber had given in to the years of neglect and was now half submerged, debris from the canal floating on the black stinking water inside it. Nothing else to see. She knelt up and searched around on the tiller deck at the stern. Kicked aside beer cans and the plastic bags that floated on the water like jellyfish. She felt all around the platform and found nothing. She hauled herself out of the barge and went back along the towpath until she found the next. This one was older and might actually have been a working barge. It sat higher out of the canal and the water inside the hull was only knee-deep. She dropped into it, the freezing, inky water soaking into her jeans. She waded a little way, letting her feet in their trainers feel every inch of the hull below her. Every rivet, every piece of jettisoned wood.

Something clinked. It rolled away from her foot an inch or two. She pushed her sleeve to her upper arm and, bending at the waist, lowered her hand into the freezing water. Groped in the muck. She found the object and pulled it out.

A mooring spike. Straightening, she shone the torch on it. It was about a foot long and shaped like a long fat tent peg with a splayed top where, over the years, it had been hammered into the banks for tying up to. Thicker than a blade and sharper than a chisel, it could easily have made the spikes in the CSM's plaster-of-paris cast. The jacker might have used it to score out his footprints.

She climbed out of the hull and stood, water streaming off her, on the towpath. She looked along the faintly gleaming canal. All the barges would have used a spike just like this. The place must be littered with them. She studied the spike in her hand. It would make a good weapon. You wouldn't want to argue with someone holding this. No. You wouldn't argue. Especially if you were only eleven years old.

21

The dog's name was Myrtle. She was threadbare, half crippled by arthritis. Her white and black tail hung off the end of her bony back like a limp flag. But she hobbled along obediently behind Caffery, got in and out of the back seat of his car without complaining, though he could tell it hurt her. Even waited patiently outside the forensics lab at HQ in Portishead while he struggled with the technicians and tried to push forward the testing of the baby tooth against Martha's DNA. By the time he was done with the lab he was feeling sorry for the damned dog. He stopped at a Smile store and got armfuls of dog food. The chew toy seemed a bit hopeful but he bought it anyway and put it on the back seat next to her.

It was late, gone ten, by the time he got back to the MCIU building. The place was still busy. He took Myrtle limping along the corridor, running the gauntlet of people poking their heads out of offices to speak to him, hand him reports, messages, but mostly to pat the dog or make wisecracks about her: *Jack, your dog looks like I feel. Hey, it's Yoda in a coat. Here, furry Yoda.*

Turner was still there, dishevelled and a bit sleepy but at least no earring. He spent a little time bringing Caffery up to date on the trawl for the Vauxhall, which still hadn't borne fruit, and gave him contact details for the superintendent who'd authorized the surveillance on the vicarage. Then he spent a longer time crouched down talking nonsense to Myrtle, who wearily lifted her tail once or twice in acknowledgement. Lollapalooza came in, still in full makeup, but she was letting her guard down: she'd taken off her high heels and rolled up her sleeves to reveal the down of fine dark hairs on her arms. She hadn't done well on the sex offenders, she admitted. CAPIT had a short list of people they thought could meet the criteria: they'd been checked on overnight. But what she *could* tell Caffery was that chondroitin was the way to go with the dog's arthritis. That or glucosamine. Oh, and cut all grains out of the poor animal's diet. By which she meant *all* grains. All of them.

When she'd gone he opened a can of Chum and let it gloop on to one of the cracked plates from the unit kitchen. Myrtle ate slowly, her old head on one side, favouring the left side of her jaw. The food stank. At ten thirty, when Paul Prody stuck his head in the door, the smell was still there. He made a face. 'Nice.'

Caffery got up, went to the window and opened it a fraction. Cold damp air came in, bringing with it the smells of drunks and takeaways. One of the shops opposite had Christmas lights in the window, Christmas officially beginning in November, of course. 'So?' He sat heavily in his chair. Arms hanging at his sides. He felt half finished. 'What've you got for me?'

'Just in the last few minutes spoke to the press office.' Prody came in, sat down. Myrtle was lying on the floor, digesting her meal, her chin on her paws. She raised her head and watched him with a vague, burned-out interest. Even Prody was showing signs of wear and tear. His jacket was creased and his tie was undone round his neck as if he'd spent a couple of hours on the sofa at home, watching soaps. 'The nationals, the locals and all the TV stations ran pictures of the Bradleys' house. The number on the door was quite clear and so was the sign: "The Vicarage". The cuttings agency is still searching, but so far all anyone can come up with is some copy about "the Bradleys' house in Oakhill". Nothing more specific than that. No road name. And no mention of the tooth. Anywhere.'

'It could be him, then.'

'Looks like it.'

'That's good.'

'Good?' Prody gave him a level look.

'Yes. It means he knows the Oakhill area – knows the A37. It's great.'

'Is it?'

Caffery dropped his hands on the desk. 'No. It's something, but it's not "great" at all. We already knew he was familiar with that area. What does it add to our intel? That he knows an estate every bastard in the area has to drive past on their way to work.'

They looked across at the map on the wall. It was covered with tiny pins, the heads coloured. The pink ones were personal to Caffery: they marked the places he knew the Walking Man had been. A pattern was emerging there: a long band stretching upwards from Shepton Mallet, where the Walking Man had once lived. But the black pins were the ones Caffery couldn't mould a pattern from – six of them: three at the places the jacker had struck, the other three at places that had some relevance – the vicarage in Oakhill where he'd left the baby tooth, the area near Tetbury where the Bradleys' Yaris had been parked briefly and the place near Avoncliff in Wiltshire where it had been abandoned.

'There's a station near where he left the car.' Caffery squinted at the black pins. 'If you look at it there's a railway line runs through there.'

Prody went to the map, tilted sideways from the waist and studied the pins. 'The line that goes from Bristol through Bath and Westbury.'

'The Wessex line. Look where it goes after Bath.'

'Freshford, Frome.' He looked over his shoulder at Caffery. 'Martha was taken in Frome.'

'And Cleo was taken in Bruton. On the same line.'

'You think he's using the train?'

'Maybe. He drove to the Bradleys today, I'm sure of it. And he must have used a car to get out to Bruton – the Vauxhall, maybe. But when he jacks someone else's car he has to come back, pick up the Vauxhall, at some point.'

'So maybe he lives near one of the stations on the line?'

Caffery shrugged. 'Well, it's tentative, but let's go with it. In the absence of anything else. In the morning I want you to get on to Railtrack, take in their CCTVs. Know the routine for that?'

'I think so.'

'And, Prody?'

'Yeah?'

'Just because Turner wears his Glasto look after six p.m., Lollapallooza thinks it's cool to go barefoot and I've got a Labrador in my office, it doesn't mean you get to lower your standards.'

Prody nodded. Did up his tie. 'It's a collie, Boss.'

'A collie. That's what I said.'

'Yes, Boss.' Prody half opened the door to leave, when something occurred to him. He stopped and came back in, closing it behind him.

'What?'

'I took the file back. Last night, like you said. No one even noticed I'd had it.'

For a moment Caffery couldn't think what he was talking about. Then he remembered. Misty Kitson.

'Good. 'S what I said to do.'

'Thought I'd really pissed you off there for a bit.'

'Yeah, well, I had a fly up my arse yesterday. Don't take it seriously.' He pulled the keyboard over. Needed to check his emails. 'See you.'

But Prody didn't leave. He hovered at the door. 'It was difficult for you. The way the case closed.'

Caffery raised his eyes and stared at him. He couldn't believe this. He pushed the keyboard away and gave him his full attention. He'd told the guy to drop it once, so where was he getting off pursuing it? 'It was difficult when the unit had to let go of it.' He switched off his lamp. Put his elbows on the table. Made his face as calm as he could. 'I can't lie to you. That part was difficult. That's why I don't appreciate you bringing files in from the review team.'

'The informer you had?'

'What about him?'

'You never did say who he was.'

'It's not in the paperwork. That's the whole point of snouts. They get their privacy.'

'You never thought he was lying to you, your contact? That doctor – the one the snout said had done Misty – they dug up his garden but they never found her. There was nothing else to connect the guy to her. So that's why I thought – maybe the snout was lying, putting you off the track?'

Caffery studied Prody, looking for signs that the guy knew any-thing – *anything at all* – about the truth he was scraping near. There was no informer. Never had been. And the digging in the garden was just another of the ways Caffery had got the force to chase its own tail over the Kitson case. He might never quite understand why he'd done it for Flea. If it wasn't for the way she froze something in him every time he saw her, if she'd been a guy, if she'd been Prody, say, or Turner, with what he knew he'd probably have turned them over in a blink. 'It wasn't my finest hour,' he told Prody steadily. 'If I had it over again I'd do things differently. But I can't, and the force has run out of resources and come to the end of too many avenues, and like I said yesterday I'd appreciate your energy going on what's happened to Martha Bradley and what that bastard has done to her. So . . .' he held up his hand, inclined his head pleasantly '. . . the CCTV footage?'

This time Prody got it. He gave a grim smile. 'Yeah. Fair enough. I'm on it.'

When the door was closed Caffery dropped back into the chair and stared blankly at the ceiling for a long time. The guy was turning out to be a prick. Wasting time. It was at least seventy hours since Martha had gone. The magic twenty-four had long been burned up and the next step, if he was truthful, was speak-ing to the Met and getting them to bring their specialist dead-body dogs up the M4. It was Caffery's job to trim the fat from any job, but he couldn't lose Prody: it'd take too long to bring someone else up to speed and, anyway, there was a tiny problem about what Prody's side of the story might be if he did turn him over to another investigation. The Kitson case would get mentioned, no doubt about it. So he'd have to bite on it for the time being. And watch Prody. Keep him focused.

Caffery's mobile was ringing. He pulled it out of his pocket. 'Flea Marley', the display said. He went to the door and checked in the corridor that no one was about to come into his office. She made him secretive like this. When he was sure he was alone he went back to his desk. Myrtle followed him with her eyes as he answered.

'Yeah,' he said sharply. 'What?'

There was a pause. 'Sorry. Is this a bad time?'

He breathed out, leaned back in his chair. 'No. It's a – a good time.'

'I'm at the Thames and Severn canal.'

'Really? How nice. I've never heard of it.'

'You won't have. It's been decommissioned for years. Listen, I want to speak to the CSM, but he won't take calls from a support-unit sergeant at this time of night. Will you speak to him?'

'If you tell me why.'

'Because I know what the jacker used to gouge out those foot-prints. A mooring spike. From a barge. I've got one in my hand now – there are probably hundreds all over this place. Dead barges everywhere. And it's only a mile from where the Yaris left the tracks.'

'We didn't search it yesterday?'

'No. It runs *just* outside the POLSA's parameters. What do you think? Will you get him to look at it?'

Caffery drummed his fingers on the desk. He'd never been easy taking advice from departments outside the unit. It could scramble your head, make you chase too many rabbits. And Flea was acting all of a sudden as though this was her unit's case. Maybe using it to find ways of polishing her reputation. And her unit's.

But a mooring spike? Fitting the cast? 'OK,' he said. 'Leave it with me.'

He put down the phone and sat staring at it. The dog tapped her tail lightly. As if she knew what it did to him to have any sort of conversation with Flea Marley.

'Yeah,' he said bad-temperedly. He reached over for the contacts list for the CSM. 'I can live without the look. Thank you very much.'

22

In the early hours of the morning the CSM had peered again at the mould of the footprints and tended to agree with Flea: the marks did look as if they could have been made by a mooring spike. The POLSA turfed out at first light and marked up a stretch of canal to be searched. Teams were given waders and a two-mile section to check either side of where the Yaris had been parked. But the Thames and Severn canal had a peculiarity that the standard search teams couldn't deal with. Two miles of it ran completely unseen and unnoticed in a tunnel deep under farmland and forests. The Sapperton tunnel. Abandoned and deeply unstable. A two-mile death trap. Nothing more, nothing less. Only one unit was trained to deal with a search like that.

By eight o'clock more than forty people had gathered at the westerly entrance to the Sapperton tunnel. On the crenellated parapet above the opening, hoping for a glimpse of what was going on below, stood about twenty journalists and a handful of plainclothes MCIU officers. They were all looking down to where Flea and Wellard were thigh-deep in the black, stagnant canal water, readying their little Zodiac inflatable, loading it with what they needed to enter the dripping tunnel – communications systems and air cylinders.

The Underwater Search Unit knew a little about the tunnel already. They'd used it years ago as part of their confined-space search training. The trust that owned the canal had given them structural information: the tunnel was seriously unstable; it ran dangerously close to the Golden Valley railway line, and every time a train went past the great slabs of fuller's earth and oolite that made up the roof were shaken. The trust wanted to make it clear that they couldn't guarantee what was going on in there: it was too dangerous to survey properly. What they could say for sure was that a massive, impassable rockfall blocked at least a quarter of a mile of the tunnel. It was vaguely visible from the surface as a long necklace of tree-filled craters and started not far from the easterly entrance, extending a long way into the tunnel. It had been relatively easy for two of Flea's men to put on hard hats and wade the couple of hundred yards to the eastern end of the rockfall and push a probe through in the faint hope it'd come out the other side to be picked up by a team coming from the westerly entrance. Now, though, they were going to have to cover the tunnel from the other end and go a mile and a quarter under-ground before meeting the rockfall from the other side. And hope none of the unstable rocks chose to shake themselves loose as they did it.

'You sure about this?' Caffery was sceptical. Dressed in a padded North Face jacket, with his hands thrust into his pockets, he peered past them into the gloom. At the rubbish and bits of trees floating on the inky surface. 'Sure the HSE are happy with it?'

She nodded, didn't meet his eye. Truth was, the HSE would have kittens if they knew what she intended doing. But the only way they'd find out was when the bastard press hounds got the news out there, and by that time the search would be over. And they'd have found Martha. 'Yeah,' she said. 'I'm sure.'

She kept her eyes just south of his as she spoke. Thought that if he saw inside them he'd know she was following that ineffable thing. A hunch. And straining at the leash to do it. Because now finding Martha wasn't just about putting a pretty feather in the unit's cap. It meant more to her. It meant making amends for not being stronger earlier.

'I don't know.' Caffery shook his head. 'A maybe match on the cast and that's all? It's kind of a flimsy justification to be putting officers through this.'

'We know what we're doing. I won't be putting either of us at risk.'

'I believe you when you say that.'

'Good. Nice to be trusted.'

The journey into the canal was slow. They pushed the boat carefully, guiding it past obstacles, past broken barges. Shopping trolleys stuck up out of the muck like skeletons. She and Wellard wore the dry suits they used for swift water rescues, with red hard hats and the wellies that had built-in steel toecaps and shanks. Each carried a small escape set: rebreathers mounted on their chests that would give them thirty minutes of clean air if they ran into a bad pocket of gas. They went in silence, using the beams from their head torches to scan the sides and bottom of the tunnel.

It had been designed for the canal lightermen to 'leg' the barges through: lying on their backs, pushing with their feet against the ceiling to move the tons of coal and wood and iron along the two miles of darkness. In those days the tunnel roof would have been claustrophobically close to the water surface and there would have been no towpath: Flea and Wellard could only walk upright now because the canal level had dropped so much that it had revealed a narrow ledge of sorts on one side that they could use.

It was warm down here – the biting cold on the surface couldn't penetrate so deep. The water wasn't frozen. In places it was so shallow it was little more than a thick black sludge around their ankles.

'It's just fuller's earth.' They were five hundred yards inside when she spoke. 'The stuff they make cat litter out of.'

Wellard stopped pushing the Zodiac and shone his torch up at the roof. 'This isn't *kitty* litter, Sarge. Not with the pressure it's under. See those cracks? Those strata are massive. And I mean massive. One of them came down it wouldn't be like cat litter, it'd be like having a Transit van fall on you. Could seriously ruin your day.'

'Don't tell me you've got a problem with this?'

'No.'

'Come on.' She looked at him out of the corner of her eye. 'Tell me. Are you sure?'

'What?' he said irritably. 'Of course I'm sure. The Health and Safety Exec hasn't got its rod shoved that far up my arse. Not yet.'

'There aren't any guarantees.'

'I hate guarantees. Why do you think I'm in this unit?'

She gave him a grim smile and they looped their gloved hands into the handles on the Zodiac, leaning against the inertia of the boat until it loosened from its spot. It lurched forward, rocking from side to side in the black water. When it was settled between them they resumed the slow march into the tunnel. The only sounds were the slosh of their boots in the water, their breathing and the tiny *ping* of the gas detectors strapped to their chests, a comfort signal that the air was clean.

Parts of the roof were brick-lined, others had been left exposed. Their head torches played over strange plants bursting through crevices. From time to time they had to pick their way over falls of clay and fuller's earth. Every few hundred yards they came to an air shaft: a six-foot-wide hole sunk more than a hundred feet from the surface to allow air in. The first hint they'd get of an approaching shaft would be a strange silver glow in the distance. Slowly, as they progressed, the light would get brighter and brighter, until they could switch off their torches and stand under the holes looking upwards, their faces bathed in the white sunlight slicing down through the plants that clung to the walls of the shaft.

It would have been easier to explore the tunnel by dropping in through these air shafts, if each hadn't been protected by a vast rusting grille at the bottom. Debris had been able to fall through the grilles. Huge piles of ancient rotting leaves, branches and rubbish sat under each. One had been used by a livestock farmer to dump animal carcasses. The weight of the dead meat had caused the grille to give way and tip a pile of stinking animal bones into the canal. Flea stopped the boat next to it.

'Nice.' Wellard covered his nose and mouth. 'Do we have to stop here?'

She ran the beam across the water. Saw bones and flesh and half-eaten animal faces. She thought about the jacker's letters: *I've rearranged her a little* . . . Slowly she stirred the mess using the steel toecap. Her foot touched rocks and old tins: she hit something big. Reached in and pulled it out. It was the blade from an old-fashioned plough. Probably been there for years. She discarded it.

'God forbid we find the poor little kid down among all this.' She wiped her gloved hands on the side of the boat, getting rid of the slime, and peered into the darkness ahead. Felt the same slow bleed of sadness and terror she'd felt the day before yesterday, imagining what it would be like for Martha. 'I wouldn't want to endure this. Not at eleven, not at any age. It's just not right.'

She checked the meter on her gas detector: the air was clean. It was safe to fire up a bigger lamp. She hauled the huge HID light out of the boat, held it up and flicked the switch. There was a loud *whoomp* as the unit came to life, then a few moments of crackling as the light grew stronger and stronger. Flooded in blue-white light the tunnel was even more eerie, the shadows bouncing around as she tried to steady the lamp. Next to her, Wellard's face was sombre, pale, as he took in what lay in front of them.

'Is that it?'

The light glinted on the canal stretching away from where they stood. Nothing to see except the water and the sides and, about fifty metres ahead, an impassable wall. So much fuller's earth had detached itself from the ceiling and dropped into the canal that the ground level had risen to the ceiling, blocking the canal.

'Is it the rockfall?' Wellard said. 'Have we reached it already?'

'I dunno.' She caught up the measuring tape and studied it. The trust's engineers reckoned the rockfall extended about a quarter of a mile from the eastern entrance. They were a little short, but this could just about be the other end of it. She leaned into the Zodiac, pushed it along, wading through the gloopy water. When she got to the scree she shone the light up to where it met the ceiling. Let the beam trail along the juncture.

'No probe,' she murmured.

'So? We knew the probe probably wouldn't come all the way

through. I think this is the other end. Come on. ' He began to push the Zodiac back the way they'd come. He'd gone a few paces before he realized she wasn't with him. She was rooted where she stood, gripping the torch, staring at the top of the fall.

He let all his breath out. 'Oh, no, Sarge. I don't know what you're thinking but let's just get the hell out of here.'

'Come on. It's worth a try. Isn't it?'

'No. This is the end of the fall. There's nothing on the other side. Now, can we just go—'

'Come on.' She winked at him. 'Thought you said the HSE rod *wasn't* up your arse. Just this last bit. Make me happy.'

'No, Sarge. This is the end. This is where I stop.'

She took a deep breath. Let it out in a long sigh. She stood for a moment dawdling the HID lamp across the rockfall, monitoring him out of the corner of her eye.

'Hey,' she hissed. 'What was that?'

'What?' Wellard frowned at her. 'What did you hear?'

'Sssh.' She held a finger up to her mouth.

'Sarge?' The communications box came to life. The voice of the officer stationed at the end of the tunnel. 'You OK?'

'Sssh.' She held her finger to her mouth. 'Quiet. Everyone.'

No one spoke. She took a few steps forward. The torch beam danced in nothingness, picking up dripping walls and the odd hunched shapes of fallen earth like the humped back of an animal protruding out of the water. She stopped, turned sideways in the tunnel and put her head back as if she was trying to open her ears. Wellard left the boat and came slowly through the water, going carefully so his boots didn't make a noise. 'What is it?' he mouthed. 'Did you hear something?'

'Didn't you?' she mouthed back.

'No. But you know . . .' He waggled a finger at his ear. The team had regular hearing tests to check the water pressure they worked under wasn't affecting their eardrums. Everyone knew Wellard's hearing was five per cent down in one ear. 'I'm not as good as you.'

She put her finger into her left ear, pretended to listen again.

But Wellard wasn't stupid and this time the act didn't work. 'Jesus.' He sighed. 'You can't even lie convincingly.'

She lowered her hand and glared at him, started to say something but stopped when she saw that something in the tunnel was changing. The water around their knees was moving very slightly. A noise like distant thunder came from overhead.

'I can hear that,' Wellard murmured. 'I can definitely hear that.'

Neither moved. They turned their eyes to the ceiling.

'A train.'

It grew louder and louder. Within seconds it was deafening: the walls shook as if the earth itself was rocking. The tunnel seemed to roar and the water wallowed around them, sending back moving reflections of the big lamp. From somewhere up ahead in the darkness came the noises of rocks splashing in the water.

'Shi-it.' Wellard hissed, ducking his head. 'Shit and fuck.'

And then, almost as quickly as it had started, it was over. For a long time neither of them moved. Then, cautiously, Wellard straightened and they stood, shoulder to shoulder, breathing hard, staring at the ceiling, listening to the sounds of one or two residual rocks falling in the darkness ahead.

'Pull back.' A voice came from the comms box. It sounded to Flea like Jack Caffery's. 'Tell them to come out.'

'Did you hear that, Sarge?' said the communications officer. 'SIO says pull back.'

Flea pushed her helmet off her face, hooked her hands into the gunwales of the Zodiac and leaned over to speak into the box. 'Tell DI Caffery that's a negative.'

'*What?*' hissed Wellard. 'Are you fucking insane?'

'There's no probe here. And, anyway, I heard something on the other side of this rockfall. Sir.' She was already pulling the equipment she needed out of the Zodiac: spade and a face mask. 'I'd like to satisfy myself of what that was. There could be spaces between this fall and the main one.'

She heard Caffery saying something to the comms officer, his voice echoey. He must have waded into the tunnel to speak to him.

'Sarge?' said the officer. 'The SIO's saying he went through it in the briefing. He says there's no hard evidence she's in the tunnel and he's not risking any lives. Sorry, Sarge, just relaying it as it is.'

'That's OK. And if you would relay back to him just as it is, though I know he's listening, that I'm a professional, I'm doing my job, and I'm not going to risk any lives. And—'

She stopped. Wellard had pulled the lead out of the comms box. The tunnel fell into silence. He was staring at her, his eyes glittering.

'*Wellard*. What the hell do you think you're doing?'

'I'm not letting you do this.'

'There might be something over that rockfall. Just on the other side.'

'No – that fall's been there for ever.'

'Look – I've got a *feeling*—'

'A hunch? Got a hunch about it, have you?'

'Are you taking the piss?'

'No. *You*'re taking the piss, Sarge. I've got a wife and kids at home and you've got no right – no right—' He broke off and stood there, breathing hard, glaring at her. 'What's the matter with you? For six months you've acted like you don't give a toss about the unit. It could have lain down and died for all you cared. Now, out of nowhere, you're so gung-ho you're going to kill us both.'

Flea was speechless. She'd known Wellard seven years. She was godmother to his daughter. She'd made a speech at his wedding, had even visited him in hospital when he'd had his hernia stitched together. They worked together brilliantly. He'd never let her down. Never.

'You're not with me, then?'

'I'm sorry. There's a limit.'

She closed her mouth, looked over her shoulder at the wall, turned back to him and shrugged, not meeting his eyes. 'Fair enough.' She took the lead from his hand and put it back in the box.

'. . . out *now*,' came Caffery's voice. 'If this goes on I'll get your own inspector down here.'

'He says come out,' the comms officer repeated tonelessly. 'Now. Says if this goes on he's going to get Inspector—'

'Thank you.' She put her face close to the box and spoke clearly. 'I heard. Tell Mr Caffery that one officer is coming out. He'll bring the boat with him. And meanwhile,' she hooked the little throat mic out of the zip pocket on the dry suit and attached it round her neck, 'I'm switching to VOX. OK? Might not have line of sight with the comms box.'

'What the fuck is going on in your head?' Caffery shouted.

She hummed to herself, blocking his voice out. When she'd crawled into the rockfall, double-checked it really was the other end and not just a smaller fall, and when she'd maybe found something that led them closer to Martha, then he'd shut up. Might even thank her.

'Nah,' she muttered under her breath. 'Say thank you? Now you're in Fairy-tale Land.'

'What was that?'

'Nothing,' she said. 'Just trying to open the throat mic.'

He didn't answer. She knew what he'd be doing. He'd be shaking his head regretfully, as if to say, *I'm a reasonable man, so what is it about me that makes me a magnet for all the nutjobs in the world?*

Wellard was loading the boat, a sick look on his face. She didn't try to catch his eyes as she pulled her trenching tool out of the elasticated loop she'd stored it in. She had a feeling they'd never talk about this moment again. She turned, carrying the spade and her other equipment, and waded to the fall. She began to scale it, the fuller's earth crumbling under her weight, sinking with every step. She had to throw the equipment ahead of her, hoping it would stay where it fell. It took three minutes to half crawl, half scramble, up the scree to the ceiling and by the time she got to the top she was panting. But she didn't stop. She started to dig, pulling at the heavy earth with the spade, hearing it roll down behind her and splash into the canal.

She'd been working for about five minutes when Wellard appeared next to her. 'You're supposed to be halfway back by now.' She twisted and glanced back at the Zodiac, which was still sitting in the black water. 'What're you doing?'

'What does it look like?' he said.

'You're not coming with me.'

'No. But I can dig. You don't have to do that part on your own.'

She let him take the spade and sat back, watching him work for a few minutes. She thought of what he'd said: *I've got a wife and kids. You've got no right, no right* . . . She felt tired. So tired.

'OK.' She put her hand on his arm. 'You can stop now. Stop.'

They sat back and looked at the hole he'd made.

'It's not very big,' Wellard said.

'It's big enough.'

She snapped the little Maglite out of the holster in her dry suit, crawled a short way into the hole on her belly and pushed the torch out in front.

'Oh, yes,' she whispered, as she made sense of what she was seeing. 'That's good. Very good indeed.'

'What?'

She let out a low whistle. 'I was right.' She pulled back out of the hole. 'There's another chamber in there.' She reholstered the torch and unstrapped her hard hat, her head lamp, the gas meter.

Wellard watched her. 'You taught us we never take these things off.'

'Well, I'm unteaching you now. I can't get through with them on.' She grappled with the Dräger rebreather.

'Not that too. I can't let you do this.'

She put the emergency set into his hands. 'Can't you? I haven't got a wife and kids. If something happens to me no one's going to cry.'

'That's not true. It's just not—'

'Sssh, Wellard. Zip it and take this.'

He rested the rebreather on a flat part of the scree without a word.

'Here. Hook me up.' She handed him the semi-static climbing rope and waited for him to attach it into the back of her harness.

He put his knee on the small of her back and gave the harness an experimental tug.

'OK.' His voice was dull. 'You're secure.'

She hoisted herself forward, pushed her head and shoulders into the dark gap. Tree roots trailed out of the ceiling, tickling her neck and back like fingers. She elbowed her way a few feet in.

'Give me a push.'

There was a pause. Then she felt him grip her feet and shove her as hard as he could. For a moment nothing happened. He tried again and this time, with a loud sucking noise, she plopped out on the other side, like a cork, covered with mud. She half commando-crawled, half rolled down the slope, tumbling the last few feet to land in the canal on the far side.

'Jesus.' She sat up, spitting and coughing. Around her the thick, stagnant water rocked lazily with the shock of her landing. Something fell down behind her from the top of the mound. She heard it bounce, leap and land at the bottom. A clink, not a splash, so it was shy of the water. She leaned over and felt in the muck. Her head lamp. 'Top man,' she shouted to Wellard. 'Top man.'

'I can only just hear you, Sarge.'

'*You deaf bastard.*'

'That's more like it.'

She clicked on the lamp and pulled herself to her feet, the stagnant water running off her. She shone the light around. It picked out the brick walls, the great scars in the ceiling where the strata had collapsed, the lines of other faults that looked precarious enough to come down at any time, the water, still moving – and up ahead, only about thirty feet away, another rockfall.

'See anything?'

She didn't answer. The place was empty, except for an old coal barge at the far end, just its stern visible, half covered by the next pile of earth. The water was so shallow that a child – or a child's body – would be visible even if it was lying in the canal. Flea waded to the barge and bent over, shining the light into it. It was full of sludge, with bits of timber floating on the surface. Nothing there.

She straightened and propped her elbows on the deck, her face in her hands. She'd come as far down the tunnel as it was possible to come. The place was empty. She'd been wrong. A total waste of time and energy. She wanted, frankly, to sit down and cry.

'Sarge? You OK in there?'

'No, Wellard,' she said tonelessly. 'I'm not. I'm coming out. There's nothing here.'

23

Caffery had borrowed some waders from the Underwater Search van. They were several sizes too big and the tops cut into his groin as he waded out into the daylight. In the short time he'd been in the tunnel the area outside had become even more crowded. Not just with the media and the hangers-on, but half of MCIU too: they were standing together about forty yards away, staring into the tunnel. Everyone had heard about the search he'd ordered and they'd all piled out to watch.

He ignored them, ignored the reporters craning over the ornate parapet, some resting cameras in the decorative alcoves. He got to the towpath, sat down on the freezing earth and tugged off the waders. He kept his face down – didn't want anyone getting a photo of how pissed off he was.

He pulled on his shoes, did up the laces. At the tunnel entrance Flea Marley and her officer appeared streaked with black mud and blinking in the daylight. Caffery got up and went along the towpath until he was directly above her. 'I am so, so fucking pissed off with you at this point,' he hissed.

She looked up at him coldly. She had faint blue bulges under her eyes as if she was very tired. 'I'd never have guessed.'

'Why didn't you come out when I told you to?'

She didn't answer. Without taking her eyes off him she began to pull off the great chunks of wet clay that clung to her body harnesses. She handed her gas meter and the emergency rebreather to a team member to hose down. Caffery leaned closer so that the reporters wouldn't hear what he said. 'You've wasted four hours of everyone's day for what?'

'I thought I heard something. There was a gap in the rockfalls. I was right about that, at least, wasn't I? She could have been there.'

'What you've done is illegal, Sergeant Marley. Breaching the parameters of an assessment that complies with the HSE's rules is technically *illegal*. You want the chief constable in the dock, do you?'

'My unit is statistically one of the most dangerous units to work on. But in three years I've never once had one of my boys hurt. No one in the decompression pot, no one in A and E. Not even for a broken nail.'

'You see, *that* –' he dug a finger at her '– *that*, what you've just said, is *exactly* what I think this morning has all been about. Your unit. You've done this just to grandstand your poxy unit—'

'It's not a *poxy* unit.'

'It *is*. Look at you – it's in *pieces*.'

The bullet was out before he knew he'd even chambered the round. It hit its target head on. He saw it clearly. Saw it find its spot, bore through bone and skin, saw the pain blossom behind her eyes. She dropped her harness, handed her helmet and gloves to a unit member, clambered up on to the towpath and walked steadily back to the unit's Sprinter van.

'Christ.' Caffery put his hands in his pockets and bit down hard, hating himself. When she'd got into the vehicle and closed the door he turned away. Prody was gaping down at him from the parapet.

'*What?*' Another, cold flare of anger went through him. It still rankled that Prody was sniffing around the Kitson case. Maybe rankled even more that the guy was acting exactly as he, Caffery, would act. Asking questions where he shouldn't. Stepping outside the box. 'What, Prody? What is it?'

Prody closed his mouth.

'I thought you were supposed to be magicking CCTV footage out of thin air, not on some coach outing to the Cotswolds.'

Prody muttered something – might have been 'sorry', but Caffery didn't much care. He'd had enough – enough of the cold and the media and the way his force was behaving.

He felt in his pocket for his keys. 'Get back to the office and take your friends with you. You're all about as welcome here as a cockroach in a salad bowl. If it happens again a little bird will be winging its way to the superintendent.' He turned smartly, walked away and mounted the steps that led up to the village green they were using as a RV point, doing up his raincoat as he went. The place was almost deserted, just a man in a torn sweater in the back garden of one of the houses, emptying leaves into a large wheelie. When Caffery was sure no one had followed he opened the door of the Mondeo and let Myrtle out.

They went under an oak tree – the dead leaves still clinging to it rustled in the breeze – and the dog squatted unsteadily to pee. Caffery stood next to her, hands in his pockets, looking at the sky. It was bitterly cold. Driving out here he'd had a phone call from the lab. The DNA from the milk tooth matched Martha's. 'I'm sorry,' he murmured to the dog. 'I still haven't found her.'

Myrtle looked back at him. Drooping eyes.

'Yeah, you heard me. I still haven't found her.'

24

The night that Thom killed Misty Kitson had been clear and warm. The moon had been up. He had been driving on a remote country lane when it happened. There was no one around and after he'd accidentally hit her, he'd bundled the body into the car boot without being seen. Drunk and with his back firmly to the wall, he'd driven to Flea's house to take refuge. On the way his reckless driving had picked him up a tail, a traffic cop who'd arrived seconds after Thom on Flea's doorstep, breathalyser kit in hand. Flea must have left her brains in a pot under the bed that night because, with almost no coercion, she'd stood in for her brother. At the time she hadn't known what was in the boot of the damned car. If she had she wouldn't have done the breathalyser for him. Wouldn't have sworn to the cop that she had been driving. Given him a nice zero reading.

The cop who'd breathalysed her was here now, a few feet away in the low-ceilinged pub, his back to her, ordering a drink. DC Prody.

She moved her half-finished pint of cider to the other side of the table, pulled her sleeves down over her hands, tucked them into her armpits and shuffled down in the seat. The pub – at the easternmost entrance to the canal, the place they'd made the first exploratory entry – was typical of the Cotswolds, stone-built, thatched, with enamel signs on the walls and soot-flashed brick-work above the fireplace. Guest ales and lunchtime menus scrawled on blackboards. But at two o'clock on this dreary

November day the only living souls in the place were an elderly whippet asleep next to the fire, the barman and Flea. And Prody. He'd notice her eventually. No way he wouldn't.

The barman gave him his lager. Prody ordered food and took a few sips of the drink. He relaxed a little, turned on the stool to look at his surroundings. And saw her. 'Hey.' He picked up the glass and came across the room. 'Still here?'

She forced a smile. 'Guess.'

He stood behind the other chair at the table. 'Can I?'

She pulled her wet jacket off the back so he could sit down. He got himself comfortable. 'Thought all your unit had gone home.'

'Yeah, well. You know.'

Prody put his glass neatly on a beer mat. He wore his hair very short. A widow's peak. His eyes were pale green and he looked as if he'd been on holiday in the last month, somewhere hot – there were white creases at his temples. He turned the glass round and round on the mat, looking at the wet mark it made. 'I didn't like hearing you get that bollocking. Wasn't necessary. He didn't need to talk to you like that.'

'I dunno. Maybe it was my own fault.'

'Nah – it's *him*. He's got his hair off over something. You didn't hear the chewing out he gave me after you went. I mean, what's his fucking problem?'

She raised an eyebrow. 'You're sulking too, then? Not just me?'

'Honest truth?' He leaned back in his chair. 'I've worked eighteen-hour days since this thing started and it'd be nice to think there was a pat on the head at the end of it. Instead I get the big fuck-off pill. So, far as I'm concerned, he can stick his CCTV warrants. Stick his overtime. Don't know about you,' he raised his glass, 'but I intend taking the afternoon off.'

Since that night in May, Flea had seen Paul Prody a few times at work – once on the day the unit had searched a quarry for Simone Blunt's car, other times around the offices the USU shared with the traffic police. Prody had struck her as a gym bunny, always on his way to the shower with a triangle of sweat down his Nike T-shirt. She'd avoided speaking to him directly – had watched him carefully from a distance – and over the months she'd become sure he had no idea what had been in her car boot that night. But that had been back when he was in Traffic. Now he was at MCIU, which would give him more reason to think back to that night. It killed her not knowing just how high in MCIU's priorities the Kitson case was, what sort of staffing level was assigned to it. Course, these weren't the sort of questions a person could just pop out indiscriminately whenever they felt like it.

'Eighteen-hour days? That'd take the smile off your face.'

'Sleeping on the sofa, some of us.'

'And . . .' She tried to melt the urgency from her words so they came out nonchalant. 'And how much manpower – sorry, *staffing* – have you got? Are you still working other cases too?'

'No. Not really.'

'Not really?'

'That's right.' Something cautious came into his voice, as if he knew she was feeling him out. 'No other cases. Just this – the jacker. Why?'

She shrugged, turned her eyes to the window, pretended to be watching the rain dripping off the woody wisteria stems that hung in front of the panes. 'Just thought eighteen-hour days must be tough on everyone. On your personal lives.'

Prody took a deep breath. 'Weird – but you know something? That comment's not especially funny. You're a bright woman, but the sense of humour box is looking empty, if you don't mind me saying.'

She shot her eyes back to him, puzzled by his tone. 'Beg pardon?'

'I said it's not funny. You want to laugh at me, do it at a distance.' He tipped back his head and drained his pint in one. There were patches of colour on his throat, as if he had a rash. He scraped the chair back and got to his feet.

'Hey!' She put a hand up to stop him. 'Wait. I don't like this. I've said something I shouldn't have said, but I don't know what.'

He pulled on his coat and buttoned it.

'Jesus. A half-decent person would at least tell me what I'd said wrong. This just came out of nowhere.'

Prody gave her a long look.

'*What?* Tell me. What did I say?'

'You really don't know?'

'No. I really, *really* don't know.'

'The jungle drums don't do USU?'

'What jungle drums?'

'My kids?'

'Your kids? No. I'm . . .' she put a hand in front of her eyes '. . . in the dark. Totally. I swear.'

He sighed. 'I don't have a *personal* life. Not any more. I haven't seen my wife or my kids in months.'

'How come?'

'Apparently I'm a wife-beater. A child-abuser.' He pulled off his coat and sat down again, the colour in his neck slowly disappearing. 'Apparently I beat my kids to within an inch of their lives.'

Flea began to laugh, thinking he was messing around, then changed her mind again and wiped the smile. 'Christ,' she said. 'Are you really? A wife-beater? A child-abuser?'

'According to my wife. Everyone else believes it too. I'm even starting to suspect myself.'

Flea watched him in silence. His hair was cut so short you could almost see the shape of his skull under it. Kids he wasn't allowed to see. Nothing to do with the Misty Kitson case. A slab of tension eased in her a little. 'Jesus. That's hard. I'm sorry.'

'Don't be.'

'I swear I didn't know.'

'Fair enough. Didn't mean to be arsy about it.' Outside, the rain fell. The pub smelt of hops, horse manure and old wine corks. The sound of beer kegs being changed came from somewhere in the cellar. The room seemed warmer. Prody rubbed his arms. 'Another drink?'

'A drink? Yeah, sure. I'll—' She looked at the cider glass. 'A lemonade or a Coke or something.'

He laughed. 'A lemonade? Think I'm going to breathalyse you again?'

'No.' She stared at him fixedly. 'Why would I think that?'

'I don't know. Suppose I always thought after that night you were pissed off with me.'

'Well – I was. Sort of.'

'I know. You've avoided me ever since. Before that you always used to say hi to me – you know, in the gym or whatever. But after that it was completely . . .' He drew a hand down his face, meaning she'd blanked him. 'I have to admit that was tough. But I was pretty tough on you.'

'No. You were fair. I'd have breathalysed me.' She tapped the cider glass. 'I wasn't drunk, but I was acting like a twat. Driving too fast.'

She smiled. He smiled back. The dull light came through the window, picking out the dust hanging in the bar. It found the fair hairs on Prody's arm. He had nice arms and hands. Caffery's arms were sinewy and hard with dark hair. Prody's were fairer and more fleshy. She thought they'd maybe be warmer to the touch than Caffery's.

'Lemonade, then?'

She realized she was staring. She stopped smiling and felt her face go numb. 'Excuse me.' She got up unsteadily and went to the Ladies, locked herself into a cubicle, peed, washed her hands and was standing with them under the dryer when she caught sight of herself in the mirror. She leaned closer across the basin and examined her reflection. Her cheeks were flushed from the cold of the day and the cider. The veins in her hands, feet and face felt swollen. She'd used the on-board shower on the unit's dive van but there was no hairdryer so her hair had dried naturally into white-blonde corkscrews.

She unbuttoned her shirt a short way. Underneath she wasn't pink and flushed. She was tanned – a sort of year-round tan she must have developed as a child from all the diving holidays with Mum, Dad and Thom. Caffery's face flashed into her head, yelling at her from the towpath. Furious. You'd never describe Caffery as congenial, but even so – that level of anger was inexplicable. She did up the buttons on the blouse and checked herself in the mirror. Then she undid the top two buttons again until a small amount of cleavage was just visible.

Back in the bar Prody was sitting at the table, two glasses of lemonade in front of him. When she sat next to him he saw the undone buttons instantly. There was an awkward, awful pause. He glanced at the window, then back again, and for a moment she saw it all clearly. She saw that she was a bit drunk, looking stupid with her tits showing, and that the wheel was about to come off the whole thing and put her in a ditch she wouldn't know how to climb out of. She turned away, putting her elbows on the table and closing off her cleavage from him.

'It wasn't me,' she said, 'that night. It wasn't me driving.'

'I'm sorry?'

She felt stupid. She hadn't planned to say it, had only opened her mouth to cover her embarrassment. 'I've never told anyone this but it was my brother. He was drunk and I wasn't so I covered for him.'

Prody was silent for a while. Then he cleared his throat. 'Nice sister. I'd like one like you.'

'No – I was stupid.'

'I'd say. That's quite something to protect someone from. A DIC charge.'

Yeah, she thought. And, believe me, if you knew what I'd really protected him from – if you knew it was much more than just a drink-driving charge – your head would spin round and your eyes would come out on springs. She sat woodenly, staring at the optics and hoping her face wasn't as flushed as it felt.

Prody's meal came then, and that saved them both. Gloucester Old Spot sausages and mash. Little red pickled onions on the side, like cloudy marbles. He ate in silence. For a moment or two she wondered if he was angry still, but she stayed anyway and watched him. Let the mood settle itself. They talked about other things – the unit, an inspector from Traffic who'd dropped dead of a heart-attack at a family wedding aged thirty-seven. Prody finished his meal and at one thirty they got up to leave. Flea was tired, her head stuffy. Outside, the rain had stopped and the sun was out but more rainclouds were banked in the west. The chalky earth of the car park was pitted with yellowish puddles. She stopped on the way to her car at the parapet above the tunnel's eastern portal and peered down into the murky canal.

'There's nothing there,' Prody said.

'Something still feels wrong.'

'Here.' He held out an Avon and Somerset business card with his phone numbers on it. 'If you remember what it is, call me. I promise not to yell at you.'

'Like Caffery?'

'Like Caffery. Now, will you go home and relax? Give yourself a break?'

She took the card but she didn't leave the parapet. She waited for Prody to get into his Peugeot and pull out of the car park. Then she stared down at the tunnel, drawn inexorably by the glint of the winter sun on the black water, until the noise of his engine had faded, and the only sounds were the clink of the barman clearing the table in the pub, and the cawing of crows in the trees.

25

At three fifty Janice Costello sat at traffic lights and stared grimly at the rain trickling down the windscreen. Everything was dark and dismal. She hated this time of year, and she hated sitting in traffic. Emily's school was only a short distance from the house, and although Cory usually drove if he picked her up from school – any mention of the greenhouse effect generally sparked off in him a diatribe about the blatant erosion of his civil liberties – on Janice's days they walked, carefully adding up the minutes and diligently reporting back to Emily's teacher as part of the Walk to School Challenge.

But today they were driving and Emily was thrilled. She didn't know it was because Janice had a plan. She'd cooked it up overnight, lying in the darkened bedroom, her heart pounding, while Cory slept dreamlessly next to her. She was going to drop Emily at a friend's house, then visit Cory at the office. On the front seat of the Audi, a bag contained a flask of hot coffee and half a carrot cake sandwiched between two paper plates. One of the things that had come up in the therapy sessions was that sometimes Cory felt his wife wasn't exactly a traditional wife. That although there was always dinner on the table and a cup of tea in bed in the mornings, although she worked and took care of Emily, he still missed the little touches. A cake cooling on a wire tray when he came in. A packed lunch for work with maybe a little *billet doux* tucked inside to surprise him at lunchtime.

'Well, we'll change that, won't we, Emily?' she said aloud.

'Change what?' Emily blinked at her. 'Change what, Mummy?'

'Mummy's going to take some nice things for Daddy. Just to show she cares.'

The lights changed and Janice shot the Audi forward. The streets were wet and treacherous. She had to brake suddenly for a gang of children who trailed over a zebra crossing without looking left or right. As she came to a halt the bag on the seat flew off and landed on the floor.

'Shit.'

'That's rude, Mummy.'

'I know, sweetheart. I'm sorry.' She groped on the floor, trying to grab the bag before the children crossed and the driver behind her leaned on the horn. Cory had chosen 'champagne' for the interior even though it was her car and she'd bought it with money she'd saved. Somehow he'd managed to have the last word on most things about it. She'd fancied a VW camper now she was working from home, but Cory said it was a shabby thing to have sitting on the driveway, so she gave in and got the Audi. And he was a killer when it came to keeping it clean. If Emily so much as crawled across the back seat in her school shoes he'd launch into a tirade about how the family had no respect for anything, and how Emily would grow up not understanding the value of money and become a leech on society. As Janice hooked up the bag and put it on the front seat a trickle of coffee dripped out of the bottom and made a long brown trail over the pale cream upholstery.

'*Shit shit shit.*'

'Mummy! I've told you. Don't say that.'

'I've got bloody coffee everywhere.'

'Don't swear.'

'Daddy'll be furious.'

'No!' Emily squealed. 'Don't tell him. I don't want Daddy to get cross.'

Janice yanked the bag off the seat and put it the first place she could think of. Her lap. Hot coffee oozed out all over her white sweater and beige jeans. 'Jesus.' She tugged at her scalding trousers, trying to unstick them from her legs. The car behind sounded its horn as she'd known it would. Someone was yelling.

'Shit, shit.'

'You're not supposed to say that word, Mummy!'

There was half a parking space at the end of a bay just past the crossing. She let the car go forward, pulled into the space and opened the window, hung the bag outside and let the coffee drain away. It was a big flask and it seemed to take for ever to drain. It was as if someone had turned on a tap. Another horn sounded. This time it was the car in the parking space ahead. It had its reversing lights on and apparently couldn't go back far enough to pull out, although there was at least a metre behind it.

'*I don't like that noise, Mummy.*' Emily put her hands on her ears. '*I don't like it.*'

'It's all right, baby. Sssh.'

Janice slammed the Audi into reverse, and eased back a fraction to let the car in front come out. As she did someone banged hard on the back window, making her jump. Rap rap rap. Rap rap rap.

'*Mummy!*'

'Hey!' a voice said. 'You're on the zebra crossing. There are kids out here.'

The car in front pulled into the traffic and Janice drove into the space. She cut the engine and dropped her head on to the steering-wheel. The woman who'd shouted at her was at the passenger window now, rapping hard on the glass. It was one of the mothers from school. She was furious. 'Hey. You've got a big car so you've got the right to park it on a zebra crossing, have you?'

Janice's hands were shaking. This was bloody awful. It was eight minutes to four, when Cory would either leave to meet Clare or she'd arrive to meet him. Janice couldn't appear at the office covered with coffee – and how would she justify turning up without it? And Emily – poor little Emily – was crying her eyes out and not understanding any of this.

'Look at me, you bitch. You can't get away from this.'

Janice raised her face. The woman was very big and red-faced.

She was bundled in a huge tweed coat and wore one of the Nepalese knitted hats that they sold in every street market, these days. She was surrounded by children in similar hats. 'Bitch.' She slammed the flat of her hand on the window. 'Petrol-guzzling bitch.'

Janice took a few deep breaths and got out of the car. 'I'm sorry.' She came round to the side of the road. She set the dripping bag down on the pavement and stood in front of the woman. 'I didn't mean to go on the zebra crossing.'

'You get a car like that I don't suppose you can afford lessons to learn to drive it too.'

'I said I'm sorry.'

'It's amazing. Whatever effort the school puts into getting us to walk home you just can't legislate for the selfish pigs of the world.'

'Look – I've said I'm sorry. What more do you want? Blood?'

'It will be blood. It will be my *kids*' blood with people like you around. If you don't run them over in your Chelsea tractors you'll *suffocate* them or *drown* them with all the shit you're pumping into the atmosphere.'

Janice sighed. 'Right. I give up. What do you want? A fist fight?'

The woman gave an incredulous smile. 'Oh, *that* just about sums up your type. You'd do that in front of kids, wouldn't you?'

'Actually . . . yes, I would.' She wrenched her jacket off, slammed it down on the Audi's boot and headed for the pavement. The children scattered, banging into each other, half giggling, half panicking.

The woman backed into the doorway of the nearest shop. 'Are you crazy?'

'Yes. I'm crazy. I am crazy enough to kill you.'

'I'll call the police.' She held her hands in front of her face and cowered in the doorway. 'I will – I'll call the police.'

Janice grabbed her by the coat lapel and put her face close to the woman's. 'Now, listen.' Janice gave her a shake. 'I *know* what it looks like. I *know* what you think I am, but I'm not. I didn't choose that car. It was my fucking husband who chose it—'

'Don't swear in front of my—'

'It was my *fucking* husband who wanted a *fucking* status symbol, even though I was stupid enough to *pay* for the damned thing. And for your information I walk my daughter to and from school *every single day*. I walk her home and that stupid beast of a car has got only *two* thousand miles on the sodding *clock* after a *year* and for your information I am having a very, *very* bad day. Now.' She pushed the woman back against the wall. 'I've apologized to you. Are you going to apologize to me?'

The woman stared at her.

'Well?'

She glanced from left to right to see if her children were near enough to overhear. Her whole face was covered with tiny broken blood vessels as if she'd spent a lifetime in the chilly weather. Probably no central heating in her house. 'For God's sake,' she muttered. 'If it's *that* important to you, I apologize. But you've got to let go of me *now* and let me get my children home.'

Janice held her eyes for a moment more. Then, with a dismissive shake of her head, she let her go. As she turned away, wiping her hands on her sweater, she glanced across the street. A man wearing, incongruously, a full-face Santa Claus mask and a zipped-up ski jacket was running across the road towards her. That's early for Christmas, she had time to think, before the man leaped into the Audi, slammed the door and pulled away on to the open street.

26

Janice Costello was probably the same age as her husband – little pinched lines around her mouth and eyes gave it away – but when she opened the door into her elegant tiled hallway she appeared much younger. With her pale skin and jet-black hair knotted at the back of her head, the jeans and casual blue shirt worn a little too big, she was like a child next to her foppish husband. Even the blotchiness of her eyes and nose from crying didn't detract from her youthfulness. Her husband tried to put an arm under her elbow to help her as they went down the hall into the huge kitchen-diner, but, Caffery noticed, she snatched it away and continued on her own, her head held high. Her awkward, dignified gait suggested someone in physical pain.

MCIU had assigned their own FLO to the Costellos, DC Nicola Hollis. A tall girl with long, pre-Raphaelite hair who couldn't have been more feminine but insisted on calling herself 'Nick', she stood quietly in the Costellos' kitchen, making tea and arranging biscuits on a plate. She nodded silently at Caffery as he came in and sat at the big breakfast table. 'I'm sorry,' he said. A child's drawings were scattered across it, with crayons and felt tips. He noticed that Janice chose a place at the table that was separated from her husband by another chair. 'I'm sorry it had to happen again.'

'I'm sure you've done your best to catch him.' Janice spoke stiffly. It must be the only way she could contain it all. 'I don't blame you.'

'A lot of people would have. Thank you for that.'

She gave a bleak smile. 'What do you want to know?'

'I need to go through the whole thing again. You told the emergency-call handler—'

'And the police in Wincanton.'

'Yes. And they've given me the basics, but I just want to get it clear in my head because my unit's going to be taking the case from here. I'm sorry to put you through it again.'

'It's OK. It's important.'

He took out his MP3 recorder and set it on the table between them. He was calmer now. Before the call about Emily's kidnap had come in he'd realized how overwrought he was getting. After the canal he'd taken time to have lunch and force himself to do something outside the case – even found himself walking around a branch of Holland and Barrett hunting down glucosamine for Myrtle. Eventually his fury with Prody and Flea had loosened up a little. 'So, it happened at around four?' He checked his watch. 'An hour and a half ago?'

'Yes. I'd just picked Emily up from school.'

'And you told the call handler the man was wearing a Santa mask.'

'It was all so quick – but, yes, a rubber one. Not one of the hard plastic sort, but softer. It had the hair and beard and everything.'

'You didn't see his eyes?'

'No.'

'And he was wearing a hoodie?'

'The hood wasn't up, but it was a hoodie. Red. Zip-up. And I think jeans. I'm not sure about that, but I do know he was wearing latex gloves. The sort doctors wear.'

Caffery pulled out a map and spread it on the table. 'Can you show me the direction he came from?'

Janice leaned over and peered at the map. She put a finger on a small side road. 'This one. It leads down to the green – the common where they sometimes have the fireworks.'

'Is it on a slope? I'm not very good with contour lines.'

'It is.' Cory swept his hand across the map. 'A steep slope all the way from here to here. It doesn't end until here, almost all the way out of town.'

'So he ran up the hill?'

'I don't know,' said Janice.

'Was he out of breath?'

'Well, no. At least, I don't think so. I didn't really see much of him – it was over so quickly. But he wasn't straining.'

'So you didn't get the feeling he'd run all the way up the hill.'

'Probably not, thinking about it.'

Caffery already had a team out combing the surrounding roads for a dark-blue Vauxhall. If the jacker had been out of breath he might have parked at the bottom of the hill. If not, they could keep the search for the car on the level streets near the abduction site. He thought of the black pins in the map in his office. 'There's no station in Mere, is there?'

'No,' Cory said. 'If we want the train we have to drive to Gillingham. It's only a few miles.'

Caffery was silent for a while. Did that blow his theory that the jacker was using the railway network to recover his car? Maybe he was using another vehicle. Or a cab. 'This road where it happened.' He ran a finger along it. 'I drove along it on the way here. It's got a lot of shops.'

'It's quiet in the day. But if you go there in the morning on the school run—'

'Yes,' Janice said. 'Or on the way home from school. Well, it's the place most people stop if they've got to pick up some last-minute groceries for supper, or in the morning if they've forgotten a drink for their kid's lunch box, say.'

'What had you stopped for?'

She pressed her lips together and moved them in and out between her teeth before she spoke. 'I had – uh – coffee all over me. I had a flask that was leaking. I stopped to get rid of it.'

Cory shot her a glance. 'You don't drink coffee.'

'But Mum does.' She gave Caffery a tight smile. 'I was going to my mother's after I'd dropped Emily with friends. That was my plan.'

143

'You were taking her some coffee?' Cory said. 'Can't she make it at home?'

'Does it really matter, Cory?' She kept the stiff smile on her face, and her eyes on Caffery. 'Under the fucking circumstances, does it *really* matter? If I'd made the coffee for Osama bin Laden would it really be *relevant*—'

'I wanted to *ask*,' Caffery said, 'about the witnesses. There were quite a few, weren't there? They're all down at the station now.'

Janice dropped her eyes, embarrassed. She pressed her fingertips to her forehead. 'Yes,' she said. 'There were a lot of people. Actually . . .' She looked at Nick, who was pouring hot water into four mugs. 'Nick? I don't think I'll have tea, thank you. I'd like a drink. Do you mind? There's some vodka in the freezer. Glasses up there.'

'I'll do it.' Cory went to the cupboard and pulled out a glass. He filled it with vodka from a bottle with a Russian label and set it in front of his wife. Caffery looked at the glass. The vodka smelt to him like the calm end to a day. 'Janice,' he said, 'you were having an argument with one of the women. That's what I've been told.'

She took a sip. Set the glass down. 'That's quite right.'

'What was the argument about?'

'I'd stopped in the wrong place. I'd stopped too near the zebra crossing. She yelled at me. And she was right to yell at me. But I didn't take it very well. I was soaked in hot coffee and I was . . . upset.'

'So you didn't know her?'

'Only by sight.'

'Does she know you? Does she know your name?'

'I very much doubt it. Why?'

'How about the other witnesses? Was there anyone you knew by name?'

'We haven't been here long, only a year, but it's a small town so you get to know faces. Not names.'

'And you don't think they know your name?'

'I don't think so. Why?'

'Have you spoken to any friends about this?'

'Only my mum and my sister. Is it a secret?'

'Where are they? Your mum and sister?'

'In Wiltshire and Keynsham.'

'I'd like you to keep it that way. I'd like you not to speak about this to anyone.'

'If you explain why.'

'The last thing we want is the media making a circus out of Emily.'

A door at the end of the kitchen opened and the woman from the Child Abuse Protection and Investigation Team came in. She was wearing soft-soled shoes and made no noise as she crossed the room and put a stapled set of notes on the table in front of Caffery. 'I don't think she should be interviewed again,' she said. She looked older than he remembered. 'I think we should leave her for the time being. There's no point in exhausting her.'

Janice scraped her chair back. 'Is she all right?'

'She's fine.'

'Can I go now? I'd like to spend some time with her. If that's OK?'

Caffery nodded. He watched her leave the room. After a moment or two Cory stood up. He finished Janice's vodka in one gulp, put the glass on the table and followed her. The CAPIT woman sat opposite Caffery and looked at him intently.

'I did exactly as you asked.' She nodded to the questions she'd asked Emily. 'It's difficult at this age to separate fact from fiction – she's in Reception but she's young even for that. They don't talk in a linear way – not the way you or I would talk. But . . .'

'But?'

She shook her head. 'I think what she told her mother is pretty much the long and the short of it. What her mother told the local cop shop, what you've got in your notes – you know, the jacker didn't talk much, he was wearing gloves, he didn't touch himself. I'm sure she's telling the truth on that one. He said he was going to hurt her toy rabbit – Jasper. That's the biggest problem for her at the moment.'

'He didn't offer her a pancake?'

'I don't think there was time for that. It was over very quickly. He said a "bad word" when he lost control of the car. And as soon as they crashed he jumped out and was gone.'

'I nearly skidded coming over here.' Nick was at the sink, studiously using a spoon to squeeze a tea bag against the side of a cup. 'It's lethal out there.'

'Not for Emily,' said Caffery. 'For Emily it may have saved her life.'

'That means you think Martha's dead,' Nick replied matter-of-factly.

'Nick, you know what I really think? I really think nothing. Not at this point.'

He unfolded the other side of the map. He used his finger to follow the route to the exact point where the jacker had lost control of the Audi and left it banked up on the side of the road. He hadn't attempted to remove Emily from it – he'd simply run away across the fields. There hadn't been any witnesses so it had been a long time before anyone else had come along and found the little girl sobbing her heart out in the back seat, clutching her school bag as if she'd been thinking of using it to defend herself. What was strange was that the road he'd chosen was a real highway to nowhere.

'It's a loop,' he said thoughtfully, to no one in particular. 'Look at that – it doesn't go anywhere.' He traced it along its length and saw that from where Emily had been taken the jacker must have driven her along the A303 and the A350, joining the A36 outside Frome – the very place where the ANPR cameras had been set up to catch the Bradleys' Yaris or the Vauxhall. Except, as luck would have it, the jacker had pulled off the A36 just before the cameras. He'd taken a detour along the tiny B road that did nothing except meander a couple of miles before it rejoined the main road. He'd crashed before the intersection that would have put him back on the A36, but even if he hadn't, he would have missed all the cameras because he'd taken the detour. Almost as if he knew they were there.

Caffery folded the map and tucked it back inside the folder he was carrying. The cameras weren't obvious to anyone. The Tactical Crime Unit used vans marked up with gas-board logos when they did a covert operation like this. The jacker had the luck of the devil. Caffery's eyes strayed to the empty glass and then he felt someone watching him. He looked up and caught the CAPIT woman's eyes.

'What?' he said. 'What do you want?'

'Would you speak to her? To Emily? She needs to know we're doing something. She's terrified. So far she's seen me and the FLO, and she needs to see there's a man in all of this, a man in authority. She just needs the reassurance that all men aren't bad.'

Caffery sighed. He wanted to say that children were a mystery to him, that other people understood and had confidence in them, but that they left him feeling sad. And scared for what could happen to them. But he didn't. Instead he got to his feet and wearily packed away the map. 'Go on, then. Where is she?'

27

Emily was in her parents' room, sitting on the enormous double bed, flanked by Janice and Cory. Her school clothes were still with Forensics, and now she was dressed comfortably in an off-white tracksuit and fluffy blue socks. She was cross-legged, holding a battered felt rabbit to her chest. Her dark hair was scraped back into a ponytail. She had a long, proud face, even at four. If Caffery'd had to choose he'd have called her Cleo and the blonde pony rider would be Emily.

He came to stand awkwardly next to the bed. Emily looked him up and down and he folded his arms because he didn't know what to do with them and because she was making him self-conscious. 'Hello,' he said, after a while. 'What's your rabbit's name?'

'Jasper.'

'How's he feeling?'

'He's scared.'

'I bet he is. But will you tell him from me that it's all over now? He doesn't need to be scared any more.'

'He does. He does need to be scared. Jasper's scared.' Her face crumpled and a couple of tears squeezed out of her eyes. She drew her knees up. 'I don't want him to come and hurt Jasper. He said he was going to hurt Jasper, Mummy. Jasper's scared.'

'I know, I know.' Janice put her arm round her daughter and kissed her forehead. 'Jasper's going to be OK, Emily. Mr Caffery's a policeman and he's going to catch that horrible man.'

Emily stopped crying and peered at Caffery again, scrutinizing him. 'Are you really a policeman?'

He opened his jacket and pulled out his set of quickcuffs. Usually they were in the glove compartment of the car. It was just luck and oversight he had them in his jacket today.

'What are those?'

'Here.' He gestured to Cory who held out his hands and let Caffery snap them on. Cory mimed a struggle to get out of them, then let Caffery release him. 'See?' Caffery said. 'That's what I do to nasty men. Then they can't hurt anyone. Especially Jasper.'

'Dad's not a nasty man.'

Caffery laughed. 'No. He's not. I won't be arresting Daddy.' He put the quickcuffs in his pocket. 'It was just for fun.'

'Have you got a gun? Can you shoot him and put him in prison?'

'I haven't got a gun,' he said. It was a lie. He did have one but it wasn't a force-issue weapon and was completely illegal. The way he'd come by it – through a dodgy connection in one of the Met's specialist units – wasn't for anyone's ears, least of all a four-year-old's. 'I'm not the sort of policeman who carries a gun.'

'How can you put him in prison, then?'

'When I find him I've got lots of other policemen who *have* got guns. I call them and they come along and put him in prison.'

'So they put him in prison but you just find him?' She didn't seem impressed.

'Yes. It's my job to find him.'

'Do you know where he is?'

'Of course I do.'

'Do you promise?'

Caffery regarded her solemnly for a while – and made a promise he couldn't keep. 'I promise I know where he is, Emily. And I promise I won't let him hurt you.'

It was left to Cory Costello to show Caffery out. Instead of stopping in the doorway he came out on to the front step and pulled the door closed behind them. 'Can I have a word, Mr Caffery? Just a moment of your time.'

Caffery pulled on his gloves and buttoned his coat. The rain had stopped but the wind was gusting now, and he could have sworn there was snow in the air. He wished he had a scarf. 'Go on.'

'How far is this going to go?' Cory glanced up at the front windows of the house to check no one was listening. 'I mean, it won't go to court, will it?'

'When we've got him it will.'

'So I'll have to get up and testify?'

'I don't see why you would. Janice, maybe. It depends how the CPS wants to handle it. Why?'

Cory tucked his lower lip under his teeth. He narrowed his eyes and let them stray away. 'Uh – there's a problem.'

'How so?'

'When all this happened . . .'

'Yes?'

'It took quite a long time for Janice to get in touch with me. It was five o'clock before I knew.'

'I know. She tried to call you. You were in a meeting.'

'Except I wasn't.' He lowered his voice. Caffery caught the glacial, oily tang of the vodka on his breath. 'I wasn't in a meeting and that's what I'm scared of. I'm scared someone's going to find out where I really was. That I'll have to stand up in court and be questioned about it.'

Caffery raised an eyebrow and Cory shivered. He wrapped his arms around the thin sweater he'd pulled on over his shirt. 'I know,' he said. 'I had to meet a client.'

'Where?'

'In a hotel room.' He rummaged in the back pocket of his trousers and handed him a piece of crumpled paper. Caffery unfolded it and held it under the porch light to read.

'Champagne? At a meeting in a hotel room?'

'Yes, well.' Cory snatched the receipt back and pushed it into his pocket. 'Don't rub my nose in it. Will it go to court?'

Caffery regarded him with a mixture of pity and contempt. 'Mr Costello. Whatever cock-up you make or are intending to make of your private life is none of my business. I can't guarantee what happens in court, but this conversation doesn't have to go any further. If you do something for me.'

'What?'

'The Bradley family. The guy found out where they lived.'

Cory's face whitened. 'Jesus.'

'Our media strategy could have been better – I admit that – but I'm clear now. There'll be no mention of what happened this afternoon in the press.'

'What did he do to them?'

'Nothing. At least, nothing to harm them physically. I don't think for a second he'll come after you – he hasn't got Emily so he's got no hold over you. But, just in case, I've put a complete block on the press. I don't want to frighten Janice and Emily – but I need you to make sure they don't talk.'

'You're not telling me he's going to turn up here?'

'Of course not. He doesn't know where you live, but that's only because the press don't know either. We're pretty good with the media, and on the whole they're pretty good with us, but we're never a hundred per cent sure.' He looked at the front garden. It was a good one. There was a long path to the gate and the house was shielded from the street by large yews planted along the perimeter. A streetlight glowed on the other side of the trees. 'You can't be seen from the road.'

'No. And I've got a top-end security system. I can set it for when we're in the house. If you think I should.'

'It's not that bad – there's nothing to panic about.' He got his wallet from his pocket and pulled out a business card. 'I'm going to have a patrol car stop by every hour or so, but if you get a hint that the press are on to you . . .'

'I'll call you.'

'That's the one. Day or night.' He handed him the card. 'You won't wake me, Mr Costello. I'm not a great sleeper.'

28

The USU men had knocked off at six. They'd showered, changed and cleaned their gear then gone, *en masse*, to the pub. They'd have made a spectacle, seven men in black warm-up trousers and Karrimor fleeces, arguing at the bar about who was going to buy the round. Flea didn't join them. She'd had enough of pubs for the day. She locked up the offices on her own and drove home with the radio switched off. It was almost eight when she got there.

She parked the car nose out to the valley, switched off the engine and sat listening to the click-click of the engine cooling. Earlier this afternoon, when she'd got back to the offices after the pub, the inspector had come in to see her again. He'd done the same routine as yesterday, put his hands on the desk and leaned over, his face close to hers, holding her eyes. But this time when she said, 'What?' and he said, 'Nothing,' she knew it was a bad nothing, not a good one. He'd heard about the morning at the Sapperton tunnel.

She rested her chin on the steering-wheel and gazed at the sky above the valley. It was clear but wispy cirrus mare's tails slipped across the moon. The earlier rainclouds – a towering bank of cumulonimbus – marched like an army into the east, gleaming orange on the underside as they passed over cities. Dad had loved the clouds. He'd taught Flea all the names: the altostratus, the stratocumulus, the 'mackerel sky' cirrocumulus. They would sit here, in this spot, on weekend mornings – Dad with his coffee and Flea with her bowl of Rice Krispies – quizzing each other on the different forms. Dad would suck his teeth if she said she didn't know, if she tried to give up. 'No, no, no. We don't give up in this family. It's against the Marley code. Ancient belief system. Bad things happen when you do – it's like flying in the face of nature.'

She took the keys out of the ignition, then pulled her kit off the back seat. It still bothered her that she was missing something about the Sapperton tunnel but however much she peered and scrutinized, she couldn't quite catch the thought and examine it properly.

We don't give up in this family. It will come . . . She could almost hear him saying it, smiling at her across his cup of coffee. *It will come* . . .

29

Nick, the family liaison officer, hung around the house for a while after Caffery had gone. Janice made her tea and talked to her because she liked her company – it diverted Emily, too, and gave Janice an excuse not to have to speak to Cory. He was restless – he kept going into the front bedrooms and peering out of the windows. He'd closed the curtains in the downstairs rooms and for the last hour he'd been in the music room at the front. When Nick left at six Janice didn't go in to him. Instead she put on her pyjamas and bedsocks, made hot chocolate and joined Emily upstairs on the big double bed.

'Are we going to bed?' Emily climbed under the covers.

'It's late. *CBeebies* is over but I've got *Finding Nemo* on DVD. The fish one?'

They sat propped up on pillows with their hot chocolate, Emily's in a pink sippy cup because Janice knew it soothed her to be a baby again, and stared at the cartoon light rippling through Nemo's water. Downstairs Cory was moving around, going from room to room, opening and closing curtains, like an animal in a zoo. Janice didn't want to see him, didn't think she could bear it, because over the course of the day – no, over the course of years – she'd realized that she would never, could never, love her husband as much as she loved her daughter. She had friends who'd as good as admitted the same thing: that they loved their husband, but the children came first. Maybe this was the great female secret, which men knew on some level but would never properly face. Somewhere in all the punditry in the papers about little Martha Bradley one thing had stuck in Janice's mind: some expert or other had said that when a family loses a child the couple's chances of staying together afterwards were nigh on zero. She knew, on some instinctive level, that it would be the woman who did the leaving. Whether she left physically or just in her heart, so that the man eventually gave up and abandoned the marriage, didn't matter. Janice knew it would be the woman who, faced with a future that included her husband but not their child, would give up on the relationship.

Next to her Emily had fallen asleep, Jasper tucked under her arm, the beaker resting on her chest, a dribble of chocolate coming out on to her nightie. She hadn't cleaned her teeth. That was two nights in a row. But there was no point in waking her now, not after what she'd been through. Janice tucked her in, went downstairs to the kitchen and put the beaker in the dishwasher. Her glass was gone so she found another, poured some vodka and took it to the music room. The light was off, the room in darkness, and it took her a moment to grasp that Cory was in there too. Something cold crossed her chest. He was standing *under* the curtains. As if he was wearing them.

'What are you doing?'

He jumped. The curtains billowed and his face appeared, shocked. 'Janice, don't creep up on me.'

'What's going on?' She threw the light switch. He dropped the curtain hurriedly. She just had time to see the twin circles of steam on the pane where he'd had his face pressed to it.

'Switch the light off.'

She hesitated, then did as she was told. The room fell into darkness again. 'Cory?' she said. 'Don't be weird. What are you looking for?'

'Nothing.' He came away from the window and gave one of his fake smiles. 'Absolutely nothing. It's a nice night.'

She licked her lips. 'What did the detective say to you? He was talking to you in the garden when he left.'

'Just chit-chat.'

'Cory. Tell me.' She couldn't keep her eyes off the curtain. 'What did he tell you? What were you looking for?'

'Don't get whiney, Janice, please. You know I can't bear it when you do that.'

'Please.' She kept her sharp reply down and instead touched his sleeve, feigning an affectionate smile. 'Just please tell me.'

'Oh, for God's sake. You have to know everything, don't you? Why can't you just trust me for once? It was about the press. Caffery doesn't want them finding us.'

Janice frowned. 'The press?' It wasn't like Cory to shy away from attention. And he was genuinely afraid of what was out there in the darkness. She went to the curtain and pulled it back, looked down the long driveway to where the streetlamp shone yellow through the yew trees. Nothing. 'It's more than that. What does it matter to him if the press see us?'

'Because,' Cory said, with exaggerated patience in his voice, 'the guy found out where the Bradleys lived and did something silly to them. Caffery doesn't want it happening to us. Happy now?'

She took a step away from the window. Stared at him.

'He *did something silly* to the Bradleys? *What* did he do?'

'I don't know. Made contact or something.'

'And now Caffery thinks he might do the same to us? Do "something silly" to us? Jesus, Cory, thanks for telling me.'

'Don't make a big thing about it.'

'I'm not making a big thing. But I'm not staying here.'

'What?'

'I'm going.'

'Janice, wait.'

But she'd gone, slamming the door behind her. She dumped the vodka in the kitchen and ran up the stairs. It took her less than ten minutes to assemble Emily's stuff – her favourite toys, pyjamas, toothbrush, her school things. A couple of changes for herself and some sleeping tablets – she had a feeling she would need them. She was in the kitchen shovelling two bottles of wine into her rucksack when Cory appeared in the doorway.

'What's happening?'

'I'm going to my mother's.'

'Well, hold on, let me get some stuff together. I'm coming too.'

Janice put the rucksack on the floor and looked at her husband. She wished she could find a way back to caring about him.

'What? Don't look at me like that.'

'Really, Cory, there's no other way to look at you.'

'What the fuck's *that* supposed to mean?'

'Nothing.' She shook her head. 'But if you're coming you'll have to get the suitcase out from under the bed. There's no room in the rucksack.'

30

Caffery got a call from a cop in Gloucestershire. The Walking Man had been arrested for loitering around a local pharmaceuticals factory. He was interviewed at the police station in the old market town of Tetbury, then cautioned and released into the open air. The duty inspector had taken him to one side before he had left and suggested, in the politest possible way, that it might be a good idea for the Walking Man not to be spotted again anywhere near the factory. But Caffery was beginning to know some of the shapes and crevices of the Walking Man's character and guessed that if he'd been interested in something he wouldn't let a little thing like an arrest stop him.

He was right. When he arrived at half past ten, parked the car with Myrtle asleep on the back seat and got out, he spotted the Walking Man almost immediately. He'd set up camp about fifty yards from the barbed-wire perimeter in a clump of trees where he could see the factory compound without being spotted from the security post.

'You haven't walked far today.' Caffery found a spare piece of bed foam and unrolled it. Usually it would be out ready for him. Usually there'd be a meal for him too. Tonight the scent of food hung in the air, but the pots and plates had been cleaned and replaced neatly near the fire. 'You started the day up here.'

The Walking Man made a low grunt in his throat. He snapped open the flagon of cider and poured some into a chipped mug, set it next to his sleeping-bag.

'I'm not here to give you more hassle,' Caffery said. 'You've already spent most of the day in the police station.'

'Five hours wasted. Five good daylight hours.'

'I'm not here on police business.'

'Not here about that nonce? The letter-writer?'

'No.' Caffery ran his hands down his face. It was the last thing he wanted to talk about. 'No. I've come for a holiday from that.'

The Walking Man filled a second mug with cider. Handed it to Caffery. 'Then, it's *her* you want to talk about. The woman.'

Caffery took the mug.

'Don't look at me like that, Jack Caffery. I've told you I'm not reading your mind. I've been wondering when you'd talk about her again. The woman. The one you're always thinking about. When you were here in the spring she was all you could talk about. You were burning for her.' He threw a log on the fire. 'I envied you that. I'll never feel like that again for a woman.'

Caffery bit the cuticle on his thumb and stared blankly into the fire. He thought 'burning' was the wrong word for the polluted, knotted mess of half-finished thoughts and impulses he had about Flea Marley. 'OK,' he said after a while. 'Let me tell you how it starts. There's a name you see in newspapers sometimes. Misty Kitson. A pretty girl. She went missing six months ago.'

'I didn't know that was her name but I know who you mean.'

'The woman – the one we're talking about – knows what happened to Kitson. She was the one who killed her.'

The Walking Man raised his eyebrows. His eyes glittered red. 'Murder?' he said lightly. 'A terrible thing. What an immoral woman she must be.'

'No. It was an accident. She was driving too fast. The girl, Kitson, stepped out of a field on to the road . . .' He trailed off. 'But you know that already, you bastard. I can see it in your face.'

'I see things. I've watched you walking the route the girl took when she left the clinic. Over and over again. The night you walked until the sun came up?'

'That was in July.'

'I was there. When you found the place it had happened – the skidmarks in the road? I was there. Watching you.'

Caffery didn't speak for a while. It didn't matter what the Walking Man said, how much he denied it, being with him was like being in the presence of God: someone who saw everything. Someone who smiled indulgently and didn't interfere when mortals made their mistakes. The night of the skidmarks had been a good one. A night when everything had fallen into place and the question had moved from being *why* Flea had killed Kitson – for a long time all Caffery'd known was that she'd disposed of the corpse – and became why the hell, if it was an accident, hadn't she just given the straight cough? Walked into the nearest cop shop and told the truth. She probably wouldn't have even done a custodial. And that was what was still eating him now, and blocking him every step of the way – why she hadn't just confessed. 'It's funny,' he murmured. 'I never had her down as a coward.'

The Walking Man finished attending to the fire. He settled down on his bedroll, the mug in both hands, his head against a log. The edges of his huge beard gleamed red in the firelight. 'That's because you don't know the full story.'

'What full story?'

'The truth. You don't know the truth.'

'I think I do.'

'I very much doubt it. Your mind hasn't properly formed around it. There's one more corner you haven't turned or even thought about turning. In fact, you can't even see it's there.' He made a small motion with his hands as if he was tying an intricate knot. 'You're protecting her and you can't yet see what a nice circle that makes.'

'A nice circle?'

'That's what I said.'

'I don't get it.'

'No. You don't. Not yet.' The Walking Man closed his eyes and smiled contentedly. 'Some things you have to work out for yourself.'

'What things? What circle?'

But the Walking Man was motionless, the light of the fire playing across his blackened face, and once again Caffery knew he wouldn't be drawn on the subject. Not until Caffery brought back to him some evidence that he'd worked at it. The Walking Man didn't give anything away for free. It irritated Caffery – this smugness. It made him want to shake the guy. Made him want to say something that hurt.

'Hey.' He leaned forward. Looked hard at the smiling face. 'Hey. Should I be asking you about the compound? Should I be asking if you're going to try to break into it?'

The Walking Man didn't open his eyes, but his smile faded. 'No. Because if you asked that question I'd ignore it.'

'Well, I'm asking you anyway. You've given me the job of second-guessing you – of trying to fathom you. And that's what I've been doing. That compound has been here ten years.' He nodded to where the arc lights shone through the trees. He could just make out the top of the barbed-wire fence, like a gulag. 'It wasn't here when your daughter was killed and you think she might be buried there.'

Now the Walking Man opened his eyes. He tilted his chin down and stared angrily at Caffery. Nothing playful in his belligerence now. 'You're trained to ask questions. Aren't you trained to know when to shut up as well?'

'You told me once that every step you walked was your preparation. You said you wanted to follow her. It was a mystery to me, why you walked, but I think I know now. You say you're not a seer, but you can tread the same piece of land I tread and read in it a hundred things I would never read.'

'You can talk all you like, policeman, but I make no promises I'll listen.'

'Then *I*'ll talk. I'll tell you everything I know about what you're doing. I know what the walking is about. Some things I haven't figured yet. The crocuses – they're in a line and that means something, but I don't know what. Then there's the van Evans dumped in the Holcombe quarry after he'd got rid of her body. That was stolen from you in Shepton Mallet and I don't know why you're so far away from where it happened. But I know everything else. You're still looking for her. For where she was buried.'

The Walking Man held his gaze. His eyes were dark, ferocious.

'Your silence,' said Caffery, 'says it all. Don't you know that you can learn more about a man from what he doesn't say than from what he does?'

'Learn more about a man from what he doesn't say than from what he does. Is that a policeman's adage? Some bargain-basement homily from the cosy offices of Her Majesty's law-keepers?'

Caffery half smiled. 'You only bait me when I've touched on something.'

'No – I bait you because I know how effete and useless you really are. You're angry, and you imagine it's because of the evil in the world when what really infuriates you is how toothless you are about that woman. How straitjacketed and hand-tied. That's what you can't stand.'

'And you're angry because you know I'm right. You're angry because, for all your insight and sixth senses, you come to something like this,' he waved at the factory compound, 'and you can't get in to search it. And there's not a damned thing you can do about it.'

'Get away from my fire. Get away from me.'

Caffery put down his beaker. He got to his feet and carefully rolled up the piece of foam, placing it next to the plates and other belongings. 'Thank you for answering my questions.'

'I didn't answer them.'

'Yes, you did. Trust me. You did.'

31

By the time Caffery got to the office the next morning it was eight o'clock and already there had been meetings, interviews and phone calls. He made a rough bed with an old towel under the radiator behind his desk, settled Myrtle there with a bowl of water and, taking sips of scalding coffee, wandered through the corridors, barely awake, his eyes bloodshot. He hadn't slept well – never did in the middle of a case. After the argument with the Walking Man he'd gone back to the isolated cottage he rented in the Mendips and spent the night combing through the witness statements on Emily's kidnapping. There'd been some Scotch somewhere along the line. Now he had a headache that could have brought down an elephant.

The office manager updated him. Lollapalooza and Turner were still busy tickling up warrants for the remaining properties out in the Cotswolds. The CSI 'surgery' had forensicated Janice Costello's Audi and come up with nothing. They'd left it in the car park downstairs and the family had collected it last night on their way to Janice's mother in Keynsham. DC Prody had taken a half-day off yesterday. In a strop, probably, but he must have seen sense overnight. He'd been back since five this morning, dealing with the CCTV footage. Caffery made a silent pact to broker a peace with him. He carried his now empty mug down to Prody's office. 'Any chance of a coffee?'

Prody glanced up from his desk. 'I guess. Have a seat.'

Caffery hesitated. Prody's tone was sullen. Don't rise to it, he thought. Just don't. He kicked the door closed, put the mug on the desk, sat and looked at the walls. The room was cheerier now. The overhead light was working, there were pictures on the walls, and in the corner there was a dust sheet with a roller tray resting on some tins. The smell of paint was overwhelming. 'Decorators been in, have they?'

Prody got up and clicked the kettle on. 'Not that I asked for it. Maybe someone decided I needed a proper welcome. Electric lights, too. Honestly? I'm just a bit disappointed I didn't get a mood board through the internal first.'

Caffery nodded. He was still hearing that sullen note in the man's voice. 'Well? What's come in overnight?'

'Nothing much.' He spooned coffee into cups. 'The streets around the place Emily was taken have been combed – the only dark-blue Vauxhall had different digits. Turned out to belong to a nice lady with two dogs and a hairdressing appointment in the area.'

'And the CCTV on the stations?'

'Nothing. No data at two, and the one where the Yaris was found – Avoncliffe? – it's a request stop.'

'A request stop?'

'You put out your arm, the train stops.'

'Like a bus?'

'Like a bus. But no one stopped the train over the weekend. He left the Yaris there and must have got away on foot. None of the local cab companies had any pick-ups either.'

Caffery swore lightly under his breath. 'How's the bastard doing it? He got past the ANPR cameras – there's no way he could have known where the units were going to be, is there?'

'I can't see how.' He clicked the kettle off and poured hot water into the cups. 'They're mobile, not fixed.'

Caffery nodded thoughtfully. He'd just noticed a familiar file on Prody's windowsill. Yellow. From the review team. Again.

'Sugar?' Prody was holding a loaded spoon above one of the mugs.

'Please. Two.'

'Milk?'

'Yes.'

He held the mug out to Caffery, who looked at it steadily, but didn't take it. 'Paul.'

'What?'

'I asked you not to look at that file. I asked you to return it to the review team. Why did you ignore me?'

There was a pause. Then Prody said, 'Do you want this coffee or not?'

'No. Put it down. Explain why you've got the file.'

Prody waited a second or two longer. Then he put the coffee on the desk, went to the windowsill and got the file. He pulled up a chair and sat, facing Caffery, with it on his lap. 'I'll fight you over this, because I can't let it go.' He found a map in the file and unfolded it on his knee. 'This is Farleigh Wood Hall and this, roughly, is the radius you initially searched. You concentrated a lot of your resources on the fields and villages in that radius. You did some house-to-house *outside* the radius too. Around here.'

Caffery didn't let his eyes drop to the map. He could tell from his peripheral vision that Prody was pointing to a place about half a mile from where Flea's accident had happened. He kept his eyes on Prody's face. Kept the huge fat fist of rage tucked under his sternum. He'd been wrong. Prody was never going to be a steady-hand cop. There was something else underneath: a hard, urban intelligence that could make him a brilliant cop in the right circumstances – and a dangerous one in the wrong.

'But mostly outside that radius you went wide, to the bigger towns. Trowbridge, Bath, Warminster. Looked at railway stations, bus stops, some of the dealers around there because she was a junkie. It occurred to me – what if she got out of this radius but didn't get as far as one of the towns? What if something happened to her on one of the roads? What if she was picked up by someone, given a lift? Taken somewhere miles away – God knows, Gloucestershire, into Wiltshire, London. But, of course, you'd thought of that. You had checkpoints set up. You inter-viewed drivers for two weeks. But then I thought, What if it was a hit-and-run? What if it happened on one of these small roads? Some of them only serve these little hamlets.' Again that finger, right over the place of the accident. 'There's hardly any traffic down there. Something happened and there'd have been no one to witness it. Seriously, have you thought of that? What if someone hit her, panicked and hid the body? Or maybe even loaded the body into the car – disposed of it somewhere else?'

Caffery took the map from him, folded it up.

'Boss, listen. I want to be a good cop. That's all this is. It's just the way I'm made – I have to put my back into everything I do.'

'Then start by learning how to take orders and how to be *respectful*, Prody. This is the last warning: you don't stop being a prick I'll get you shifted to that prostitute murder the others are working on. You can spend your days down at City Road interviewing the slag meth dealers if you prefer.'

Prody took a breath. His eyes went to the map in Caffery's hand.

'I said, *is that what you'd prefer?*'

There was a long silence. Two men fighting without saying a word or moving a muscle. Then Prody breathed out. Let his shoulders droop. Closed the file. 'But I don't like it. I don't like it at all.'

'Oddly enough,' Caffery said, 'I really didn't think you would.'

32

Twenty minutes after Caffery's meeting with Prody, Janice Costello appeared unannounced at his office door in a rain-streaked coat, her hair untidy, her face flushed. She looked as if she'd been running. 'I've called nine nine nine.' She was holding a piece of paper in her right hand. 'But I wanted to show you in person.'

'Come in.' Caffery got up and pulled back a chair. On her bed under the radiator Myrtle pricked her ears and blinked at Janice. 'Sit down.'

She took a step inside and, ignoring the chair, pushed the crumpled paper at him. 'It came through the door at my mother's. We'd been out. The note was on the doormat when we got back. We didn't stay in the house for a second after that. We got straight out and came here.'

Her hand was trembling and Caffery knew, without having to ask, what the paper was. Almost knew what it would say. A long, slow wave of nausea came up from his stomach. The sort of nausea that could only be sent away by cigarettes and Glenmorangie.

'We need you to put us somewhere safe, somewhere we're protected. We'll sleep on the floor of the police station if we have to.'

'Put it down.' He went to a filing cabinet and found a small box of latex gloves, pulled on a pair. 'That's it – on the table.' He bent and straightened it. Some of the ink was smudged from the rain on Janice's hands, but he recognized the writing instantly.

Do not believe it is over. My love affair with your daughter has only just begun. I know where you are – I will always know where you are. Ask your daughter – she knows we're supposed to be together . . .

'What do we do?' Janice's teeth were chattering. The rain in her hair scattered the fluorescent light. 'Has he been *following* us? *Please* – what the hell's going on?'

Caffery gritted his teeth hard and fought the desire to close his eyes. He'd put a lot of energy into making sure the story wasn't leaked. And everyone, from the FLO to the press office, was telling him it was watertight. So how in Christ's name had the jacker found out not only where they lived but where her damned *mother* lived? Trying to keep a step ahead of him was like trying to stop lightning.

'Did you see anyone? Any reporters? Outside your house?'

'Cory spent all afternoon watching. There wasn't a soul.'

'And are you *sure* – one hundred per cent cast-iron *sure* – that you haven't told anyone?'

'I'm sure.' Tears were in her eyes. Tears of real fear. 'I swear. And my mother hasn't either.'

'No neighbours saw you coming or going?'

'No.'

'And when you went out?'

'It was just to the local shops first thing this morning. In Keynsham. Just to get bread for breakfast. Mum had run out.'

'You didn't try to go back to Mere?'

'*No!*' She paused, as if her vehemence had shocked her. She pushed her sleeves up her arms, shivering. 'Look – I'm sorry. It's just I've gone over and over it. And we haven't done anything. I swear.'

'Where's Emily now?'

'With Cory. In the office downstairs.'

'I'm going to find you somewhere. Give me half an hour. I can't guarantee it'll be as nice as your place – or your mother's –

or that it'll be close to Keynsham. It could be anywhere in Avon and Somerset.'

'I don't care where it is. I just want to know we're safe. I want my mother to come too.'

Something occurred to Caffery as he picked up the phone. He replaced the handset and went to the window, put a finger on a blind slat and peered out into the street. Dark and rainy, the streetlamps on still, even though it was morning. 'Where's your car?'

'Outside. Round the back.'

He looked a little longer at the street. One or two cars were parked – empty. Another went past slowly, headlights making silver domes in the rain. He released the blind. 'I'm going to get a driver to take you.'

'I can drive.'

'Not the way this driver can.'

Janice was quiet. She looked at the blind. At the darkness beyond it. 'You mean he can do evasive driving, don't you? You think he might have followed us here?'

'I wish I knew.' Caffery picked up the phone. 'Go and wait with Emily. Go on. Give her a hug.'

33

The team did a sweep of the rainy streets outside the offices and found nothing. No cars loitering. No dark-blue Vauxhalls, registration ending in WW. No one taking off at the sight of the cops and gunning it down the high road. Of course, there wouldn't be. The jacker was too sharp for anything so pre-dictable. The Costellos were calmed down and given a safe-house, this one down in Peasedown St John, thirty or more miles away from the Bradleys. A specialist driver turned up and drove the family car for them. He called Caffery half an hour later to say they were settled – Nick and a local PC putting on a protective show for them.

When Caffery sat and thought about it – about just how the hell the jacker had found the family – the headache that had dogged him all morning ratcheted up a notch. He wanted to close the blinds, switch off the lights and curl up on the floor next to the dog. The jacker was like a virus, changing and evolving at a terrifying rate, and Caffery couldn't get all the unanswered questions to stop screaming at him. He had to turn away from it. Just for a while.

He took the yellow box file back to the review team – told them in future to let him know before they passed it out to any-one under inspector rank. Then he put Myrtle into the car and drove out through the miserable suburbs, along the ring road, with its soulless industrial estates and hypermarkets, past the multiplexes with their tinsel Christmas trees mounted above the billboards. He stopped in Hewish, where the jets flew low over the Somerset Levels, and parked outside a breaker's yard.

'Stay there,' he told the dog. 'And don't cause trouble.'

Back in his probationary days in London one of the duties Caffery had liked least had been spot checks on the Peckham scrap-dealers. The sheer quantities of stolen metal that got fenced through the yards were awesome – lead from churches, phosphor bronze from lathes and ships, even cast-iron street manhole covers. In the last ten years the role had been passed to the local authorities so he had no authority in the yards now. Didn't matter. The car that had hit Misty Kitson needed to be in the crusher, out of harm's way.

He stopped just inside the gates and looked at the low light on the frosted mountains of metal, the huge hydraulic crusher crouched in the middle. In the distance the towering carcasses of scrapped cars rose like intricate metal termite mounds against the flat grey sky. The car he wanted was at the front of a pile of five shells stacked one on top of another. He picked his way towards it and stood for a while next to it in the freezing cold. A silver Ford Focus. He knew it well. The front end was destroyed, the engine block and the firewall crumpled. The engine was beyond repair – no one would be taking that for the reconditioned market. All that was keeping the car sitting there, waiting quietly for the end, were the other bits and pieces that could be scavenged: sills, door handles, instrument panels. Its decomposition had been slow so far. Caffery came here every week to check it, buying a door or a seat to speed its journey to the crusher. Nothing too obvious, though. He didn't want to draw attention to it.

He ran a gloved hand over the crumpled bonnet, up the shattered windscreen and on to the roof. He let his fingers trail down into the familiar dent. He knew it like the back of his hand. He pictured Misty's head colliding with it, bursting red in the night. Pictured her flying over the bonnet on a lonely country lane, making contact with the roof. A sloppy bag of slack muscle and bone by the time she hit the tarmac. Already dead, neck broken.

A German shepherd on a chain barked noisily as Caffery approached the reception building. Outside were parked three four-by-fours: *Andy's Asphalt and Fascias*, their flanks said. Tiring and familiar to him. Still a cop wasn't even supposed to *think* the word 'pikey'. The job slang, with its way of getting round any obstacle, had shifted its terminology to TIB. Call them TIBs and they'd never know you were calling them thieving itinerant bastards. The TIB who owned the scrapyard was about as much the stereotype as you could get and not be in a cartoon: overweight, grease-stained overalls, a diddicoy ring in his ear. He sat behind the desk, a two-bar fire warming his legs, playing penny bets on the filthy, oil-stained computer. When Caffery came in he killed the screen and twisted round in the chair. 'What can I do you for, mate?'

'A tailgate. Ford Focus, Zetec. Silver.'

The man pushed himself off the chair and stood, hands on his sides, to peer up at the rows and rows of car parts ranked on the huge Dexion shelves mounted above the desk. 'I've got a couple up there. Can do you either of them for a ton.'

'OK. But I'll have it from a car out on the yard.'

The owner turned. 'One from out on the yard?'

'That's what I said.'

'But these are already cut.'

'Don't care. I want it from out in the yard.'

The TIB frowned. 'Have you been in here before? Do I know you?'

'Come on.' Caffery held the door open. 'I'll show you.'

Disgruntled, the man came out from behind the desk, pulling on a stained fleece and following him out into the yard. They stood next to the silver Focus, their breath steaming white in the freezing air.

'Why this one? I've got dozens of Focus tailgates inside. Silver ones too. The Focus is my biggest seller. It's a clit car.'

'A what?'

'A clit car. Every cunt's got one. And for me they're arse cars too, because I've got them coming out my arse. Clits coming out me arse. I'm a biological marvel.' He gave a phlegmy laugh. Stopped when Caffery didn't join in. 'But you want this one, you're looking at another thirty on top. You want something specific you've got to pay for your tastes. With the merchandise inside, I don't have to do anything, just pass them over to you. This one, I've got to get the boys out with the cutting torch.'

'They're going to do it anyway. Eventually.'

'A hundred and thirty or walk away.'

Caffery looked at the dent in the roof. He wondered if he should warn Flea about Prody. He didn't know what he'd say, how he'd go about it. 'A hundred for the tailgate,' he said. 'But when you've taken it off I want to watch you crush the car.'

'It's not ready for crushing.'

'Yes, it is. If the tailgate goes there's nothing else. The gearbox has gone, the offside headlamp, the seats, the wheels, even the trims. Take the tailgate away and the car's ready for the chomper.'

'The seatbelts.'

'Nothing special about them. No one'll want those. Throw them in with the tailgate for a ton. There's a nice man.'

The TIB gave him a sly look. 'I know what your sort would call me in private. You call me a TIB. A thieving itinerant bastard. But the thing is you're wrong. I might be itinerant but I'm not thieving – and I'm not thick either. And in my world when someone asks me to crush a car it makes alarm bells go off.'

'In my world if someone bothers to cut cars up and stack the parts in a shed without getting any orders *that* makes alarms go off. Why the tidy lines inside? Why did you bother cutting them up before you knew they'd be wanted? And where are the shells? I know what happens in your midnight crushing sessions. I know how many VIN numbers get mashed up of a night out here.'

'Who the fuck are you? I've seen you round here before, haven't I?'

'Just crush the car, OK?'

The man opened his mouth, then closed it. He shook his head. 'Jesus,' he said. 'What is the world coming to?'

34

The house was an unremarkable little box on a bedraggled windswept estate. For years it had been the local bobby's, but now the force had no use for it and a weatherbeaten FOR SALE sign was planted in the unkempt garden. Today, probably for the first time in ages, there were lights on inside. The heating had even come on – the upstairs radiators and the gas fires in the living room were working. Janice had got the kettle on and made tea for everyone. Emily – who'd cried on the way over – had been allowed hot chocolate and a jelly and had cheered up. Now she was watching *CBeebies* in the living room, sitting on the floor and giggling along to Shawn the Sheep.

Janice and her mother watched her from the doorway.

'She'll be fine,' said her mother. 'A couple of days off school won't hurt her. I sometimes kept you off at that age just because you were tired or grumpy. She's only four.' With her wide-necked Fair Isle sweater and her short, boyishly cut white hair pushed back off her tanned face, she was still beautiful. Periwinkle-blue eyes. Very soft skin that always smelt of Camay soap.

'Mum,' Janice said, 'do you remember the house at Russell Road?'

Her mother raised an eyebrow, amused. 'I think I can cast my mind back. We lived there for ten years.'

'Do you remember the birds?'

'The birds?'

'You kept telling me not to have the window open in my

bedroom. Of course I ignored you. I used to sit up there and throw paper planes out of it.'

'Wasn't the last time you disobeyed me.'

'Well, we went away for the weekend to that campsite in Wales. The one with the cove at the bottom of the lane? I made myself sick on Opal Fruits? And when we got home there was a bird in my bedroom. It must have come in when I'd had the window open and when we shut them to go away it got trapped.'

'I think I remember.'

'It was still alive but it had babies in the nest outside the window.'

'Oh, God, yes.' Her mother put her hand to her mouth, half delighted to have this memory delivered to her, half horrified too. 'Yes. Of course I remember. Poor little things. The poor mother. She was sitting at the window looking at them.'

Janice gave a small, sad laugh. Tears pricked the back of her eyes just thinking about the bird. At the time she'd felt sorry for the babies dead in the nest. She'd buried each one under a white pebble in the flowerbed, crying with guilt. She'd had to grow up and have her own baby to understand that the greatest suffering had been for the mother bird, watching its babies die. Not being able to do anything to help. 'Yesterday when the car drove off I just couldn't stop thinking about that bird.'

'Janice.' Her mother put an arm around her, kissed her head. 'Sweetheart. She's safe now. It might not be very nice here, but at least the police are looking after us.'

Janice nodded. She bit her lip.

'Now, you make yourself another cup of something. I'm going to clean that awful bathroom.'

When she'd gone, Janice stood where she was for a long time, the door half open, her arms crossed. She didn't want to go to the kitchen. It was tiny and depressing, and Cory was sitting in there with a cup of coffee and his iPhone, answering work emails. All morning he'd been at it. He hated having to take time off work – just hated it. He'd spent a long time muttering darkly about lost hours, about the recession, jobs being hard to come by and about ingratitude, as if he resented Janice for what had happened to them, as though she had planned the upheaval just to keep him away from work.

In the end she went upstairs to the small bedroom at the front. There were two single beds, hastily made up with sleeping-bags she and Cory had grabbed as they left the house and sheets that Nick had managed to rustle up from somewhere. She looked at the beds: it would be the first time in ages that she'd sleep on her own. Even after all this time together, and all the things they'd been through, Cory still wanted sex. In fact, if anything, he seemed to want it even more since Clare had been on the scene. Even when all Janice wanted was to lie still and silent in the dark and let dreams play out across the backs of her eyelids, she'd still let him do what he needed to. It spared her the bad moods, the veiled insinuations that she wasn't living up to the wife he'd hoped for. But she was silent when it was happening. She never pretended to enjoy it.

Outside a car stopped. Instinctively she went to the curtain and lifted it. It was parked on the opposite side of the road, with a dog – a collie – on the back seat and DI Caffery in the front. He killed the engine and paused for a while, looking across at the house, his face expressionless. He was good-looking, any idiot woman could see that, but there was something contained and guarded in his face that made her feel out of her depth. Now he was oddly still and it dawned on her that he wasn't just gazing into space but focusing on something in the garden. She put her head to the window-pane and glanced down. Nothing odd. Just her car parked in the driveway.

Caffery got out of his car, slammed the door and looked up and down the deserted street, as if he suspected a sniper was trained on him. Then he pulled his coat round him, crossed the road and stopped on the driveway in front of the Audi. It had been cleaned before it was returned to them – the dent on the off-side front wing where the jacker had crashed it wasn't that bad. But something about it had caught Caffery's interest. He was studying it carefully.

She opened the window and leaned out. 'What?' she whispered. 'What is it?'

He turned his face up to hers. 'Hello,' he said. 'Can I come in? We need to speak.'

'I'll come down.' She pulled a sweater on over her T-shirt, jammed her feet into her boots, not bothering to zip them up, then went lightly down the stairs. Outside, in the freezing drizzle, Caffery was waiting. He was facing her, his back to the car as if he was guarding it.

'What is it?' she hissed. 'You've got a weird look on your face. What's wrong with the car?'

'Is Emily OK?'

'Yes. She's just had her lunch. Why?'

'You're going to have to interrupt her. We're moving on.'

'Moving on? Why? We've only just got . . .' And then it dawned on her. She took a step back into the shelter of the porch. 'You're joking. You mean he knows where we are? He's found this place too?'

'Can you just go inside and get Emily ready?'

'He's found us, hasn't he? He's out there, watching us now. You're telling me he's found us.'

'I'm not telling you that. You've been very helpful so far, so, please, keep calm. Go inside and get everything packed. I've got an unmarked car coming down from Worle. It's completely normal in cases like this. We move people from time to time. It's standard practice.'

'No, it isn't.'

A burst of static from Caffery's radio. He turned his back on her, pulled away his jacket and bent his head to mutter into it. She couldn't hear what he was saying but she caught a couple of words from the other person: the name of the street and 'low-loader'. 'You're taking the car again. Why? What's he done to it?'

'Just get back inside and get your daughter ready, please.'

'No. You tell me what it is.' Angry now, angry enough not to care if the jacker really was out there with a bloody rifle trained on her, she stepped on to the driveway. She glanced up and down the empty street. No one. She went to the back of the Audi and crouched to inspect it, looking at it carefully, wondering what she was missing. She went around the side, not touching, but leaning close enough to pick up the smallest anomaly. It hadn't been easy, getting into the car so soon after the jacking. Yesterday when she'd got it from the unit car park she'd found herself seeing the interior with new eyes. Trying to trace, on the handles and head-rests, a shadow of the man who'd taken Emily. But there'd been nothing physically different about it. Now she went past the passenger door, around the front, past the dent in the right bumper, back past the driver's door. She stopped where Caffery stood, arms folded. 'Could you step back? I want to look at this bit.'

'I don't think it's necessary.'

'I do.'

'No. What is necessary is that you go inside and get your daughter ready to leave.'

'This isn't helping, protecting me like this. Whatever you're doing you're not helping me by hiding things. Can you step back, please? You might be the police, but this is still my property.'

For a couple of seconds Caffery was motionless. Then, without changing his expression, he took one step away. He stood side on to her, facing the house as if that had suddenly diverted his interest from the Audi. Slowly, checking him warily over her shoulder, she studied the area he'd been hiding. There was nothing – nothing odd or out of place. No scratches or dents. No attempt to break the locks. When she was absolutely sure there was nothing she took a step back and simply stood on the driveway, not speaking, not moving, working silently on unknotting this conundrum. It took a moment or two but at last something in her head fitted into place. She crouched, hand on the rain-soaked driveway and peered under the car. Sitting there, like a barnacle, was a dark square shape about the size of a small shoebox.

She jerked upright.

'It's OK,' Caffery said calmly. 'It's not a bomb.'

'Not a bomb? What the hell is it?'

'It's a tracking device.' He made it sound as if it was the usual sort of thing you found attached to the bottom of a family saloon car. 'Switched off now. Won't hurt you. Don't worry – the squad car'll be here any time. We'll have to go straight away. Suggest you get your family to—'

'Oh, *Christ*.' She marched inside, down the hallway, until she could see Emily, cross-legged on the floor, smiling at the TV screen. Caffery followed. Janice drew the door closed and turned to him.

'How the hell did he do it?' she spoke in a low whisper. 'A *tracking device*. When on earth did he have the chance to put that on?'

'You picked it up from us, didn't you, yesterday? The forensics team delivered it to the offices at MCIU?'

'Yes. I signed for it. Cory wanted Emily to get back into it as soon as possible. Didn't want her to get a problem with it. I didn't have any idea there was a—'

'You didn't stop anywhere on your way to your mother's?'

'No. We went straight there. Cory was in his car behind us.'

'And at your mother's? What did you do with it there?'

'I put it in the garage. There's never been a chance for anyone to get near it.'

Caffery shook his head. There was something shuttered about his eyes that she didn't understand. 'Has Emily talked about what happened? In any detail?'

'No. The woman from CAPIT said not to push it. She said it would come out when Emily was ready. Why? Do you think he had a chance to put it on when he had her?'

'I don't know. Maybe.'

'But your forensics people. If he'd done it then they'd have . . .' Suddenly she got it. Suddenly she knew why his eyes were so guarded. 'Oh, my God. Oh my God. You mean your men didn't check the bloody car properly.'

'Janice, just get Emily ready, will you?'

'I'm *right*. I know I am. I can see it in your face. You think the same thing. He put it on when he – I don't know – when he crashed the car maybe and *they* didn't find it. *They didn't find a bloody tracking device stuck right up under the car.* Well, what else did they miss? Did they miss his DNA too?'

'It was a thorough job. A very thorough job.'

'A thorough job. A *thorough job*? Would Martha's parents think they'd done a "thorough job"? Hmm? If they heard your men swept the car and missed something like that, would they have any faith left in you at all?' She stopped and took a slight step back. He hadn't moved but she'd seen something in his face and realized that he wasn't just riding this thing carelessly, that it was biting him too. 'I'm sorry,' she muttered stupidly, holding up a hand in apology. 'I'm sorry. That wasn't necessary.'

'Janice, believe me, you can have no idea just how sorry I am. About all of this.'

35

It took less than an hour for Caffery to get the guilty parties assembled. Both of the MCIU's briefing rooms were in use so he held the meeting at a desk in the open-plan HOLMES computer room, all the computer inputters trying to get on with their jobs around him. He seated the crime-scene manager and the guy who had driven the Costellos to the house in Peasedown at a low coffee-table towards the edge of the room where the HOLMES girls had their lunch and coffee breaks. DC Prody was there too – at a nearby desk, half listening, half leafing through some paperwork. Paperwork from the jacker case, not from the Kitson review file. Caffery had already checked.

'Would Martha's parents think you'd done a thorough job?' The first person whose wings Caffery really wanted to pin was the crime-scene manager, a thin guy who bore more than a passing resemblance to Barack Obama. His hair was cut short and neat, which made him look too distinguished for this profession, as if he should be a high-level corporate lawyer or a doctor. He'd been the one who'd taken the car into the forensics 'surgery' in Southmeads and combed it for the jacker's DNA. 'Would they? Hmm? Think you'd been thorough? Would they see the job you did on the Costellos' Audi and say, "There's a fine job. We've got confidence in this force. They're pulling out all the stops"?'

The CSM looked back at Caffery stonily. 'The car was *done*. From top to bottom. I've already told you.'

'So tell me this. Where's the "bottom" of a car? Where is the

181

legal bottom of a car in your head? The door sills? The exhaust pipe?'

'It was checked. There was no tracker on it when it came into my surgery.'

'Let me tell you a story.' Caffery sat back in his chair, twirling a pencil in his fingers. He was being an arse, he knew, a showman, but he was furious with the guy and wanted to make a spectacle of him. 'Back in London when I was on the Murder Squad – the Area Major Investigation Team, as they called it in those days – I knew a forensics guy. He was quite high up. I won't repeat his name, because if I did you might have heard of him. Now, some muppet in Peckham had offed his wife. We didn't know where the body was but it was sort of clear what had happened – she was missing, he was found trying to hang himself from a tree out on Peckham Rye, and the walls in their flat were covered with blood, including some handprints. Now, both Mr and Mrs Muppet had form, drugs stuff, so their dabs were on file – you can see where I'm going with this, can't you?'

'Not really.'

'I figured I'd get the fingerprints from the wall, match them to the missus and then even if the body never turned up we'd at least have the makings of a case to pass to the CPS. So the flat's been photographed, et cetera, and now my forensics guy's got a free rein. He can do whatever it takes to get a nice print off the wall. Some of the prints are up high – still don't know how they got there, if maybe the husband was lifting her up or what, but somehow the poor unfortunate woman got her hands up almost eight feet in the air. Well, as you know, the science boys are supposed to carry tread-plates – but on this occasion my man's left them somewhere, or used them all up, or whatever. So, he sees this pine chest, with a TV on top of it, about a foot away from the prints he wants. He pulls it out of the corner, stands on it, gets the dabs off the wall and pushes the chest back. Bingo – they belong to Mrs Muppet. Except two days later a relative's clearing up the flat and notices a nasty smell coming from – you guessed it – the trunk. When it's opened the wife's body's in there, and on the carpet under it is blood, with a mark, *in blood*, where the trunk's been pulled out and pushed back. When we go back to the forensics guy what does he do?'

'I don't know.'

'He shrugs and says, "Oh – I thought it was a bit heavy when I pulled it out." *I thought it was a bit heavy!*'

'What's your point?'

'My point is that there are some people in your profession – and of course I wouldn't make assumptions about you – but *some* people who are so tunnel-visioned they fail to spot the glaringly bloody obvious. Kick aside the sodding great confession note just to get to the blood spatter on the wall.'

The CSM pursed his lips, gave him that slightly superior look again. 'The car was *checked*, Mr Caffery. It came into the morning's surgery and went straight to the top of the list – you'd put an express order on it. We cleaned it top to tail. Everything. *There was nothing under it – not a thing.*'

'Were you personally overseeing the surgery?'

'Don't try to nail me on that. I don't personally supervise every job that gets done.'

'So you didn't see it happen?'

'I'm telling you it was done thoroughly.'

'And I'm telling you it wasn't. You didn't check it. At least have the grace to admit it.'

'You're not my line manager.' The CSM pointed a finger at Caffery. 'I'm not a cop, I don't work by your rules. I don't know how you run your debriefs round here, but I don't have to take it. You're going to regret talking to me like this.'

'Maybe. But I doubt it.' He held out a hand, indicating the door. 'Please, feel free to leave. Make sure the door doesn't hit you on the arse as you go.'

'Funny man. Funny.' The CSM crossed his arms. 'That's OK, thank you. I think I'll stay. I'm getting to like it here.'

'Suit yourself. Give the HOLMES girls some entertainment.' Caffery turned to the surveillance driver who'd taken the Costellos to the first safe-house. He wore a suit, a neat tie, and was sitting forward, his elbows on his knees, staring intently at a point on Caffery's chest.

'Well?' Caffery leaned forward and turned his head sideways to try to meet the guy's eyes. 'What about you?'

'What about me?'

'Isn't part of your training to check the car you're getting into? I thought that was the deal – you never get into a car you haven't completely checked. Thought it was habit. Instinct – drummed into you.'

'What can I say? I'm sorry.'

'Is that it? *I'm sorry?*'

The driver puffed out a breath and sat back. He opened his hands to indicate the snotty crime-scene manager. 'You just told him to have the grace to admit it, and I'm admitting it. I didn't check, only had half my mind switched on, and now I'm sorry. Very sorry.'

Caffery glared at him. There was no answer to that one. The guy was right. And he, Caffery, was the twat: sitting like old Nero in the gladiators' ring, twirling his damned pencil. Whatever their mistakes, whatever the force's shortcomings, the point was that the jacker was outsmarting them. And that was scary. 'Shit.' He threw the pencil down. 'This is all going to shit.'

'Yours maybe.' The CSM got to his feet. He turned in the direction of the far door. 'Not mine.'

Caffery twisted round and saw, coming through the room, making her way between the tables, a plump young woman in a black trouser suit. With her sternly straightened blonde hair and orange tan she had the same look as some of the HOLMES indexers. But he didn't recognize her, and the tentative look on her face said she was new. She was clutching a plastic envelope in one hand.

'Thank you.' The CSM stood and took it from her. 'Stop here for a bit. I'm not going to be long. We can drive back together.'

The girl waited awkwardly next to the low sofas while the CSM sat down and shook the contents of the envelope out on to the table. A dozen photographs fell out and he sorted through them with his fingertip. They all showed a car from different angles: interior, exterior, rear view. It was a black car with champagne interior. The Costellos' Audi.

'I think that's the view you're after.' He pulled out a photograph and pushed it across the table to Caffery. It showed the car's underside, exhaust pipe and floor pan, clearly date-stamped from yesterday: 11:23 a.m. Caffery stared at it for a second or two. He wished he'd taken a paracetamol. It wasn't just his head any longer: now his bones were aching from sitting outside in the cold with the Walking Man last night. The car in the photo was clean. Completely clean.

The CSM said, 'Do I get an apology? Or is that too much to ask?'

Caffery picked up the photograph. Held it so tightly the nail on his thumb went white. 'You brought it over here, didn't you? The Costellos collected it from here.'

'They didn't want to come all the way to the surgery. They're in Keynsham? Somewhere near it? They decided it was easier to pick it up here. I had it driven over. Thought I was doing you a favour.'

'You signed it in with my office manager?'

'Yes.'

'Who must have signed it out . . .' Caffery studied the photograph. Somewhere between here and the Costellos' the car had picked up a tag. Which meant – the hairs went up on his arms – the only time, the *only* time, it could have picked up something was while it was here, downstairs in the car park. A secured car park that even a pedestrian couldn't get into. Unless they had an access code.

Caffery raised his sore eyes. He looked at the people in the offices. The warranted officers and the police staff. The auxiliaries. There must be a hundred people who had access to this place. Something else hit him. He remembered thinking the jacker had had the luck of the devil to skirt past the ANPR point. Almost as if he'd known where the cameras were.

'Boss?'

He rotated his head slowly. Prody was sitting forward, a strange look on his face. He was white. Very white. Almost grey. In his hand he was holding one of the jacker's letters. The one that had gone to the Bradleys. The one that talked about rearranging Martha's face. 'Boss?' he repeated quietly.

'Yeah?' Caffery said distantly. 'What is it?'

'Can I have a word with you in private?'

36

The Underwater Search Unit was trained for general support work and for specialist searches. Its responsibilities towards finding Martha Bradley ended there. So, with the disastrous canal search completed, the offices at Almondsbury outside Bristol slipped back to their routine business and PC Wellard at last found time to do the computer-based diversity training each officer was required to complete. A two-day course of sitting in front of a screen clicking buttons to say, yes, he understood it was wrong to judge, wrong to discriminate. When Flea arrived he was in a room off the main office, staring grumpily at the screen. She knew not to speak about yesterday at the canal. She put her head round the door and smiled. Pretended it hadn't happened. 'Afternoon.'

He held up a hand to acknowledge her. ''Ternoon.'

'How's it going?'

'Just about getting there. I think it's working. You won't catch me calling a nigger a nigger any more.'

'*Jesus*, Wellard. For crying out loud.'

He held both hands up. Surrender. 'I'm sorry, Sarge, but this is an insult. Being taught to do the things that're supposed to come naturally? Even the black guys on the force – sorry, *the British individuals of Afro-Caribbean descent* – think it's an insult. The decent human beings in the force don't need to be taught this shit, and the bastards who do need to be told it just tick the boxes, smile and say the right thing. Then they're off to their BNP meetings, shaving their heads and getting the George Cross tattooed where the sun don't shine.'

She took a deep breath. Wellard was hard-working, uncomplaining and totally colour-blind, loved every guy in the team as much as the next. He of all people didn't need this training. He was right. It was an insult to people like him. But there were others who needed it rammed home.

'I can't get into this, Wellard. You know that.'

'Yeah – and that's what's wrong with the world. No one will say it. It's bloody McCarthyism all over again.'

'I don't give a stuff about McCarthyism, Wellard. Just finish the sodding thing. You only have to tick the right bloody boxes. A trained seal could do it.'

He returned to clicking around the screen. Flea closed the door and went to her desk, where she sat, gazing blankly through the open door into the locker room, trying for the hundredth time to focus on the idea sitting just out of her line of vision.

A Christmas card was taped to one of the lockers, the first, as solitary and naked as a January snowdrop. Everything else – the boots on the rack in the corner, the noticeboard with all the filthy postcards and stupid cartoons – had been there for months. Years. They'd been there when Thom had run Misty over – she was sure of that because she remembered sitting in exactly this place trying to work out what the rotten-meat stench was. She hadn't known at the time that it was coming from her own car parked outside. That the smell of decomposing flesh in the boot was being carried into the building by the air-conditioning system.

Air-conditioning. She drummed her fingers on the table. Air-conditioning. She felt the electromagnetic field crackle around her skull and her neck, pushing goosebumps up on her arms. What alarms were kicking off in the back of her head? The exchange of gas. The replacement of old air for new. She thought of where Misty was now: the way the air made its way up from the cave deep in the rock, along unseen passages, tiny crevices no wider than a finger, and out, out, out into the open.

And then, in a rush, it came to her. She stood and pulled out her project file, a loose-leaf folder full of all the things that needed doing in the unit day after day, leafed quickly through it until she found the notes from the search yesterday. Shakily she pulled them out, spread them on the desk and stood with her hands on the table, poring over them, the whole thing slotting into place in her head.

Air shafts. That's what she'd been missing. The fucking air shafts.

Someone knocked at the door.

'Yes?' Half guiltily she shovelled the paper back into the file, turned her back to the desk. 'What?'

Wellard appeared. He was holding a pad with a message written on it in his untidy handwriting. 'Sarge?'

'Yes, Wellard.' She leaned back on the desk to hide the file. 'What can I do for you?'

'Got a job. Just got the call.'

'What sort of job?'

'Arrest warrant.'

'Who are we supposed to be arresting?'

'Don't know. They told us to expedite our journey to the RV point. No firearms coding, but sounds pretty hefty all the same.'

She looked at him steadily. 'You do it, Wellard, you act up for me. I'm taking the afternoon off.'

Wellard always stepped in as acting sergeant when she couldn't be there but usually a handover would be scheduled in advance. He frowned. 'You're rostered for today.'

'I'm ill. I'll self-certify.'

'You're not ill.' He looked at her suspiciously. 'Hey. It's not 'cos of what I said, is it? You know, when I said you won't catch me calling a n—'

She held up a hand to stop him, her heart racing. 'Thank you, Wellard. No. That's not why.'

'Then, what?'

If she told him the way her mind was careening along he'd lose it with her. He'd tell her she was obsessed and that she should let it go. He'd make fun of her or, worse, threaten to tell the inspector. Or give her a lecture. Or even try to come with her. Anyway. She'd be fine. Nothing was going to happen. 'Because I'm sick. Swine flu – whatever looks good on the forms. I'm going home now to put my feet up.' She bundled the file into her rucksack and swung it over her shoulders, straightened and gave Wellard a bright smile. 'Good luck with the arrest. Don't forget to put in for the acting's allowance.'

37

'It's not just the car park he'd have had access codes for,' said Turner. 'He'd have been able to walk round the whole building, in and out of all the offices. He might as well have been invisible.'

Caffery, Turner and Prody were crammed into Prody's office. The heating was on full and the windows were steamed up. The smell of paint and sweat hung heavy in the air.

'There's CCTV in the car park.' Caffery was standing in the corner, hands in his pockets. 'If he put the tracker on the car we'd have footage of it. Has anyone looked at that?'

The two other men were silent.

'What?'

Turner shrugged. Didn't meet his eyes. 'Camera's broken.'

'*Again?* That was the excuse when the sodding unit car was stolen. You're telling me it's happened again?'

'Not again. It just never got fixed in the first place.'

'Oh, great. How long's it been on the blink?'

'Two months. He was the handyman – it was kind of his job to fix it.'

'And how long has this wanker been working for us?'

'Two months.'

'Christ, Christ, Christ.' Caffery put his knuckles to his head. Dropped them, exasperated. 'I hope we folded his fucking napkin when we served Martha up to him on a plate.'

He picked up the paperwork on Prody's desk that had been faxed over from Human Resources. A photo was stapled to the top. Richard Moon. Thirty-one. Employed by the police as a 'maintenance officer' for the last year and at MCIU for the last eight weeks, doing general jobs around the building: painting, fixing lights, nailing skirting-boards, replacing broken lavatory cisterns. Planning Martha's abduction and how best to indulge his habits without being caught.

It was Prody who'd made the connection. He'd remembered a note he'd found on his desk that morning and had crumpled up in his wastepaper basket. A message from the handyman Moon: *Sorry about the smell of paint. Don't touch the radiator.* The Barack Obama CSM, who knew a little about handwriting, was sure they'd been written by the same person who'd sent the notes to the Bradleys. Then someone had pointed out that the notes to the Bradleys and the Costellos had been written on paper that looked suspiciously like the notepads issued to them from HQ. The jacker had been using the force's own stationery to write his sick messages on. How brilliant was that?

Moon had been at work this morning. But he was rostered off duty at midday and had left the building just as the meeting with the CSM had started. He'd been here, right under their noses. Caffery stared at his photo, remembering the guy he'd seen around the place a couple of times. Tall, if he recalled rightly, overweight. Usually dressed in overalls, though in the photo he wore a khaki T-shirt. He was white, with an olive skin, a broad forehead, wide-spaced eyes, a full mouth. Dark hair cut close, probably a number three, not a number two. A number two took maintenance. Caffery looked at the eyes. He tried to see something reflected in them. The eyes that had seen God-only-knew-what happen to Martha Bradley. The mouth that had done God-only-knew-what to her.

Christ, he thought, what a total feast of snakes this was. Heads would roll.

'He's got no cars registered to his name,' Turner said, 'but he was driving himself to and from work. Lots of the boys remember seeing him.'

'I saw him too,' Prody said dully.

The two men turned to him. He was sitting in his chair, his

shoulders slumped. He hadn't spoken much. He was furious with himself that he hadn't picked it up sooner. For a while Caffery had been tempted to use it as a stick to beat him with, to ram home the point that if he'd had his head properly locked on this case they might have picked up Moon earlier. But Prody was ashamed enough already. If there were lessons to be learned, he was doing all the teaching himself.

'Yeah – he had a car.' Prody gave them a thin, sick smile. 'And guess what it was?'

'Oh, please,' Caffery said faintly. 'Don't tell me. A Vauxhall.'

'I saw him driving it one day. Noticed it because it was the same blue as my Peugeot.'

'Jesus.' Turner shook his head, deflated. 'I can't believe this.'

'Yeah, OK. No need to look at me like that. I know I'm a cunt.'

'You worked on relocating the Costellos today,' said Caffery. 'Tell me he wasn't in the room when you did it. Tell me he didn't overhear that conversation.'

'He didn't. I'm sure.'

'How about when you were ordering up all the ANPR points? You're sure he couldn't have . . . ?'

Prody shook his head. 'That was late at night. He'd have gone.'

'How did he know about it, then? Because he definitely knew where those cameras were.'

Prody started to say something but stopped and closed his mouth as if something had dawned on him. He turned to the computer and shook the mouse. The screen lit up and he stared at it, his face going dark red. 'Great.' He threw his hands into the air. 'Fucking great.'

'What?'

He pushed his chair bad-temperedly away from the desk, swivelled it to face the wall, and sat there with his arms folded, his back to the room, as if he'd come to the end of his patience.

'Prody. Don't act like a fucking child.'

'Yeah, well, feel like one at the moment, Boss. He's probably been into my computer. That's why it never seemed to time out. It's all in there.' He waved a hand at it over his shoulder.

'Everything. The works. All my emails. That's how he did it.'

Caffery chewed his lip. He checked his watch. 'I've got a job for you. You need to go and see someone.'

Prody turned his chair back. 'Yeah? What?'

'The bean-counters are whining about budgets – throwing their toys out of the pram about the staffing levels on the new safe-house. Go over there and give the PC the afternoon off. Speak to the Costellos and Nick. Give them an update on what's going on – try to calm Janice down because she's going to lose it when she hears about this. When you've done all that – and you can take your time about it, hang around if you have to – get the local shop to send someone back to cover you.'

Prody regarded him balefully. Go and explain to a woman who had nearly lost her daughter that they knew who the bastard was? That something could have been done about it a long time ago? Not exactly the soft option. A hidden punishment in there. Still, he pushed his chair back, got his raincoat off the hook and found his keys. He walked to the door without a word, not looking at anyone.

'See you,' Turner shouted to him. But he didn't answer. He closed the door, leaving the two men standing in silence. Turner might have spoken to Caffery at that point, but his phone rang. He answered it. Listened. Finished the call, put the phone in his pocket, and looked sombrely at the DI.

'They're ready, I take it?' Caffery asked.

Turner nodded. 'They're ready.'

They held each other's eye. Each knew what the other was thinking. They had Richard Moon's address, a witness who said Moon was at home right this second, and now a forced-entry team standing by. And no reason to think Moon knew they were coming. He might be at home, just sitting on the sofa in front of the TV with a cup of tea, not expecting anything to happen.

Of course it wouldn't be like that. Both Turner and Caffery knew it. So far Moon had outsmarted them at every turn. He was cunning and deadly. There was no reason to think he was going to change now. But they had to make the effort. Really, there wasn't anything else they could do.

38

'Jasper doesn't like it here. Jasper thinks that man's going to come in those windows.' In the flat DI Caffery had transferred the Costellos to, little Emily was sitting on the bed, toy rabbit clutched against her chest. They'd had lunch, spaghetti and meat sauce, and now they were making up the beds. Emily frowned at her mother. 'You don't like it here, do you, Mummy? You don't really like it, do you?'

'I don't *love* it.' Janice pulled Emily's Barbie sleeping-bag out of the dustbin liner she'd used to transport it and gave it a shake. This bedroom was nicer than the last one. In fact, the whole flat was better than the police house. Cleaner and tidier with cream carpets and white woodwork. 'I don't *love* it, but I don't hate it. And I do know *something* very special about it.'

'What?'

'I know it's safe. I know no one is going to hurt you while we're here. Those windows are special safe windows and Nick and the rest of the police have made sure of that. The nasty man can't get you here. Can't get Jasper either.'

'Or you?'

'Or me. Or Daddy, or Nanny. None of us.'

'Nanny's bed's too far.' Emily pointed out of the room, down the corridor, past the living room and bathroom to the door at the back of the flat. 'Nanny's bed's all the way down there.'

'Nanny likes her new room.'

'And my bed's too far from yours, Mummy. I won't be able see you in the night. I was scared last night.'

Janice straightened and looked at the little trundle bed Nick had set up in the corner for Emily. Then she looked at the rickety pine bed she and Cory would sleep on. Last night at her mother's Cory had fallen asleep easily. While he snored and grunted she'd lain awake, watching car headlights pass on the ceiling, waiting for one to stop, waiting for footsteps, straining her ears at the tiniest noise outside. 'I tell you what.' She went to the T-shirt and joggers Cory had worn last night. They were in an untidy tangle in his suitcase where he'd thrown them this morning. She picked them up and dropped them on to the trundle bed. Then she pulled Emily's pyjamas out from the rucksack, crossed to the double bed and put them under Cory's pillow. 'How's that?'

'I sleep with *you*?'

'That's right.'

'*Great*,' said Emily, bouncing eagerly. '*Great*.'

'Yeah – really great.' Cory stood in the doorway. He was wearing a suit, his hair slicked back from his forehead. 'I get the camp bed. Thanks a bunch.'

Janice put her hands on her hips and gave him a long look, up and down. The suit was the most expensive one he owned – YSL – and had cost them a small fortune. Last night, in the time she'd been grabbing toys, food, sleeping-bags and clothes for Emily, he'd been getting this suit out of the cupboard. Now he was busily fitting the tiny Paul Smith cufflinks she'd bought him for Easter last year. 'You look nice,' she said coldly. 'Where are you off to? Hot date?'

'Yeah – really hot. I'm going to work. Why?'

'*Work?* Jesus, Cory.'

'What's the matter with that?'

'Well, *Emily* to start with. She's terrified – you can't just go.'

'There are four of you – Nick's not going anywhere and there's an officer sitting outside. You are being looked after. Watertight – *watertight*. In the meantime, my job is not quite as secure. In the meantime, *Janice*, our livelihood, our house, *your* car – everything is not quite *as* watertight. So forgive me for applying myself to the problem.'

He headed back down the hallway. Janice leaped up, closed the door behind her so Emily wouldn't hear and hurried down the corridor to where Cory was standing at a little smeared mirror next to the front door, checking his tie was straight. 'Cory.'

'What?'

'Cory, I—' She took a deep breath. Closed her eyes and counted to ten. Emily had had enough to put up with. She didn't need to hear her parents tearing each other's heads off. 'I am very grateful to you for how hard you work,' she said tightly. She opened her eyes and smiled. Bright. Patted his lapel. 'That's all. Just very grateful. Now, you have a lovely time at work.'

39

The high street was typical of a thousand others in England, with a Superdrug and a Boots interspersed with a couple of local retailers. The shop lights battled with the rain and the beginnings of dusk. Eight men were waiting for Caffery when he arrived at the RV point in a supermarket car park two hundred yards down the street from Richard Moon's flat. They were dressed in protective gear: Kevlar vests, shields, helmets in their hands. He recognized some of them: the Underwater Search Unit, out on the regular support-group duties they did from time to time.

'Where's your sergeant?' Their van's lights were still on, the doors open. 'She on board, is she?'

'Afternoon, sir.' A shortish man with cropped blond hair stepped forward, his hand out. 'Acting Sergeant Wellard. I spoke to you on the phone.'

'You're acting? Where's Sergeant Marley, then?'

'She's back on tomorrow. You can get her on her mobile if you need her.' Wellard positioned himself with his back to the rest of the men so he couldn't be heard. He lowered his voice. 'Sir? I don't know who's been talking but some of the lads've got it into their head that this is the carjacker we're doing today. Are they right?'

Caffery raised his gaze past Wellard, down to where the little street they stood on met the big thoroughfare and the entrance to the flat. 'Tell them I don't want excitement. I want them to keep their respect for this job. Make sure they're ready for the

198

unexpected. This guy is clever, clever, clever. Even if he's in there it's not going to be fairy dust.'

The house with Moon's flat in it was a two-storey plain Victorian terrace with a Chinese takeaway – 'The Happy Wok' – on the ground floor. The stairs from the flat, as with most buildings like this, ran down the side of the takeaway and opened straight out on to the pavement, where pedestrians were passing, hurrying home from work, heads down, fighting the cold. The back of the flat overlooked a small car park where the takeaway owner dumped his empty containers and probably sold off his used cooking oil to the local boy-racers. The curtains were drawn tightly at all the windows. But they'd already made enquiries with the takeaway owner, who said Richard Moon did live upstairs and that there had been movements up there all afternoon. Already members of another unit were assembling at the back of the building. More cops still were discreetly diverting the pedestrians. A rash of sweat prickled on Caffery's upper lip.

'How do you want us to work it?' Wellard stood in typical support-group stance: arms folded at chest height, feet planted wide. 'Do you want us to knock on the door or do you want to handle that part with us backing you up?'

'I'll do the knock. You back me up.'

'You want to do the caution, do you?'

'Yes.'

'And if he doesn't answer?'

'Then it's the big red key.' He nodded to where two men were unstrapping the red battering ram. 'Whatever way, I'm going in with you. I want to see it first hand.'

'If you do, sir, please come in behind us. Stay back, give us space. When we've found the target, I'll assess it and give you a shout. I'll tell you one of three things: compliant, non-compliant or deranged. We'll cuff him if it's a non-compliant—'

'No. You'll cuff him even if it's a compliant. I don't trust this guy.'

'OK – I'll cuff him for either of the first two and you can come in to do the caution. If it's a deranged, you know the routine. It'll be Armageddon in there. He'll be up against the wall, two shields on him, squashed. We'll take him down by the back of his knees if we have to. That'll be the point you might want to think about letting me do the caution.'

'No. I'll do it.'

'Whatever. But stand clear till we've got him completely cuffed. Shout it at him from the doorway if you have to.'

As they walked down the street – Caffery, Turner and the Underwater Search Unit – the mood was superficially calm. Casual, even. The USU guys chatted among themselves, fiddling with gear, checking the channels on their radios so the only communication they'd get would be from officers on this operation. One or two squinted up at the curtained windows, assessing the flat. Only Caffery was silent. He was thinking of what the Walking Man had said: *This man is cleverer than any of the others you've brought to me before. He's laughing at you.*

It wasn't going to be straightforward. He just knew it. It couldn't be this simple.

They stopped at the shabby little front door. The support officers fell instantly into time-tested formation around Caffery, who stood, hand poised, ready to press the bell. To his left three men grouped together as a shield entry team, riot shields rigid in front of them. To his right Wellard spearheaded the rest, batons and CS gas at the ready. Caffery turned his eyes to Wellard. They exchanged a small nod. Caffery took a breath, and rang the bell.

Silence. Five seconds of nothing.

The men held each other's eyes, expecting at any moment the familiar crackle of the radio to tell them their target had jumped from a back window. But nothing happened. Caffery licked his lips. Rang again.

This time there was a noise. A footfall on the steps. From the other side of the door came the sound of bolts being pulled back, a Yale lock turning. The men around Caffery stiffened. He took a step back, feeling in his pocket for his warrant card. He flipped it open, held it up in front of his face.

'Yeah?'

Caffery lowered his card. He realized he'd been squinting, half expecting something to explode in his face. But standing in the doorway was a small man in his sixties. He wore a filthy vest, trousers held up with braces. His head was completely bald. You'd have mistaken him for someone at a BNP meeting if it wasn't for the slippers.

'Mr Moon?'

'Yeah?'

'I'm DI Caffery.'

'Yeah?'

'You're not Richard Moon?'

'Richard? No, I'm Peter. Richard's my boy.'

'We'd like to speak to Richard. Do you know where he is?'

'Yes.'

There was a pause. The team exchanged glances. It never went this smoothly. There'd be a pay-off. 'Then would you like to tell me where he is?'

'Yeah – he's upstairs in bed.' Peter Moon stood back from the door and Caffery peered past him into the hallway and up the stairs. The carpet was shabby and covered with mud. The walls were marked with years of use and nicotine, lines of brown at waist height where hands had scuffed and trailed over the years. 'Do you want to come in? I'll go and get him.'

'No. I want you to step outside, sir, if you don't mind. You can wait here with my colleagues.'

Peter Moon stepped out into the street, shivering at the cold. 'Jesus. What's going on?'

'Any questions, Sergeant Wellard?' said Caffery. 'Got any queries for him?'

'Yes. Mr Moon, there aren't any firearms on the premises as far as you know?'

'Not in a million years.'

'And your son's not armed?'

'Armed?'

'Yes. Is he armed?'

Peter Moon looked carefully at Wellard. His eyes were dead. 'Give me a break.'

'Yes or no?'

'No. And you're going to frighten the crap out of him. He doesn't like unexpected visitors. That's just Richard's way.'

'I'm sure he'll understand. Under the circumstances. He's in bed, then? So how many bedrooms are there?'

'Two. You go through the living room down the corridor – there's one on the left, then a bathroom and the door at the back is his bedroom. Mind you, I wouldn't go too near the bathroom at the moment. Richard's just been in it. Smells like something crawled up inside him and died. Don't know how he does it.'

'End of the corridor.' Caffery jerked his head at the door. 'Wellard? You got it? We good to go?'

Wellard nodded. On a count of three they went: the three-man shield team first, running up the stairs, shouting at the top of their voices: '*Police, police, police!*' The hallway filled with noise and the smell of sweat. Wellard followed with three of his men, and Caffery brought up the rear, taking the steps two at a time.

At the top a large room was heated by a paraffin stove, and crowded with cheap MFI furniture and pictures. The team swarmed all over it, dragging out sofas, checking behind curtains and on top of a large cupboard. Wellard held up a hand flat – the unit's signal for a clear. He pointed at the kitchen. They searched and cleared it. They continued down the corridor, switching on lights, past the bathroom: 'I'd do them a favour and open a fucking window if I didn't think he'd use it as any excuse to leg it,' Wellard muttered, under his breath. They cleared the second bedroom and arrived outside a flimsy veneer door at the end of the corridor.

'Ready?' Wellard murmured to Caffery. He nodded to the bottom of the door, getting Caffery to register there was no light coming from under it. 'This is it.'

'Right – but remember. Expect the unexpected.'

Wellard turned the knob, pushed the door open a crack and stepped back. 'Police,' he said loudly. 'We are the police.'

Nothing happened so he pushed the door wider with his foot, reached in and clicked on the light.

'Police!'

He waited again. The team stood in the corridor with their backs to the wall, sweat on their foreheads, only their eyes moving, darting around, coming back to Wellard's face. When there was no answer from inside Wellard gave them a signal and pushed the door wide. Immediately the team ran in, adopting the defensive stance behind their shields. From where Caffery stood in the hallway he could see the vague reflection of a room on their polycarbonate visors. A window, curtains open. A bed. No more. Behind the reflection, the officers' eyes flicked back and forth, assessing what was in front of them.

'Duvet,' an officer mouthed to Wellard.

He leaned into the crack in the door and shouted, 'Throw the duvet off, please, sir. Please throw the duvet on to the floor in front of my officers so they can see it.'

There was a pause, then the soft sound of it falling. Caffery could see it on the floor – a dingy cover with a geometric design.

'Sir?' The nearest man relaxed his hold on the shield a little. 'It's a compliant. You can come in.'

'A compliant,' Wellard told Caffery, pulling his quickcuffs from his body armour. 'You can do the caution.' He shouldered the door aside and paused when he saw what was inside the room. 'Uh.' He turned to Caffery. 'Maybe you need to come in.'

Caffery put a hand on the door and stepped cautiously inside. The bedroom was small and smelt stale. Men's clothing was scattered everywhere. There was a cheap chest of drawers with a smeared mirror. But it was the man who lay on the bed that was drawing everyone's eyes. He was mountainous – and naked. He probably weighed close to thirty stone. His hands were at his sides and he was shaking as if an electric current was going through him. A high-pitched whine, a kind of stridor, came from his mouth.

'Richard Moon?' Caffery held up his card. 'Are you Richard Moon?'

'That's me,' he wheezed. 'It's me.'

'It's nice to meet you, sir. Do you mind if we have a chat?'

40

Janice insisted that Nick let them go shopping. She couldn't sit around any more without some home comforts. She got the joint credit card out, and Nick drove them to Cribbs Causeway. She bought sheets, duvets and a Cath Kidston teapot in John Lewis and a carrier bag of cleaning equipment from a pound store at the end of the mall. Then they trailed around Marks & Spencer, buying anything that took their fancy: nightgowns for Janice's mother, slippers with pompoms for Emily, a lipstick and a cardigan for Janice. Nick found a 'Juicy' T-shirt she liked and Janice insisted on buying it for her. They went into the food hall and loaded their baskets with exotic tea bags, Eccles cakes, a punnet of cherries, half a salmon she'd cook tonight with dill sauce. It was good, seeing the bright lights, the shoppers with their colourful clothes. Made her feel Christmas might be quite good this year.

When they got back to the little flat a man in a charcoal suit was waiting for them in a blue Peugeot. As Nick pulled up he got out, holding up his warrant card. 'Mrs Costello?'

'That's me.'

'I'm DC Prody, MCIU.'

'I thought I recognized you. How are you?'

'All right.'

Her smile faded. 'What? Why are you here?'

'I've come to see if you've settled in.'

She raised her eyebrows. 'Is that all?'

'Can I come in?' he said. 'It's cold out here.'

She gave him a long, thoughtful look. Then she handed him a carrier bag and made for the front door.

The central heating was on and the flat was warm. While Emily helped Nick and Janice's mother unload the shopping, Janice put on the kettle. 'I'm going to make some tea,' she told Prody. 'I've been desperate for a decent cup and now I'm going to have one. Emily's got some reading to do – she can do that with my mum while you sit down with me and tell me what's happening. Because I'm not stupid. I know something's changed.'

When she'd made the tea they went into the front room. It bordered on pleasant, with a modern brushed stainless-steel gas fire, a sea-grass carpet and clean furniture. A table near the window bore a bowl of silk flowers. Corny, but it made the place feel as though someone had actually spent some time on it. It was a little musty and cold but with the fire on it soon warmed up.

'Well?' Janice unloaded the cakes and the Cath Kidston teapot from the tray and arranged them on the table. 'Are you going to tell me, or are we going to have a little dance first?'

Prody sat down, his face serious. 'We know who it is.'

Janice paused. Her mouth was suddenly dry. 'That's good,' she said carefully. 'That's very good. Does it mean you've got him?'

'I said we know who it is. That's a very significant step.'

'That's not what I want to hear – it's not what I was hoping to hear.' She finished unloading the tray, filled their cups with tea, handed him a plate and put a cake on her own. She sat down and looked at it, then put the plate back on the table. 'So? Who is he? What does he look like?'

Prody reached into his pocket and brought out a folded sheet of paper. At the top left-hand corner there was a photograph of a man – the sort taken in photo-booths. 'Ever seen him before?'

She expected the face to bring with it some emotional punch, but no: he just looked like an ordinary bloke. A chubby guy in his twenties, his hair cut very short and a constellation of spots at either corner of his mouth. She saw the neckline of a khaki T-shirt. She was about to hand the paper back to Prody when she noticed some details on the form. 'Avon and Somerset', it said. 'What's this? Some kind of arrest . . .' she trailed off. She'd just seen the words 'POLICE STAFF' at the bottom.

'I may as well tell you, because you'll find out eventually, that he works for us. He's a handyman.'

She put a hand to her throat. 'He's a . . . He *works* for you?'

'Yes. One of our part-time staff.'

'Is that how he put the device on our car?'

Prody nodded.

'Christ. I can't . . . Did you know him?'

'Not really – I saw him around the place. He painted my office.'

'You spoke to him, then?'

'A few times.' He shrugged. 'I'm sorry. There's no excuse – I was a prat. My mind was elsewhere.'

'And what was he like?'

'Unremarkable. Didn't stand out in a crowd.'

'What do you think he's done to Martha?'

Prody folded the paper. Once, twice, three times, making the creases very neat with his thumbnail. He put it back into his pocket.

'Mr Prody? I said, what do you think he's done to Martha?'

'Can we change the subject?'

'Not really.' The fear, the absolute rage, was building in her. 'Your unit's made a God-awful balls-up and I nearly lost my little girl through it.' It wasn't his fault, she knew, but she wanted to fly at him. She had to force herself to bite her lip and lower her face. She picked up the plate and pushed the cake around with her finger, waiting for the anger to fizzle away.

Prody bent his head a little, trying to see her expression under the fall of her hair. 'This has been awful for you, hasn't it?'

She raised her eyes and met his, which were somewhere between brown and green with gold flecks. Seeing the compassion in them, suddenly, out of nowhere, she wanted to cry. Shakily, she put the plate down. 'Uh . . .' She pushed up the sleeves of her top and rubbed her arms. 'Well, yes. Without sounding too dramatic, these have been some of the worst days of my life.'

'We'll get you through it.'

She nodded and picked up her plate again. She fingered the cake, moved it sideways, broke it in half but didn't eat. There was a knot in her throat and she didn't think she could swallow. 'So how come you got the fuzzy end of the lollipop?' She gave a weak smile. 'Why did you have to come out and get my wrath between the eyes?'

'It was lots of things. Maybe the tipping point was that my DI thinks I'm an arse.'

'Are you?'

'Not in the way he thinks.'

She smiled. 'Can I ask you something? Something really inappropriate.'

He gave a small laugh. 'Well, I'm a man. Men don't always agree with women about what's inappropriate.'

Her smile grew wider. Out of nowhere she felt like laughing. Yes, Mr Prody, she thought. In spite of how bloody horrible this has been, one thing I can see for sure is that you're a man, a nice one. Strong and sort of good-looking too. Meanwhile Cory, my husband, feels like more of a stranger to me than you do at this precise moment.

'What?' Prody said. 'Have I put my foot in it?'

'Not at all. I was going to ask you . . . if I went to Mr Caffery and said I was really scared – scared of my own shadow – would he let you stay here for a few hours with me and Emily and Nick and Mum? I know it'll be boring for you – but it would make things feel so much easier. You don't even have to talk to us – just watch the TV, make phone calls, read the newspaper, whatever. It'd just be nice to have someone around.'

'Why do you think I'm here.'

'Oh. Is that a yes?'

'What does it sound like?'

'Sounds like a yes.'

41

Caffery had the taste of tobacco in his mouth. While scrawny little Peter Moon had helped his son get dressed, supported him as he walked down the corridor into the living room, Caffery had gone outside to where his car was parked, stood next to the window nearest to Myrtle and rolled his first cigarette in days. His fingers were shaking. The rain made the paper dissolve. But he kept at it and lit it, his hand round the lighter flame. He blew the smoke upwards in a thin blue line, Myrtle watching him steadily. Caffery ignored her. He didn't know what trick he'd expected of the jacker, but it wasn't this at all.

The tobacco helped. When he went back into the living room he felt toxic and tight, but at least he wasn't still trembling. Peter Moon had made tea, strong and not too milky. The pot sat on the scruffy little peeling veneer table, along with a plate of Battenberg cake, carefully sliced. Caffery hadn't seen a Battenberg in years. It made him think of his mother and *Songs of Praise* on a Sunday. Not of mean little council flats like this. Next to the cake lay Moon's photo ID, which the force's HR department had hung on to. It showed the handyman – soft jaw, dark hair. Overweight, but nothing like the Richard Moon who sat on the sofa, wheezing, as his father busied himself around him, supporting him with cushions, getting his legs raised, putting a mug of tea into his swollen hands.

Turner had been in touch with the employment agency the force used for casual staff and the manager who'd hired Moon – put him through his CRB clearance, interviewed him – was here now. A middle-aged Asian man in a camel coat with the beginnings of grey in his hairline. He looked anxious. Caffery wouldn't have wanted to be in his shoes.

'He's nothing like the man I employed.' He scrutinized Richard Moon. 'The man I employed was a quarter this weight. He was healthy and reasonably fit.'

'What ID did he give you?'

'A passport. A utility bill from this address.' The folder he'd brought was full of paperwork: photocopies of all the ID evidence he had for Richard Moon. 'Everything the CRB dictates.'

Caffery sorted through the paperwork. He pulled out the photocopied sheet of a UK passport. It showed a young man of about twenty-five, grim-faced, a fixed hardness to his face. Richard F. Moon, Caffery held the photograph at arm's length, compared it to the man on the sofa. 'Well?' He pushed it across the table. 'Is that you?'

Richard Moon couldn't lower his head enough to look at it. He could only swivel his eyes to squint at it. He closed his eyes and breathed hard. 'Yes.' His voice was high and feminine. 'That's me. That's my passport.'

'That's him,' his father said. 'Twelve years ago. Before he gave up on his life. Look at that photo. Is that the face of someone who doesn't give a toss? I don't think so.'

'Stop it, Dad. It hurts when you talk to me like that.'

'Don't use your therapist speak on me, son. I'll give you the meaning of *hurt*.' Peter Moon looked his son up and down as if he couldn't believe the monstrosity the world had visited upon him. 'Seeing you turning into a garage in front of my eyes. That's the meaning of hurt.'

'Mr Moon,' Caffery held up his hands to quieten them, 'can we take this slowly?' He studied the face in the photo. It was the same forehead, the same eyes, the same hairline. The same dirty blond hair. He looked at Richard. 'You mean it's taken you twelve years to go from this,' he tapped the photo, 'to what you are now?'

'I've had problems—'

'*Problems?*' his father interrupted. '*Problems?* Well, you'd win the understatement of the year, son. You really would. You're a fucking vegetable. Face it.'

'I am not.'

'You are. You're a vegetable. I've driven cars smaller than you.'

There was a pause. Then Richard Moon put his hands to his face and began to cry. His shoulders shook, and for a few moments no one spoke. Peter Moon crossed his arms and scowled. Turner and the agency manager looked at their feet.

Caffery picked up the handyman's ID card and compared it to the passport photo. The two men were not dissimilar – same wide forehead, same small eyes – but the agency manager must have really been asleep if he hadn't noticed they weren't the same man. But bollocking him here and now, in front of the Moons, wouldn't get them anywhere, so he waited for Richard to stop snivelling and held out the ID card. 'Know him?'

Richard wiped his nose. His eyes were so swollen they were barely visible in his face.

'Not a friend of yours you've helped out? Someone you've loaned your squeaky-clean record to?'

'No,' he said dully. 'Never seen him before in my life.'

'Mr Moon?' He flipped the ID card round.

'No.'

'You sure? He's a dangerous, dangerous bastard, and he's using your son's name and identity. Have another think.'

'I dunno who he is. Never seen him in my life.'

'This guy is seriously warped – more so than anyone I've ever dealt with before. People like him, in my experience, don't respect anyone, not their victims, not their friends – and certainly not the ones who help them. You help someone like that and nine times out of ten it comes back to bite you on the arse. 'He looked from father to son and back again. Neither man met his eye. 'So, have another think. Are you sure one of you hasn't got some idea of who he is?'

'No.'

'So how did *this*,' he put the passport photocopy on the table, 'come to be presented as ID documentation for a Criminal Records Bureau search?'

Peter Moon picked up his mug and sat back on the sofa, one leg crossed over the other. '*I* haven't seen that passport for years. Have you, son?'

Richard sniffed. 'Don't think so, Dad.'

'In fact, have you seen it since that break-in?'

'Eh?'

'Not that you've needed it, you being the way you are. Don't need a passport to get to the television set and back, do you, son? But have you seen it since the break-in?'

'No, Dad.' Richard shook his head very slowly, as if the effort might wear him out.

'What break-in?' said Caffery.

'Some lowlife did the window at the back. Had away that much stuff I didn't know if I was coming or going.'

'Did you report it?'

'With the way you'd have dealt with it? No disrespect, but it never crossed my mind. You lot've got a fine line in ignoring people. A diploma in looking the other way. Then, of course, the fire happened and that put things out of our heads for while. You know – the way a fire that destroys your life will.'

Caffery was studying Richard. His face was too loaded with flesh to give much away but his father had a con's face, pure and simple, the look of someone with serious form. Yet there was nothing on the CRB check that flagged them up. 'This fire – it'll be in our records, I take it?'

'Too effing right it will. Arsonist. Not nice. Council paid to have the place redone, but a bit of paint? That was never going to undo what happened.'

'Finished Mother,' Richard whispered breathlessly, 'didn't it, Da? Finished her.'

'She survived the fire, but couldn't take what it did to us as a family. Finished you too, son, didn't it, in a way?'

Richard tipped his weight on to his left buttock, breathing hard at the effort. 'S'pose it did.'

'Smoke inhalation.' Peter Moon's knee was suddenly twitching, jumping up and down as if he had a motor running in his body. 'Lung damage, asthma, plus, of course, the –' he made inverted commas with his fingers '– cognitive and behavioural problems. They came from the carbon monoxide. Makes him moody – depressed. Makes him sit around day after day watching the telly and eating. Crisps and Twix bars. Pot Noodle if he's on a health kick.'

'I do not sit around all day.'

'You do, son. You do nothing. And that's what's got you to the state you're in.'

Caffery put his hand up. 'We're going to stop now.' He put his mug down and got to his feet. 'Under the circumstances I'm going to give you a choice. You can either accompany me to the station or—'

'You'll take us there over my dead body. My son hasn't been out of the flat in over a year and he's not going now. It'll kill him.'

'Or I'll leave one of my men here. Just in case that burglar suddenly gets Christian on us and decides to return the passport to its rightful owner, eh?'

'We've got nothing to hide. And my son needs to go to bed now.' Peter Moon got to his feet and went to stand in front of his son. He hoisted his braces up on to his shoulders and bent at the waist, his arms out. 'Come on, son. You stay out here for too long and it'll be the death of you. Come on.'

Caffery watched Richard, sweating in his vest and jogging trousers, put his arms up to meet his father's. He watched the sinews in the older man's arms stretch and harden as he hauled the weight off the sofa, heard the soft exhalation of effort.

'Need some help?'

'No. Been doing it years. Come on now, lad. Let's get you to bed.'

Caffery, Turner and the agency manager watched in silence as the son was lifted to his feet. It shouldn't have been possible for this small guy, with his bald head and stooped back, to do it. But he lifted Richard to his feet and half carried him, step by painful step, to the corridor.

'Follow them,' Caffery murmured to Turner. 'Make sure they haven't got a mobile on them. I'll send a support officer up to take over. Then I want you back at the office. Do a complete search on them. Criminal records on the dad – every logged incident relating to this address. And find out about that fire – if there really was one. I want them cross-referenced on HOLMES and a list of every known associate. Wring them dry.'

'Will do.'

Turner headed for the door to follow the Moons, leaving Caffery and the manager together. Caffery felt in his pocket for his keys. He ignored the tobacco pouch sitting there like a bomb. For the first time in ages he was thinking about his own parents, wondering where they were and what they were doing. He hadn't kept track of them for years and now he wondered if they were old enough for infirmity to have set in. And if they were, who was helping whom when it came time at the end of the day to struggle to bed?

He decided his father would be helping his mother. She had never got over losing Ewan and she never would. She'd always need help.

That was just the way it was.

42

It was gone seven. Cory hadn't made an appearance, but Janice didn't care. She'd had a great afternoon. Truly great – under the circumstances. Prody had been as good as his word and had stayed on. He hadn't watched television or made phone calls but had spent most of the time sitting on the floor with Emily, playing snakes and ladders and 'Tell me'. Emily thought Prody was hysterical: she'd used him as a climbing frame, charging into him, hanging on to his shoulders and pulling herself up by his hair in a way that would have infuriated Cory. Now Nick had gone, Emily was in the bath, supervised by her grandmother, and Janice was in the kitchen with Prody. The salmon was in the oven.

'I think you've got kids.' Janice was using her thumbs to push the cork out of the bottle of prosecco they'd bought in Marks & Spencer. 'You're, you know, sort of natural.'

'Yeah, well . . .' He shrugged.

'*Yeah, well?*' She raised an eyebrow. 'I think you need to explain that to me.' She popped the cork, poured the wine into two of the tumblers she'd discovered in the back of a cupboard and handed one to him. 'Come on. The salmon's got a bit longer to go, so we're going into the living room and you're going to tell me all about "Yeah, well".'

'Am I?'

She smiled. 'Oh, yes. Indeed you are.'

In the living room, Prody pulled the mobile out of his pocket, switched it off and sat down. The room was strewn with Emily's toys. Ordinarily Janice would have raced around tidying up so that the place wasn't a mess when Cory got home. Today she sat with her shoes off, her feet curled under her and her arm on a cushion. To start with, Prody needed prompting. These were things he didn't like talking about, he said, and, anyway, didn't she have enough problems of her own?

'No. Don't worry about it. It helps keep my mind off my own situation.'

'It's not a pretty picture.'

'I don't mind.'

'Well . . .' He gave an awkward smile. 'It goes like this. My ex got full custody of the kids. It never went to court because I pulled out of the case, gave way to what she wanted. She was going to tell the court I'd been beating her and my sons ever since they were born.'

'Had you?'

'I smacked the eldest once.'

'What do you mean, "smacked"?'

'On the back of his legs.'

'That's not beating him.'

'My wife was desperate to get out. She'd met someone else and wanted the boys. She got friends and family to lie for her. What could I do?'

'The kids would have said if it wasn't true, wouldn't they?'

Prody gave a small, harsh laugh. 'She got them to lie too. They went to a solicitor and told him I was hitting them. As soon as they did that everyone was on her side – the social workers, even the teachers.'

'But why would the children lie?'

'It wasn't their fault. She told them *she*'d hate them, take away their pocket money, if they didn't. And if they did there'd be a trip to Toys R Us. That sort of thing. I know because my oldest told me. He sent me a letter two weeks ago.' Prody pulled a piece of folded blue paper out of his pocket. 'He said he was sorry what he'd told people but Mum had promised him a Wii.'

'She sounds – and I'm sorry to say it because she is your ex-wife – like a right bitch.'

'There was a time I'd have agreed with you – I thought she was just plain evil. But now I think she was probably doing what she felt she had to.' He put the letter back in his pocket. 'I could have been a better dad, could have stopped work taking over like it did – the hours, the shift work. And call me old-fashioned but I always wanted to be the best at my job. No point doing something if you don't do it perfectly.' He kneaded his hands, pressing his knuckles into the palms. 'I suppose I just never saw what it would take from my home life. I was missing school plays, Easter-egg hunts . . . Privately I think that was why the kids said what they did – it was their way of teaching me a lesson.' He paused. 'I could have been a better husband too.'

Janice raised her eyebrows. 'Girlfriends?'

'God, no. Not that. Does that make me a mug?'

'No. It makes you . . .' she watched the bubbles breaking in her glass '. . . faithful. That's all. It makes you faithful.' There was a long silence. Then Janice pushed her hair off her forehead. She felt flushed and warm from the prosecco. 'Can I . . . can I tell you something?'

'After you've let me bump my gums like that? I s'pose I could give you a moment or two.' He looked at his watch. 'You've got ten seconds.'

She didn't laugh. 'Cory's having an affair. Has been for months.'

Prody's smile faded. He lowered his hand slowly. 'Christ. I mean . . . I'm sorry.'

'And do you know the worst thing?'

'What?'

'That I don't love him any more. I'm not even jealous he's seeing someone. I've gone way past that. It's just the injustice of it that gets to me.'

'Good word, injustice. You put everything into something and get nothing out.'

They were silent for a while, lost in their own thoughts. The curtains were still open even though it was dark, and on a scrappy stretch of common opposite the flat the wind had piled fallen leaves into a long drift. In the streetlamp they were like tiny skeletons. Janice gazed at them blankly. They reminded her of the leaves that used to pile up in the garden at Russell Road. Back when she was a child. Back when everything was possible and there was still hope. Still so much hope in the world.

43

It was raining again, a light drizzle. Even though it was dark the clouds had a brooding quality, low and damp – as if they were pressing the night air down on to the ground. Flea was at home, in her all-weather Berghaus jacket, the hood up. She was lugging her father's caving gear out of the garage to the car.

She had no idea how she'd overlooked the air shafts. It was as if there'd been a block in her head. The tunnel was supplied by twenty-three shafts dropping directly from the surface. Four dropped into the landslide, leaving nineteen in the open sections. She and Wellard had passed under eighteen: two coming from near the pub on the easterly entry and sixteen on the longer, westerly entry. So where was the nineteenth? Maybe she'd assumed that the last shaft entered the tunnel somewhere in the quarter-mile rockfall. But the detailed paperwork the trustees had given her made it clear: the stretch of canal under all but the four air shafts was free of debris for at least twenty yards in each direction. So, the last shaft was somewhere outside the rockfall.

Which meant only one thing: that the last wall she'd come to after squeezing through the tiny gap, the fall that had almost covered the old barge, wasn't the end of the long blockage. It was an intermediary fall. Beyond it there must be another, hidden, section with another air shaft. And, as far as she was concerned, the USU couldn't claim to have cleared the tunnel out until that lost area had been searched. They couldn't say with certainty that the jacker hadn't put Martha – or her body – into the tunnel.

She was going alone, which sounded insane, but after all the derision and criticism that'd been heaped on her over the tunnel affair, the self-preservation route was to keep it to herself until she had a result. She pushed her rucksack into the boot of the car, threw in a pair of caver's wellies, then took down the immersion suit that hung from the garage rafters. She paused. On top of an old refrigerator was a sagging cardboard box full of odd-ments. She went to it and peered inside. Old diving masks, a pair of fins, a regulator with the rubber perished by salt water. A glass jar of sun-bleached shells. A dead sea anemone. And an old-fashioned caver's lamp, brass carbide with a battered glass reflector.

She pulled it out and unscrewed it. Inside was a small com-partment: the generator, the place explosive acetylene gas was produced and fed to a small reflector, where it was ignited to pro-duce a powerful light. She screwed it back together and rummaged inside in the box again until she found a grey-white lump about the size of her fist, wrapped inside an old Co-op carrier bag. Calcium carbide. The crucial ingredient.

Be careful, Flea. Her father's voice came to her across the years. *Be careful with that. It's not a sweetie. Don't touch it now. And, whatever you do, don't get it wet. That's what releases the gas.*

Dad. The adventurer. The madman. The climber, the diver, the caver. Hated most modern sports equipment, jerry-rigged his way through life – and would never have let her go into the tunnel without something to pick up the pieces when the 'over-engineered modern shit' pooped out. Thanks, Dad. She rested the calcium carbide and the lamp on top of the immersion suit and carried it all out to the car, put it in the boot, slammed the lid and got in, rain dripping off the Berghaus.

She pulled off the hood, got out her phone and scrolled through the numbers, pausing at Caffery's name. Not a chance. There would be a lecture the size of a cow if she dared mention the subject of Sapperton tunnel. 'Prody' rolled past. She stopped, went back to it, considered it for a moment or two, thought, Oh, sod it, and dialled the number.

It went into answerphone. His voice was nice. Calming. It almost made her smile. He was at work, maybe in a meeting about the jacker. She moved her thumb to hang up, then remembered the number of times she'd diverted incoming calls to her voicemail because she was in a meeting and how it pissed her off later when she found people hadn't left a message. 'Hi, Paul. Look, you're going to think I'm nuts, but I remembered what I was missing about the tunnel. There's another air shaft – about a third of a mile from the eastern entrance.' She checked her watch. 'It's six thirty now, and I'm going back for a look. I'll go in the same way I went yesterday because I'm not an abseiler and those air shafts are more dangerous than the tunnel itself, whatever the trust says. Just for the record, I'm not doing it on the firm's time – I'm off duty. I'll call you at eleven tonight to tell you what happened. And, Paul . . .' She looked through the rainy kitchen windows, where she'd left a light on inside. The warm yellow glow. She wasn't going to be long. Not long at all. 'Paul, you don't need to call me about this. Really. I'm going to do it anyway.'

44

At eight o'clock Janice put Emily to bed in the new pyjamas she'd bought at Marks & Spencer. Her hair was still slightly damp from the bath and smelt of strawberry shampoo. She was clutching Jasper.

'Where's Dad?'

'He's working, poppet. He won't be long.'

'He's always working.'

'Hey, not that again. Come on, hop up here.' Emily got into the double bed and Janice tucked her in, bent over to kiss her. 'You're such a good girl. I love you so, so, much. I'll be back later, give you another hug.'

Emily curled up, Jasper tucked under her chin, thumb in her mouth, and closed her eyes. Janice stroked her hair gently, a half-smile on her face. Her head was light with bubbles and she felt a little drunk. Now that the jacker had a name and a face, she was less scared of him. As if his name, Richard Moon, had diminished him.

When Emily's breathing had changed to the regular, soft rhythm of sleep, Janice got up and tiptoed out, closing the door carefully. She found Prody standing in the hallway in the half-light, his arms folded.

'In Mum's bed? What's the single one for?'

'Her dad.'

'Well, call me out of order, but I'd say he deserves it.' He was standing with his back to the wall. He'd taken his jacket off and she noticed for the first time how tall he was. Much taller than she was. And broad. Not fat, just wide in the places a man should be. He looked as if he worked out. Suddenly she put a hand to her mouth as if she might hiccup or giggle. 'I've got a confession to make. I'm a bit drunk.'

'Me too. A bit.'

'*No!*' She smiled. 'That's terrible! So irresponsible! How on earth are you going to get home?'

'Who knows? I used to be a traffic cop so I know the danger spots – could get home if I really wanted to. But I expect I'll do the right thing – sleep it off in the car. It won't be the first time.'

'That sofa in the living room is a pull-out and I got some bed linen this morning in John Lewis.'

He raised his eyebrows. 'Beg your pardon?'

'In the living room. Nothing incriminating about that, is there?'

'Can't say I'm mad about the back seat of the Peugeot.'

'Well, then?'

He was about to answer when the doorbell rang. She sprang away from him as if they'd been kissing and went into the bathroom. She looked out of the window. 'Cory.'

Prody straightened his tie. 'I'll let him in.' He went down the stairs, plucking his jacket from the hook and pulling it on. Janice slung the empty prosecco bottle into the bin, put the glasses into the sink and cantered down the stairs after him. Prody took one last second to straighten his jacket, then put the chain on and opened the door.

Cory was standing on the step, his coat buttoned up and a scarf round his neck. When he saw Prody he stepped back and peered at the number above the door. 'I've got the right place, haven't I? They all look the same.'

'Cory.' Janice stood on tiptoe and spoke over Prody's shoulder. 'This is Paul. He's with MCIU. Come in. Mum, Emily and I've eaten but I've kept some salmon for you.'

He came into the little hallway and began to take off his coat. He smelt of rain and cold and car exhaust. When he'd hung up the clothes, he turned, held out his hand to Prody. 'Cory Costello.'

'Good to meet you.' They shook. 'DC Prody, but you can call me Paul.'

Cory's smile faded. His hand was still in Prody's but he stopped moving it. His body got a little tighter across the shoulders. 'Prody? That's an unusual name.'

'Is it? I don't know. I've never done a family search.'

Cory regarded him coldly, his face an odd, ashen colour. 'Are you married, *Paul?*'

'Married?'

'That's what I said. Are you married?'

'No. Not really. I mean . . .' he glanced at Janice '. . . I *was* married. But that was then. I'm separated, almost divorced now. You know how it is.'

Cory turned stiffly to his wife. 'Where's Emily?'

'Asleep. In the bedroom.'

'Your mum?'

'In her room. Reading, I think.'

'I'd like a word, please.'

'OK,' she said hesitantly. 'Come upstairs.'

Cory pushed roughly past them and went up the stairs. Janice gave Prody a look – *I'm sorry. I don't know what this is about but, please, don't go* – then hurried after her husband. In the flat he was walking down the corridor, pushing at doors, looking into rooms. He stopped when he found the kitchen with the two glasses in the sink and the plate of salmon covered with clingfilm.

'What, Cory? What is it?'

'How long has he been here?' he hissed. 'Did you let him in?'

'Of course I did. He's been here, I don't know, a couple of hours maybe.'

'Do you know who he is?' Cory slammed his laptop bag on to the worktop. 'Well? Do you?'

'No.'

'That's Clare's husband.'

Janice's mouth fell open. For a moment she wanted to laugh. At the sheer ridiculousness of the whole thing. '*What?*' she said, her voice a little shrill. 'Clare? From the group? The one you're fucking, you mean?'

'Don't be stupid. Keep your mouth clean.'

'Well, Cory, how else would you know he's her husband? What? Has she shown you a picture? That's cosy.'

'The *name*, Janice.' He sounded pitying. As if he felt sorry for her, having such a low mind. 'Not many Paul Prodys around. Clare's husband's a cop too.' He jabbed a finger at the hallway. 'That's him. And he's a bastard, Janice. A full-blown, card-carrying blot on the face of humanity. The things he did to his kids – to his wife!'

'Oh, Christ, Cory – you *believe* her? Why? Don't you know what women are like?'

'What? What are women like?'

'They're *liars*, Cory. Women *lie*. We lie and we cheat and we flirt, and we play hurt and wounded and betrayed and wronged. We are *good actresses*. We are brilliant at it. And this year's Oscar goes to the whole of womanhood.'

'You include yourself in that?'

'*Yes!* I mean, no – I mean . . . sometimes. Sometimes I lie. We all do.'

'That explains it, then.'

'Explains what?'

'Explains what you were really saying when you said you'd love me more than anything. That forsaking all others you'd love me. You were lying.'

'I'm not the one who cheated.'

'You never went out and shagged anyone but you might as well have done.'

'What the *hell* are you talking about?'

'About the way the whole world stops when it comes to *her*. Doesn't it, Janice? When it comes to her I might as well not exist.'

Janice stared at him, incredulous. 'Are you talking about Emily? Are you actually talking about your daughter like that?'

'Who else? Ever since she came along I've been second best. Deny it, Janice. Deny it.'

She shook her head. 'Do you know what, Cory? The only thing I feel for you right now is sorry. I feel sorry for you that, gone forty – and looking every day of it, by the way – you're still condemned to live in such a narrow, sad little place. It must be hell.'

'I don't want him here.'

'Well, I do.'

Cory looked at the two glasses in the sink. 'You've been drinking with him. What else have you done? Fucked him?'

'Oh, shut up.'

'He's *not* staying the night.'

'I've got news for you, Cory. He *is* staying the night. He's going to sleep on the pull-out bed in the living room. The carjacker is still out there somewhere and – newsflash, Cory – I don't feel safe with you. In fact, if I'm honest, I'd just as soon you pissed off to Clare's, or wherever it is you go, and left us to it.'

45

There had been two rainfalls that day and the canal was deeper than it had been yesterday. The air smelt heavier and greener, and the constant plink-plink-plink of water filtering through the rock and falling into the tunnel wasn't as musical as it had been. Tonight it was loud, insistent, like standing in a shower. Flea had to wade through the silt in her leaded boots with her head down, the water bouncing off her helmet and trickling down the back of her neck. It took her almost an hour to get back to the rockfall she and Wellard had burrowed through. The hole they'd made was still there, and by the time she'd squeezed through the gap and come down the other side she was wet and filthy. Mud clung to every inch of the immersion suit, there was grit in her mouth and nose, and she was cold from the water. Very cold. Her teeth were chattering.

She pulled her dive light out of the rucksack and shone it at the far end of the section, to where the back of the barge was visible, wedged under the next rockfall. Maybe the missing air shaft was on the other side, in a hidden section of the tunnel. She waded to the bottom of the fall and clicked off her head torch and the dive light. The canal fell into blackness so quickly she had to put her hand out to steady herself in the dizzying darkness. Why the hell hadn't she thought to switch off the torch yesterday? Because there *was* light – from about ten feet above the ground. A faint blue glow. Moonlight. Coming through the loose earth at the top of the scree. This was it, then. The nineteenth air shaft on the other side of the rockfall.

She tightened the rucksack on her back and clambered up in the dark. The marker line unreeled behind her, slapping against the backs of her legs. She didn't need a torch: the blue chink of moonlight was enough for her to see what she was doing. At the top she used her hands as spades and fashioned a ledge in the clay for her knees. She dug a second ledge for the rucksack. Then she knelt and pushed her face into the gap.

Moonlight. And she could smell what was on the other side, a sweet scent: the mixed odours of vegetation, rust and accumulated rain. The smell of the shaft. She could hear the echoey, dripping space. She pulled back and rummaged in the rucksack until she found the chisel her father used to use for cave digging.

The fuller's earth at the top wasn't packed but friable – quite dry. The chisel went through the loose stones quickly – she scrabbled them away in handfuls, hearing them clunk down the scree behind her and splash into the water. She'd cleared a gap about a foot from the ceiling and could see the moonlight lying blue ahead of her when she hit rock. A boulder. She slammed the chisel into it once. Twice. It bounced away. A spark flew off. It was too big to move. She sat back, breathing hard.

Fuck it.

She licked her lips, examined the hole. Not big, but it might just be wide enough to get through. No harm trying. She took off her helmet, rested it alongside the chisel, and inched her right arm through the gap. It moved forward a foot. Two feet until it was stretched out as far as it would go. Her head now. She turned slightly to the left, eyes screwed shut, and pushed her face in, bracing with her knees, pulling herself along with her fingertips until her hand was through and she could feel the cool air on it. The sharp chips of stone in the clay scratched her cheeks. She imagined her hand at the top of the rockfall – disembodied, clenching and unclenching in the moonlight. She wondered if it was being watched. And stopped wondering straight away. That sort of thinking could paralyse you in a second.

Clay fell from the ceiling and down the back of her neck, granules running into her ears and settling on her eyelashes. She braced her knees and levered herself further. There was no room to pull her left arm through – it had to stay trapped at her side. Her leg muscles tightened, but with one more push of her aching calves her right arm and head popped out into the light.

She coughed, spat, rubbed the muck out of her eyes and mouth, shook it off her hand.

She was looking down at another section of canal, which was dominated by a column of moonlight streaming from the massive air shaft above. Strange humps lay in the water where fuller's earth had tumbled into the canal and half dissolved. The rockfall she lay on wasn't that wide: six feet below her, the front end of the barge poked out, lifted up in the water by the weight of the rocks on its mid-section, the deck slightly buckled under a rusting windlass. About fifty yards ahead, just visible in the darkness, were the footings of yet another wall of rock and earth. Maybe *that* was the westerly end of the long rockfall she and Wellard had been looking for. So this new section was also enclosed, like the one she'd crawled in from, which meant the only access to this area was via the shaft.

She stared up at it. Water plinked steadily down – tight little sonic dots in the silence. The grille at the bottom was half-broken, hanging precariously from the roof and matted with dripping plant debris. But it was what was hanging through the gap in the grille that caught her eye. A length of climbing rope attached to a hook, with a karabiner that was looped into the handles of a huge black kitbag that cast a mangled shadow into the water below. It was strong enough to lower a large object down into the canal. A body for example. And there was something else out of place in the tunnel. A smudge of light further out in the water, its colour slightly different from that in the rest of the tunnel. She lowered her chin and concentrated. Something was floating among the debris on the water, just past the column of moonlight. A shoe. She knew the type: a cross between a plimsoll and a Mary Jane. Pastel-printed and soft, with a little buckle over the top. The sort of thing a child would wear. And exactly what Martha had been wearing when she disappeared.

A line of adrenalin shot down Flea's chest and out to the ends of her fingers. This was really it. He'd been here. Maybe he was here now, somewhere in the shadows . . .

Stop it. Don't *imagine*. Act. He couldn't follow her back through this hole – the only smart thing was to withdraw, retrace her steps back down the canal, and raise the alarm. She began to pull back but halfway through found she was stuck, her shoulders wedged in the tiny gap. She tugged frantically at her right arm, twisting sideways, trying to loosen it that way, but her ribs were jammed into the roof, her lungs squashed. She forced herself to stop, reminding herself not to panic. In her mind she was screaming. But she let her head go slack on one side and took the time to calm herself, keeping her breathing slow to allow her lungs to open against the pressure.

From somewhere in the distance came a familiar sound. Like thunder. She and Wellard had heard it the other day. A train racing along the track – she could picture it – the air flying off it, earth and rock shuddering under it. She could picture, too, the metres and metres of stone and clay sediment above her. And her lungs: two vulnerable oval spaces in the darkness. The smallest movement of the earth could squash them to a place where nothing would open them again. And Martha. Maybe little Martha's body somewhere ahead in the canal.

A rock fell, close to Flea's head. It tumbled down the scree into the water with a splash. The tunnel was shaking. *Shit shit shit.* She took the deepest breath she could, jammed her knees against the opening, braced her left hand against the boulder and pulled with all her strength. She came through into the first chamber in a rush, reversing feet first, scraping the underside of her chin on the boulder. The caving line slipped down the slope and she toppled after it, the rucksack with her, landing on her backside in the water.

All around her the chamber creaked and screamed. She fumbled for the torch in the rucksack, clicked it on and shone it upwards. The whole cavern was vibrating. A fracture in the ceiling lengthened in a shot – like a snake going through grass – and a deafening crack ricocheted around the little chamber. Bent double, she staggered through the water to the only shelter she could see – the stern of the barge. She had just managed to squeeze herself into the space behind it before the air was filled with the roar of falling debris and the whistle of rock racing past her ears.

The noise seemed to last for ever. She sat in the muck, hands over her head, eyes closed. Even when the noise of the train had dwindled she stayed there, listening to little rockfalls somewhere in the darkness. Every time she thought it was over there would come another trickle of small stones slithering down and splashing into the water. It was at least five minutes before the chamber was quiet and she could raise her head.

She wiped her face on the shoulders of the immersion suit, shone the torch around and began to laugh. A long, low, humourless laugh, like a sob, that echoed around what was left of the chamber and sent noises back that made her want to cover her ears. She dropped her head against the hull of the barge and rubbed her eyes.

What the fuck was she supposed to do now?

46

Moonlight crept out from behind shredded clouds, the cold canopy of stars reflected in the quarry fading in the blue glare. Sitting in the car on the track at the edge of the water, Caffery watched in silence. He was cold. He'd been here more than an hour. He'd snatched four hours' dense, uncomplicated sleep at home and snapped awake just before five with the certainty that something out in the freezing night was expecting him. He'd got up. He knew staying at home, wakeful, would only lead to trouble – would probably lead to his tobacco pouch and the whisky bottle – so he'd put Myrtle in the back seat and driven around a bit, expecting to see the Walking Man's camp over the hedgerow. Instead, somehow, he'd ended up out here.

It was a big quarry, about the size of three football fields, and deep too. He'd studied the schematics. At one point it was well over a hundred and fifty feet deep. The underwater rocks were scabby with plants, abandoned stone-cutting machinery, submerged niches and hidey-holes.

Earlier this year there had been a time when he had been plagued by a man, a Tanzanian illegal immigrant who had followed him round the county, watching him from the shadows like an elf or a Gollum. It had gone on for almost a month and then, as quickly as the man had started, he had stopped. Caffery had no idea what had become of him – whether he was alive or dead. Sometimes he caught himself looking out of the window late at night, wondering where he was. In some perverse, lonely corner of his psyche he missed him.

For a while the Tanzanian had been living here, in the trees around this quarry. But there was more about this place that made Caffery's skin prickle at every noise, every shift of light around the car. This was where Flea had dumped the corpse. Misty Kitson's body was somewhere in the silent depths.

You're protecting her and you can't yet see what a nice circle that makes.

A nice circle.

A single winter cloud moved across the moon. Caffery stared at it – at the moon. A faint fingernail in white, a tentative but perceptible wash of light on its dark side. Riddle me this, riddle me that. The Walking Man, the clever bastard, always fed him clues. Kept him crawling along, his tongue to the ground. Caffery didn't think the Walking Man's anger would last. Not in the long run. Still, Caffery hadn't found him tonight, and that fact alone felt like a rebuke.

'Obstinate old shit,' he told Myrtle, who was on the back seat. 'The miserable, obstinate old shit.'

He pulled out his phone and keyed in Flea's number. He didn't care if he woke her or what he was going to say. He just wanted to put an end to it. Here and now. Didn't need the Walking Man and his mumbo-jumbo, riddles and clues. But her line went straight to answerphone. He hung up and put the mobile back into his pocket. It had been there for less than ten seconds when it rang. He snatched it out, thinking it was her calling back, but the number was wrong. It was a withheld number.

'It's me. Turner. At the office.'

'Jesus.' He rubbed his forehead tiredly. 'What the hell are you doing at this time in the morning?'

'I couldn't sleep.'

'Thinking about all the overtime you could finesse?'

'I've got something.'

'Yeah?'

'Edward Moon. Known as Ted.'

'Who is . . . ?'

'Who is the younger brother of the fat bastard.'

'And I should be interested in him because?'

'Because of his rogues'-gallery shots. You'll have to look at them, but I'm ninety-nine point nine. It's him.'

The hair went up on the back of Caffery's neck. Like a hound with the first scent of blood in its nose. He blew air out of his mouth. 'Rogues' gallery? He's got form?'

'Form?' Turner gave a dry laugh. 'You could say that. He's just done ten years at Broadmoor under Section 37/41 of the Mental Health Act. Does that count as form?'

'Christ. That sort of sentence, it must have been . . .'

'Murder.' Turner's voice was calm, but there was an edge of excitement in it. He'd got the scent of blood too. 'A thirteen-year-old. A girl. And it was brutal. Really nasty. So . . .' A pause. 'So, Boss, what would you like me to do now?'

47

'My colleagues are having a look around your place. You've seen the warrant, it's all kosher. You can stay here as long as you don't try to obstruct the search.'

It was just before seven in the morning and Caffery was back in the Moons' damp little flat. There were the remains of a fried breakfast on the table, ketchup and Daddie's sauce bottles, with two smeared plates. Dirty pans were piled in the sink in the kitchen. Outside it was still dark. Not that they could see out: the little paraffin heater in the corner had steamed up the windows and condensation ran in wriggling rivulets down the glass. The two men, father and son, sat on the sofa. Richard Moon wore a pair of joggers that had been split at the ankle cuffs to allow his enormous calves to fit through and a navy T-shirt, with the word 'VISIONARY' on the chest and sweat-stains under the arms. He was staring fixedly at Caffery, sweat beading on his upper lip.

'Odd, isn't it,' Caffery sat at the table, regarding him carefully, 'that you never mentioned your brother yesterday?' He leaned forward, holding out the photo ID Ted Moon had used to get in and out of MCIU's offices. 'Ted. Why didn't you mention him? Seems odd to me.'

Richard Moon glanced at his father, who raised his eyebrows warningly. Richard lowered his eyes.

'I said, it seems odd, Richard.'

'No comment,' he muttered.

'No comment? Is that an answer?'

Richard's eyes shifted around, as if there were lies in the air and they needed a place to hide. 'No comment.'

'What is this no-comment shit? Have you been watching *The Bill*? You're not under arrest, you know. I'm not recording this, you haven't got a brief, and the only thing you'll achieve with your no-comments is to royally piss me off. And then I might change my mind and decide you are under arrest. Now, why didn't you tell us about your brother?'

'No comment,' said Peter Moon. His eyes were cold and hard.

'You didn't think it was relevant?' He pulled out the sheet Turner had printed from the *Guardian*'s database. The CPS were going to pull their files to fill in the details but the stark facts on this printout were quite enough to tell Caffery what they were dealing with. Moon had killed thirteen-year-old Sharon Macy. He'd concealed the body somewhere – it had never been found – but he'd been convicted anyway on the DNA evidence. According to the intelligence there hadn't been any problem with that because Sharon's blood had been all over Ted Moon's clothes and bedding. The bedroom floor had been so deep in blood it had soaked through the boards in some places. The stains on the ceiling in the room below had still been spreading when the team arrived to arrest him. He'd done ten years for it until, a year ago, the home secretary had agreed with what the RMO, the responsible medical officer, had said: that Moon was no longer a danger to himself or to others. He had been released from Broadmoor on a conditional discharge.

'Your brother did that.' Caffery pushed the database printout in front of Richard Moon's face. 'What sort of bitter pig kills a thirteen-year-old girl? Do you know what the coroner said at the time? That her head would have had to have half come off to make that much blood. Don't know about you but it makes me queasy just thinking about it.'

'No comment.'

'Here's the deal. You tell me now where he is and we can talk about you bypassing an obstruction charge for not mentioning it earlier.'

'No comment.'

'Do you know how long you can get banged up for obstruction? Eh? Six months. How much of that time do you think you'd last, fat boy? Especially when they hear you were protecting a nonce. Now, where is he?'

'I don't—'

'Richard!' His father silenced him. He put a finger to his lips.

Richard Moon looked at him for a moment, then dropped his head back. Sweat was running down into the neck of his T-shirt. 'No comment,' he muttered. 'No comment.'

'Boss?'

They turned.

Turner was standing in the doorway holding a bulky envelope wrapped in a freezer bag. 'This was in the lavvy cistern.'

'Open it, then.'

Turner unzipped it, poked around dubiously. 'Papers. Mostly.'

'What are those doing in your cistern, Mr Moon? Seems a strange place to keep your filing.'

'No comment.'

'Jesus. Turner, give me that. Have you got any gloves?' Turner put the envelope on the table and got a spare pair from his pocket. Caffery pulled them on and shook out the contents of the envelope. It consisted mostly of bills, the name Edward Moon popping up over and over again. 'And . . . ah – what's this?' He raised his eyebrows. 'It looks fascinating.' Using his thumb and forefinger he pulled out a passport. Flipped it open. 'The missing passport. As I live and breathe. What are the chances of that? Some arsehole breaks in here, steals all your stuff, comes back years later and leaves it in the bog. I love happy endings.'

The Moons stared back at him dully. Peter Moon had gone a deep, almost bluish red. Caffery couldn't tell if it was anger or fear. He threw the passport on to the table with the bills. 'Did you let your brother use this to get him through that CRB sweep? You're clean but he's dirty. Particularly dirty, if you ask me.'

'No comment.'

'You're going to have to make a comment eventually. Or start praying your pad-mate hasn't got AIDS, fat boy.'

'Don't call him that.'

'Ah.' Caffery turned to the father. 'You going to speak to me now, are you?'

There was a pause. Peter Moon closed his lips and moved them up and down as if he was fighting the words. His face was like a red fist.

'Well?' Caffery put his head politely on one side. 'Are you going to tell me where your son is?'

'No comment.'

Caffery slammed his hands on the table. 'Right – that does it. Turner?' He raised his chin at the two men sitting on the sofa. 'Take them in. I've had enough of this. You can come in and do the real thing, Mr Moon. You can have your own brief, give him the no-comment treatment and then we'll see about whether . . .' He trailed off.

'Boss?' Turner, who had pulled out his quickcuffs, was waiting for Caffery to give him instructions. 'Where are we taking them? Local shop?'

Caffery didn't answer. He was transfixed by one of the bills.

'Boss?'

Caffery raised his eyes slowly. 'We need to speak to Ops,' he murmured. 'I think this might be something.'

Turner came to him. Studied the piece of paper Caffery was holding. He let out a low whistle. 'Christ.'

'Christ indeed.' It was a commercial property-leasing statement. It showed that for at least the last eleven years Ted Moon had been renting a lock-up garage in Gloucestershire. It had a secure steel roller door and a hundred square metres of storage. It was all there in the spec. And the address was in Tarlton, Gloucestershire.

Just half a mile from the Sapperton tunnel.

48

Caffery didn't believe in coincidences. In his book Ted Moon's lock-up was about as concrete a lead as ever winged its way to an officer of the law. While another DC got the Moons cautioned and into the car, Caffery sat in the shabby little flat making phone calls. Within ten minutes he had two support units on their way to meet him at the lock-up. 'No time for a warrant,' he told Turner, as he swung into the Mondeo. 'We'll Section 17 it. Threat to life and limb. No need to bother the nice beak. See you up there.'

He drove as fast as he could through the morning traffic, row after row of red brakelights coming on and off in the queues, down the A432 and along the M4 behind Turner's Sierra. They were less than four miles from the lock-up when Caffery's phone rang. He shoved the dongle in his ear and answered. It was Nick, the Costellos' FLO, sounding panicky: 'I'm sorry to keep hassling you but I'm really worried now. I've left three messages and I do think it's serious.'

'I've been a bit tucked up here. Had the phone on silent. What's up?'

'I'm at the Costellos', the new flat in—'

'I know.'

'I was due to turn up for an hour, just to see how they were doing, but I'm here now and I can't get in.'

'They're not there?'

'I think they are, but they're not coming to the door.'

'You've got keys, haven't you?'

'Yes, but I can't open the door. They've got the chain on inside.'

'Isn't there a PC with them?'

'No. He got stood down last night by DC Prody. But Prody must've forgotten he was supposed to tell the local shop when he left because no one was rostered to replace him.'

'Call him.'

'I have. His phone's switched off.'

'The Costellos, then. Have you tried them?'

'Of course. I've spoken to Cory but he's not in the flat. Says he didn't even spend the night there. I think he and Janice had a disagreement. He's on the way over now. He's called Janice, too, but she's not picking up for him either.'

'*Shit.*' Caffery tapped the steering-wheel. They were just coming up to the exit for the A46. He could either go left to Sapperton, or right to Pucklechurch, where the Costellos' flat was. 'Shit.'

'I've got to tell you – I'm scared.' Nick's voice was wobbly. 'Something's wrong here. All the curtains are closed tight. There's no reply at all.'

'I'll come over.'

'We'll need an entry team. These chains are solid.'

'Will do.'

He swerved the car to the right, got on to the southbound A46 and pulled out his phone. Thumbed in Turner's number. 'Change of plan, mate.'

'How so?'

'Get the units assembled and the lock-up covered. Ring it – wide – but don't do anything yet. Wait for me. And I want you to get another entry team over to the Costellos' place. Something's gone seriously Pete Tong down there.'

'Three entry teams? Ops are going to love us.'

'Well, tell them their reward'll be in heaven.'

49

The road to Pucklechurch had a forty-miles-per-hour speed limit. Caffery did sixty whenever the dreary trails of commuters thinned enough to let him. When he arrived it was getting light and the streetlamps had been switched off. Nick was standing on the front path wearing a houndstooth coat and smart high-heeled boots. She was looking up and down the road, biting her finger-nails. She shot to the kerb when she saw him and tugged open his door. 'I can smell something. I got the door open just enough and got my head through the crack and there's a smell.'

'Gas?'

'More like a solvent. The way glueheads always smell – you know?'

Caffery got out of the car and looked up at the flat, the closed windows, tight curtains. Nick had left the front door open as far as it would go on the two chains. He could just see the blue carpet on the stairs inside, a few scuffmarks on the walls. He glanced at his watch. The entry team should be here any minute. They didn't have far to come.

'Hold this.' He pulled off his jacket and handed it to her. 'And look the other way.'

Nick took a few steps back and held up her hand to shield her eyes. Caffery threw himself at the door, half turning so his shoulder made the contact. The door leaped on its hinges, shuddered noisily, but the chains held and he ricocheted back on to the path. He hopped a little, got his balance and came back at it. He gripped the wooden frame that lined the small porch with both hands, braced himself and shoved his foot at the door. Once. Twice. Three times. Each time it shivered, made deafening splintering noises, and each time it bounced straight back into the frame.

'Fuck.' He stood on the path, sweating. His shoulders were aching, his back was jarred from the kicks. 'Getting too old for this.'

'It's supposed to be a safe-house.' Nick took her hands from her eyes and looked at the door dubiously. 'And it is. Safe, I mean.'

He looked up at the windows again. 'I hope you're right.'

A white armoured Mercedes Sprinter pulled up. Caffery and Nick watched six men in riot gear pile out – 727: Flea's unit.

'We meet again.' As the rest of the team pulled the red battering ram out of the van Wellard came forward to shake Caffery's hand. 'Starting to think you fancy me.'

'Yeah, well, the uniform's kind of rugged. You acting again?'

'Looks like it.'

'Where's your sergeant?'

'Honestly? I don't know. Never turned up at work today. It's not like her, but recently nothing's like her.' He tipped his visor back and looked up at the side of the house. 'What've we got here? Think I know this place. This the old rape suite, is it?'

'We've got a vulnerable family inside, lodged for witness protection. Lady over here,' he gestured to Nick, 'turns up half an hour ago. She's expected but no one comes to the door. Chains are on inside. There's a smell too. Like a solvent.'

'How many souls?'

'Three, we think. Woman in her thirties, another woman in her sixties and a little girl. Four.'

Wellard raised his eyebrows. He looked at the flat again, then at Nick and Caffery, and silently beckoned to the men. They trotted over, carrying the battering ram between them. They flanked the door and swung the ram at it. With three deafening thuds the door splintered in two, one half hanging off the two security chains, the other on the hinges.

Wellard and two of his men stepped over the door and into the hallway, shields at the ready. They streamed up the stairs, yelling as they had in the Moons' flat – '*Police, police!*'

Caffery followed, face screwed up at the astringent fumes. 'Open some windows, someone,' he yelled.

As he got to the top of the stairs he saw Wellard at the end of the landing, holding a door open. 'Your lady in her sixties.'

Caffery looked through the door and saw the woman on the bed – Janice's mother. In cream pyjamas, her short white hair pushed back from her tanned face, she lay on her side, one arm stretched up, the other drooped across her face. She was breathing in a slow, depressed way that made Caffery think of hospices and RTCs. She stirred at the noise and half opened her eyes, her hand lifting vaguely, but she didn't wake.

Caffery leaned over the staircase and yelled to the men below, 'Someone get some paramedics ASA.'

'Adult male here,' called another officer. He was in the kitchen doorway.

'Adult male?' Caffery joined him. 'Nick said he's not . . .' He didn't finish the sentence. The window in the room was slightly open. There were some washed dishes and mugs on the draining-board, a plate of food covered with clingfilm on the side and an empty wine bottle on top of the fridge. A man lay on the floor, his head bent at a strange angle against the cabinets, vomit covering his white shirt. But it wasn't Cory Costello. It was DC Prody.

'Jesus Christ – Paul? *Hey!*' Caffery crouched and shook him. 'Wake up. Wake the fuck up.'

Prody moved his jaw up and down. A long line of drool dangled from his lip. He lifted a hand and made a weak effort to brush it away.

'What the hell happened?'

Prody's eyes half opened, then closed again. His head drooped. Caffery went back into the hallway, his eyes watering at the fumes.

'Are those paramedics on their way?' he yelled down the stairs. 'They'd better be. And, for the second time, will someone open the fucking windows?' He stopped and looked to the end of the landing. An officer – Wellard, still with his visor down – was standing at another opened door, at the front of the flat this time. It must be the room that looked out over the road. He was beckoning slowly. He was doing it without turning because what-ever was in front of him had him riveted.

Caffery experienced a moment of pure, full-on fear. Suddenly he wanted out. Suddenly the last thing he wanted to know was what Wellard was looking at.

His heart bumped low and hard in his chest as he crossed the landing and came to stand next to him. The room in front of them was dark. The curtains were drawn and the windows closed. The chemical smell was much stronger. There were two beds in plain sight: a single pushed up against the window – empty – and a rumpled double bed. A woman lay on it: Janice Costello, from the tangle of dark hair. Her back rose and fell.

Caffery turned to Wellard, who gave him a strange look. 'What?' he hissed. 'It's a woman. Isn't that what you expected?'

'Yes, but what about the little girl? I've seen two women and a man but I haven't seen a little girl. Have you?'

50

Dawn broke over the tiny hamlet of Coates. It was a half-hearted, wintry dawn with no orange or speckled skies, just a featureless, ashen light that lifted listlessly over the roofs, past the tower of the neighbourhood church, across the heads of the trees and came down like mist on a tiny clearing deep in a forest on the Bathurst estate. In a grass-choked air shaft, a hundred feet above the canal, the black border between day and night crept slowly down. Heading for the bowels of the earth, it reached a cavern formed by two rockfalls at either end of a short space of tunnel. The swarmy, diffuse light found the black water, formed a shadow under the kitbag that hung motionless at the end of the rope and settled on the humped rocks and debris.

On the other side of one rockfall, Flea Marley knew nothing about the dawn. She knew nothing except the cold and the old, stale silence of the cavern. She lay on a rough ledge at the foot of the fall. Curled in a ball, like an ammonite fossil, she kept her head tucked in, her hands shoved inside her armpits in an effort to keep warm. She was half asleep, her thoughts flat and exhausted. The darkness pressed on her eyelids, like fingers. Something complex in the optical pathways lit up with dancing lights, with strange and pastel images.

No caving lights for now. The big torch and her little head lamp were all that had survived the rockfall. She kept them switched off, rationing the batteries, before she had to turn to Dad's old carbide lamp. There was nothing to see anyway. She knew what a torch beam would pick out: the yawning hole in the ceiling where tons of earth and rock had been dislodged. The debris had brought the floor level up about three feet in some places and covered the original screes at either end of the tunnel section in earth and stone. Both her escape routes had vanished. This time digging by hand wasn't enough. She'd tried. And exhausted herself. Only a pneumatic drill and earth movers would tunnel through those barriers. If the jacker came back, he'd never get to her now. But that hardly mattered because for her there was no going back. She was trapped.

Still, she was learning a lot down here. She'd learned that just when you thought you couldn't get any colder, you could. She'd learned that even in the early-morning hours trains ran along the Cheltenham and Great Western Union Railway. Goods trains, she imagined. Every fifteen minutes one would thunder along, rattling the ground like a dragon in the night, shaking out a few stones from invisible recesses in the tunnel. Between trains she slept, fitful, dozing, and woke, shivering and electric with fear and cold. On her wrist her waterproof Citizen clicked through the minutes, marking off the increments of her life.

A picture of Jack Caffery was in her head. Not Jack Caffery yelling at her, but Jack Caffery talking to her quietly. The hand he'd once put on her shoulder – it had been warm through her shirt. They'd been sitting in a car and at the time she'd thought he'd touched her because she was standing at an open door, ready to step through into a completely new world. But life ducked and wove and the only ones who weren't thrown every now and then were the strongest and most capable. Then Misty Kitson's face came to her, smiling out from the front pages of newspapers, and Flea thought that maybe this was the big catch: that because she and Thom had got away with concealing what had happened to Misty, something higher than them had decided they had to pay. Ironic she'd end up paying by being entombed the same way Misty's corpse was.

Now she stirred. She pulled her freezing hands out from her armpits and touched the mobile phone in the waterproof pocket of her immersion suit. No signal. Not a chance. She knew from the schematics roughly where she was. She'd punched out scores of texts in rapid fire with approximate co-ordinates and sent them to everyone she could think of. But the texts all sat there in the outbox, the 'resend scheduled' icon hovering over them. In the end, scared she'd lose the battery, she'd switched the phone off and tucked it back into its plastic wrapper. Eleven o'clock, she'd told Prody. That was seven hours ago. Something had gone wrong. He hadn't got the message. And if he hadn't got the message then God's harsh truth was this: the caving line was in the entrance to the tunnel. She'd left the car at the very edge of the village green, where it wouldn't get reversed into. It could be days before someone noticed either and drew any conclusions about where she was.

Painfully she uncurled herself. She shifted, opened her feet wider, and slid down the last few inches of the landslide. The splosh of her boots echoed around the chamber as she landed in the water. She couldn't see anything, but she knew rubbish was floating in it. Rubbish that must have been dropped down the shaft before the rock fall that had sealed off the chamber, then been driven by the wind to where she stood now. She took her gloves off, bent over, scooped a little of the water into her freezing, chapped hands and sniffed it. It didn't smell of oil. It smelt of earth. Of roots and leaves and sunlit glades. She tested it with her tongue. It was slightly metallic.

Something opaque rested in the corner of her eye. She let the water slip from her hands and turned stiffly to her left.

About ten feet away there was a faint, cone-shaped glow. The dimmest, most spectral of lights. She twisted and fell against the rockfall, scrabbling for her rucksack, and dragged out her cave light. She put her hands over her eyes and fired it up. The cavern whoomped into light. Everything was outlined in a fizzing blue-white: too big, the edges too defined. She dropped her hand and trained her eyes on where the light had been. The hull of the abandoned barge.

She clicked off the light and kept looking at the hull. Slowly the shapes and burn marks in her retinas faded. Her pupils dilated. And this time there was no mistake. Daylight was coming through the barge from the other side of the rockfall.

She turned the cave light back on and jammed it into the clay, illuminating the edge of the fall while she repacked her kit. She pulled her gloves on, slung the rucksack on to her back and waded to the barge, crouched and pushed the light inside, shining it around. The barge extended under the rockfall, its bows protruding into the section of tunnel where the shaft was. It would have been made more than a hundred years ago – the hull and deck were sheets of iron riveted together. Good engineers, the Victorians, she thought, peering up at the underside of the deck: in spite of the weight of the rockfall it hadn't bowed. Instead the entire barge had been driven down into the soft mud, tilted backwards a little, so that, in the next cavern along, its bows were higher. Here in the stern the water level was less than a foot from the underside of the deck – but the tilt made the deck slope upwards so that head space increased further forward into the hull.

About eight feet in, the big beam picked out a bulkhead blocking her way to the bows. She shone the light around the rest of the hull, looking for an exit. It threw the rivets and the drooping cobwebs of the ceiling into sharp relief, picked out odds and ends of floating rubbish: carrier bags, Coke cans. Something that looked furred. A bloated rat probably. But no hatches or exit points in here. She clicked off the lamp and this time her eyes didn't need time to get used to the change. Immediately she saw where the daylight was coming from: there was the outline of a rectangle in the bulkhead. She let out all her breath. 'You fucking lovely bastard thing.'

A hatch in the bulkhead, half submerged in the water. Probably for moving the coal between compartments. There was absolutely no reason for it to be locked. The carjacker hadn't been in the next section of tunnel earlier, but that didn't mean he hadn't come back in the last few hours. Still, her choice was clear – get through the barge and face him, or die, trapped down here.

From the rucksack she rummaged out her old Swiss Army

knife, and the mooring spike she'd found the other night, and shoved them both into the little waterproof tackle bag with the drawstring she carried on her wrist.

She strapped on the elasticated head torch and knelt down in the muck, letting herself sink slowly until the water was up to her chest. She went into the hull on her knees, hands stretched out under the water, sweeping for any obstacles, head brushing the rust-crusted cobwebs, chin up, keeping her mouth out the water. If he was in the next section of tunnel, she wasn't concerned about him seeing the beam of her torch bouncing around, it would be too bright on the other side for it to be visible, but he might be able to hear her. She let her fingers graze across the mooring spike, making sure it was at the ready.

She moved carefully, breathing through her mouth, the bitter whiff of her breath coming back to her in the tiny space. The smell of a night of fear and no food, mingled with the faint tarry scent of coal from inside the hull.

She got to the bulkhead and found that at least two feet of the hatch were under water. She could feel most of it through her gloves. The rest she had to guess at with the numb clumpy toes of her boots. She found a latch halfway down the seam: open. The only thing holding the hatch closed as far as she could tell was decades of rust. There'd be no pressure in the water on either side. As long as she cleared this side, it shouldn't be impossible to open. The trick was to open it as low down as possible.

Tongue between her teeth she slid the blade of the Swiss Army knife into where the door met the bulkhead, and quietly levered away the rust. The silt at the bottom of the hull she cleared with her feet. She didn't dare take her gloves off – her fingers were clumpy and painful as she wedged them behind the lip of the hatch. She lifted one heavy foot so she had purchase against the bulkhead and pushed all her energy into her fingers, gritting her teeth and pulling. The pop was sudden and loud. A little spray of rust confettied down on her and a rush of warmer water snaked through the hatch around her stomach.

The noise of the hatch popping felt like a hand punching inside her ear. Too loud, and for the first time in ages she lost her nerve. She found she couldn't move. She just stayed exactly where she was, crouched, half-submerged, eyes wide, waiting for an answering noise from the other side of the hatch.

51

Blue lights flashed across the walls of the houses in the narrow street, sirens wailed mournfully in the distance: ambulances with Janice and her mother nosing their way out into the morning traffic. About fifty people from the neighbourhood were standing in the street at the outer cordon, trying to see what was happening at the nondescript building where the police were gathered.

Everyone on the front lawn was white-faced – silent and serious. No one could quite believe it had happened: that Emily had been snatched from under their noses. The force had been put on its hind legs. Rumour had it that the chief constable himself was on his way down to witness at first hand the staggering cock-up they'd made. Press calls were coming thick and fast and the person at the centre of the storm was DC Paul Prody.

He sat on a small picnic bench placed incongruously on the diseased patch of grass at the front of the house. He had accepted someone's offer of a T-shirt so he no longer smelt of puke – his own shirt was in a knotted carrier bag at his feet – but he'd refused to let the paramedics touch him. He couldn't keep his balance. He had to sit with his arm on the table, concentrating on a point on the floor. Every now and then his body would weave a little and someone would have to prop him up.

'They think it was a kind of chloroform, made from bleach and acetone, maybe.' Caffery had given in again to the call of tobacco. He sat on the other side of the bench, smoking a tightly rolled cigarette and watching Prody through narrowed eyes. 'Knock-out gas. Old-fashioned. If you were hit hard enough it'll get your liver. That's why you should be in hospital. Even if you think you're OK.'

Prody shook his head jerkily and even that small movement looked as if it might unbalance him. 'Fuck off.' He spoke as if he had a bad cold. 'You think Janice'll want me in the same hospital?'

'A different one, then.'

'No fucking way. I'm just going to sit here. And breathe.'

He made a show of pulling air into his lungs. In, out, in, out. Painful. Caffery watched in silence. Prody had spent the night with Janice Costello, a vulnerable person, which had pissed Caffery off almost as much as the stuff about the Kitson case. If the circumstances had been any different he might have enjoyed seeing Prody fuck up like this, but he couldn't help feeling a bit sorry for him at the balls-up he'd made. He understood why the guy wouldn't want to be in the same hospital as Janice and her mother. Not after he'd failed to stop Emily being taken.

'I'm going to be OK. Give me ten and I'll be ready to go.' He looked up with bloodshot eyes. 'They said you know where he is.'

'We're not sure. We've got a lock-up in Tarlton, near the canal. They've searched it.'

'Any sign?'

'Not yet. They've pulled back. Maybe he's going to head up there now with Emily. But . . .' He narrowed his eyes and looked down the street to where the houses dwindled into the distance. 'No. He won't do that, of course. That would be too easy.'

'You know he took my phone?'

'Yep. It's switched off but we've already got a ping site analysis started. If he switches it on we can get a triangulation on it. But, like I said, he's too clever. If he switches it on there'll be a reason.'

Prody shivered. Head still lowered, he glanced darkly up the road, then the other way. It was a cold but sunny day. The people who were going to work had already left. The mothers who'd dropped their kids at school were now at home, cars parked neatly on driveways. Instead of going inside they'd wandered over to the cordon to stand, arms crossed, staring at the police vans and the ambulances. Their eyes were like nails, pinning Caffery and Prody where they sat. Wanting answers.

'I never even saw it coming. Don't remember a thing. I cocked up.'

'Tell me about it. You cocked up big-time. But not because you didn't stop this arsehole. Not for that.' Caffery pinched the end of the cigarette so the ash fell into a paper handkerchief Nick had given him. He folded it, pressing hard to kill the heat and put it, with the butt, into his inside pocket. No one was in the flat. They'd searched it thoroughly for Emily – even the loft – and the moment they were sure she wasn't there they'd cordoned it, leaving the scene as pristine as it could be for the crime-scene boys who still hadn't arrived. When they did come he wasn't going to ruffle their feathers by dropping butts all over the place. 'No. Your headline balls-up was being there in the first place. You're a DC on this case. You shouldn't have been there in the evening after hours. How the hell did that happen?'

'I came over in the afternoon, like you asked me. She was . . .' He waved a weak hand. 'She was – you know. So I stayed on.'

'She was what? Attractive? Available?'

'On her own. He'd fucked off to work.'

'Nice language.'

Prody stared at him as if there was something he'd like to say but couldn't. 'He'd *gone* to work when his wife and daughter were in the middle of this whole thing – left them on their own. Scared. What would you've done?'

'In the Met I had this drummed into me in training. You take advantage of a woman like that – someone who's already a victim – and it's hunting wounded animals. Hunting wounded animals.'

'I didn't take advantage, I took *pity*. I didn't sleep with her. I stayed because I *thought* it'd save you some staffing budget, and because *she* said she'd feel safer with me there.' He shook his head ironically. 'Lucky I never let her down, isn't it?'

Caffery sighed. Everything about this case had the dank, fetid smell of defeat about it. 'Take me through it again. Costello goes out in the afternoon? To work?'

'One of the squad cars took him. Nick organized it.'

'And he never comes home?'

'Yeah – he did. For about ten minutes. It was about nine at night. Boozed up, I think. And the moment he's through the door he lays into her.'

'Why?'

'Because—' Prody broke off.

'Because what?'

His face tightened a fraction. He seemed to be about to say something – something bitter. But he didn't. After a moment or two he got his face flattened down again. 'Dunno. Some domestic stuff, none of my business. They're both upstairs and the next thing I know she's screaming at him and he comes running down the stairs swearing and he's off. Slams the door. She comes leaping after him and runs all the chains on the door. I'm, like, "Mrs Costello, I really wouldn't, you'll antagonize him," and she's just, "I couldn't give a toss." Sure enough he comes back half an hour later, finds the chains on and starts yelling abuse up the stairs and rattling the door.'

'What did you do?'

'She asked me to ignore it so I did.'

'But eventually he goes? Leaves you be?'

'Eventually. I think he . . . Let's put it this way, I think he has somewhere else he can spend the night.'

Caffery pulled out the wrapped-up napkin from his pocket. Inspected the remains of the cigarette. He folded it again and put it back into his pocket. 'We found you in the kitchen.'

'Yeah.' He looked up at the open window. 'I remember going in. I'd made some cocoa for us all and I took the cups in to wash them up. I remember that far.'

'What time?'

'Christ knows. Maybe ten o'clock? Emily had woken up with all the noise.'

'The window was forced. There're marks in the grass. A ladder.'

He nodded to where the entry team had rigged up some police tape tied to three temporary barriers that cordoned off an area. 'Less visible round the side. He would have taken you first. In the kitchen. No one would have heard in the rest of the—' He broke off. A police Beemer slowed in the street and stopped at the kerb. Cory Costello got out. His overcoat was unbuttoned to reveal an expensive suit. He was neat and tidy – shaved and showered. So wherever he'd spent the night it hadn't been a bench. Nick, who had been sitting in Caffery's Mondeo making phone calls, instantly jumped out and stopped Cory in his tracks. They spoke for a moment, then Cory glanced around the assembled police officers and onlookers. His eye fell on Caffery and Prody. Neither man moved. They simply sat there and let him look at them. For a while a hush seemed to fall on the entire street. The father who'd lost a daughter. And the two cops who should have done something about it. Cory began to walk towards them.

'Don't speak to him.' Caffery pushed his face close to Prody's, spoke hard and fast: 'If there's anything to be said, let me say it.'

Prody didn't answer. He kept his eyes locked on Cory, who stopped a few feet away.

Caffery turned. Cory's face was quite smooth, no wrinkles or creases in his forehead. A small jaw, feminine nose and very clear grey eyes fixed on the side of Prody's face. 'Cunt,' he said quietly.

Caffery sensed Nick, somewhere to his right, getting frantic, panicking about what was going to happen.

'Cunt. Cunt. Cunt.' Cory's face was calm. His voice was almost a whisper. 'Cunt cunt cunt cunt cunt cunt cunt.'

'Mr Costello . . .' Caffery said.

'Cunt cunt cunt cunt cunt.'

'Mr Costello. That's not going to help Emily.'

'Cunt cunt cunt cunt CUNT.'

'*Mr Costello!*'

Cory shuddered. He took half a step back and blinked at Caffery. Then he seemed to remember who and where he was. He straightened his cuffs and turned to look around the street, a polite, reasonable expression on his face, as if he was thinking of buying the house and sizing up the neighbourhood. Then he took off his overcoat and dropped it on the ground. He unwound the scarf he was wearing, dropped that on top of the coat. He stopped to consider the pile, as if he was mildly surprised to see it there. Then, without any warning, he took three steps round the side of the picnic bench and launched himself at Prody.

Caffery had time to leap to his feet before Prody was wrestled off the bench and thrown on his back on the grass. He didn't resist: he let Cory get on with it and lay there, his arms half raised across his face, allowing the man in the business suit to rain punches on him. Almost patient, as if he accepted this as his punishment. Caffery dodged round the picnic bench and got to Cory, grasped the backs of his arms as Wellard and another officer came steaming across the lawn.

'Mr Costello!' Caffery yelled into the back of the guy's head – into his perfect haircut. The two other officers grappled for his hands. '*Cory*, let him go now. You have to let him go or we'll have to cuff you.'

Cory managed to land two more punches in Prody's ribs, before the support-group guys got his arms behind his back and pulled him away. Wellard rolled Cory away across the ground, gripping him from behind, lying on his side, spooning him with his face pressed against the back of his neck. Prody managed to get to his hands and knees and crawl a few paces away. He stopped there, panting.

'You didn't deserve that.' Caffery squatted next to Prody, got him by the shirt and pulled him upright so he rocked back on his heels. His face was slack, his mouth bleeding. 'You really didn't deserve that. But you still shouldn't have been there.'

'I know.' He wiped his forehead. Blood was trickling down from his scalp where Cory had managed to pull out a clump of hair. He looked as if he might start crying. 'I feel like shit.'

'Listen – and listen carefully. I want you to go to that nice young paramedic over there and tell her you want to go to hospital, get checked over and patched up – you hear? And then I want you to discharge yourself and call me. Tell me you're OK.'

'And you?'

'Me?' Caffery straightened up. Brushed off his jacket, the knees of his trousers. 'S'pose I'll have to go and have a sniff around this bloody lock-up. Not that we'll find him there. Like I said.'

'Too clever?'

'Exactly. Too effing clever.'

52

The area was quiet, rural and very pretty. At the edge of the Cotswolds, it was scattered with cottages and manor houses built from the local sugary brown stone. The lock-up Ted Moon rented was among a development so out of character with its surroundings it couldn't be long before the developer's wrecking ball paid a visit. It comprised five squat breezeblock buildings, each roofed with moss-covered corrugated iron. They must have been cattle sheds once. No commercial signage and no activity. God only knew what they were used for.

Ted Moon's lock-up was the last of the buildings at the western end where the development gave way to farmland. To look at it now, dark and featureless in the sparkling autumn sunlight, you wouldn't guess it was only half an hour out of one of the most intensive and fraught police searches conducted in years. The entry teams had broken in through a side door and within minutes the place had been swarming with cops. They'd stripped the place to its bones, found nothing. Now, however, they were nowhere to be seen. The place was quiet. The cops were still there, though. Somewhere out in the silent trees a team of surveillance officers surrounded the building. Eight pairs of eyes watching and waiting.

'What's the signal like inside?' In a lay-by near the entrance, sheltered from the road, Caffery sat in the front seat of one of the entry team's Sprinter vans, twisted round, his elbow on the back of the seat, quizzing the team sergeant. 'Did the radios drop out at all?'

'No. Why?'

'I'm going to have a look round. Just want to be sure that if he makes an appearance I get the heads up.'

'Fine, but you won't find anything. You've seen the evidence list. Ten stolen cars, five stolen mopeds, a stack of moody numberplates and some respectable citizen's brand-new Sony widescreen TV and a Blu-ray still in their boxes.'

'And the unit's Mondeo?'

The sergeant nodded. 'And a Mondeo believed to have been taken without consent from the MCIU car park. There's a four-by-four that – from the brake discs – has been driven in the last twenty-four hours and, apart from that, just some bits of rusting agricultural stuff in the corner. And the pigeons. It's a giant nesting box for them.'

'Just make sure the surveillance teams know to give me some warning.' Caffery jumped out of the van. He checked that the radio clipped to his belt was showing a signal, pulled his coat on and raised his hand to the sergeant. 'OK?'

The sun on the cracked driveway made the world feel almost warm for the first time in days. Even the ragwort stems that grew out of the ballast seemed to be straining upwards to the sky, as if they were aching for spring. Caffery walked quickly, head down, feeling the urge to hurry. At the side window of the building – which had just one neatly broken pane and no police tape or other signs they'd been here – he covered his hand with his coat sleeve, pushed his arm through, and unfastened the latch. He was careful as he climbed in. In just a year he'd gone through two good suits in the course of his job and wasn't about to ruin another. He closed the window behind him, and stood, silently, looking around him.

On the inside the place looked more like a bomb bunker. The little light there was came through cracked, cloudy windows and fell in dusty squares on the floor. A single electric bulb had been strung up from a hook in the ceiling and cobwebs traced graceful rainbows from it. The cars – a range of sizes and colours – were parked in three rows facing the door. All polished and gleaming as if they were in a showroom. Moon had gathered the rest of the stolen goods into one corner, huddled them together as if that might make them less conspicuous. The agricultural equipment lay at the far end. Beyond the cars, in the very centre of the unit, sat an old Cortina, like a prairie corpse half dismantled by vultures, its innards on show.

Caffery crossed the echoey building to the rusting ploughs. He crouched to peer into the mangled mess, making sure nothing was there. Then he made his way across to the other side of the shed and checked through the collection of stolen goods. Everywhere he went his feet crunched through pigeon droppings that formed little stalagmites. Miniature cities crumbling with every step. The Cortina must have been one of the last made. It had a vinyl roof and slatted tail-lights and had obviously been parked there for years. Cobwebs linked the opened bonnet to the chassis. Why, with all the other cars polished and gleaming, this one had been left so was anyone's guess. Caffery went back to the other corner and, using his penknife, slit away a piece of cardboard from the box of the Sony TV. The exhibits officer would get the hump, but rather that than another suit buggered. He carried the cardboard back to the Cortina, threw it on to the floor and lay on it. He used his toes to push himself a few inches further under the car.

So that was why the Cortina hadn't been moved.

'Uh—' He pulled the radio closer to his mouth. Hit the transmit button. 'Did anyone notice the inspection pit under the car?'

There was a pause, then a rattle of static, and the sergeant's voice: 'Yeah, we noticed that – had one of our lads down in it.'

Caffery grunted. Patted his trouser pockets. On his key-ring he had a tiny LED torch. Meant to help find the lock on a car door at night, it didn't throw out much of a light. Holding it down into the hole he could just make out the sides, lined with MDF panels that looked like parts of a cannibalized kitchen cabinet. He let the torch play over them for a few seconds and then, because he was the sort who never had been able to walk past an open door without looking inside, he shuffled out from under the car, turned the cardboard so it lay lengthways along the edge of the hole, lay down on it again and rolled himself into the pit, landing with a bone-jarring thud on both feet.

It was instantly darker. The rusting Cortina above him blocked out what little light there was in the lock-up. He switched the torch on again and shone it around himself, examining the panels, the cheap oil-stained cabinet mouldings, the marks where the handles must have been. He checked the concrete floor. Stamped on it. Nothing in there. He slung the bunch of keys on to the cardboard and was just about to haul himself up when something made him stop. Carefully he pulled the keys back, crouched in the pit and held up the torch.

All the panels had been nailed to batons drilled into the concrete. But there wasn't any good reason to line a pit like this. Unless it was to hide something. He ran his fingers along the bottom of the panel at the rear of the pit. Tugged at it. It held solid. He wriggled his knife between the panel and the baton, pulled it back and saw the gap behind it.

Caffery's heart was thudding. Someone had said there were holes and caves under this area. It had been the guy from the Sapperton tunnel trust, briefing Flea Marley's team. He'd said there were interconnecting tunnels and hidey-holes all over the place. A man as strong as Ted Moon could carry a four-year-old girl like Emily a long way through those tunnels. Maybe to somewhere he'd prepared. A place where he could do what he wanted undisturbed.

Caffery pulled himself out of the pit and went back to the window, turning the volume down on his radio as he did. 'Hey.' He leaned out of the window and hissed into the unit: 'When your someone went into the inspection pit did they notice the boarded-up entrance?'

There was a long silence. Then: 'Say again, sir. Think I missed something there.'

'There's a bloody escape hole down here. A way out of the inspection pit. Didn't anyone notice?'

Silence.

'Oh, Christ. Don't answer. There is something down here. I'm going to have a look. Get someone in here, will you? Don't have them breathing down my neck – I don't want a hundred kilos of armed police clanking its way after me but it'd be nice to know someone's sitting in the pit so my backside is covered.'

Another pause. Then: 'Yeah – that's not a problem. They're on their way.'

'But keep the outside as clean-looking as it has been. If Moon does turn up I don't want him seeing the place crawling with men in black.'

'Will do.'

Caffery crunched back through the pigeon shit and rolled himself into the hole. With the top of the panel half prised off the baton the remainder came away easily. He put the wood to one side and bent over, peering at what it had revealed.

It was a tunnel big enough for a man to get into. Even a tall man would only have to stoop a little to walk straight through. Filthy newspapers lay on the ground for as far as Caffery could see. He shone the tiny torch in: it showed a ceiling of soil buttressed with two-by-four like something out of the world's best war movies, *The Great Escape*, maybe. The walls were about two foot wide. The construction was crude, but effective. Someone had worked very hard to build themselves a secret underground passage.

He took a few steps in, following the beam of the torch. It was warmer down here than up on the surface, the air thick with the peaty smells of plant roots. Silent and muffled too. He took a few more cautious paces, pausing every now and then to listen. When the light of the inspection pit behind him had dwindled to a small grey hole he switched off the torch and stood quite still for a while, eyes screwed tight. He concentrated on opening his ears, listening to the darkness around him.

When he was a kid, sharing a room with Ewan, they had played a game at lights out: when their mother had closed the door and gone down the creaking stairs Ewan would tiptoe across the bare floorboards and creep into bed with Jack. They'd lie together on their backs trying not to giggle. They were too young for it to be girls they were talking about – it was dinosaurs and bogey men, and what it'd be like to be a soldier and kill someone. They tried to scare the living crap out of each other. The game was for each to tell the scariest story he could. Then he got to put his hand over his brother's chest and feel if it had made his heart beat faster. The one whose heart beat fastest lost the round. Ewan was the oldest so usually he won. Jack had a heart like a steam-hammer, a great meaty organ that would keep him alive into his nineties, the doctor said, if he didn't pickle it in Glenmorangie. He'd never learned to keep it quiet. Now it was bounding out of his chest, racing the blood through his veins because he had the feeling, a completely unwarranted sensation, like cold water on his skin, that he wasn't alone down there.

He looked back at the tiny point of light at the entrance. The back-up teams were on their way. He had to trust that. He clicked on the torch and shone it further into the hole. The weak beam fragmented to shadows. There was nothing here. Couldn't be. That panel had been nailed closed. Still, he could imagine some-one breathing in the darkness around him.

'Hey, Ted,' he tested. 'We know you're here.'

His voice came back to him. *We know you're here.* Dulled by the soil walls, it sounded flat. Unconvincing. He continued on, torch pushed out in front of him, arm stiff. The hairs were stand-ing up on the back of his neck. The Walking Man's face came to him in the gloom: *He is cleverer than any of the others.* Within about eight yards he found himself up against a wall. He'd come to the end of the tunnel. He turned and looked back towards the entrance. He shone the torch all around, up at the girders and the wooden supports. A dead end?

No. About two yards back the way he'd come he saw a hole in the side of the wall at about waist height. He'd walked straight past it.

He went back a few paces, bent at the waist, and shone the torch into the hole. It was an opening to another tunnel. It shot off at an angle of about forty-five degrees, but it went too far for the torch beam to pick out the end. He sniffed. There was a smell of something like stale, unwashed clothes. 'Are you here, you shit-hole? Because if you are I've got you.'

He went into the opening, bent over, hands up in front of him. His back and shoulders brushed the ceiling – so much for the suit. The tunnel sloped slightly downhill for about ten feet, then opened into a small room that had been hollowed out, wider here than the rest. He stopped at the entrance, body braced in the defensive stance, ready to back straight up if anything came fly-ing at him. The torchlight played through the small cavern. His heart was still bouncing in his chest.

He'd been right in thinking he wasn't on his own down here. But it wasn't Ted Moon he was with.

He scrambled back into the tunnel, pushed the radio out so he had line of sight with the entrance. 'Uh – those units backing up? You getting me?'

'Yup – loud and clear.'

'Don't come into the tunnel. Repeat: don't come into the tunnel. I need the CSI down here and . . .' He dropped his face. Put his fingers to his eyes. 'And, look, better get someone from the coroner's office too.'

53

The CSI team had been on a job just two miles away and were the first to arrive, even before the doctor. They sealed off the entrance and set up fluorescent tubes on tripods to flood the cave with light. They wandered in and out wearing their Andy Pandy suits. Caffery didn't say much to anyone. He went out and met them at the inspection pit, put on boots and gloves, then went back down the tunnel with them and stood in the room, his back against the wall, arms folded.

The cave was littered with newspapers and old food containers. Beer cans and batteries. At the far wall two industrial pallets were stacked one on top of the other. A form wrapped in a dirty sheet, stained and brittle, covered with dead insects, lay on them. The shape was unmistakable. A human lying on its back, arms folded across its chest. From top to bottom it probably measured about five feet.

'You haven't touched anything?' The crime-scene manager came in, dropping tread-plates in a line from the entrance to the body. It was the distinguished-looking, aloof one. The one who'd done the Costellos' car. 'You're too clever to have done that, of course.'

'Put my face close to it. Didn't touch the wrapping – I didn't need to. You can tell when something's dead. It doesn't take much, does it, even for a thick-as-shit cop?'

'You're the only one who's been in here?'

Caffery rubbed his eyes. He lifted a hand vaguely in the direction of the body. 'That's not an adult, is it?'

The CSM shook his head. He stopped next to the piled pallets and scanned the body. 'That's not an adult. Definitely not an adult.'

'You can't tell how old, can you? Could she be ten? Or could she be younger?'

'She? How do you know it's a she?'

'Do you think it's a he?'

The CSM turned and gave him a long look. 'They told me this is the jacker case still? They told me you've got Ted Moon in the frame for it.'

'They told you right.'

'That murder – the girl, Sharon Macy – it was the first job I did on the force, eleven, nearly twelve, years ago. I spent a day cutting her blood out of floorboards with a scalpel. Remember it like it was yesterday – I still get nightmares about him.'

The doctor arrived, coming through the entrance bent double, A woman with nicely cut hair and a belted raincoat. She'd put bootees on over her smart shoes and gloves. In the room she straightened, throwing her head back, one hand raised against the glare of the lights. Caffery nodded at her, gave her a tight smile. She had natural straw-coloured hair tied back and she looked too young and nice to be doing this. She looked as if she should be selling patisserie or helping people with dental hygiene.

'Is this anything to do with those car jackings?' she asked.

'You tell me.'

The doctor raised her eyebrows at the CSM for more information. But he just shrugged and went back to his boxes and tread-plates. 'OK.' Her voice had a low, nervous shake to it. 'Fair enough.' She crossed the room cautiously, keeping to the tread-plates. At the head of the corpse she stopped. 'Uh – can I cut this? Just to get a look at the face?'

'Here.' The CSM gave her a pair of Toughcut scissors from his kit. He pulled one of the fluorescents down to light what she was doing and got out a camera. 'Just let me get a couple of shots as you're doing it.'

Caffery pushed himself away from the wall and came across

the tread-plates, stopping next to the doctor. Her face was pale in the greenish light. There were faint pink circles on her cheeks.

'Right.' She gave him a sickly smile and he saw that she was completely out of her depth. Too young. Trying to act grown-up. Maybe it was her first time. 'So, let's see what we've got.'

When the CSM had his photos, she gripped the sheet in her gloved fingers and tried to insert the scissors. A slight tearing sound came from the cloth. Caffery exchanged glances with the CSM. Something was stuck to the underside of the sheet.

It's not you, Emily. It's not you . . .

The doctor wrestled the scissors, struggling to make a hole in the sheet, her hands shaking. It seemed to take for ever before the blade pushed through the fabric. She paused for a moment. Put the back of her wrist to her forehead. Smiled. 'Sorry about that. It's tough.' Then, almost to herself, 'Right . . . what next?' She snipped a line into the sheet, about ten inches long. Very carefully opened it. There was a pause. Then she looked at Caffery, her eyebrows raised as if to say, *There. That's not what you were expecting, is it?* He took a step forward and shone the little light into the shroud. Where he'd pictured a face, he saw instead a skull, stuck to the sheet and coated with powdery brown matter. It wasn't Martha either. But maybe he'd already known that from the condition of the shroud. This body had been dead for longer than a few days. This body had been dead for years.

He looked up at the CSM. 'Sharon Macy?'

'That's where my money would be.' He fired off a few more shots. 'If I was a betting man. Sharon Macy. As I live and breathe. Swear I never thought I'd see her body. Ever.' Caffery took a step back. He scanned the roughly hewn walls, the primitive buttresses. Moon must have been building it since before he was banged up. It took intelligence and strength to do something like this, to construct something so complex and efficient. The entrance to this chamber had been well hidden – Caffery'd nearly missed it. There could be other tunnels, other places. There could be a whole ants' nest system right under their feet. Maybe Emily and Martha's bodies were down here too somewhere. There, he thought, you used the word *bodies*. So you do think they're dead.

'Inspector Caffery?' A man's voice from the tunnel behind. 'Inspector Caffery – are you there?'

'Yeah? Who is it?' He crossed the tread-plates to the entrance and shouted down the tunnel. 'What's up?'

'Support group, sir. I've got a phone call for you. Young lady. Can't get through on your phone – says it's urgent.'

'On my way.' He held up his hand to the doctor and the CSM, turned and bent to walk back down the low tunnel. The support-group officer was standing in the car pit, his huge frame blocking out the light. Caffery could see the flashing light of the phone he was holding aloft under the Cortina chassis. 'Need to be out here to keep the signal, Boss.'

Caffery took the phone from the officer and, using the light-weight steps the CSI team had put up, scrambled out of the pit, crossed the lock-up to the window and leaned there, blinking, in the freezing daylight. 'Inspector Caffery – how can I help?'

'Sir, can you get over here ASAP?' It was the Bradleys' FLO. The tall brunette with the shiny hair. He recognized the slight Welsh lilt immediately. 'Like now.'

'Get over where?'

'Here – to the Bradleys' safe-house. Please. I need some advice.'

Caffery put a finger in his other ear to block out the sounds of the CSI team behind him. 'What's up? You need to speak slowly.'

'I don't know what to do. There's nothing in my training to cover this. It came ten minutes ago and I can't hide it from her for ever.'

'Hide *what* from her for ever?'

'OK.' The FLO took a few deep breaths, got herself under control. 'I was sitting at the breakfast table – usual scene, Rose and Philippa on the sofa, Jonathan making another cup of tea, and Rose's phone's on the table in front of me and suddenly it lights up. Usually she has the ringer on but maybe she doesn't get many texts because she's got that alert turned off. So, anyway, I look at it, just casually – and . . .'

'And what?'

'I think it's from him. It has to be from him. Ted Moon. A text.'

'Have you read it?'

'I haven't got the balls. Just haven't. I can only read the subject heading. And, anyway, I don't think it's a text text. It's an MMS.'

A photograph. Shit. Caffery stood up straight. 'Why do you think it's from him?'

'From the subject heading.'

'Which is?'

'Oh, Christ.' The FLO's voice dropped a notch. He could picture the look on her face. 'Sir – it says, "Martha. The love of my life".'

'Don't do a thing. Don't move, don't let Rose see it. I'll be there within the hour.'

54

On the way back to his car Caffery palmed two paracetamol into his mouth, washing them down with scalding coffee from a support-group officer's Thermos. He ached everywhere. He had a list of calls to make as he drove the twenty-five miles to the Bradleys' safe-house, Myrtle lying sleepily on the back seat. House-keeping calls: his superintendent, the Silver commander of the support groups at HQ, the press office. He put in a call to the office and found that Prody had discharged himself from the hospital already, had been debriefed and was back in the incident room, champing at the bit to do something to make up for last night. Caffery told him to find out from Acting Sergeant Wellard whether Flea had turned up anywhere.

'If she hasn't . . .' He pulled up outside the safe-house at HQ. It looked fairly normal. Curtains open. One or two lights on. A dog was yapping inside. '. . . speak to the neighbours, find out who her friends are. She's got some weird shit-for-brains brother somewhere – speak to him. Find yourself a chuck-away phone or one from the unit and text me your number. And call me when you know something.'

'Yup, OK,' Prody said. 'I've got a couple of theories already.'

It was the FLO who opened the door and he could tell right away, just from her face, that things were even worse than when she'd made the phone call. She didn't give him her sarcastic, appraising raised eyebrows. She didn't even comment on his filthy suit. She just shook her head.

'What? What's up?'

She stepped back in against the wall, opening the door wide so he could see along the hallway. Rose Bradley was sitting on the stairs in a pink housecoat and slippers. Her arms were tucked into her stomach, her head drooping. A thin, mewling sound was coming from her mouth. Philippa and Jonathan stood in the living-room doorway watching her helplessly, their faces like stone. Philippa held Sophie by the collar. The spaniel had stopped barking but was eyeing Caffery suspiciously, her hindquarters twitching.

'She got the phone,' the FLO murmured. 'She's like a bloodhound when it comes to the damned thing. She managed to get it off me.'

Rose rocked back and forth. 'Don't make me give it to you. You're not going to see it. It's *my* phone.'

Caffery took off his coat and dropped it on to a chair next to the door. The hallway was hot and slightly damp. The walls were covered with blue-swirled anaglypta wallpaper. This was supposed to be accommodation for visiting police chiefs but it was awful. Truly awful. 'Has she opened it?'

'*No!* No, I haven't.' She rocked harder, her forehead on her knees, tears soaking into the housecoat. 'I haven't opened it. But it's going to be a picture of her, isn't it? It's going to be a picture of her.'

'Please.' Jonathan had his finger against his temple. He looked as if he might fall over at any moment. 'You don't know that. We don't know what it is.'

Caffery stood on the staircase two steps down from Rose and looked up at her. She hadn't washed her hair and an unpleasant, spicy odour was coming from her. 'Rose?' He held out a hand. Either for her to put her own hand into, or the phone. 'You know that whatever it is, whatever is on the photograph, it could help us find her.'

'You saw that letter. You *know* what he said he was going to do to her. It was terrible what he said he'd do. I know because if it hadn't been awful you would have let me see it. What if he's done one of the things he said he'd do and what if this is a photograph of it?' Her voice rose. It was tight and sore, as if the vocal cords were chafing against each other from constant grief. *What if that's what the photograph is? What if that's what it is?*'

'We won't know until we've had a look. Now, you've got to give me the phone.'

'Not unless I can see what's on it. You're not hiding anything else from me. You can't.'

Caffery glanced at the FLO, who was standing with her back to the door, her arms folded. When she saw his face, realized what he was going to do, she raised her hands resignedly, as if to say, *It's your funeral.*

'Philippa,' he said, 'you've got a laptop, haven't you? Have you got a USB for the phone?'

'No. It's Bluetooth.'

'Then, get it.'

She hesitated, moving her lips as if her mouth had dried. 'We're not going to look at it, are we?'

'Your mother won't give me the phone otherwise.' He kept his face still, expressionless. 'We have to respect her wishes.'

'Oh, Jesus.' She shuddered. She pulled Sophie into the living room. '*Jesus.*'

They sat at the dining table and waited while Philippa assembled the laptop. Her hands were shaking. Jonathan had gone into the kitchen and was banging around, probably doing more washing-up. He was having none of this. Only Rose wasn't trembling. An icy calm had come over her and she was sitting at the table, quite steady, staring into the middle distance. When the laptop was assembled she unfolded her arms and placed the phone in the centre of the table. For a moment everyone stared at it in silence.

'OK,' Caffery said. 'I can take it from here.'

Philippa nodded and turned away. She threw herself on to the sofa and sat with her knees drawn up, a cushion pressed to her face, her eyes above it wide, as if she was watching the most appalling movie and couldn't quite drag them away.

'Are you sure, Rose?'

'Quite sure.'

He established the Bluetooth pairing and transferred the jpeg across. *Martha, the love of my life.jpg* Everyone sat with their eyes glued to the screen as the photo slowly downloaded, from the bottom up, the picture filling itself in line by line. At first it showed a blue carpet. Then the divan drawer of a child's bed came into view.

'Her bed,' Rose said matter-of-factly. 'Martha's. He's taken a picture of her bed. The stickers on the base. We had an argument about them. I—' She broke off. Her hand went to her mouth as the rest of the photograph filled in.

'*What?*' Philippa said from the sofa. 'Mum? What is it?'

No one answered. No one breathed. They all inched a little closer to the screen. The picture showed Martha's bed: white, covered with stickers, pink bed linen. On the wallpaper behind it there was a border, ballerinas pirouetting along it. But no one was looking at the walls, or the bedcovers: they were looking at what was on the bed. Or, rather, *who* was on the bed.

A man in jeans and a T-shirt, his muscles clearly defined. His hands were gripping his crotch. His face and neck were covered with a full-bearded Santa Claus mask. Caffery didn't need to see under the mask to know what Moon's face would be like. Underneath it he'd be grinning.

55

As the day wore on past midday, a bank of cumulus clouds that had been lowering on the western horizon eventually began to move east. Caffery glanced at them from time to time on the way to the vicarage in Oakhill. They looked like the towers of wild heathen cities, trundling across the sky. He rode on the passenger seat of an unmarked Mercedes van driven by a traffic officer, who'd taken off his epaulettes and tie. Caffery had dropped Myrtle back in his office at Kingswood, parked there and ordered the lift. Behind him, on the bench seat, sat Philippa and Rose; Jonathan and the FLO were in a Beemer behind. Rose was still convinced Martha would try to call her and didn't want to be more than a few steps away from her phone, but Caffery had managed to finesse it away from her by saying it needed to be with a professional in case Moon called. Truth was, the only professional who should have had the phone was a hostage negotiator. Caffery didn't mention that. From the get-go he'd been determined not to cede the case to one of those. The phone was tucked into his back pocket, all alerts switched to loud.

They arrived at the vicarage just before one o'clock. The driver switched off the engine and Caffery sat for a moment, looking at the scene. The curtains were closed, there was still an empty milk-bottle holder on the front step, but apart from that the place was nothing like it had been the day he'd evacuated the Bradleys. Now it was swarming with cops, lights flashing, blue and white tape fluttering, vans parked everywhere. A unit from Taunton had come out and checked the place over. There was a dog handlers' van parked outside, dogs staring out through the back-window grilles. Caffery was secretly pleased not to see the dogs out. He hadn't expected Moon to be waiting there for them in the vicarage, his hands up, but he didn't need to be reminded by a dog how clever the bastard was. What a piss-poor show the force had put up so far. He didn't think he could stand another tracker German shepherd turning in confused, whining circles.

An unmarked Renault van was parked about ten metres away, three plainclothes officers lingering around it, smoking cigarettes and talking among themselves. The surveillance team who had been watching the house since the Bradleys had left, hoping Moon would come back, show his face.

Caffery unsnapped his seatbelt, got out of the car and crossed to them. He stood a few feet away, his arms folded, not saying a word. He didn't need to speak. The force of his expression was loud enough. The men's conversation died and, one by one, they turned to him. One put his cigarette behind his back and gave Caffery a brave smile; the second stood to attention, looking at a point over Caffery's shoulder, as if Caffery was a drill sergeant. The third just lowered his eyes, began nervously to smooth his shirt. Oh, great, Caffery thought, the three monkeys.

'I swear,' one began, holding up his hand, but Caffery cut him off with a look, shook his head disappointedly. He turned and walked back to the house, where Jonathan stood, pale and drawn.

'I'm coming in with you. I want to see her bedroom.'

'No. That's not a good idea.'

'Please.'

'Jonathan, what's it going to achieve?'

'I want to check he hasn't . . .' he looked up at the window '. . . done anything in there. Just want to be sure.'

Caffery wanted to look at the room too. Not for the same reason. He wanted to see if he could do what the Walking Man could: soak up something about Ted Moon just by being there. 'Come on, then. But don't touch anything.'

The front door was open and they went in. Jonathan's face was a mask. He stood for a moment, gazing around the familiar hall, the surfaces covered with black fingerprint dust. A member of the CSI team that had been through – dusting the place, tweezering hairs from Martha's pillow, removing all the bed linen – wandered past in his spacesuit, collecting up bits and pieces of equipment. Caffery stopped him. 'Found a forced entry?'

'Not yet. It's a mystery at this point.' He did the *na na na na, na na na na Twilight Zone* theme and realized too late that the two men were gazing at him stiffly. He made his face go serious and pointed sternly at their feet. 'You coming in here?'

'Give us some bootees and nitriles. We'll be good.'

The CSI gave Caffery a pair of each and passed a set to Jonathan. They pulled them on and Caffery held out a hand to indicate the stairs. 'Shall we?'

Caffery went up first, Jonathan following him despondently. Martha's room was just as the jacker's photo had shown it: pictures framed on the walls, ballerinas twirling along a pink border, Hannah Montana stickers on the divan drawer. Except now the mattress was bare, stripped right back. And the divan, walls and windows were covered with fingerprint dust.

'Looks shabby.' Jonathan turned slowly, taking it all in. 'You live somewhere for so long and you don't notice it's getting shabby.' He went to the window, his gloved finger resting on the pane, and for the first time Caffery noticed the guy had lost weight. Just like that – in spite of the lectures on keeping up the family's strength, in spite of his apparent loading on of food, Jonathan was the one, not Rose or Philippa, who was becoming scrawny around the neck, trousers a bit baggy. He'd taken on the look of a sick, ageing vulture.

'Mr Caffery?' He didn't turn away from the window. 'I know we can't talk in front of Rose and Philippa but, man to man, what do you think? What do you think Ted Moon has done with my daughter?'

Caffery studied the back of Jonathan's head. The hair he'd once thought curly seemed thin. He decided the man had a right to be lied to – because the truth, Mr Bradley, is this: he has raped your daughter. He's done it as many times as he could manage. And he has killed her – to shut her up, stop her crying. That part has already happened – probably some time on the day after the kidnap. There's nothing human left in Ted Moon so he might even have used her body after he killed her. He probably went on doing that for as long as he could, but that part's over too by now. I know that because he took Emily. He needed another. What's probably happening to Martha now is he's trying to decide what to do with her body. He's good at building tunnels. He makes fine, well-engineered tunnels . . .

'Mr Caffery?'

He looked up, his thoughts broken.

Jonathan was watching him. 'I said – what do you think he's done to my daughter?'

He shook his head slowly. 'Shall we do what we came to do?'

'I'd hoped that wasn't what you thought.'

'I didn't say I thought anything.'

'No. But you do. Don't worry. I won't ask again.' Jonathan tried a brave smile and failed. He shuffled away from the window to the centre of the room.

They stood for a few minutes, side by side, neither speaking. Caffery tried to let his mind empty. He let the sounds and smells and colours come into his head. He waited for things to do something – to send a message like a banner shooting into his consciousness. Nothing happened. 'Well?' he said eventually. 'Has he changed anything?'

'I don't think so.'

'Where do you think the camera was when he took that photo?' Caffery pulled out Rose's mobile, looked at Moon lying on the bed and turned it at arm's length until he got the right angle. 'He must have had it on a tripod: it's taken from high up.'

'Maybe he put it above the door. Rested it on the frame?'

Caffery took a step nearer the door. 'What are those in the wall? Screws?'

'I think there was a clock up there years ago. I can't remember, to be honest.'

'Maybe he put a bracket in the wall.' Caffery got a chair from under Martha's desk, pushed it against the door and stood on it. 'To hold the camera.' He put on his glasses and peered closely at the screws. One was silver, poking out about half a centimetre, but the second wasn't a screw: it was a hole. He dug his finger into it and something inside moved. Swearing under his breath, he fished in his pocket for his penknife, pinched out the tweezer tool with his nails and, very carefully, pulled out the object.

He got off the chair, and came to Jonathan with his index finger held up. On top of it rested a tiny black disc, the size of a penny, faint shapes of electrical circuitry embedded in it. On one side was the silvery slip of a lens. It probably weighed less than twenty grams.

'What's *that*?'

Caffery shook his head. Still computing. And then, in a second, it came to him. 'Fuck.' He got up on the chair and shoved the thing back into the hole. He got down and led Jonathan out of the room.

'What?' Jonathan was staring at him, bewildered.

Caffery put a finger to his lips. He was scrolling through numbers in his phone. The hairs were standing up on the back of his neck.

'What *is* it?'

'Ssh!' He dialled the number, held it to his ear, listened to it ring.

Jonathan looked at Martha's door, then back at Caffery. He put his face close to Caffery's and hissed, 'Tell me, for heaven's sake.'

'Camera,' Caffery mouthed. 'That thing's a camera.'

'Which means what?'

'Which means Ted Moon is watching us.'

56

The noise of the hatch opening had shocked Flea so much that it had taken her almost half an hour to get up the courage to move any further. She was paralysed, picturing the sound reverberating around the tunnel ahead, seeing it like waves of black water pulsing up the air shaft and announcing her presence. When at last nothing had happened, and she was sure the jacker wasn't there, she got her shoulder into the gap and braced herself against the bulkhead, dragging the hatch wide with a long glooping sound. A long, cool draught of daylight and air rushed around her, making her hold her breath – pressing down the crazy fear floating up inside her.

In front of her the forward section of the hull was empty. It was raised slightly by the pressure of the rocks on top of the barge, a low shelf or bench was visible above the water. An iron box was welded to the underside of the deck – an old rope locker to keep the rope dry – and there were two holes where a mooring line should have run. Sunlight came from these, the beams crisscrossing the cavity like the laser sightings of two guns. The hundred-year-old evidence of coal was here too – the inside of the hull was lined with black crystals that would chip off if knocked. She raised her eyes. Above her, another hatch was outlined in light.

She eyed it silently, and thought, achingly, of the space and light on the other side. If it could be opened she could crawl out. With her climbing equipment she could be up the air shaft in less than half an hour. It might all be so straightforward. If she was on her own down here.

She lifted her arm out of the water and forced herself to concentrate on the watch hand going round. No sound from the canal ahead. Just the steady drip, drip, of water coming from the saplings and weeds in the air shaft. When ten minutes had elapsed and her teeth were chattering, she began to get some confidence flowing. She turned and crawled silently on her knees to collect her rucksack. The water around her made no noise, just bobbed and wallowed. The dead rat bumped lazily into the hull and started a slow, meandering pirouette.

Rucksack lifted in front of her above the water, she came quietly back through the doorway and into the warmer water of the forward compartment. Three more paces on her knees, and she was able to brace a hand against the hull and push herself to her feet. She continued, bent over, until she was in the very tip of the bows and could stand up, her head brushing the rusty, cobwebby underside of the deck. She waited for a while, with the surface of the water at her waist, the light from the holes bathing her face, her breathing bouncing back at her in the enclosure.

There was a hook in the underside of the deck to which she attached the rucksack so it stayed dry. She fumbled out the mobile, unwrapped it from the plastic she'd protected it with, switched it on and checked the signal. Nothing. The mast icon was crossed out. Keeping her breathing very slow, her mouth open to reduce the noise, she inched herself to one of the holes in the hull. At first she stayed shy of it, just kept her ear near to it, letting her imagination crawl out into the echoey tunnel, searching the sound patterns for any hint that she wasn't alone. Then, still breathing carefully, she put her face to the hole and peered out.

About five yards away the bag on the hook hung solid and shadowed. Now she could see it properly, she saw there was no moss or debris on it. It had been used recently. She hadn't had time to notice that last night. By pressing her body flat against the hull and wedging her cheek hard into the hole, she could see another section of the tunnel. Could see the pale dab of light. The child's shoe. The electrostatic prickle she'd felt earlier was stronger here than it had ever been. She was close. Martha had been down here. No doubt about it. This may have been the place she'd been raped. The place she was killed, even.

Flea pushed the mobile through the hole in the hull. Held it at arm's length as far out into the tunnel as she could. Tilted it to face her.

No signal. So – she licked her lips and glance upwards – it was the hatch.

She switched off the mobile, returned it in its plastic to the rucksack and put her hands on the underside of the deck. The hatch opened from above. Not as easy as the last one. It was rusted too. She got the chisel out of the rucksack and used the handle to thump the hatch. A few flakes of rust and coal dust came down, but the hatch didn't move or rattle. She fished her Swiss Army knife out of the immersion suit and began to chip at the rust around the join. It was harder and more encrusted than it had been on the bulkhead hatch. She had to bend her knees, pull part of the dry suit down and wedge it into the knife to stop the blade folding itself up. At the tough bits she had to bring the knife down from over her head as if she was using a mallet, catch-ing the deck at a glancing angle.

When the joints were clear she gave the hatch three more blows with the chisel handle. Still nothing happened. There was no rust left so it should be ready to give. She unfolded the knife again, gave it another go round, her left hand placed over the right to give it more force. But the knife wasn't man enough for the job and on the sixth thump it snapped, deflecting her hand, which plunged down and landed on her thigh. The broken blade penetrated the immersion suit and sank deep into her flesh.

She jerked her leg up, her back arcing with the pain. The steel blade was buried in the muscle, just the little enamel handle visible, sticking out of the blue neoprene. Forgetting her first-aid training, she pulled it out instantly, letting it clatter away in the muck. She dropped on to the shelf and unzipped the suit, swung her feet in their heavy boots on to it and lifted her backside so she could peel the legs down. The skin on her thighs was white and mottled, like a freezer chicken's, the hairs standing up individually, stiff and stark. There was a dull blue area where the knife had sunk in. She put her thumbs on either side of the patch and peered at it. As she did so a thin crescent of red appeared. It thickened then, all at once, bloated up and the blood broke over the surface. It ran down her raised thigh in two rivulets and soaked into her underwear.

She clamped her hands over the wound, biting her lip. It wasn't the femoral artery. If it had been it'd be shooting blood into the air, hitting the hull sides. Still, any bleed she couldn't afford. Not down here in this cold. She ripped off her T-shirt and pressed it to the wound, tied the fabric using a clove hitch knot at the back of her thigh. Then she put the leg straight on the bench, rested her hands in her groin, and leaned as much pressure on it as possible.

She sat there for a long time, like a ballet dancer doing a warm-up exercise, pushing back against the pain, pushing her mind into pictures of getting out.

A noise came from the air shaft. The screech of metal on rock. She raised her head. Another noise – this time she knew she wasn't imagining it. A pebble or something hard had just bounced down the shaft and landed with a plink in the water. And then more: stones, some leaves and a branch.

It wasn't someone throwing things down. It was someone climbing down.

57

'You're wrong. He's not watching you. You can relax.'

Caffery was in the kitchen with the guy from the high-tech unit at Portishead, a tall, sculpted, ginger-haired guy who didn't look as if he worked for the police. He wore a skinny tie, a weird sixties suit with narrow lapels, and the bag he carried was fake crocodile skin. He'd turned up in some vintage Volvo number, like an extra from a Sean Connery flick. But he seemed to know his stuff. He made Caffery remove the camera from the slot in the wall and rest it on a piece of card on the kitchen table. Then the two men stood together, peering down at it.

'I promise you he's not watching.'

'But the gubbins on the back. That's a radio transmitter, isn't it?'

'Uh-huh. He's probably got it linked to a high-speed USB receiver so he can record directly to the hard drive. I dunno, maybe his plan was to be sitting somewhere out there in a car just watching the whole thing on his laptop, but he's not there now.'

'You sure?'

The guy smiled. Calm. 'One hundred and twenty per cent. We scanned it. Anyway, this little thing's nothing impressive. Very low end, off the shelf, cheap as chips. The stuff the security services use is about a hundred times more powerful – uses microwaves – but this? He'd have to be somewhere on the estate to pick it up and the units have run the whole diameter. There's no one out there. Sorry. I have to admit I was excited for a bit.

Actually thought we might find the bastard sitting in his car tapping away on the keys of a nice little Sony.'

Caffery looked him up and down. The high-tech unit had already traced the phone number Moon had sent the the photo from. It was a pay-as-you-go, purchased in a Tesco somewhere in the south of England at least two years ago. Switched off, but they'd already been able to say where the text was sent from. Near junction sixteen of the M4. Halfway between anywhere and anywhere. Then the unit had sent this red-haired character to the vicarage. There were winklepickers on his feet and his black-framed glasses were out of *Alfie*. Caffery studied the shoes. Then his face. 'What do we call you, then? Q?'

The guy laughed. An unamused, nasal sound. 'Never heard that one before. Never, ever, ever. It's true what they say about MCIU – you guys really are a stitch. A laugh a minute.' He unzipped the bag and produced a small box with a circular red LED display. 'No, I'm just an anorak. Two years in high-tech and before that two years in the technical support unit at Serious Crime – you know, SOCAT, who've got the covert-surveillance boys?'

'Doing things we don't admit to the Crown Prosecution Service?'

'Hey-hey.' He touched the knot of his tie. He had freckles across his nose. Pale eyes. Like an albino. 'See, I know that's a joke. I can tell by the cute way your eyes crease.'

Caffery bent to peer again at the camera. 'Where would some-one pick up a bit of kit like this?'

'That? Anywhere. A few hundred quid, probably less. Off the Internet. They'd ship it, no questions asked.' He smiled, revealing very small, evenly set teeth. 'Nothing illegal about having an enquiring mind.'

'What I'd like to know is why he wants to get a view of an empty bedroom. He knows they're not here any more.'

'Sorry, mate. I'm from the gadgetry department. Psychology's second door on the right.' He straightened, ran his hands down his tie and glanced around the kitchen. 'But there's another one – in here. If that's of any interest.'

Caffery stared at him. '*What?*'

'Yes. There's one in here too. Can you see it?'

Caffery scanned the walls, the ceiling. He couldn't see anything.

'It's all right. You won't be able to. Look at this.' He held out what looked like a small hand torch. A little circle of red diodes danced across the top of it. 'I had my own budget at SOCAT, never had to go through Procurement. Believe me, I didn't waste a penny. Everything I bought has made its money back in saved time and man hours. This is the Spyfinder.'

'You really are out of a Bond movie.'

'You know what? I've got an idea. How about we *abandon* that source of amusement – just for the time being.' He held the unit at an angle for Caffery to look at. 'That *Close Encounters* dance? That's light reflecting off a camera optic.'

'Where?' Caffery's eyes ran over the walls, the fridge, the cooker. The row of Martha's birthday cards on the windowsill.

'Concentrate.'

He followed the direction Q's attention was locked on.

'Inside the clock?'

'I think so. Inside the number six.'

'Fuck fuck fuck.' Caffery went to stand in front of the clock, hands at his sides. He could see a glint in there but it was wasting. Tiny. He turned back to the kitchen: the old veneer cupboards, the frayed curtains. The carton of cream Jonathan had poured on the apple pie still sitting there, going rancid. And the pile of newspapers, the smell of vomit. Why the hell would Moon want to watch this empty kitchen? What would he be getting out of it? 'How long would it have taken to put them in?'

'Depends on how good he is with the technology. And he'd have to have gone outside to check they were working, that he was picking them up on his receiver.'

'He'd have been coming and going? In and out?'

'To get it right. Yes.'

Caffery sucked air through his teeth. 'A surveillance team is one of the biggest expenses the force can carry. Makes me wonder why we bother.'

'I think I know.'

The two men turned. Jonathan was standing in the doorway. He was holding Philippa's laptop in both hands. He wore an odd expression. His head was on one side, as if he was listening for the first knockings of madness.

'Jonathan. You're supposed to be in the car.'

'I was. I'm not there now. Moon put the cameras in to look at Martha. He put them in before he took her. They've been here for more than a month. That's why the surveillance team didn't see anything.'

Caffery cleared his throat. He glanced at the techie, then beckoned to Jonathan.

'Put it down.' He moved things off the table. 'Here.'

Jonathan came stiffly into the kitchen, put the laptop on the cleared space and flipped it open. The computer paused for a moment, then came to life. The photo of Moon in the Santa mask, lying on the bed, came up on the screen. It had been zoomed in so that only part of the wall and part of his shoulder were in the frame. 'That.' Jonathan tapped the screen. 'See it?'

Caffery and Q gathered round. 'What are we looking at?'

'That picture. That drawing.'

Pinned to the wall above the bed was a felt-tipped picture – a young girl's image of a mythic land. Martha had drawn clouds and hearts and stars and a mermaid in the top corner. She'd drawn herself standing to one side, holding the reins of a white pony. Near her, dislocated as if floating in space, were two dogs

'Sophie and Myrtle.'

'What about them?'

'No necklace. No flowers.'

'Eh?'

'Philippa's birthday is on November the first. Martha dressed Sophie up for the day. And when it was over she came up here and drew flowers and necklaces on Sophie in the picture. Rose remembers her doing it. So does Philippa. But look. No roses, no necklaces in this picture.'

Caffery straightened. Hot and cold needles pricked along his back. Everything he'd thought he was certain of was wrong. Wrong, completely wrong, and built on foundations of sand. The whole case had just turned upside-down.

58

The kitbag clunked fitfully against the dripping canal wall, the sound echoing off the barge. In the bows Flea breathed shallowly, shaking uncontrollably. She peeled the T-shirt off her leg. It came slowly, parts of it sticking to the already drying blood. The wound had settled to a crusty red line. She gave it an experimental squeeze. It held. Quickly she unstuck the T-shirt and pulled it over her head, feeling the dried blood crack and flake. She peeled her immersion suit back up, zipped it carefully and slipped silently off the bench to crouch in the water at a place where she could see out of the hole.

The rope swayed and circled, casting long, ugly shadows. She dropped deeper into the water and began stealthily to move her hand through the muck. She was used to searching silt and water using touch alone – it was her profession: her fingers were trained for it even in the thick gloves. She found the broken Swiss Army knife quickly, wiped it on her T-shirt and opened it to the flathead screwdriver. She waded silently to the hole and stood with her back to the hull, her head tilted so she could see all the way up into the shaft.

Someone was on the grille. A man. She could see him from behind, his feet in brown hiking boots. Brown cargo trousers tucked inside. A black bumbag around his waist. He was gripping the plants that sprouted from the walls of the shaft to steady himself as he took a couple of steps nearer the edge of the grille and peered down into the tunnel. His back was to her, she couldn't see his face, but from his posture he seemed dubious, as if he really wasn't sure he was doing the right thing. After a moment or two pondering he sank to a sitting position and shuffled his feet to the edge of the grille. Gravity took over and he began to slide. He grabbed the chain and slowed his descent, so he could lower himself into the dirty water below.

He stood in the shadows, both arms out defensively, looking carefully around. Then he bent at the waist, straining to see into the darker recesses of the cavern. His head and shoulders came momentarily into the light and Flea let all the air out of her lungs at once. It was Prody.

'*Paul!*' She pushed her face into the hole, her breathing loud and shaky. '*Paul* – I'm here.'

He jerked in the direction of her voice, his hands flying up defensively. He took a step back and peered at the barge as if he couldn't quite believe what he'd heard.

'*Here*. In the boat.' She pushed her fingers through the hole and wiggled them. 'Here.'

'Shit. *Flea?*'

'Here!'

'Christ.' He waded towards her, his boots and trousers getting soaked in the muck. 'Jesus, Jesus.' He stopped a foot away, blinking stupidly at her. 'Jesus, look at you.'

'Oh, fuck.' She gave a shiver. A body-length shiver like a dog coming out of water. 'I really thought I was stuck here. I thought you hadn't got my message.'

'Message? I didn't. I lost my phone. I saw your car in the village and put it together with the way you . . .' He shook his head. '*Christ*, Flea. Everyone's shitting bricks over what's happened to you. Inspector Caffery – everyone. And . . .' He looked up and down the barge as if he still couldn't quite believe she'd been stupid enough to get down here. 'What the hell are you doing in there? How the fuck did you get *in?*'

'From the stern. The barge goes back under the rockfall. I came through the tunnel on the other side. I can't get out.'

'Through the *tunnel?* Then, how come . . .' Something seemed to occur to him. He turned slowly and looked back at the air shaft. 'You didn't drop that rope down the shaft?'

'Paul, listen,' she hissed. '*This is it*. This is where he brought her. He carried her across the fields. That's *his* climbing kit, not mine.'

Prody pressed his back up to the barge as if he expected the jacker to come up behind him. He took a deep breath and let it out with a loud *hoah*. 'Right. OK. Fair enough.' He fumbled in the little traveller's bumbag and pulled out a pen torch. '*OK.*' He clicked it on and held it out in front of him as if it was a weapon. His breathing was fast.

'It's OK. He's not here now.'

Prody swept the light around the darkest corners. 'You sure? You haven't heard anything?'

'I'm sure. But look – over there in the water. The shoe. See it?'

Prody turned the torch on to it. He was silent for a long time, just the sound of his breathing coming through the hole. Then he pushed himself away and waded back through the water, stopping next to the shoe. He bent to study it. She couldn't see his face but he was still for a long time. Then he straightened abruptly. Stayed for a moment, angled a little bit back at the waist, a fist planted on his chest as if he had indigestion.

'*What?*' she whispered. 'What is it?'

He pulled a phone out of his pocket and jabbed the keyboard with his thumb. His face was ashen in the pale-blue glow of its screen. He shook the phone. Tilted it. Held it in the air. Waded to a point directly under the shaft and held the mobile aloft, squinting at the screen, hitting the call button with his thumb over and over. After a few minutes he gave up. He put the phone in his pocket and came back to the barge. 'What network are you?'

'Orange. You?'

'Shit. Orange too. Pay-as-you-go at the moment.' He took a step back, looked up and down the length of the barge. 'We need to get you out of here.'

'Hatch on the deck. I've tried, can't budge it. Paul? What's with the shoe?'

He put both hands on the gunwales and levered himself up, supporting himself on trembling arms, his body dangling against the hull. After a moment or two he let himself slither back into the water.

'What's with the shoe, Paul?'

'Nothing.'

'I'm not stupid.'

'Let's concentrate on getting you out. You're not coming through the hatch. There's a sodding great windlass on top of the deck.'

He walked along the side of the barge, his hand on the hull, stopping at places to examine it. She heard him hammer on it further down near the rockfall. When he came back there was a light sheen of sweat on his forehead. He was wet and muddy and, suddenly, looked terrible.

'Listen.' He didn't meet her eyes. 'Here's what we do.' He bit his lip and peered at the shaft. 'I'm going to climb back up, get a signal.'

'Was there one in the shaft?'

'I . . . Yes. I mean, I think so.'

'You don't know for sure?'

'I didn't check,' he admitted. 'If there's not one in the shaft there will be at the top.'

'Yeah.' She nodded. 'Course there will.'

'Hey.' He bent at the waist so his face was level with the hole and he could hold her eyes. 'You can trust me on this. I'm not going to leave you alone. He won't be back – he *knows* we've been searching the tunnel and he'd be crazy to come here. I'm only going to be at the top.'

'What if you have to leave the entrance to get a signal?'

'Then it won't be far.' He paused. Stared at her. 'You look pale.'

'Yeah.' She hunched her shoulders and gave an exaggerated shiver. 'I'm . . . you know. It's fucking freezing. That's all.'

'Here.' He rummaged in the bumbag. Pulled out a squashed sandwich in cellophane and a half-full bottle of Evian. 'My lunch. Sorry – bit manky.'

She pushed her hand through the hole and took the sandwich. The bottle of water. Tucked them in the rucksack hanging under the deck. 'No whisky in there, I s'pose?'

'Just eat it.'

He was halfway across the canal when something stopped him. He looked back to her. There was a pause. Then, without a word, he waded back and put his hand through the hole. She looked at it for a moment – his warm white fingers against the blackened inside of the hull – then lifted her own hand and rested it in his. Neither said anything. Then Prody pulled his hand away and waded back to the chain. He paused for a moment, to scan the tunnel one last time – the nameless bumps and mounds in the water – then hauled the rope away from the wall and began to climb.

59

Janice Costello had a sister who lived out near Chippenham and Caffery headed over there in the afternoon. The village was sleepy, with hanging baskets outside the cottages, a pub, a post office and a plaque that read: *Best Kept Wiltshire Village 2004*. When he got to the house – a stone-built cottage, with a thatched roof and mullioned windows – it was Nick who appeared in the low doorway. She was wearing a soft mauve dress, her high-heeled boots replaced with turquoise Chinese slippers she must have borrowed. She kept putting her fingers to her lips to get him to keep his voice down. Janice's mum and sister were upstairs in the bedroom and Cory had taken off, no one was quite sure where.

'And Janice?'

Nick made a face. 'You'd better come to the back.' She took him through the low-ceilinged cottage, past an inviting fire dancing in the grate, two Labradors asleep in front of it, and out into the cold of the back terrace. Here the back lawns sloped away to where a low hedge met the great oolite plain at the south of the Cotswolds, its furrowed fields lay frosty, the skies lead grey.

'She hasn't spoken to anyone since she left the hospital.' Nick pointed to a figure sitting on a bench at the bottom of a small rose garden, her back to the cottage, a duvet wrapped around her shoulders. Her dark hair had been pushed back off her face. She was staring out across the fields to where the autumn trees touched the sky. 'Not even her mother.'

Caffery buttoned up his coat, shoved his hands into his pockets and made his way down the narrow, yew-lined path to the lawn at the end. When he came and stood in front of Janice she raised her eyes to his and gazed at him, trembling. Her skin was naked of makeup, her nose and chin red. Her hands clutching the duvet at her neck were grey with cold. Emily's toy rabbit was on her lap.

'What?' she said. 'What is it? Have you found her? Please say it, whatever it is – just *say* it.'

'We don't know anything – we still don't know anything. I'm sorry.'

'Jesus.' She sank back on the bench, her hand on her forehead. 'Jesus, Jesus. I can't bear this. I just can't bear it.'

'The moment we hear something you'll be the first to know.'

'Bad or good? Do you promise me I'll be the first, bad or good?'

'Bad or good. I promise. Can I sit down? I need to talk to you. We can get Nick to sit in if you'd rather.'

'Why? She can't change anything, can she? No one can change it. Can they?'

'Not really.'

He sat on the bench next to her, legs pushed out and crossed at the ankles, arms folded. His shoulders he kept hunched against the cold. On the ground at Janice's feet was an untouched mug of tea and a hardback copy of *À la recherche du temps perdu* in a library's plastic dust jacket. 'Isn't that the difficult one?' he said after a while. 'Proust?'

'My sister found it. It was in some Sunday paper's top-ten list of things to read in a crisis. It's either that or Kahlil Gibran.'

'And I bet you can't read a word of either of them.'

She bent her face and touched the end of her nose. Stayed like that for what seemed almost a minute, concentrating. 'Of course I can't.' She took her hand away and shook it, as if it was polluted. 'I'm sort of waiting for the screaming in my head to stop first.'

'The medical staff are going crazy. You shouldn't have

discharged yourself like that. You look OK, though. Better than I expected.'

'No, I don't. That's a lie.'

He shrugged. 'I've got to apologize, Janice. You've been let down.'

'Yes, I have. I've let me down. Emily's been let down.'

'On the force's behalf I apologize for Mr Prody. He should have done better than he did. And he shouldn't have been there in the first place. His behaviour was entirely inappropriate.'

'No.' She gave a pained, ironic smile. 'There was nothing inappropriate about Paul's behaviour. What is inappropriate is the way you've handled this. And that my husband is having an affair with Paul's wife. That's what's *inappropriate*. Really totally bloody inappropriate.'

'I beg your—'

'Yes.' She gave a sudden hard laugh. 'Oh – didn't you know? My wonderful husband is fucking Clare Prody.'

Caffery turned away, looked at the sky. He wanted to swear. 'That's . . .' he cleared his throat '. . . *difficult*. For all of us – that's difficult.'

'Difficult for you? Try the fact that my daughter is missing. Try the fact that since she went my husband hasn't even fucking spoken to me. That,' she held a finger out at him, tears in her eyes, 'is what's fucking difficult. That my husband hasn't spoken to me. Or even said Emily's name. He's forgotten how to say her *name*.' She dropped her hand and sat for a minute looking at her lap. Then she lifted the rabbit and pressed it against her forehead. Tight. As if the pressure would stop her crying.

The hospital registrar had said it was odd her mouth and throat were free of the blisters they'd have expected from gas. They still hadn't worked out what substance Moon had used to subdue them. Rags soaked in turpentine had been left in some of the rooms. They were what had been filling the flat with fumes, not chloroform. But turps hadn't knocked everyone out.

'I'm sorry.' She wiped her eyes. 'Sorry – I don't mean to . . . It's not your fault.' She put the rabbit to her nose, breathed in the smell. Then she opened the neck of her sweater and pushed it inside, as if it was a living creature that needed body warmth. She kept her hand in her sweater and worked the toy around, until it was sitting in her armpit. Caffery let his eyes travel across the garden. Coppery leaves had been swept into a pile in the corner where the low picket fence met the farmland. A spider's web shivered lightly in the slight breeze that came up, smelling of manure from the fields. Caffery watched the web, trying to picture the way it would be frosted and dewed in the morning. He thought of the skull in the sheet. Of the fuzzy yellow-brown matter staining the cloth.

'Janice, I've tried speaking to Cory. He's not taking my calls either. Someone needs to answer some questions. Will you do it for me?'

Janice sighed. She pulled her hair back and looped it in a knot at the nape of her neck, then ran her hands down her face, smoothing the skin. 'Go on.'

'Your house has never been broken into, Janice?' He pulled his pocket book out of his jacket, clicked a biro on his knee and wrote the date and time there. The book was only a prop. He wouldn't fill it in now – only later. Having it there just helped him focus. 'In your house? No burglaries?'

'I'm sorry?'

'I said, you've never had any burglaries in your house, have you?'

'No.' She stared at the pocket book. 'Why?'

'You've got an alarm system, haven't you?'

'Yes.'

'And it was on when you left that day to go to your mother's?'

'It's always on. Why?'

Her eyes were still on the book. Suddenly he understood why, and immediately felt like a prize dick. The book made him seem inexperienced, like a probationer. He closed it and put it back in his pocket. 'Your sister says you had some work done on the house, that you didn't have the alarm system until then.'

'That was months ago.'

'You stayed here with your sister for a lot of the time, didn't you, when the house was being worked on? Left the place empty?'

'Yes.' Janice's eyes were still on the pocket where the book had gone. 'But what's that got to do with anything?'

'Detective Prody showed you a picture of Ted Moon, didn't he?'

'I didn't recognize him. Neither did Cory.'

'You're sure he wasn't one of the people who came in? Worked on the house?'

'I didn't see all of them. There'd be people in and out – sub-contractors, that sort of thing. We sacked one lot of builders, brought in another. I lost track of all the faces – all the cups of tea I made. But I'm sure – almost sure – I never saw him.'

'I'd like, if possible, when Cory turns up, to get the details of all those workmen. The names of the builders you sacked. I'd like to be speaking to them as soon as possible. Have you got it all in a file at home? All the details? Or can you remember them?'

She sat for a few moments with her mouth half open, staring at Caffery. Then she let the air out of her lungs, dropped her head and rapped her forehead with her knuckles. One-two-three. One-two-three. One-two-three. Hard: making the skin redden. As if she wanted to knock some thoughts out of her head. If it had gone on any longer he'd have grabbed her hand. But the rapping stopped as abruptly as it had started. She composed herself – eyes closed now, hands folded primly on her lap. 'I know what you're telling me. You're telling me that he'd been watching Emily.' She kept her eyes closed and spoke rapidly, as if she had to concentrate on getting every word out before she forgot it. 'That he'd . . . *stalked* her? That he was in our *house*?'

'We found some cameras in the Bradleys' house today. So we went back to Mere – looked at your place. And we found the same thing.'

'*Cameras?*'

'I'm sorry. Ted Moon was able to install a CCTV system in your house without you knowing.'

'There weren't any *cameras* in my house.'

'There were. You'd never have seen them – but they were there.

They were put there long before all this started, because there's no sign of a break-in since you left.'

'You mean he put them there when we were here, staying with my sister?'

'Probably.'

'So he was *watching* her? He was watching Emily?'

'Probably.'

'Oh, Christ. Oh, Christ.' She put her face into her hands. 'I can't bear this. I can't bear it. I just can't do it.'

Caffery turned away and sat there, pretending to focus on the horizon. He was still thinking about all the assumptions he'd made, and the avenues he'd ignored. About how stupid he'd been not to see it all before. He should have known, when Moon came back for Emily and didn't just drop it, that he'd chosen her a long time before the kidnap. That she wasn't a random hit. But most of all Caffery was thinking that of the times he was grateful to be alone, childless and loveless, this was one of them. It really was true what they said: the more you have, the more you have to lose.

60

Flea wasn't hungry but she needed the fuel. She sat on the ledge in the hull, her legs in the sludge, and listlessly chewed the sandwich Prody had left her. She was shivering, her whole body convulsing. The meat in it was greasy and heavy-tasting, with tiny bits of cartilage and other gristle. She had to follow each mouthful with a gulp of water to wash it down her sore throat.

Prody was dead. No doubt in her mind. At first she'd watched the rope moving back and forward, leaving a scar in the moss and slime on the wall. That had gone on for fifteen minutes. It had stopped when he'd got to the top of the forty-foot shaft. 'Going for a walk,' he'd yelled down at her. His voice echoed and bounced around the tunnel. 'No signal.'

Of course there's not, she thought bitterly. Of course not. But she'd wet her lips and yelled, 'OK. Good luck.'

And that had been that.

Something had happened to him on the surface. She knew what the top of the air shaft was like. Years ago, on the training exercise, she'd been there. She recalled woods, bridle-paths, grassy glades and yard after yard of impenetrable undergrowth. He'd have been tired. Would probably have sat down at the top of the shaft to recover after the climb. Easy pickings for Martha's kidnapper. And now the day was on the wane. The great circle of daylight powering down from the shaft had moved slowly across the canal, throwing down the shadows of plants. It had thinned to an irregular sliver on the moss-covered wall, like a smiling mouth. All the shadows in the tunnel were starting to run into another so when she looked through the hole she couldn't see the corners of the tunnel any more. Could hardly see Martha's shoe.

Prody had reacted badly to the shoe. He'd been in Traffic, first on the scene to all the unimaginable accidents. He was supposed to be unflappable, but something about the shoe had shocked even him.

She lifted her arm and studied her hand. Her fingers were patched purple and white – one of the early symptoms of hypothermia. The body-racking shivering wouldn't last. That would go as she sank nearer to death. She balled up the cellophane, pushed it inside the bottle. There was hardly any light left. If she was going to get out of here she had to do it now. She'd spent an hour sculling around the sludge and had already found an old acrow – an iron pit prop – lying in the sump hole. It was covered with slime but not too rusted and she'd lodged its top plate under the hatch. She'd found a sturdy six-inch nail that she could wedge into the acrow-winding mechanism and for the last two hours she had been laboriously tightening it, pushing the prop up into the hatch. She planned to dislodge the windlass. And then what? Crawl to the surface and be picked off like a First World War soldier going over the top? Better than dying from cold down here.

Hey? You know how to make God laugh? Tell him your plans.

She got to her feet, legs creaking and aching. Wearily she put the bottle into the net pocket of the rucksack, then reached for the nail to start winding the acrow. It was gone.

It had been on the ledge – right here next to her. She moved her hands frantically, skimming over the rivets and the slime. Half an hour it had taken to find that nail, feeling around in the muck at the bottom of the barge sump. She fumbled for the head torch in the rucksack, pulled it out and the nail came with it. Fell, *plink-plink*, on to the ledge.

She froze. Stared at the nail. It had been in the rucksack. But she'd left it on the ledge. She remembered making a careful decision to put it on there. Or did she really remember that?

She put her hand to her head, momentarily dizzy. She did remember putting it on the ledge, she was sure. It meant her memory was slipping. Another symptom of hypothermia shutting her system down.

She picked up the nail in numb fingers. It wasn't quite thick enough for the hole in the acrow and she pushed it easily into the mechanism. There were tender gullies in her palms where the nail had dug in earlier, even through the gloves, and now she lined it up with those channels, ignoring the pain, and leaned all her weight on the nail. It didn't move. With a grunt she did it again. And again. It didn't move. Fucking thing. She rammed at it again. Still nothing. And again.

'Shit.'

She sat on the ledge. Sweat prickled under her arms in spite of the cold. The last time the nail had moved was more than an hour ago. And then it had been less than half a centimetre. A sign like that was telling her to give up.

But she had no other choice.

The right ankle cuff on her immersion suit felt wrong. She submerged her hand in the water and touched the ankle carefully. The cuff itself was OK but, above it, the neoprene bulged tight as if water was trapped in there. She used her hands to lift her leg out of the muck, rest it on the ledge. She strapped on the head lamp and she leaned over to study the suit. Above the ankle it ballooned out. When she moved her leg she could feel fluid sloshing around. Gingerly she slid a finger under the cuff and pulled it. Something like water gushed out. Warm. Red in the torch beam.

Fuck. She leaned her head against the bulkhead, took deep, slow breaths to stop the giddiness. The wound in her thigh had opened and that was one hell of a lot of blood to lose. If she'd seen someone else lose that much she'd be getting them to hospital. And fast.

This wasn't good. Not good at all.

61

Damien Graham wasn't doing himself any favours when it came to cracking people's prejudice. When Caffery arrived at his tiny terraced house, just past six in the evening, he was standing in the open doorway surveying the street and smoking, of all things, a cigarillo. He was wearing wraparound Diesel shades and a long camel pimp coat draped around his shoulders. All that was missing was the purple-velvet fedora. Part of Caffery couldn't help feeling a trace of pity for the guy.

As he came up the path Damien took the cigarillo out of his mouth, nodded an acknowledgement. 'Mind if I smoke?'

''S long as you don't mind if I eat.'

'Nah – you're safe, man, safe.'

This morning, catching a shave in the mirror at MCIU, Caffery'd thought he'd looked haggard. Along with his other notes he'd made an internal memo to eat something. Now he had a passenger seat full of service-station sandwiches and chocolate bars – Mars, Snickers, Dime. Typical man's solution to the problem. He'd have to remember to sweep them somewhere safe before Myrtle next got into the car. He pulled out a Caramac and peeled it, snapped off two sections and put them into the corner of his mouth to melt. He and Damien stood with their backs to the house and looked blankly at the vehicles in the street. The CSI van. Q's insane retro Vauxhall.

'You gonna tell me what's going on?' said Damien. 'They're in there taking the place apart. Saying there's some kind of camera system in my house.'

'That's right.' Damien wasn't the only one. The Blunts had the same set of paraphernalia in theirs. Turner was over there now, talking to them. In fact, everyone was out in the field. Everyone except Prody. Caffery couldn't reach him on the phone. He'd have liked to know where he was – what he'd found out about Flea. He'd have liked to be sure that was what he was doing – looking for Flea and not nosing around the review team's Kitson file again. 'Damien,' he said, 'these cameras. I don't suppose you have any idea how they came to be there?'

Damien made a noise of contempt through his teeth. 'What're you saying? You think I put them there?'

'No. I think someone got into your house and put them there. But I don't know how they had the opportunity. Do you?'

Damien was silent for a while. Then he flicked the stub of the cigar into the scrappy front lawn. 'Yeah,' he admitted, pulling the coat closer around his shoulders. 'Maybe I do. Been thinking about it.'

'Well?'

'A break-in. Long time ago. Before the car got jacked. Me, I always thought it was something to do with my missus – she had some dodgy friends back in those days. We reported it, but it was weird – nothing got nicked. And now I'm thinking about it I'm starting to . . .you know . . . wonder.'

Caffery put the last of the Caramac into his mouth. He glanced past Damien at the photos on the hallway wall: framed black-and-white studio shots of Alysha, her hair pulled back in a wide Alice band. He felt the sickening disorientation of a case that had turned a slow somersault in a matter of hours. The team was switching its focus: it had stopped studying Ted Moon and was instead studying his victims because Moon was choosing the girls in advance, and that made it a completely different investigation. Worse, everyone had the uneasy sense it wouldn't be long before he did the whole thing again. That there was another family out there with surveillance cameras already in their house.

All MCIU had to do was find out where that family was – and Caffery was sure the key lay in working out why he'd chosen Alysha, Emily, Cleo and Martha.

Damien said, 'What's going on? Feels like I'm being haunted. I don't like it.'

'Don't suppose you do.' Caffery crumpled up the wrapper and stuck it, with hardwired crime-scene instinct, in his pocket. 'What's going on is we've climbed up a few steps. Seen Ted Moon from a different perspective. He's clever. Right? Look at what he's done in your house. He could have abducted Alysha – any of the others – at any time he chose. But he didn't. He staged it. Took the girls in a public place to make it look random. He did that to hide the fact that he already knew your girls.'

'Already knew her?' Damien folded his arms and shook his head. 'No. I don't buy that. I've seen the bastard's photo. I don't know him.'

'Maybe not. But *he* knows Alysha. Somehow. Maybe he met her through friends. Did she used to stay away – at her friends' houses?'

'No. I mean, she was little in those days. Just a little girl. Lorna kept her with us all the time. We haven't got family here, even. Mine are all in London, hers are in Jamaica.'

'No close friends she went out with?'

'Not at that age. I dunno what her mother lets her do now.'

'Any times she was left on her own maybe?'

'No. Really, I mean it. Lorna – for all her scabby ways – was a good mother. And if you want to know more about that time she's the one you need to speak to.'

Caffery wished he *could* speak to her. With all the Interpol searches Turner had initiated, the Jamaican police had come up with nothing. He swallowed the chocolate. His mouth was furred and dry with all the sugar. It made him feel wrong and dis-ordered and added to the maddening sense that something else was lingering on the periphery of his consciousness that he was *still* missing. 'Damien. Can we go upstairs?'

Damien let out a sigh. 'Come on.' He stepped inside and closed the front door. He took off the pimp coat, hung it on a peg in the hall and beckoned to Caffery to follow. Up the stairs he went, ticker-tacker, fast, with his hand on the banister and his toes pointing out, his massive legs too big and strong on the old wood. Caffery followed, more slowly. On the landing they found Q. In a suit that had the glint and gleam of taffeta, he was tinkering with a tiny electronic unit that was resting on the banisters. He didn't look up or acknowledge them as they passed and went along the landing.

The master bedroom at the front of the house was over-decorated. Three walls were painted a truffle brown, with air-brushed canvases of naked women, and the fourth was papered in flock silver and black wallpaper. The bed had a black suede headboard and silver scatter cushions, and there was an off-the-peg wardrobe system with mirrored doors.

'Nice.'

'D'you like it?'

Caffery pulled a Twix out of his pocket and unwrapped it. 'Bachelor room. Not what you had when you were with Lorna, is it? Did you and she sleep here?'

'I changed it when she'd gone. Got rid of some of her shit. But this used to be our room. Why?'

'And before that. This was never Alysha's room?'

'No. She always had the one at the back. Since she was a baby. Do you want to see it? I got nothing in there, just Alysha's stuff. For if she ever comes home.'

Caffery didn't want to see it. He'd already been fed news on which of the rooms Moon had covered with his cameras. Damien didn't know it yet, but there was a unit somewhere in the ceiling above his room. Q was expecting a ladder to arrive so he could get into the loft and strip the damned thing out. It was the same as it was at the Costellos' and the Blunts' and it didn't entirely make sense: the cameras were not in the places Caffery'd antici-pated. He'd have thought Moon would focus on places where the girls would undress. The bedrooms and the bathroom. But apart from Martha Bradley's room there hadn't been one camera in the girls' bedrooms. Instead they'd been in the kitchens, the living rooms, and – most odd of all – in the parents' bedrooms. Like here.

'Damien, thank you for your consideration. Someone'll be in touch. With an expense claim. For the – you know . . . mess.' He pushed the Twix bar into his mouth, wiped his hands and went back on to the landing, past Q, and down the stairs, chewing as he went. At the bottom he glanced up at Alysha's photographs. Three pictures, three outfits, but the poses weren't any different. Hands under her chin. Teeth on display. A little girl trying her best to smile at the camera. He had the front door half open when something about the photos made him pause, stand still and consider them seriously.

Alysha. Nothing like Martha. Nothing like Emily. Alysha was black. Ticking away in the back of Caffery's head was what the literature said – that paedophiles had types. Colourings and age ranges. It came up time and time again. If Moon was going to the trouble of selecting these girls, then why weren't they more similar? All blonde and eleven? All brunette and four? Or all black and six?

Caffery ran his tongue around his mouth, dislodging the chocolate from his teeth. He thought about Martha's tooth in the pie. And then he thought about the letters. Why, he thought, did you send those letters, Ted? Out of nowhere he thought of what Cleo had said – that the jacker had asked about her parents' jobs. And then everything settled on Caffery all at once. He closed the front door and stood shakily in the hallway, his hand on the wall. He understood. He knew why things had felt so wrong for such a long time. And he knew why the jacker had asked Cleo the question. He'd been double-checking he had the right child.

Caffery glanced up at Damien, who was standing at the foot of the stairs lighting a cigarillo from a flat tin. He waited until he'd got it lit, then gave the guy a tight smile. 'Don't suppose you've got a spare one of those knocking around?'

'Yeah, sure. You OK?'

'I will be when I've had a smoke.'

Damien opened the tin and held it out. Caffery took one, lit it, drew in the smoke and paused, giving it time to damp down his pulse.

'Thought you were on your way? Changed your mind? Stopping?'

Caffery took the cigarillo out of his mouth, blew the smoke in a long, delicious stream in front of him. Nodded. 'Uh-huh. Can you put the kettle on? I think I'm going to be here a bit longer.'

'How come?'

'I need to talk to you seriously. I need to ask you about *your* life.'

'My life?'

'That's right. Yours.' Caffery turned his eyes to Damien. He was tasting the low, easy glow of things falling into place. 'Because we were wrong. It was never Alysha he was targeting. He's not interested in what happens to her. Never has been.'

'Then what? What's he interested in?'

'You, mate. He's interested in *you*. It's the parents he wants.'

62

Janice Costello sat at her sister's big wooden table in the huge kitchen at the back of the house. She'd been there most of the afternoon, ever since Nick had helped her in from the freezing garden. Cups of tea had been made, food had been offered, a bottle of brandy had appeared from somewhere. She'd touched none of it. It all looked unreal to her. Like something meant for someone else. As if there as an invisible barrier in the physical world and that everyday things – like plates and spoons and candles and potato-peelers – were meant to be used only by people who were happy. Not by those who felt like her. The day had dragged. At about four o'clock Cory had appeared out of nowhere. He'd come into the room and stood in the doorway. 'Janice,' he'd said simply. 'Janice?' She hadn't answered him. It was too much effort even to look at him and eventually he'd left the room. She didn't wonder where he went. She just sat there, arms wrapped around herself, Jasper the rabbit squashed hard into her armpit.

She was trying to remember the last moment she'd spent with Emily. They'd shared the bed, she knew that much, but she couldn't remember if she'd been lying on her side, spooning Emily, or if she'd been on her back, her arm around her, or even, and this thought stung her more than anything, if on that occasion she'd fallen asleep with her back to Emily. The cold truth was that a bottle of prosecco had been shared and Janice's thoughts had been more with Paul Prody asleep on the pull-out in the living room than on holding Emily, breathing her in as deeply as she could. Now she struggled towards the memory, stretched forward to it, like an exhausted swimmer straining for the shore. Searched and searched for just one scrap of Emily. The smell of her hair, the feel of her breath.

Janice leaned forward and rested her forehead on the table. Emily. A tremor went through her. The overwhelming urge to bang her head against the wood. Skewer herself. Shut her thoughts up. She screwed her eyes tight. Tried to focus on something practical. The parade of workmen who had wandered in and out of the house during the renovations – Emily had loved them: they'd let her climb their ladders, go through their tools and lunch boxes, examine the wrapped sandwiches and packets of crisps. Janice tried to find Moon's face among them, tried to see him standing in the kitchen at the breakfast bar, drinking a cup of tea. Tried and failed.

'Janice love?'

She jerked her head up. Nick was standing in the doorway, holding her red hair up in a coil behind her head, massaging her neck wearily.

'What?' Janice's face was like ice. She couldn't have moved it into an expression if she'd wanted to. 'What is it? Has something happened?'

'Nothing. No news. But I do need to speak to you. DI Caffery's got some questions he wants me to ask.'

Janice put her hands on the table, two lumps of dead meat, and pushed the chair back. Slowly, woodenly, she got to her feet. She must look like a marionette, she thought, walking with her arms slightly outstretched, her feet heavy. She shuffled through into the big formal living room – the fire in the inglenook made up but unlit, the big comfy chairs, all sitting in silence, as if they were waiting, the smell of woodsmoke in the air. She sat lumpenly on her sister's sofa. Somewhere at the other end of the cottage she could hear a television playing. Maybe her sister and her husband were sitting in there, the volume turned up so they could say 'Emily' without Janice hearing. Because then she might scream, might fill the cottage with her screaming, until the windows rattled and broke.

Nick switched on a small table light and sat opposite her. 'Janice,' she began.

'You don't need to, Nick. I know what you're going to say.'

'What?'

'It isn't Emily, is it? It's *us*. It's us he's after, isn't it? Me and Cory. Not Emily. I've worked it out.' She jabbed a finger at her forehead. 'My brain is sweating, Nick, trying to put everything together. I've got all the information the well-meaning but ever so slightly inefficient police will give me. I've put it together, added two to two, and come up with ten. It's *us*. Cory and me. Jonathan Bradley and his wife. The Blunts, the Grahams. The adults. It's what the police think too. Isn't it?'

Nick folded one hand over the other. Her shoulders were sloped, her head drooped. 'You're smart, Janice. Really smart.'

Janice sat quite still, staring hard at the top of Nick's head. At the far end of the cottage someone on the television cheered. A car went past on the lane, its headlights briefly illuminating the lonely furniture. Janice thought of DI Caffery sitting next to her on the bench in the garden earlier. She thought of his notebook with the scribblings in blue biro. It had made her feel sick, that book. A flimsy square of card and paper – the only tool to bring Emily back.

'Nick,' she said after a long time. 'I like you. I like you very much. But I don't trust your force. Not as far as I could throw it.'

Nick raised her face. She was pale and her eyes were hollow with tiredness. 'Janice, I don't know what I'm supposed to say, I don't know what I'm supposed to do. I've never been in this position before. The force? It's an institution just like any other. It's got "public servant" writ large in its manifesto, but I've never confused it with anything other than a business. Except I can't say that, can I? I have to look you in the face and tell you the investigation is being run perfectly. It's the most difficult thing I have to do. Especially when you get to like a family. When that happens it's like lying to friends.'

'Then, listen.' Speaking felt like the most enormous effort to Janice. Exhausting. But she knew where she had to go next. 'There's a way to sort this out, but I don't believe your unit will do it. So I'm going to do it instead. And I'll need your help.'

The corner of Nick's mouth twitched. 'Help,' she said non-committally. 'I see.'

'I need you to find some contact details for me. I want you to do some phoning. Will you? Will you help?'

63

'My son is not a nonce. He's a bad boy, a very bad boy, but he's not a fucking nonce.'

It was nearly midnight. The lights were still on in the MCIU building. Still the clatter of keyboards in distant offices, the noise of phones ringing. Turner and Caffery sat in the meeting room at the end of one of the corridors on the second floor, the blinds drawn, the fluorescent tubes on. Caffery was fiddling with a paperclip. Three cups of coffee sat on the table, and Peter Moon was seated at the other side of the desk on a swivel chair, dressed in a diamond-design jumper and saggy blue sweatpants. He'd agreed to talk on condition they released him from the cell overnight. He didn't want to talk under caution, didn't want a lawyer present, but he'd been thinking about it all night and now he wanted to set the record straight. Caffery let him do it. He didn't plan to let the guy off. He planned to bang him up again the moment he'd coughed.

'Not a nonce.' Caffery looked at him dully. 'Then why have you been covering for him?'

'The cars. His problem is with cars – he's like a little kid with them. He's nicked scores of them. It's like he can't help himself.'

'We found most of them in his lock-up.'

'That's why he got a job here.' Peter looked thin and defeated. Embarrassed. Here was a man whose only legacy to the world was two sons, one of whom would die at home in bed before he was thirty, and the other in prison. An A4 blow-up of Ted was pinned to the whiteboard on the wall. It had been taken from the police-staff pass. Ted stared down into the room with his blank dead eyes, his shoulders hunched slightly forward, his forehead lowered. Peter Moon, Caffery noticed, avoided looking at it. 'He's stolen so many he thought you were on to him. Thought if he worked here he could – I dunno – get into your computers. Change the records or whatever.' He put his hands in the air. 'God knows what ideas he had – that he was some computer genius or something.'

'He went into our system – but to find out what we knew about his stolen cars?' Caffery looked at Turner. 'Does that sound right to you? That he was looking for stolen cars?'

Turner shook his head. 'No, Boss. Doesn't sound right to me. To me it sounds more like he was doing it to find the places we'd housed that family. The one he's targeted. And the traffic-surveillance cameras.'

'Yes – those traffic cameras. Amazing how he avoided them.'

'Amazing,' Turner agreed.

'See, Mr Moon, your son's kidnapped four children now. Two he hasn't given back. He's got good reason to want to stay ahead of us.'

'No, *no, no*. I swear on the heads of all the saints, he's not a nonce. My son is not a nonce.'

'He killed a thirteen-year-old girl.'

'Not for nonce reasons.'

On the desk there was a single sheet covered with Caffery's handwriting – the scribbled notes he'd made of a phone conversation earlier this evening. After the post-mortem on Sharon Macy's remains, Caffery'd had a brief informal call from the pathologist. The man wasn't going to say anything official, that would be in the report later, but he could give him a few things on the QT. Sharon Macy's body was so decomposed that no one could be 100 per cent sure of anything, but if he'd been a betting man he'd say she had been killed either by the blunt-force trauma to the back of the skull or by blood loss from the enormous gash in her throat. There was evidence she'd struggled: one of her fingers was broken on the right hand, but when it came to evidence of sexual assault the pathologist had drawn a blank. The clothing wasn't disturbed and her body hadn't been displayed in a sexual way.

'I know,' Caffery said now. 'I know he's not a nonce.'

Peter Moon blinked. 'You what?'

'I said I know he's not a paedo. The fact he's taken girls? All under the age of thirteen? It's a red herring. Coincidence. They could just as well been boys. Or teenagers. Or babies.'

Caffery shook a set of copied photographs out of an envelope, stood and began very carefully taping them to the whiteboard, one by one, lined up under Ted Moon's picture. Caffery had got one of the DCs to print out little tags with all the relevant information he could think of: name, age, appearance, socioeconomic class, job, background, etc. He stuck the tags beneath the faces. 'You're here because your son has got a list of victims. A whole catalogue of people he's got something against. But it's not the kids he hates, it's the parents. Lorna and Damien Graham. Neil and Simone Blunt. Rose and Jonathan Bradley. Janice and Cory Costello.'

'Who the fuck are they?'

'Your son's victims.'

Peter Moon stared at the pictures for a long time. 'You're honestly saying my boy's supposed to have attacked these people?'

'In a manner of speaking. What he's done with the children he abducted, God knows. I've given up hoping. But I can't see him worrying much about their human rights, because they're incidental. Dispensable. He knows the facts of life: hurt the young and you may as well kill the parents. And *that*'s what he wants. All these people.' Caffery sat down, waved a hand at the photos. 'They're the ones who mean something to your son. *They*'re the ones we're looking at now. Ever heard of victimology?'

'No.'

'You should watch more TV, Mr Moon. Sometimes we investigate crime by studying the people it's happening to. Usually it's to learn who our perpetrator is. In this case we don't need to know *who*'s doing it, we know that already, in this case we need to know why he's choosing the people he is, and we need to do that because he's going to do it again. And soon. Something – *something* – in your son's head is telling him he has to do it again. Look at these faces, Mr Moon. Look at their names. What do they mean to your son? This guy on the left is Neil Blunt. Neil works for the Citizens Advice Bureau. When I was with him this evening he said he knew he'd pissed people off now and then, and he's had a couple of threats from clients at work. Has Ted had any dealings with the CAB?'

'My wife went to the CAB when we had the fire. But that was eleven years ago.'

'What about since he's been out of the slammer?'

'Not that I know of.'

'He works as a handyman. But when we went to check out his references they were all faked. So what experience did he have as a general builder?'

'He's good. Really good. He can turn his hand to any—'

'I didn't ask you how good he is. I asked you what experience he had.'

'None. That I know of.'

'Never did any work over in Mere? All the way down near Wincanton? Gillingham? A nice place. Family house. Name Costello. That's them at the bottom.'

'Costello? It doesn't ring a bell. I swear it doesn't.'

'Look at the man on the left.'

'The black geezer?'

'He works in a car showroom in Cribbs Causeway – BMW. Does that ring any bells? With Ted's fondness for cars?'

'No.'

'His name's Damien Graham.'

Moon stared at the photo, shook his head. He pointed to Jonathan Bradley's face. 'Him.'

'Yes?'

'Vicar bloke.'

'You knew him?'

'No. I seen him in the news.'

'Ted didn't know him?'

'How the hell would Ted know someone like that?'

'Before Mr Bradley was ordained he was a headmaster. At St Dominic's School. Did Ted have any connections in that area?'

'I told you – he's not a paedo. He doesn't hang out at schools.'

'What about Farrington Gurney, Radstock? Why does he feel so at home out there? He knows the roads round there like the back of his hand.'

'Ted wouldn't know Farrington Gurney if it was the last place on earth. Arsehole of the Mendips, innit?'

Caffery turned to Ted Moon's photograph. Looked into his eyes – stared into them, trying to draw something out. 'Look at the pictures again, Mr Moon. Really concentrate. Is there anything? Anything at all? You don't need to feel stupid. Just say it.'

'No. I told you. Nothing. I'm trying to help here.'

Caffery chucked down the paperclip he was fiddling with. He got to his feet. His stomach hurt with all the bloody junk food he'd been shovelling down the hatch. It was the place these cases always got you. In the belly. He went to the window and opened it, stood for a moment with his hands on the frame, feeling the cool air on his face.

'OK. This is where I need you to have an open mind, Mr Moon. Where I've got to ask you to dig deep.' He turned and went to the whiteboard. He uncapped a marker pen and placed it next to Janice Costello's name. He drew a slow line from her face across to Rose Bradley's. 'Look at the women – Simone Blunt, Janice Costello, Lorna Graham, Rose Bradley. Now, I want you to do something difficult. I want you to think about your wife.'

'Sonja?' Moon made a noise in his throat. 'What about her?'

'Is there something about these women that reminds you of her?'

'You're joking, aren't you?' Moon was incredulous now. 'You *are* joking?'

'I'm just asking you to keep an open mind. To help me.'

'I can't help you. None of them looks like her.'

Peter Moon was right, of course. If there had ever been a time Caffery'd clutched at straws this was it. The women couldn't have been more different: Janice Costello was fresh-faced, straight-forwardly nice-looking, Rose Bradley was fifteen years older and two stones heavier – their colouring wasn't even similar. The ultra-groomed Simone looked like a harder-edged blonde version of Janice, it was true, but Lorna Graham, the only one he hadn't met, was black. If he was honest she looked more as if she should be hanging on to the arm of some R&B dude, with her polished nails and hair extensions.

The husbands, then. Something with the husbands? He put the marker pen next to Cory Costello's name. He'd love to know what had happened between Janice Costello and Paul Prody the night Moon had broken in. He probably never would. And maybe it wasn't his business to be pissed off with Prody. But Cory Costello whoo-hooing with Prody's missus? Funny guy, Prody, he thought. Private. To talk to him you wouldn't know he had any family at all. He went back to Cory's face, looked at it again. Into his eyes. Thought – *affairs*. 'Mr Moon?'

'What?'

'Tell me – because it'll never go outside this room, I can guarantee that – did you ever have an affair? When Sonja was alive.'

'Jesus. No. Of course not.'

'Of course not?' Caffery raised an eyebrow. The answer had been there. Right in Peter Moon's mouth. Waiting. 'Are you sure?'

'Yes. I'm sure.'

'You weren't seeing Sharon Macy's mother, were you? Even just casually?'

Peter Moon's mouth opened, closed, then opened again. His face went tight and he moved his head forward on his neck. Like a lizard. Trying to crick a spasm out of his head. 'I don't think I heard you right. What did you say?'

'I said you weren't seeing Sharon Macy's mother? Before Sharon was killed?'

'You know something?' He closed his mouth briefly, as if he was struggling to hold himself together. 'You have no idea – no idea – how much that question makes me want to land one on you.'

Caffery raised an eyebrow. 'I'm just trying to make that link, Mr Moon.' He capped the pen. Threw it on to the desk. 'Still trying to connect the families together. The Macys with these people.'

'The Macys? The shagging *Macys*? None of this has got anything to do with the Macy family. Ted never killed Sharon because of her shagging parents.'

'Yes, he did.'

'No! No, he fucking didn't. He done it because of the *fire*. Because of what she did to Sonja.'

'What *Sharon* did to *your wife*?'

Moon looked from Caffery to Turner and back again. 'You don't fucking know, do you? It was Sharon done it. She was the bloody arsonist, little bitch. Tell me you know that much at least?'

Caffery glanced at Turner, who met his eyes and shook his head slowly. The psychiatric reports from the hospital and the probation officers' reports on Ted Moon's release weren't in the paperwork that had come down. In the suspect interview transcripts Moon had refused to say why he'd killed Sharon Macy. He'd refused to speak even to deny it.

Peter Moon sat back in his seat, arms crossed. Angry that the police were so damned useless. 'The fucking system. Lets you down every time, don't it? If it can't fuck you one way it asks you to turn round and has a good look at you to see if it can fuck you some other way. Did it to us back then. No one even told us Ted had it up here.' He tapped his temple. 'Schizophrenia. People just thought he was simple. Brain-dead Ted. Sharon Macy thought that made him fair game so he turns round one day, calls her a couple of names, and *she* turns round and pours petrol through our letterbox. Sets fire to the fucking place. At first we're thinking it's something to do with the Chinky lot downstairs, but then there's Sharon gloating about it to my lads, saying as how it served them right. Course, there wasn't a person in Downend would stand up in court and swear it was her. If you'd met her and her family you'd know why.'

Caffery had a photo of Sharon Macy from those days pinned to the giant corkboard on the opposite wall. When he'd first seen it, his instinctive thought had been that if ever the word 'dysfunctional' needed a human face to illustrate it, then Sharon Macy's was the one. By thirteen there had already been an abortion and a line of police cautions jostling for position. You could see her past and her future written in her slack eyes. He'd had to force the professional in him to wade in and remind him that she was a victim. That he had the same duty of care to her as to anyone else.

'You're thinking what I'm thinking, ain't you?' Moon's eyes were hard. 'You're thinking that if ASBOs had been handed out in those days Sharon would've got herself a whole fucking trophy cabinet. I mean, she could take care of herself, that one, and she was a big girl too. Broad, you know. Course, Ted was bigger. And madder. My Sonja tops herself – don't make me go there with what that was like. Having my whole entire *heart* pulled out through my *mouth* was what it was like, losing her, because, no, I wasn't having an affair whatever your filthy cop brains are telling you – but she tops herself and if that was bad for me it was even worse for Ted. He's like *that*.' Moon jutted his head forward, teeth bared, one fist balled. The sinews on his neck stood out, high tensile, rigid. 'Next thing I know he turned around to me and Richard and goes, "I ain't sitting still no longer, Dad." Never bothered to hide what he did next. He dragged that girl through the streets – everyone saw it, thought it was boyfriend and girlfriend arguing, sort of thing you'd see a lot round there. They look the same age so no one calls it in, do they? So he's off then, getting away with it, and before anyone knows it he does her in the bedroom. In his own bedroom. With a kitchen knife.' He shook his head. 'Me and Richard weren't there. The neighbours, though, they heard the whole thing through the walls.'

There was a long silence. Moon looked from Caffery to Turner and back again. 'He killed her.' He held his hands up in the air. 'I'm not saying he didn't. He killed Sharon Macy. But not to piss the parents off. And I wasn't having an affair with that slag of a woman. Definitely not. Cut me open.' He tapped his chest. 'Cut me open and give me to your scientists. They'll tell you what's on my heart and what ain't. *I wasn't having an affair with her.*'

Caffery smiled lightly, meaning, yeah, yeah, yeah. You keep going with your fantasy, Peter, but we'll get to the truth of it. 'Sure there's nothing you want to add?' he said. 'Bearing in mind we're speaking to the Macys tonight?'

'Nothing.'

'Just here's me thinking we're going to hear a totally different story from them.'

'You won't.'

'I think we will. I think we'll hear that you were schtupping the Macy mother, and that your son killed Sharon because of it. I think we're going to hear a whole catalogue of what he did to them later. The letters he sent them after the event.'

'No, you won't. Because he never did. He was banged up straight after.'

'We will.'

'You won't. It's *not* him,' Moon said. 'It's not my son.'

There was a knock. Caffery let his eyes rest on Moon a bit longer. Then got up and went to the door. He found Prody standing in the corridor, slightly out of breath. He had a scrape on his cheek that Caffery didn't remember seeing at the safe-house this morning. His clothing was a bit awry.

'Jesus.' Caffery closed the door behind him. He put a hand on Prody's arm and led him a few steps down the corridor, away from the meeting room to the very back of the building where it was quiet and they couldn't hear the phones ringing in the main offices. 'You OK?'

Prody took a handkerchief out of his pocket and mopped his face. 'Just about.' He looked exhausted, completely drained. Caffery almost said to him: *Hey, about the missus. I'm sorry.*

Don't let it get to you. But he was still pissed off about a lot of things. Mostly the staying-overnight thing. And about Prody not calling him with progress on what the hell had happened to Flea. He took his hand away from Prody's arm. 'Well? Have you found something?'

'It's been an interesting afternoon.' He shoved the handkerchief back into his pocket and ran a hand across his bristly haircut. 'I spent a long time at her office – turns out she was rostered today and never showed. So people are starting to get a bit antsy, saying it's not like her, et cetera, et cetera. So I went to her house but it's all shut up – locked. No car there.'

'And?'

'Spoke to the neighbours. Now it turns out *they* are a bit calmer about the whole thing, put it all into perspective. Said they saw her yesterday morning packing the car – diving equipment, suitcase. She tells them she's going on a weekend break – away for three days.'

'She was supposed to be at work.'

'I know. All I can think is she's got the roster wrong, got a dud DMS printout, thinks she's on a long annual or something. The neighbours were absolutely clear about it. They spoke to her. Unless one of them's cut her up and put her under the floorboards.'

'They didn't have the name of the place she's staying?'

'No. But maybe it's somewhere out of signal range. No one can get her on her mobile.'

'Is that all?'

'That's all.'

'What about that?' He gestured at the scrape on Prody's face. 'Where'd you get that little artefact?'

Prody pressed his fingers to it gingerly. 'Yeah – Costello really gave it to me. Suppose I deserve it. Is it that bad?'

Caffery thought about what Janice had said: 'My husband is fucking Paul Prody's wife.' God, life was never easy.

'Go home, mate.' He put his hand on Prody's back. Patted him. 'You haven't had a break in two days. Go home and put something on that. Don't want to see you in the office until the morning. OK?'

'I guess. I guess. Thank you.'

'I'll walk you down to the car park. Dog needs a pee break.'

They stopped at Caffery's office and collected Myrtle from her place under the radiator. The three of them walked silently through darkened corridors that sprang to life with light as they entered, the men letting the old dog set the pace. In the car park Prody got into his Peugeot. Started the engine. Was about to pull away, when Caffery banged on the window.

Prody paused, sitting forward in the seat, his hand on the key. A look of annoyance crossed his face, and for a moment Caffery was reminded of the thing he didn't trust about Prody. That the guy was a usurper. Trying to step into his own shoes. But he cut the engine. Patiently unwound the window. His pale eyes were very still. 'Yeah?'

'Something I wanted to ask you. About the hospital today.'

'What about it?'

'The tests they ran – they can't find what Moon used to knock you out. None of you are testing positive for any of the major inhalant groups. And you had different reactions from the Costello women. You were the only one who heaved. Can you maybe speak to the hospital? Give them a bit more information.'

'A bit *more*?'

'Yeah. Maybe just give them the shirt you were wearing if you haven't washed it. They'll test your stomach contents. Just give them a call, mate. Make the men in the white coats happy?'

Prody let all the air out of his lungs. Still his eyes hadn't moved. 'Jesus. Yes. Of course. If I have to.' He wound up his window. Started the car again and drove out into the street. Caffery followed a few steps behind, then stopped with one arm looped wearily over the gate, watching until the little Peugeot lion logo, lit red by the brakelights, disappeared from view.

He turned to Myrtle. Her head was down. She wasn't looking at him. Caffery wondered if she felt as empty as he did. As empty and as scared. There wasn't much time. He didn't need a profiler to tell him what was next. Somewhere there was a family with cameras in their kitchen. In the parents' bedroom too. He could sense it. Could smell it coming. In fact, if he had to put a stopwatch on it, he'd say there was less than twelve hours left before it happened again.

64

Jill and David Marley were sitting in the tops of the plane trees that bordered the garden. 'London planes. The lungs of London.' David Marley was smiling as he spoke. He was drawing tea from an elaborate samovar into a delicate bone-china cup. 'Breathe in, Flea. Have to keep breathing in. No wonder you feel so sick.'

Flea began to climb the tree to her parents. But it was hard going – the leaves were in the way. Too thick, too choking. Each had a different colour and a different texture that she sensed as a taste in her mouth, either thin and acid or smooth and suffocating. Fighting her way through just a foot of them took for ever.

'Keep breathing,' came her father's voice. 'And don't look down at yourself.'

Flea knew what he meant. She knew her stomach was swelling. She didn't need to look down to know. She could feel it. Multicoloured worms as thick as fingers weaving their way through her intestines. Breeding and rolling and growing.

'Shouldn't have eaten it, Flea.' Somewhere overhead in the trees her mother was calling. 'Oh, Flea, you shouldn't have touched that sandwich. You should have said no. Should never trust a man with clean trousers.'

'Clean trousers?'

'That's what I said. I saw what you were doing with that man in the clean trousers.'

Tears ran down Flea's face, a sobbing noise was coming out of her mouth. She'd climbed all the way up the tree. Except now it wasn't a tree. It was a staircase – like an Escher painting, a staircase that started in a rickety Barcelona building, then twisted and stretched into the air above the roofs, sticking out naked and unsupported in the blue where clouds raced by. Mum and Dad were at the top. Dad had walked down a few steps and was holding his hand out to her. At first she'd reached for it gladly, knowing that taking Dad's hand was salvation, but now she was crying because, no matter how hard she tried to grasp it, he was subtly avoiding letting her do it. He wanted her to listen.

'I told you it's not a sweetie. It's not a sweetie.'

'What?'

'*It's not a sweetie, Flea. How many times do I have to tell you . . .*'

Her eyes flew open. She was back in the barge. The last of the dream battered itself futilely against her eyes, Dad's voice ringing around the echoey barge – *it's not a sweetie*. She lay there in the darkness, her heart thudding crazily. Moonlight was coming through the two portholes in the hull. She checked the Citizen. Three hours since she'd crawled up here, aching and light-headed from exhaustion and blood loss. The T-shirt was wrapped tightly around the wound: it seemed to be holding back the blood for the time being, but what she'd already lost had done the damage. Her skin was clammy, her heart was having moments of jittery palpitations, as if she'd mainlined pure adrenalin. She'd dismantled the acrow prop from under the hatch and laid it across the shelf. Then she'd crawled between the acrow and the hull and, just as she could feel the blood loss pulling her under, had lain on her side, one arm stretched out, pinioned against the hull.

The acrow prop may have stopped her falling into the water in her unconscious state, but it was useless as a tool for getting her out of here. She'd struggled with it for hours though she knew, in her heart, it was never going to hoist the hatch open with the weight of the windlass on it. There had to be another way.

It's not a sweetie, Flea . . .

She twisted her head to look at the hatch she'd come through. Behind her the barge slanted downwards, the water in the stern compartment nearly touching the roof. *Not a sweetie*. Acetylene – the gas the chunk of calcium carbide would produce if it was thrown into water – was slightly lighter than air. She pushed herself up on her elbows and considered how the water lay, then the underside of the deck with its cobwebs and rust. She turned her chin upwards and eyed the rope locker. There was a small hole rusted through it. She'd be wasting her time punching that open because the egress to the surface that the rope would have been fed through was tiny – she'd already had her light up there and studied it and it was the size of a fist. Even so the rope locker was making things stir in her head. Acetylene would rise to the top of a box like that. There'd be leakage into the hull but it might – *might* – not get under the lip above the hatch into the stern. If she was back there, behind the bulkhead. And if the gas was in here . . .

It was dangerous, it was insane, and it was the sort of thing Dad would have done without a second's hesitation. With a grunt she levered the acrow off the ledge, let it fall into the water. She swung her legs down. Felt the exhausting, killing drain of blood away from her head into her torso, the stammer of her heart and blinding waves of static circling her skull. She had to sit, her eyes closed, breathing in a slow, concentrated rhythm until the barge stopped swaying around her.

When her heart had settled back to where it belonged she reached up and found the lump of calcium carbide in the rucksack. She'd almost peeled it from the carrier bag when a noise came from out in the tunnel. The familiar clink-clink-clink of a pebble falling down the air shaft. A splash in the water. She sat, head turned, mouth slightly open, her heart hammering again. Cautiously she returned the chemical ball to the rucksack. And then, almost as if whoever it was had crept up stealthily, she heard the grunt of the grille giving way to human weight and the splash of water. Two splashes. Three.

In absolute silence she tipped herself off the ledge into the water. Put her hand against the hull for support and inched her way slowly to the other side of the barge. Every now and then the faintness came buzzing back and she'd stand still, breathing hard and silently through her mouth, fighting to lock down the nauseating swaying sensation. Six inches from the hole she stopped, her back to the hull so she could see out. The tunnel looked empty. Moonlight streamed in. But on the far wall the rope was swaying. She held her breath. Listened.

A hand came through the hole, holding a torch. She shot back. 'Flea?'

She got her balance. Breathing hard.

Prody? She fumbled the head torch from around her neck, put her hand around his in a fist and shoved it back through the hole, stepped forward and powered the beam into his face. He stood there, knee deep in the water, blinking at her. She let all the air out of her lungs at once.

'I thought you were dead.' Tears came to her eyes. She put a finger to her forehead. 'Shit, Paul. I really thought he'd got you. I thought you were dead.'

'Not dead. I'm here.'

'Fuck, fuck, fuck.' A tear ran down her face. 'Fuck, this is horrible.' She pushed the tear away. 'Paul – are they coming? I mean, seriously, I need to get out soon. I've lost a shitload of blood and it's getting to the point . . .' She paused. 'What's that?'

Prody was holding a large object, wrapped in a plastic sheet.

'What? This?'

'Yeah.' She wiped her nose shakily. Swept the torch down to study it. It was a weird shape. 'What've you got there?'

'Nothing, really.'

'Nothing?'

'Really. Nothing much. I went to my garage.' He unwrapped the plastic sheeting and laid it carefully on the bottom of the scree under the chain. Inside was an angle grinder. 'I thought it might help get you out. Battery-operated.'

She stared at it. 'Is that what they said to . . . ?' She raised her eyes to his face. He was sweating. And the sweat didn't look right. Long snail trails of it, like fingers, stained his shirt. The poisonous worms in her intestines moved and flicked again. He'd called the police, then gone all the way to his house to collect the angle grinder And the rescue services weren't here yet? She shone the torch into his face. He looked back at her steadily, his teeth just visible through his slightly opened lips.

'Where are the others?' she murmured distantly.

'The others? Oh – on their way.'

'They let you come back on your own?'

'Why not?'

She sniffed. 'Paul?'

'What?'

'How did you know which air shaft to come down? There are twenty-three.'

'Eh?' He put his leg forward and rested the angle grinder on his thigh. Began to fit a disc to it. 'I started at the west end and went down them all till I found you.'

'No. I don't think that's right.'

'Hm?' He looked up mildly. 'Beg pardon?'

'No. There are nineteen shafts coming from that end. Your trousers were clean. When you came down they were clean.'

Prody lowered the angle grinder and gave her a quizzical smile. There was a long, still moment while they held each other's gaze. Then, without a word, he went back to fitting the disc as if there had been no communication between them at all. He screwed down the disc and, after a few seconds, satisfied it was secure, he stood. Smiled at her again.

'*What?*' she whispered. '*What?*'

He turned and walked away, his body going forward, his head turning eerily back on his neck, so he could keep his eyes fixed on hers. Before she knew what was happening he had stepped out of her eyeline round the side of the barge. Instantly the tunnel dropped into silence.

She clicked off the torch, plunging herself into darkness. Heart racing, she took a couple of steps backwards, floundering around, wondering desperately what to do. Fuck, fuck, fuck. *Prody?* Her head balled up like a knot. Her legs turned into columns of sand, making her want to sit down and pant. *Prody?* Seriously – *Prody?*

From about ten feet to her left came the sound of a motor. A whine that put talons into her head. The angle grinder. She took a confused step sideways, flailing for something to hold on to, banging into the rucksack, making it swing crazily. The grinder disc bit the metal with a high-pitched scream. Through the hole the cascading sparks lit the tunnel like Guy Fawkes night.

'*Stop!*' she yelled. 'Stop!'

He didn't answer. The hemisphere of the grinder disc showed through into the hull, a slice of moonlight coming with it. It was at a point halfway between her and the hatch. It moved slowly down, gnawing at the iron hull. Moved about ten inches. Then hit something immovable. The grinder jumped, rattled madly, shooting sparks into the air. A particle ricocheted around the hull, pinging into the water somewhere in the dark. The disc recovered, bit into the metal again, but something was wrong with it. The motor stuttered. Ground noisily at the iron. Whined and decelerated to silence.

On the other side of the hull Prody swore softly. He pulled the disc out and spent a moment or two tinkering with the machine, she listening to him, hardly breathing. He started the grinder again. Again it stuttered. Coughed. Whined and juddered to a halt. The acrid, burning-fish smell of failing machinery wafted into the hull.

A stray sentence went through her from nowhere. *I saw a little girl thrown out of a windscreen once: did the last twenty feet on her face.* That had been Prody speaking on the night he'd breathalysed her. In retrospect there had been something creepy about the way he'd said it. A note of pleasure in there. Prody? Prody? *Prody?* An MCIU detective? The guy she used to see coming from the gym with his kit over his shoulder? She thought about the moment in the pub – how she'd looked at him, thought about something happening between them.

Sudden silence outside. She raised her head. Looked with watering eyes at the hole. Nothing. Then a splash about twenty yards away. She tensed, ready for the whine of the angle grinder. Instead his footsteps faded – as if he was going to the very end of the chamber near the furthest rockfall.

Clumsily she wiped her mouth, swallowed the sour taste and, taking care not to move too fast and set her head spinning, carefully knelt up on the ledge. Clutching the lip of the porthole on the starboard side she steadied herself and peered out.

The section of the tunnel that reached to the rockfall was visible from this side of the barge. The water in the canal shone dully: the moon had moved and was now shining directly down the shaft. The walls narrowed at sickening angles, making her head lurch, but she could see Prody clearly. About twenty feet away from her. Almost in the darkness. Focus, her exhausted mind said, watch – he's doing something important.

He was a long way down the chamber, at the edge of the tunnel where the water level had lowered over the years to reveal a strip of ground about a yard wide – the same path that ran the length of the canal, and that she had walked with Wellard on Tuesday. Prody had his side to her. His shirt was filthy with black canal water, his face not visible in the bad light, and he was studying something in his hand. Martha's shoe. He put it into the pocket of his fleece and closed the popper to keep it secure. Then he dropped to an ugly crouch and began to study the ground. Flea gripped the edges of the hole tighter and pressed her face into it, breathing open-mouthed, straining to see.

He was pushing away the leaves and the muck, scooping it in great handfuls and letting it pile behind him the way a dog would, digging a hole. After a few minutes the scooping stopped. He shuffled a little nearer on his haunches and began to scrape carefully. The ground there was soft – like the rockfalls, it was mostly fuller's earth, with one or two boulders lodged in it – but she didn't think it was a rock he was cleaning around. It was too regular. Too clearly a shape. If anything it was corrugated iron. A wave of weakness passed through her. It choked her and sent pins and needles sparkling through her head. It was a pit. She hadn't noticed it before – would never have noticed it – because he'd covered it so well with earth, but she knew instinctively what it was. A grave. Somehow Prody had sunk a pit into the floor of the canal. It would be where Martha was buried.

He sat for a few moments contemplating the shape. Then, seemingly satisfied with what he'd seen, he began to scoop the earth back. Flea's trance broke. She ducked under the rucksack and waded back towards where she'd dropped the acrow. Arms out in the dark water she groped blindly for it. She could drag it through into the aft compartment. Wedge it somewhere and tighten it against the closed hatch. That would give her some time. But not long enough. She straightened, eyes darting from side to side. The rope locker caught her eye.

It's not a sweetie, Flea . . .

Stealthily she snaked her hand into the rucksack, pushing past the hard, salty chemical ball, feeling around the other things. The chisel, the climbing cams, the length of green parachute line that went everywhere with her because her father had sworn by it. *Never underestimate the problems para line can get you out of, Flea.* Her fingers found something small and plastic – a cigarette lighter. Another of Dad's must-haves. She usually carried two – no, today it was three: there was an extra one at the bottom. Teeth clenched, she raised her eyes again to the rope locker.

Outside she heard a splash. Closer to the barge than she'd have expected. Another. Closer yet. And another. By the time she'd realized he was running towards her the impact had already come: the barge seemed to lift nightmarishly, tremble and shudder, as he hurtled into the hull. She heard him bounce away into the water, splashing. She shrank back from the rucksack, cringing. Saw a flicker of light and dark go past the hole. Then silence again.

She began to pant with fear. She couldn't help it. She looked across at the bulkhead – it seemed miles away. At the other end of a very long, narrow tunnel. The walls were seesawing from side to side. Nothing was real. It was like something she had dreamed.

Another series of splashes. This time from behind. She cramped herself forward. Tensed. Prody landed exactly behind the place where she stood. She actually felt his weight on the hull. Felt it echo through her own muscle and organs like a sonic boom. As if he wanted to shake the barge out of the water.

'*Hey!*' He banged on the hull. A series of sharp hammerings. '*Wake up in there. Wake up!*'

She groped numbly for the ledge, sat on it and put her head into her hands, trying to stop the blood falling away from her brain. Her chest rose and fell convulsively; shivers ran up and down her arms.

God, God, God. This was death. This was her death. This was how it was going to end.

65

The woman standing in her dressing-gown on the gravelled driveway had gone through most of her life with the name Skye Blue. But, then, what else would hippie Mr and Mrs Blue have called their only daughter if not 'Skye'? It was obvious, and really she should count herself lucky their name hadn't been Brown. It was only in the last year, when a good and decent man with the sensible name of Nigel Stephenson had come along and made her his wife that she'd stopped having to make defensive little anti-hippie jokes every time she signed her name.

Skye Stephenson had a lot more to thank Nigel for than just a name, she thought, as the lights of his taxi disappeared at the end of the road. A lot more. She had peace, fun, great sex and great cuddles whenever she put out her arms for one. She had a beautiful house too, she thought, pulling the dressing-gown around her and going back down the silent garden path to the opened front door – a detached Victorian with bay windows, a front garden full of peonies and a real feel of home. The windows needed replacing and they'd probably have to put in a new heating system before next winter, but to her it was exactly how she imagined a family home. She smiled down the road after Nigel, closed the door behind her and put the chain on because he would be two days on his business trip and the door couldn't be seen from the street, which sometimes made her feel vaguely insecure.

She inched the draught excluder into place with a toe, stop the cold air coming in and snaking meanly around the downstairs rooms.

Skye's stitches had healed now and she could move like a normal human being again. She'd stopped wearing the sanitary towel ten days ago and now she really was back to her old self. Still, habit made her go up the stairs slowly, her body still feeling a little full, cumbersome. Her breasts ached all the time. Just the tiniest brush against something and they'd be leaking everywhere. Sometimes she thought she was more eager to get the feeding done than Charlie was.

She waddled down the long, cold corridor to the nursery, stood in the doorway and took a moment to look at him, fast asleep on his back, arms above his shoulders, head turned to the side, mouth making little sucking movements. Charlie – the biggest and most important thing she had to be thankful to Nigel for. She went to the cot and smiled down at him. If it had been left to her she'd let Charlie sleep in bed with her. It would be easier to soothe him when he woke. To wrap an arm around his head and push a nipple into his sleepy mouth. But the screaming brigade of health visitors, relatives and childcare books had trampled her down. Reminded her she was the product of hippies and that, really, if she didn't set the boundaries now, Charlie would never know which was his bed and which was Mum and Dad's. He'd be scarred for life and end up a hopeless tangle of separation anxieties.

'But a few minutes now won't hurt, will it, little boy? Promise you'll go back afterwards?'

She lifted him from the cot, grateful not to feel the tug of stitches any more. Put him over her shoulder and wrapped the blanket round him. Then, one hand on his tiny warm skull, the other on his bottom, and moving carefully because sometimes it terrified her that she might trip, drop him maybe, she padded next door to her and Nigel's bedroom at the front of the house. She kicked the door closed behind her and sat on the bed. The light was off, but the curtains were open, and the room was filled with the yellow light of the streetlamp at the top of the drive.

Careful not to wake Charlie, she lowered her face and gave his bottom a sniff. Nothing. She unsnapped the poppers on the legs of his sleepsuit and wormed a finger in to check his nappy. Damp.

'Nappy change, little man.'

With an effort, not using her hands, she tipped herself back on to her feet. Carried him across to the baby-changing station by the window. It was quite a number, in green and orange, with a strap to hold him safe and lots of drawers for different things: nappies, bags for the dirty ones, wipes, cream. Skye's colleagues had bought it for her. She thought the gift showed a tenderness towards babies uncharacteristic of the mostly male solicitors with whom she worked and she was sure they'd only done it out of pity. Probably they were thinking that Charlie signalled the end of her useful career as a divorce lawyer.

Maybe they were right, she thought, as she unsnapped the Babygro – because these days the thought of going back to work made her want to cry. It wasn't just the long hours she dreaded. Or the backbiting. It was the thought of existing at the sharp end of people's cruelty, as if Charlie's birth had skinned her of a protective layer. She didn't think she'd be able to face seeing naked human nature at its rawest any more. It was more than just the few occasions where she'd heard, in the course of the divorces, accusations of child abuse. It was the acrimony, the loading of blame, the feral struggle for *self*. In just a few short weeks her faith in her job had evaporated.

'Hey, little guy.' She smiled down at Charlie, who had half woken up and was moving his fists weakly up and down, opening his mouth ready to cry. 'Just a nappy change. Then a cuddle. Then back to your nasty old cot.' But he didn't cry and she managed the change with him still half asleep. She dressed him and laid him on the blanket on her bed. Puffed the pillows up against the headboard. 'Now listen, little Charlie, you mustn't get used to Mummy's bed. The Nazis will come after Mummy if you do.'

She kicked off her slippers, pulled off the dressing-gown, and crawled across the bed on all fours to him. She thought he might wake up, want to feed, but he didn't. After a few seconds he stopped agitating his arms and moving his mouth, and his eyes closed. His face slackened. She lay on her side, her cheek resting on her hand, and watched him sleep. Little Charlie. Little Charlie, who was everything to her.

The bedroom was quiet. The streetlight came in from the window and reflected off points in the room: a glass of water on the bedside table, the mirror, the row of nail varnishes on a shelf high up. Each surface sent back dull, reflective glimmers. But there was an extra glint in the room that she wouldn't have recognized even if she'd noticed it. High above her head, among the ornate folds and creases of the plaster ceiling rose, nestled a tiny glass disc. The tireless, unblinking lens of a surveillance camera.

66

Bang. The barge shuddered. The squeal of rusting metal echoed in the tunnel. *Bang.*

Prody wasn't in the water any more. He had crawled up on to the deck of the barge and was rocking the windlass, trying to dislodge it from the hatch. Three feet beneath him Flea stared up at the hatch. Every time he moved, the stripes of moonlight that criss-crossed their way through the dark were blotted out. She closed her eyes. There was a hard knot in her stomach – a hard knot from thinking about Martha's shoe. About her grave and about the angle grinder, the way the motor had seized. Because of what? Because it had already been used to chew through meat and bone? And what had been in that sandwich? There was nothing she would put past Prody. *Nothing.*

She opened her eyes, twisted her head back and looked at the bulkhead hatch, then up at the rope locker. There wasn't time to just sit here. She had to—

Above her Prody stopped rocking the windlass.

Silence. She stared clear-eyed at the outline of the hatch, holding her breath. There was a long pause, then he fell heavily on the deck, blocking the moonlight outline. He was lying directly above her. Inches away on the other side of the hull. She could hear his breathing. She could hear the *shush-shush* of his nylon jacket. She was surprised she couldn't hear his heart pounding.

'Oh, look! I can see your head.'

She flinched. Pulled herself back as tight into the hull as she could.

'I can *see* you. What's the matter? You're very quiet all of a sudden.'

She put her fingers to her forehead, felt the pulse there, screwed up her face and tried to put all this insanity into place. When she didn't answer he shifted so his mouth was to the crack in the hatch. His breathing changed, became spasmodic. He was masturbating – or pretending to. The knot in her belly tightened – thinking about a little girl who probably didn't even know what sex was, let alone why a grown man would want to do it to a small child. A little girl, or what was left of her, lying in a grave less than fifty yards away. Overhead Prody was sniffing, making a noise as if he was sucking the insides of his cheeks. Something – a drop of moisture – leaked through the gap and hung on the underside of the deck. A tear or saliva, she wasn't sure which. It trembled in the moonlight, then broke off and fell with a tiny *plink* into the barge.

She lowered her hand and gazed coldly at the hatch. The drop had been liquid but it hadn't been semen. Yet she'd been meant to think it was. He was tormenting her. But why bother? Why not just get it over and done with? Her eyes went to the place where moonlight sliced into the hull through the scar he'd made with the angle grinder. She thought she understood why. He was doing it because he knew he couldn't get to her.

Energy flowed back into her body. She pushed herself away from the wall.

'What are you doing now? Bitch?'

She breathed in and out slowly through her mouth, moving quietly to the rucksack.

'Bitch.'

He hammered on the deck again – *bang bang bang* – but she didn't flinch. She was right. He couldn't get to her. He really couldn't get to her. She began taking things out. The calcium carbide, the parachute line and the cigarette lighters. She put them all on the ledge just under the rope locker. The trick was going to be to seal the hole that went from the locker up to the deck. She could do it with her bloodied T-shirt – but she'd have to wait for him to get off the deck. The time would come. She was sure of it. He wasn't going to stay up there for ever. She found the empty bottle he'd given her, uncapped it and submerged it in the water, squeezing it gently until it was full. Reaching above her head she squirted it into the locker, refilled it and repeated the process.

'What're you doing, bitch?' He shifted around on the hatch. She could feel him above her, moving like an awful giant spider, trying to see what she was up to. 'Tell me or I'll come in there and find out.'

She swallowed. With about a litre of water in the rope locker she shook the bottle and placed it, neck down, in the webbing of the rucksack to dry out. Working in the moonlight, she found the chisel and the six-inch nail she'd been using with the acrow prop. She took her time, lining up the nail, and popping the plastic casing of the lighters with a neat tap of the chisel. Prody was listening to everything, his breathing right over her head. She could almost feel his cold eye swivelling to follow her as she bent and carefully tipped the contents of each lighter into the water bottle.

She straightened and gave the bottle a shake, watched the contents swishing around. The lighters had been full but there wasn't much fluid – under a hundred millilitres. It would be enough to soak part of the para line and make a wick of sorts that would reach into the next compartment. The rest she'd have to sacrifice to the rope locker to give the acetylene the extra explosive jolt it needed.

'*Tell me what you're fucking doing or I'm coming in.*'

She swallowed. She put her thumb and forefinger on her throat and pressed lightly. Tried to stop her voice shaking as she said, 'Go on then. Come in and see.'

There was a pause. As if he couldn't believe what she'd said. Then he began to claw and hammer and tear at the hatch, shouting and swearing and kicking. She raised her eyes to it. He can't get in, she told herself. He cannot get in. Eyes locked on the hatch, she began searching through the rucksack, trying to find something she could put the lighter fuel in to protect it from the water in the rope locker. Prody stopped screaming at her. Breathing hard, he slithered to the edge of the deck and dropped off into the canal. She could hear him walking around the barge, pacing, trying to find a way in. He wouldn't. Unless he got the angle grinder started again, or unless he climbed back up the hole and somehow found himself another power tool, he wouldn't get back in. She was going to beat him at his own game.

She found the plastic tray that had contained batteries for her torch. She took it to the ledge and had turned for the bottle of lighter fuel when a long wave of nausea and weakness came over her.

Immediately she set the bottle on the ledge and sat down, breathing hard to steady herself. She opened her mouth and sucked in air, but her body was at the end of its resilience. The fumes of the lighter fuel, the stench of rot and fear overwhelmed her. She just had time to tip herself down on to the ledge when a dense and bitter pull rose up through her chest and neck and dragged her feet first downwards until everything, every thought, every impulse, was reduced to nothing more than a tiny red point of electrical activity at the pulpy centre of her brain.

67

At four thirty Charlie Stephenson blinked, opened his mouth and began to howl. In the room at the front of the house Skye stirred. She rubbed her eyes and reached sleepily for Nigel, but found cold empty sheets instead of his warm mass. She groaned and rolled on to her back, tilting her head up to see the numbers projected on to her ceiling – 4:32. She let her hands drop across her face. Four thirty. Charlie's favourite time.

'Oh, God, Charlie.' She pulled on her dressing-gown, sleepily shoved her feet into slippers. 'Oh God.'

She shuffled into the nursery, the walking dead moving towards the soft glow of his Winnie the Pooh nightlight. The nursery was dark. And cold – too cold. The sash window was open. Drowsily, she padded to it and closed it. She couldn't recall leaving it open – but her brain was mush these days. She paused to look into the moonlit alley that ran along the side of the house. At the dustbins lined up. They'd had a break-in a couple of months ago. Someone had got in through the french windows in the living room. Nothing had been taken, but in a way that had freaked her out more than if everything had gone. Afterwards Nigel had put locks on the windows downstairs. She really ought to remember to close them.

In the cot Charlie screwed up his face. The sobs made his little chest jerk up and down.

'Oh you little tyke.' She smiled. 'Waking Mummy up.' She reached in and wrapped his blanket around him, swaddled it around his arms, lifted him up and carried him into her room, murmuring to him all the way, about how he was going to be the death of her, how she'd remind him of this when he was eighteen and dating. It was windy outside. The trees in the front were making strange moving shapes on the ceiling as they bent and swayed. The draught coming through the windows ruffled the curtains. They popped and lifted.

Charlie's nappy was dry so she rested him on a pillow and climbed sleepily on to the bed next to him. She began to unhook the maternity bra. She stopped. Sat upright, eyes wide, suddenly completely awake, her heart thudding. In the alley outside Charlie's window something had clattered.

She held a finger to her lip. 'Stay there, Charlie.' She tipped silently out of bed on her bare feet and went back into the nursery. The window was rattling. She went to it, pressed her forehead to the glass and peered down into the alley. One of the dustbin lids lay on the ground. Taken off by the wind.

She closed the curtains, went back into the bedroom and climbed on to the bed. That was the problem when Nigel was away. Her imagination ran riot.

'Silly Mummy.' She pulled Charlie into her arms, jammed down her bra to expose her nipple and got him latched on. Lay back and dreamily closed her eyes. 'Silly old Mummy and her silly old imagination.'

68

As dawn came Caffery slept, fully dressed, half curled up on four chair cushions he'd dropped on to the office floor at three a.m. He dreamed, incongruously, of dragons and lions. The lions looked like real ones. Their teeth were a hard-grained yellow, coated with blood and saliva. He could smell their hot breath and see the matting in their manes. The dragons on the other hand were two-dimensional, children's tin dragons, as if they were wearing armour. They clanged and clattered across the battlefield, carrying their streaming banners. They reared and rolled their long metallic necks. They were huge. They crushed the lions like ants.

From time to time he half woke. Surfaced a little to a place where the caustic remnants of worry sat. Niggles he hadn't untangled before he'd slept. Prody's sour face in the car as he drove away last night and how that had rankled. Flea going off for three days' climbing and how that hadn't sounded right. Worse, the whole sad, fat fact of Ted Moon still out there. Martha and Emily still missing six days into the case.

He came awake properly, lay with his eyes closed, feeling the cold, the stiffness in his body. He could smell Myrtle's comfortable old-dog scent rising from where she lay a few feet away under the radiator. He could hear traffic outside, people talking in the corridors and mobile phones ringing. So it was morning.

'Boss?'

He opened his eyes. The office floor was dusty. Paperclips and screwed-up balls of paper congregated under the desk. And, in the open doorway, a pair of good, feminine ankles ending in well-polished high heels. A man's shoes and trousers next to them. He raised his eyes. Turner and Lollapalooza. Both holding sheaves of paper. 'Jesus. What time is it?'

'Seven thirty.'

'Shit.' He rubbed his eyes, propped himself up on an elbow and blinked. On her makeshift bed under the window Myrtle yawned, sat up and gave herself a little shake. The office was blitzed, packed with the evidence of Caffery's up-all-nighter. The whiteboard covered with the photos and notes he'd been studying – everything from Sharon Macy's autopsy shots to the pictures of the kitchen at the Costellos' safe-house, the window broken, the washed-up cocoa mugs on the draining-board. His desk, too, was crammed with stuff – pile after pile of paper, different-coloured plastic envelopes containing photographs of crime scenes, reams of hastily scribbled notes and countless half-finished cups of coffee. The melting pot that nothing had come out of. No clue. No way of knowing where Moon was going next.

He rubbed his sore neck and squinted up at Lollapalooza. 'Got any answers for me?'

She made a sour face. 'Got more questions. Will that do?'

'Come in.' He sighed, beckoning to them. 'Come in.'

They came into the office. Lollapalooza folded her arms and leaned back against the desk, her feet pushed primly together. Turner turned a chair round and sat astride it, rodeo style, elbows resting on the back, looking down at his boss.

'Right. First things first.' Clearly Turner hadn't slept much either. His tie was a bit crooked and his hair hadn't seen a shower recently. But still no earring. 'Overnight the Met's dead-body dogs've been searching Moon's little rabbit warren under the lock-up.'

'And found? Oh.' Caffery waved his hand dismissively. 'Don't answer that. I can see from your face. Nothing. Next?'

'Moon's tribunal psychiatric evaluation arrived. Sitting in my mailbox this morning.'

'He talked? When he got into the slammer?'

'Couldn't stop him, seems like. Anyone who stood still for more than a second would get it. A confession every day of his ten years' stir.'

This was important. Caffery pulled his legs round and sat upright, trying to make the room stop blurring. 'So? He talked?'

'But it's just like his dad said. Ted killed Sharon because of the fire, because of Sonja dying. No excuses, no justification. Black and white. All the psychiatric reports say the same thing.'

'Fuck. What about the Macys? Did you find them?'

Turner lowered his chin at Lollapalooza. Made a face that said, Your turn in the dock, girl.

She cleared her throat. 'OK. So one of my men finally tracked the Macys down at two o'clock this morning – coming home from the pub. I've just had breakfast with them.' She raised an eyebrow. 'Nice couple. Nice level of sophistication. You know, believe cars belong on bricks and that the right place for a refrigerator is the front garden. Must do a lot of outdoor entertaining is all I can think. But they did speak to me.'

'And?'

'Nothing happened. After Sharon disappeared they didn't hear anything from Moon. Not a dickie.'

'No notes? No letters?'

'Nothing. Not even when Ted was arrested. As you know, he didn't say a word at his trial and as far as the family are concerned they don't expect to hear anything from him. Neither of them would even say his name. They let your friend from the high-tech unit look around. Q? He told me that was his name, though personally I think he's got a warped sense of humour. He used every gizmo he had, couldn't find a thing. No cameras, *nada*. The Macys have been in the place years, had it decorated a few times, but never found anything suspicious.'

'What about Peter Moon and Macy's mother? Any urty-urty going on there?'

'No affair. I believed her too.'

'Fuck.' He pushed his hair back off his face. Why was it that when it came to Ted Moon every alley Caffery turned down seemed to have a stonking great brick wall at the end of it? Fitting Moon and his actions together just wasn't smooth. Not like the best cases where the connections, when they came, felt as liquid and natural as honey. 'What about the others? The Bradleys, the Blunts?'

'No. And that's straight from the FLOs, who, as we know, usually get to the truth. Statistical anomaly maybe, but these might be the only couples in the whole UK who aren't doing the bad thang on the side.'

'Damien? He's not with his wife.'

'But it wasn't him called time on that marriage. It was Lorna. If it was a marriage. He says they were married, but we can't find any record of it. Call it more of an international arrangement, shall we?'

Caffery got to his feet and went to the whiteboard. He studied the pictures of the Costellos' safe-house Moon had broken into: the kitchen, the empty double bed where Emily and Janice had slept. There should be progress by now. There should be a new perspective. He stared at the mock-up of the dark blue Vauxhall, the pictures of the Costellos' car in the CSI surgery. He scrutinized the faces – Cory Costello looking seriously into the camera – and all the lines he'd drawn between the photos, connecting them to Ted Moon at the top. Caffery lifted his face and looked into Moon's eyes again. He felt nothing. No flicker.

Without a word he took a chair and placed it at the window. Sat with his back to the room, facing out into the dismal street. The sky was a uniform lead colour. Passing cars swished through puddles. He felt old. So old. Once he'd fought this case, what would be next? Another mugger or rapist or child abductor to strip the skin from his back, make his bones ache?

'Sir?' Lollapalooza began, but Turner stopped her with a sssh.

Caffery didn't turn to them. He knew what that *sssh* meant. It meant Turner didn't want Lollapalooza to interrupt him. Because he believed Caffery sitting at the window meant he was thinking, was taking all the information he'd been given and was making alchemy of it with his brilliant brain. Turner really, really thought

Caffery was going to spin round on his chair and pull out a theory, like a bright bunch of circus flowers from a hat.

Well, he thought despondently, welcome to the land of crashing disappointment, mate. Hope you like it here, because we're going to be making it our home for a while.

69

Not long after dawn and the huge garden in Yatton Keynell was covered with frost. But inside the cottage it was warm – Nick had built a fire in the living-room grate and Janice sat near it, in a chair next to the window, the bleak winter sunlight throwing her into sharp silhouette. She didn't move as her sister opened the front door at the appointed time and showed the guests through. No one pointed Janice out, but they all knew immediately who she was. It must have been something to do with the way she was sitting. They automatically came forward and introduced themselves to her, muttering things under their breath.

'I'm so sorry to hear about your little girl.'

'Thank you for calling. We really wanted to speak to someone else.'

'The police have pulled our place apart. I can't believe he's been watching us.'

Janice nodded, shook their hands and tried to smile. But her heart was cold. The Blunts came first. Neil was tall and slim, with Cory's Scottish colouring – sandy hair, eyelashes and brows. Simone had blonde hair, slightly olive skin, brown eyes. Janice studied them. Had some similarity in their appearances tipped something in Moon's mind? Made him target them? Rose and Jonathan Bradley were even more worn down than they'd looked in the newspaper photos. Rose had fine-blonde hair, her skin so washed out and thin you could see the veins through it. She was wearing sensible stretch trousers, soft shoes, a pink floral sweater and a pink scarf tied at the neck. There was something pathetic about that scarf – about the attempt to keep up appearances. She and Jonathan shook Janice's hand and slouched almost apologetically into their chairs, sitting a pace away and clutching the cups of tea Janice's sister had poured from the pot standing next to the fire. Then Damien Graham came in and Janice knew for sure that the idea of physical similarities was nuts. He was tall and black with powerful thighs and shoulders, his hair cropped close to his skull. Nothing like Cory, nothing like Jonathan, nothing like Neil.

'Alysha's mum can't make it.' He was a little shy, out of place in this delicate country room. He settled on the last chair – a fragile, ornate winged affair that made him look even more powerful – and sat self-consciously plucking at the creases on his trousers. 'Lorna.' He crossed one leg over the other, making the little chair creak.

Janice stared at him dully, an enormous weariness coming over her. People talked about feeling empty, numb, at times like this. She wished she could feel either of those things. Either would be better than this hard, sharp ache under her ribs where her stomach used to be. 'Look. I should introduce myself to you all properly. I'm Janice Costello. That's my husband Cory over in the corner.' She waited for everyone to turn and hold their hands up to him in greeting. 'You won't have heard our names because they kept it quiet when our little . . . little girl was taken.'

'The papers said there's been another,' said Simone Blunt. 'Everyone knows it's happened. Just no one knows your name.'

'They kept it quiet because they were protecting us.'

'The cameras,' Rose murmured. 'Did he put cameras in your place?'

Janice nodded. She rested her hands on her lap and looked down at them, at the veins on the backs, showing through the skin. She couldn't inject any expression or enthusiasm into her voice. Every word out of her mouth was an effort. Eventually she lifted her head again. 'I know the police have spoken to you. I know they've gone through it over and over again and they can't see what we've got in common. But I thought maybe if we got together we might work out why he's chosen us. We might be able to guess who he's going to do it to next. Because I think he will do it again. And the police do too. Even if they're not saying it. And if we could figure out who's next that might be a chance to catch him – to find out what he's done to our . . .' She took a breath, held it. Avoided Rose's eyes, knowing what would be in there and that just glimpsing it would unhitch the spring coiled inside her. When her voice was under control again she released the breath. 'But now I've met you all I'm starting to think I'm just an idiot. I sort of hoped that maybe we'd be really similar. I thought we'd look the same, maybe, like the same things, live in similar houses, have similar situations, but we don't. I can just see from looking at us that we couldn't be more different. I'm sorry.' She was exhausted. So exhausted. 'Really sorry.'

'No.' Neil Blunt sat forward, pushing his head out so she was forced to look at his face. 'Don't be sorry. You've got a feeling about it so hang on to that. Maybe you're right. Maybe there really *is* something connecting us. Something not obvious.'

'No. Look at us.'

'There *has* to be something,' he persisted. 'Something. Maybe we remind him of someone. In his childhood.'

'Our jobs?' Simone said. 'Something about our jobs.' She turned to Jonathan. 'I know what you do, Jonathan, it's been in all the papers. But, Rose, what do you do?'

'I'm a medical secretary. I work for a team of osteopaths in Frenchay.' She waited for someone to comment. No one did. She gave a sad smile. 'Not very interesting, I know.'

'Damien?'

'I work for BMW. Working my way up through sales. Always think sales is where it's at. If you can do well in sales you can have the world in your hand. But you got to want the chase, got to love the kill—' He broke off – everyone was staring at him silently. He sank back, his hands up. 'Yeah, well,' he muttered, 'that's me. Car sales. BMW. In Cribbs Causeway.'

'You, Janice? What do you do for a living?'

349

'Publishing. I used to be a copy-editor. Now I'm freelance. And Cory's a—'

'Consultant to a printing company.' Cory didn't look at anyone when he spoke. 'I advise them in marketing strategy. Tell them how to greenwash their image.'

Simone cleared her throat. 'Financial analyst. And Neil works for the Citizens' Advice Bureau in Midsomer Norton. Specializes in custody cases during divorce. But that doesn't ring any bells for any of you. Does it?'

'No.'

'Sorry. No.'

'Maybe we're looking at it all wrong.'

Everyone turned. Rose Bradley was hunched in her chair, slightly embarrassed, slightly stubborn. She'd pulled her cardigan high around her shoulders so it came halfway up the back of her head – like a scared lizard in oversized skin. Her pale eyes peered out uncertainly from under lowered eyebrows.

'I beg your pardon?' said Simone.

'I said maybe we're looking at it all wrong. Maybe we *do* know him after all.'

Everyone exchanged glances.

'But we've just agreed we don't,' said Simone. 'None of us has even heard of Ted Moon.'

'What if it's not him?'

'What if *who*'s not him?'

'The kidnapper. The person who's doing all this. I mean, we're sitting here assuming the police are right. That it's Ted Moon. What if they're wrong?'

'But . . .' said someone, then let the sentence die. Everyone in the room had stopped talking and moving. Their faces had gone slack. There was a long pause as this idea worked its way into their heads. One by one everyone turned away from Rose to Janice with expectant expressions. It was the exact way children would look at a teacher. Waiting for the person in control to come along and sort out the mess they'd got themselves into.

70

The baby seat had been another of the storm of presents that had hailed down on them at Charlie's arrival. From Nigel's parents this time. It was blue with yellow anchors embossed all over it. At eight fifteen on that cold morning it was sitting on the hallway floor, waiting to be picked up and strapped into the car. Charlie's bag sat next to it, all ready: nappies and toys and a change of clothes.

Skye was gulping down a third cup of coffee, standing in the kitchen in her huge sweater, looking blankly at the condensation on the windowpanes. There was frost on the trees in the garden and she could feel the freezing air from outside coming through the gaps in the rattly sash windows. She thought about last night. About the opened window. The dustbin lid. She rinsed the cup and put it on the draining-board. Turned the thermostat up a little and checked that the windows were locked. In the hallway her red coat hung on the peg near the door, and next to it her handbag. Going out this morning made sense. A visit to the office. Just to show off Charlie to the partners. Why not?

Yes. It all made perfect sense.

71

In spite of the fire Janice was freezing. Her head was like stone. Cold and hard. Everyone was staring at her, expecting her to do or say something. She folded her arms and tucked her hands under her armpits to stop them trembling. Tried to gather herself.

'Maybe – uh – maybe Rose is right.' Her teeth were chattering. Banging together uncontrollably. 'It wouldn't be the first time the police were wrong. Maybe Ted Moon is the wrong man.' She thought of all the men Emily had come into contact with over the years. A string of faces unfurled in her head – teachers at school, a lanky football coach with bad skin who was always too friendly with the mums, the milkman who sometimes spoke to Emily on the doorstep. 'Maybe we're all connected to someone else. Someone we haven't even thought of.'

'But who?'

'I don't know . . . I don't know.'

A long silence descended on the group. Outside, Janice's sister and Nick were showing Philippa Bradley the garden. She had brought her spaniel to play with the Labradors. From time to time the three women could be seen from the french windows, muffled in their coats and scarves, walking back and forth, throwing balls. They made black footprints in the frosted lawn. Janice stared at them. She remembered Emily playing out there as a toddler, laughing because she could hide behind the lavender beds and make Janice come out and act scared, say: *Oh, no! My little girl's gone! Where's my Emily? Has the monster got her?*

Not Ted Moon? If so, then who? Who connected her and Cory to these five other people?

From the corner Damien spoke in a subdued voice. 'Look.' He opened his hands, turned to face the people behind him. 'I ain't never met that son-of-a-bitch in the photo neither, but I ought to say something.' He levelled a finger at Jonathan. 'You, man. Sorry to say it, but I know you from somewhere. Been thinking it since I came in.'

Everyone looked at Jonathan. He frowned. 'From the papers, you mean? I've been all over the papers this week.'

'No. I saw the pictures on the news and I never recognized you otherwise I'd've said something to the police. But when I came in just now I saw you and I thought, I do – I know that man from somewhere.'

'From where?'

'I can't remember. Maybe I'm imagining it.'

'Do you go to church?'

'Not since I was a kid. The Deptford Seventh Day Adventists. Not since I got away from home. No disrespect but you wouldn't catch me dead.'

'And your child,' Jonathan said. 'Your daughter. What was her name?'

'Alysha.'

'That's right. The police asked me. I did know an Alysha once, but it wasn't Alysha Graham. It was Alysha Morefield, or Morton. I can't remember.'

Damien stared at him. 'More*by*. Alysha Moreby. Moreby's her mother's name – the name Lorna schooled her under.'

Colour crept into Jonathan's face. Everyone in the room had inched forward a little and was staring at the two men. 'Moreby. Alysha Moreby. I know her.'

'Where do you know her from? We never took her to church.'

Jonathan's mouth was half open. As if a terrible, terrible truth was about to reveal itself. Something that had been there all along and could have saved the world if only he'd thought of it early enough. 'School,' he said distantly. 'Before I was ordained I was a headmaster.'

'Got it.' Damien slapped his thighs. Dug a finger in the air. 'Mr *Bradley* – of *course*. I remember *you*, man. I mean, I never met you, like – Lorna always did Alysha's school stuff. But I seen you. I seen you – at the gates an' shit.'

Janice sat forward, heart thumping. 'Someone at the school. You both knew people at the school.'

'No. I never came to anything at the school,' said Damien. 'Hardly anything. It was Lorna's thing, the school run.'

'No PTA meetings?'

'No.'

'Fêtes or fairs?'

'No.'

'You really didn't meet the other parents?'

'I swear – just never got involved. That's how it's always been in our family – woman does the school thing.'

'But your wife,' Jonathan said woodenly, 'she was friendly with the other parents. I know because I remember her well. She always had a group of friends at the school gates.'

'Anyone in particular?' said Simone.

'No. But . . .' Jonathan's eyes rolled up as if he was recalling something.

'What is it?' Janice was half out of her chair. 'What?'

'She got involved. In an incident.' He looked at Damien. 'Do you remember?'

'What sort of incident?'

'With one of the other parents. It got unpleasant.'

'The sweetie jar? Is that what you're talking about?'

Jonathan loosened his collar and turned bloodshot eyes to Janice. The room was suddenly hot. As if it was full of electricity. 'It was the Monday after a fête. Lorna, Mr Graham's partner, came into my office. She was holding a sweetie jar. She said she'd bought it at the fair. I remember it clearly because it all seemed so very *odd* at the time.'

'A sweetie jar?'

'I'd asked the parents to bring old jars filled with sweets to sell at the fair. For a pound, or whatever. It was to raise funds for the school roof that year, but when Mrs Graham got her jar home she found—'

'A note in it,' said Damien. 'A little Post-it. Some writing scribbled on it.'

'Lorna, Mrs Graham, read the note and brought it straight to me. She would have taken it to the police, but she was concerned it could have been a prank. She didn't want the school in trouble.'

'What did the note say?'

'It said,' he looked at her gravely, ' "Daddy hits us. He locks Mummy up." '

'*Daddy hits us. Locks Mummy up?*' The words put ice into Janice's veins and made her want to stop breathing. 'Did you find out who wrote it?'

'Yes. Two of my pupils. I remember them very well, brothers. I think their parents were going through a divorce. I took it very seriously and, yes, I got Social Services involved. It didn't take long to find out it was true. Two boys being abused by their father. Months before the sweet jar they'd been off school for a week. Came back looking very subdued.' He rubbed his arms as if the memory made him cold. 'Once Social Services were on board the mother got custody of the children. Father never went to court. He was police, I seem to recall. Backed down and never fought the custody case . . .' He trailed off. Janice, Cory and Neil Blunt were sitting forward, their faces white. 'What?' he said. 'What have I said?'

In her chair, her legs still crossed at the ankles, Janice began to shake.

72

A man, quite a large man, crouched unnoticed in the lee of an old olive-green telephone switching box on a residential street in Southville and stared intently at a front garden on the other side of the road. He wore jeans, a sweatshirt and a nylon jogging jacket. Nothing remarkable, really, but from his back pocket hung a length of coloured rubber. A face, sloppy and limp. The grinning mouth of a rubber Santa Claus mask – the sort of thing that could be picked up from any novelty shop for a few pounds. His dark-blue Peugeot was parked a few hundred yards away. Since the woman in Frome had seen him outside her house he'd learned to keep his distance better.

A woman came out of the front door, dressed in a bright-red coat and carrying two bags and a blue and yellow baby seat. She loaded up the car: baby seat first, safely strapped to the back seat, blanket all tucked in neatly. Then handbag on the front seat, nappy bag in the footwell. She got an ice-scraper from the glove compartment and leaned across the bonnet to get to the windscreen. Her back was turned to the man for a moment and he took the opportunity to creep from the shadow of the switching box. He walked calmly across the street, back straight, checking all around him as he did. He ducked into a neighbour's front driveway and crossed the frosted lawn. He stopped in the line of shrubs that divided the two houses and watched as the woman walked around the back of the car, lifted the rear wiper to scrape the glass. The woman gave the windows one last brush and went

356

to the front. Paused to wipe the wing mirrors and got into the driver's seat, blowing on her cold hands, fumbling with the key.

The man pulled on the Santa Claus mask, stepped over the low stone wall – a wolf taking its time – and walked calmly to her side of the car. Opened the door.

'Get out.'

The woman's response was to throw her hands into the air. It was an instinctive thing, to protect her face, and it succeeded only in clearing the way for him to reach over and unfasten her seatbelt. By the time she realized her mistake it was too late. He was already pulling her out of the car.

'Get out, bitch.'

'No! No! *No!*'

But he was strong. He took her by the hair and dragged her out, her hands scrabbling at her scalp, legs kicking, frantically trying to find purchase. She got a knee wedged up under the steering-wheel and her left hand into the sill above the door, but she couldn't hold it. With one wrench she was out, staggering, dropping once, cutting her knee through the tights. She got her fingers into his gloved hands, tried to get him to release her hair, but he dragged her backwards, ignoring her nails in his hands. She bounced her feet off the ground, kicked and screamed. He could feel little pieces of hair popping out all over her scalp as he flung her up against the front door of the house.

'Fuck off.' She pushed him away with all her might. '*Get away from me.*'

He gave her a shove, sent her staggering across the porch. Her arms went up, pinwheeled, slammed into the brick pillar, scraping the skin on her hands. Her left leg shot out, almost stopped the forward momentum, failed. She stumbled, went down, landing on her right shoulder. She rolled on to her side in time to see the man jump into the driver's seat and start the engine. The radio came to life, pumping 'When A Child Is Born' into the cold air. The engine revved, a cloud of fumes shot out of the exhaust, the handbrake came off and he twisted in his seat to reverse the car rapidly out of the driveway.

The car stopped in the middle of the road just long enough for Prody to change gear, then screamed away. It was only then, with the almighty squeal of brakes rocking round the street, that any of Skye Stephenson's neighbours realized what was happening. One or two came running out of their doors, down their paths, but it was too late. The cherry-red four-by-four had turned the corner at the end of the road and disappeared from sight.

73

Clare Prody didn't wear makeup and she didn't colour her lifeless blonde hair. She dressed nicely and plainly in neutral and pastel separates from mid-price high-street stores like Gap. Flat shoes. She looked as if she might come from the same socioeconomic bracket as Janice Costello. But then she opened her mouth and it was pure country bumpkin that came out. A Somerset girl, Bridgewater, and the furthest she'd strayed out of the area had been the train to London twice – once for *Les Mis* and once for *The Phantom*. She'd been a trainee nurse at Bristol Royal, dreaming of working with children, when Paul Prody had walked into her life. He'd married her and cajoled her into giving up work and staying at home with the two children, Robert and Josh. Paul had a good job, and Clare was dependent on him. It had taken her years of abuse to get up the courage to leave.

Caffery scrutinized her where she sat on the other side of his desk. She'd arrived at the offices wearing the first things she'd had to hand when his call came – a jogging T-shirt and khakis. For some reason she also wore a chequered blue blanket around her shoulders, clasped at her chest in bloodless fingers. It wasn't because she was cold. It was something more. It was because she felt like a refugee. Someone in the permanent process of running away. Her face was pale, as if there wasn't enough blood in her body, but her nose was an awful chapped red. Since she'd arrived half an hour ago she'd cried enough to break a person's heart. She simply couldn't believe this was happening to her. Just couldn't believe it.

'I can't think of any more.' Her eyes were fixed on the names scrawled on the whiteboard over his shoulder. Her lips were quivering. 'I really can't.'

'It's OK. Don't push yourself. It'll come.'

Clare had written the most comprehensive inventory of every person she could think of – anyone her husband might include in his appalling vendetta. Some of the names the team had already thought of, some they hadn't. A few doors down the corridor a whole room of officers was frantically working through them. Getting on to the local police. Phoning direct warnings. MCIU was at its tensest ever because there wasn't a person in the unit who wasn't seized with the absolute conviction that Prody would strike again. And that their biggest hope lay in pinpointing his next victim. Caffery, who, because of his fury, believed he sensed Prody more keenly than anyone in the building, thought it would be soon. Very soon. This morning, maybe.

'They were lucky.' Clare's eyes had travelled away from the list of names and had come to rest on the photos pinned up. She looked at Neil and Simone Blunt. At Lorna and Damien Graham. 'So lucky.'

'He let them off lightly.'

She gave a dry, hopeless laugh. 'That's Paul for you. He's very precise. The punishment always fits the crime. If you'd really upset him you'd get it worse. He wasn't as angry with Alysha's mum, with Neil . . .' she squinted at the name '. . . Blunt. I suppose he must have introduced himself at the Citizens' Advice Bureau, I just don't remember. I sort of recognize his face but I would never have known his name. I do remember that day, though, because afterwards Paul was waiting for me outside. Threatened to kill me.' She shook her head as if she still couldn't quite fathom her own stupidity. 'I missed it all. Jonathan Bradley used to be Robert and Josh's *headmaster* – the boys and I even went up to Oakhill when Martha was kidnapped and left flowers outside his house and I *still* didn't make the connection.'

'He's very, very clever, Clare. Your husband is very clever. Don't blame yourself.'

'*You* knew. *You* worked it out.'

'Yes, but I had help. And, anyway, I'm the police. I'm supposed to make connections.'

While Caffery wished he could claim some subtle sleuth's sleight-of-hand here, he couldn't. It had been a simple phone call from the hospital lab, something routine, that had started the slats falling in his head. Paul Prody still hadn't brought his shirt in to be tested. The technicians had run out of tests to do for inhalants and were starting to ask themselves if the jacker had used an oral sedative. Prody's stomach contents would make a very welcome addition to their pipettes and beakers. After the phone call Caffery hadn't been able to stop thinking about the clean look of Janice's mouth in the garden yesterday. White and pink and scab-free. Unsettlingly so. And then he'd understood what it was in the photo of the safe-house kitchen that had been bugging him. It was the little line of beakers on the draining-board. The last thing Paul Prody had done in the safe-flat was serve cocoa to the family. To Janice, her mum and Emily.

Caffery got to his feet, went to the window, where Myrtle lay on her bed, and looked out at the watery sky. He'd managed a quick rinse in the men's, with pump-dispenser soap and hand-dryers, and a shave with the disposable razor he kept locked in his filing cabinet, but his suit was crumpled and somehow he still felt dirty. As if Paul Prody had crawled inside his skin. Waiting to hear was like waiting for a storm to come. Not knowing which direction it would be, which roofs the dark clouds would tower above. But he could feel Prody out there like a vibration in his skin, on this rainy winter's day, moving nimbly around in the cold city and the countryside. Things were already happening out there: already the force had its tentacles out. They were going to find him today. And when they did they'd find Flea Marley too. Caffery was a hundred per cent sure of that awful reality. A junior DC had left the offices an hour ago to check her house and the whole of the Underwater Search Unit were being woken from their beds by the telephone team in the next office. But everyone suspected the answer lay with Prody.

'He was a bastard to me,' Clare said behind Caffery. 'A bastard. I lost count of the black eyes.'

'Yes.' Caffery rested his fingers on the window, thinking, You're coming to us, Prody. You're coming. 'It's a shame you didn't tell the police.'

'I know. Of course now I can see how stupid it was, but I believed everything he told me – so did the boys. We never thought the police would help us, that's how brainwashed we were – we thought you were like a club. All in it together and you'd never turn on your own. I was more scared of the police than I was of Paul. So were the boys. It's just—' She broke off. There was a moment's silence. Then he heard her suck in a small, shocked breath.

He turned. She was staring at a point in the middle of the air, an expression of dawning horror on her face. 'What is it?'

'Christ,' she said faintly. 'Oh, Christ.'

'Clare?'

'Dehydration,' she murmured.

'Dehydration?'

'Yes.' She turned her eyes to him. They were glittering. 'Mr Caffery, do you know how long it takes to die from dehydration?'

'It depends,' he said cautiously, coming to sit opposite her, 'on the conditions. Why?'

'We'd had an argument. The biggest of them all. Paul locked me in a toilet – the downstairs one where there was no window I could shout out of. He sent the boys to his mother's and told everyone I'd gone away on holiday with friends.'

'Go on,' Caffery said, feeling something loosen in his chest that had been clenched from the moment he'd walked into Rose Bradley's kitchen. 'Go on.'

'He switched off the water. For a while I drank from the toilet cistern, and he switched that off too.' Her face was stark and rigid. 'He kept me there for four days. I don't know but I think I nearly died.'

Caffery breathed slowly and quietly. He wanted to put his head down on the desk and yell. Because he knew instinctively that

Clare was right: it was what Prody had done to Martha and Emily. Which meant they could still be alive. Just. Emily had a good chance. Martha – probably not. Caffery'd had reason, on a case back in London, to speak to doctors about dehydration and knew that, whatever the bushcraft rule said – a person could only live three days without water – the limit of life without water could be more than ten days. Martha was a child and that would limit her chances but if, as a dumb cop, he'd had to play the doctor he'd say five, maybe six days tops. If the universe was shining its good grace on her.

Six days. He looked at the calendar. She'd been gone exactly that. Six days. All but six hours.

The phone on the desk rang. Both he and Clare stared at it, immobilized. Even Myrtle sat up, ears pricked, suddenly all attention. It rang again and this time he lifted the handset. Listened, his heart thudding. He put the phone down and looked at Clare. She was gaping at him, her eyes wide.

'Skye Stephenson.'

'*Skye?* The solicitor? *Shit.*'

Caffery hooked his jacket off the back of his chair. 'I've got a job for you.'

'She's got a baby. Skye's got a baby. A little boy. I never thought of her—'

'I'll get you an escort. DC Paluzzi. She'll drive you out there.'

'Drive me where?' Clare gripped the desk – as if to stop herself being moved. The blue blanket flopped and fell to the floor, revealing her thin shoulders in the black jogging T-shirt. 'Where's she driving me?'

'Out to the Cotswolds. We think we know where he is. We think we might've got him.'

74

Outside the MCIU offices it was raining. The side turning that led from the main street to the car park was packed with vehicles. There were people on the pavement, men in suits, uniformed officers. There was an armoured Sprinter van with the back doors open. Cold blue lights turned on vehicle roofs.

Janice already knew that MCIU had figured out about Prody: at the same time as she'd been with the families, Caffery had been putting it together. But as the four of them – Janice, Nick, Cory and Rose Bradley – pulled up in the Audi, she could tell from the seriousness in the men's faces that something more had happened. There was something terrible about the way the officers were concentrating, talking in neat, nipped sentences. Urgent. That serious intent was the worst thing for Janice. It meant it wasn't a dream. Maybe it meant they'd got him. Found the girls.

Nick saw it too. She unclipped her belt, her face fixed. 'Wait here.' She got out and walked fast in the direction of the offices.

Janice hesitated, then unbuckled her seatbelt and got out. She set off across the street after Nick, her shoulders hunched in the rain, her coat half hitched up over her head. Past the vehicles, through the gates that stood wide open and into the car park. She had almost passed a long black car parked against the wall when something about it caught her eye. She came to an abrupt halt. She stood, facing ahead for a moment, motionless.

Someone was sitting in the back seat of the car. A woman. A

woman with pale hair and a sorrowful, drawn-down face. Clare Prody.

Janice turned very slowly. Clare stared back at her from behind the rain-spattered window. She had a blanket around her shoulders as if she'd been rescued from a fire, and there was pure horror in her eyes – to be face to face suddenly with Cory's wife. With Emily's mother.

Janice couldn't move. Couldn't turn away, couldn't go forward. All she could do was stare back. Her eyes were dry – dry and sore as if they'd never close. There was nothing to say. Nothing adequate to express how it felt to be standing there wretchedly in the rain. Hopeless. Watched by the woman who was sleeping with Cory and whose husband had stolen Emily. She'd never felt so transparently weak and miserable in her life.

Her head dropped forward. She didn't have it in her any more – even standing was too much effort. She turned to trudge back to the Audi. Behind her the window of the black car opened with a shushing sound. 'Janice?'

She stopped. She couldn't take another step, couldn't turn back. Dog-tired.

'Janice?'

Painfully she lifted her chin and twisted her head. In the car Clare's face was so white it was almost luminous. There were black tracks on her cheeks where she'd cried her mascara off. Her expression was pinched and cloudy with guilt. She half leaned out of the window and checked quickly around the car park that no one was watching her. Then she leaned further towards Janice and whispered, 'They know where he is.'

Janice's mouth opened numbly. She shook her head. Not getting it. 'What?'

'They know where he is. They're taking me now. I'm not supposed to be saying anything, but I know.'

Janice took a step back towards the car. '*What?*'

'He's somewhere called Sapperton. I think it's in the Cotswolds.'

Janice felt her face widen. Felt a squeezed-up part of her head come to life. Sapperton. Sapperton. She knew that name. It was the tunnel where the teams had searched for Martha.

'Janice?'

She wasn't listening. She was running back to the Audi, as fast as her legs would carry her, splashing crazily through the puddles. Cory was out of the car now, a strange look on his face. He wasn't looking at her, but at Clare sitting in the car. Janice didn't stop. She didn't care. She opened her arm out behind her. 'She's all yours, Cory. All yours.'

She jumped into the car. Rose was leaning forward from the back seat, her face full of questions.

'They've found him.'

'*What?*'

'The Sapperton tunnel. The place they searched for Martha? They don't want us there but that doesn't matter.' She jammed her keys in and started the engine. The windscreen wipers came on, cannoning back and forth with urgent squeaks. 'We're going too.'

'Hey.' The passenger door opened and Nick peered in, dripping rain everywhere. 'What's going on?'

Janice clicked on the sat nav, tapped in 'Sapperton'.

'Janice. I asked you a question. What the hell's going on?'

'I think you know the answer to that. They've told you.'

The sat nav was crunching the instructions. And now the map came up on the screen. Janice fiddled with the toggle button, zooming out to get a perspective.

'Janice, I don't know what you're thinking of doing.'

'Yes, you do.'

'I can't let that happen. You'll have to abduct me if you want me to stay with you.'

'Then you're abducted.'

'Jesus.' Nick jumped into the front seat and slammed the door. Janice put the car into gear, took the handbrake off and began to pull forward. But she had to slam her foot on the brake. At the end of the bonnet, half obscured by the rain, stood Cory. His eyes were hooded miserably, his body was half hanging, as if his arms and hands had got too heavy for him. She stared at him, not understanding what was happening. Beyond him Clare was in the black car, looking stonily in the opposite direction. With colour in her face at last. Her cheeks were red. Janice got it. There'd been an argument.

She took the car out of gear and Cory came round to the driver's side. She opened the window and gave him a long, appraising look. Studied his tan, which had been sprayed on in a booth in Wincanton. Was he as pale under it as she felt? It was hard to tell. She studied the suit – pressed and neat because he'd had time to do all that somehow, whereas she'd have to look down at herself if she wanted to know what she was wearing. And he was crying. In all the time Emily had been gone he hadn't cried. Not once. It had taken Clare to make him cry.

'She dumped me. I don't know what you said to her, but she dumped me.'

'I'm sorry.' Janice kept her voice calm. Quiet. 'I'm really sorry.'

He held her eyes, his mouth shaking a little. Then his face crumpled. His shoulders came up. He dropped his head forward, put his hands on the side of the car, and began to sob. Janice watched him in silence, saw the vulnerable bald spot on the top of his head. She felt nothing for him. No pity, no love. Just a cold, hard wedge of nothing. 'I'm sorry,' she said again, and this time she meant she was sorry for everything. For him, for their marriage, for their poor, poor little girl. She was sorry for the world. 'I'm sorry, Cory, but now you have to get out of my way.'

75

The rain in the city hadn't reached the countryside to the north-east of Bristol. Persistent wind had kept the sky clear and the temperatures down so that even by midday most of the fields were still covered with frost. Turner drove Caffery's Mondeo, taking it fast up the little lanes that led to the wood near the Thames and Severn canal where Prody had dumped Skye Stephenson's four-by-four. Caffery sat silently in the passenger seat, not speaking. His head jiggled slightly, bumping with the movement of the car. The body armour he wore under his suit was digging into his back.

'Lion,' he said distantly. 'That's what I was missing.'

Turner shot him a look. 'Beg pardon?'

'A lion.' He nodded. 'Should have seen it.'

Turner followed his eyeline. Caffery was gazing at the emblem on the steering-wheel. 'Peugeot? The lion?'

'Prody's car is a Peugeot. I saw it when he drove out of the car park last night. It reminded me of something.'

'What?'

'You could mistake it for a dragon, couldn't you? If you were a woman in your sixties who didn't know much about cars?'

'Mistake it for a Vauxhall?' Turner put his indicator on. They'd reached the RV point. 'Yeah. You could.'

Caffery thought of the miles of streets the units had searched, always looking for a Vauxhall, when Prody's car was a dark-blue Peugeot. Walking down the wrong road: looking for a dragon and ignoring all the lions they walked past. If they'd had the chip from the shop's CCTV they'd have known it was a Peugeot. But Prody had taken care of that too. Caffery was willing to bet who the first attending officer had been taking the camera chip out for the robbery investigation and who had forgotten to switch the CCTV back on. Plus Paul and Clare Prody had lived for ten years in Farrington Gurney – at the time it hadn't struck Caffery as a co-incidence. Now he thought of the last six days, pictured them spread out behind him like a trail. He saw every wasted second. Every bitter lapse of concentration. Every cup of coffee he'd stopped to make and drink, every piss he'd taken. All measured against the time – minutes or hours – Martha might have left. He put his forehead to the window and stared out. This morning Ted Moon had tried to hang himself from the same tree his mother had. He was in hospital now, surrounded by his family. Did things get any bleaker?

Turner pulled into the car park of a pub that sat near the easterly entrance to the Sapperton tunnel. The place was crawling with cops: dog vans, CSI vans, support unit vans. The roar of an Air Support Unit helicopter rattled the air above them. Turner pulled on the handbrake, turned to Caffery, his face grave. 'Boss. At the end of the day my missus always makes me dinner. We sit down and open some wine and then she asks me what happened at work. What I want to know is, am I going to be able to tell her?'

Caffery peered out of the windscreen to where the afternoon sky was cut at mid-section by the tops of the forest trees, and above it the tail rotor of the helicopter. The trees started about fifty yards from the car park – the vague white smear of the inner cordon tape was already in place, lifting lazily in the wind. He sat back. 'I don't think so, mate,' he said quietly. 'I don't think she's going to want to hear any of this.'

They got out of the car, went past the people in the car park, and signed in with the outer cordon loggist. The containment area was enormous and there was a long way to walk – along a rutted track overhung with dripping trees, past the five-bar gate Prody

369

had smashed through being chased by two road policing unit vehicles – until they came to the place where he'd crashed and continued on foot. They walked in silence. They were only a quarter of a mile from where Prody had parked the Bradleys' Yaris the night he'd kidnapped Martha. You know this area, Caffery thought, as they picked up the trail the CSI's tread-plates made into the wood, don't you? And you're not far from here right now. You can't have gone very far at all now you're on foot.

By the time they arrived at the crash site the helicopter had stopped circling and was hovering a few hundred yards to the south, over an area of dense woodland. Caffery squinted up at it, noting its position. Wondered what it was focusing on and when he'd hear something. He flashed his badge and ducked under the inner cordon, Turner behind him, to where Skye Stephenson's four-by-four sat inside its own taped-out containment area. Caffery pocketed his card and stood for a moment, staring at the scene, measuring himself. Trying to get his heart to sit down a bit: trying to stop it battering its way out of his chest.

The vehicle was a dark almost cherry red, its flanks scarred with mud churned up in Prody's frantic effort to drive it down this tiny lane. He'd known by then he was being followed. Its off-side bumper was smashed, the tyre tread split wide to show the radial wires inside. The passenger door and both rear doors stood open. From the sill on the passenger side a blanket trailed slackly, connecting the car to a baby seat that was tipped over, its under-side facing Caffery and Turner. Blue, with yellow anchors. Baby clothes lay strewn around. A small arm was just visible in the curve of the seat: a clenched fist.

The crime-scene manager looked up. He saw Caffery and came towards him, pulling down his hood. His face was ashen. 'The guy is sick.'

'I know.'

'The officers on his tail think he knew about them for the last ten miles. He could have opened the window and thrown the baby seat out. But he didn't. He kept it in the car.'

Caffery eyed the seat. 'Why?'

'He was pulling the damned thing apart as he drove. Furious with us, I guess.'

They went to the seat and looked down at it. The life-size baby doll Skye had dressed in Charlie's clothes had been reduced by Prody to a pile of plastic limbs, deposited in the baby seat. A foot away, half covered by Charlie's Babygro, lay the doll's head. Squashed flat. A muddy footprint stamped across it.

'How is she doing?' asked the CSM. 'The stand-in?'

Caffery shrugged. 'She's in shock. I don't think she really believed it was going to happen the way we said it would.'

'I know her. Through the force. She's a good officer but if I'd thought she'd volunteer for a stunt like that I'd've told her to go have a lie-down in a darkened room and rethink it. Still,' he said grudgingly, 'that was some good bet. To guess where it would happen.'

'Not really. I was lucky. Very lucky. And lucky everyone played their part. That it worked.'

Only now was Caffery realizing that for once in this god-forsaken case something in the great unknowable universe had come down on his side: even before Clare had got to the office and given them her list of Prody's possible victims, Caffery, Turner and Lollapalooza had already written down three names they thought could be next. People who'd been contacted by the police and warned. Who'd spent the morning with covert surveillance units outside their houses. Skye Stephenson had been the one the team had been rooting for because she was the only person they could use a substitute with. Prody had never met her personally until today – he'd known her only from her address and from a photograph on the company website. The unit's fortunes were changing.

Caffery bent over, hands on his knees, to study the tracking unit Q had attached to Skye's four-by-four in case the tail cars outside her house had lost Prody.

'What?' said the CSM.

'Are these the ones the force always uses?'

'I think so. Why?'

He gave an ironic shrug. 'Nothing. It's the same as Prody used on the Costellos' car. Must've half inched it from the technical department. Sly sod.'

'Knows his stuff, then.'

'You could say that.'

From the other side of the wood a dog began to bark. Loud enough to be heard above the helicopter. Every person at the crime scene stopped what they were doing. Straightened and stared out across the trees. Caffery and Turner exchanged a glance. They recognized the familiar note in the yap. A tracking dog made a sound like that for one reason and one reason only. It had found its target. The two men turned without a word, ducked under the tape and headed fast along the path in the direction of the noise.

As they moved through the woods, other figures in uniform appeared in the surrounding trees, all converging on the place the dog was barking. Caffery and Turner came through a soft and silent pine forest, their footsteps cushioned by the carpet of henna red needles, the clatter of the helicopter rotors growing louder the nearer they got. There was another sound too – the bellow of a loudhailer. Caffery speeded up. Sprinted through a glade littered with felled silver birch, back up a short slope, mud and leaves all over his trousers now – and out on to a cleared track where the thin winter sun glanced down in blades. He stopped. A tall man in riot gear, his visor up, was coming towards them, his arm held aloft to halt them. 'Inspector Caffery? The SIO?'

'Yes?' Caffery flashed his warrant card. 'What's happening? Sounds like the dogs've got a knock over there.'

'I'm the Bronze commander for today.' He put his hand out. 'Good to meet you.'

Caffery took a long, deep breath. He made himself return the card to his pocket and shake the hand calmly. 'Yes. Very nice to meet you. What's happening here? Have the dogs got him?'

'Yes. But it's not good.' Sweat was popping out on the guy's face. The Silver and Gold commanders on an exercise like this would be at HQ, organizing the operation from the safety of their seats, while this poor bastard, Bronze, was at the bottom of the pile. The tactical commander, the guy on the ground, he had to take Silver and Gold's orders and translate them into action. If Caffery was in his shoes he'd be sweating too. 'We know where he is, but we haven't effected an arrest yet. It's not a good place at all. There are air shafts all over this place – they feed the Sapperton tunnel.'

'I know.'

'Well, he's got a belay rope in one of them. Went down like a fucking rabbit.'

Caffery let all his breath out at once. Flea'd been right. All along she'd been right. And suddenly he felt her – like he'd hear a shout in the darkness. A tug at his instinct. As if she was near by. He looked around at the empty expanse of trees. There hadn't been anything yet from the PC in Bath sent out to check her house. Flea was definitely here somewhere.

'Sir?'

He turned and there, as if Caffery had magicked him up from the strength of his anxiety for Flea, stood Wellard. Also dressed in dark-blue cargoes and an opened riot helmet. He was panting, his breath white in the freezing air. He had bluish circles under his eyes and Caffery knew from his face that the guy was thinking about exactly the same thing. 'You haven't heard from her?'

Caffery shook his head. 'You?'

'No.'

'So what are we supposed to think about that?'

'I don't know.' Wellard put a finger to his throat. Swallowed. 'But, uh, look, what I do know is the tunnel. I do know about that. I've been down there before, I've got the schematics. That shaft he's gone down is between two rockfalls. He's a rat in a trap down there. Really. No way out.'

They turned expectantly to the Bronze commander. He unbuckled his helmet and used his sleeve to wipe the sweat off his forehead.

'I'm not sure. He's not responding to our challenges.'

Caffery laughed. 'What? Someone with a megaphone yelling at him? Course he won't.'

'Best to establish communications first. Bring in a negotiator. His wife's on her way, isn't she?'

'Fuck the negotiations. Get a rope-access team in there now.'

'I can't do that. It's not that simple – we need risk assessments.'

'Risk assessments? Do me a fucking favour. The suspect knows the area – we think he brought one of the vics here. She could still be alive. Tell that to your Silver and Gold. Use the words "grave and immediate danger". They'll get the drift.'

He pushed past the commander, headed along the track, his feet squelching in the mud, cracking the ice on the puddles. He'd gone a few yards when a noise louder than the helicopter, the dogs and the megaphone put together lifted from under his feet. The ground seemed to move beneath them. The bare branches quivered with the shock and a few dry leaves fluttered down. A flock of rooks took to the air, cawing.

In the silence that followed, the three men stood facing the air shaft. There was a pause, then, from inside the trees, dogs began to howl. A high-pitched, terrified sound.

'What the fuck was that?' Caffery turned and looked back down the track at Wellard and the commander. 'What the *fuck* was that?'

76

Janice switched off the Audi engine and looked at the crowded pub car park. It was full of response cars and specialist trucks. There were people everywhere, moving around, their faces grim, their breath steaming the air. From somewhere over the forest came the din of a helicopter.

'The team will want us to stay here.' Nick peered out of the windscreen at a track that disappeared into the woods. 'They won't want us any nearer than this.'

'Won't they?' Janice took the keys out of the ignition and pocketed them. 'I see.'

'Janice,' Nick said warningly, 'I'm supposed to stop you doing this. You'll get yourselves arrested.'

'Nick,' Janice said patiently, 'you are lovely. You are one of the loveliest people I have ever met, but you haven't got a clue about this. Whatever your training, you don't even know the half of it. You can't until it happens to you. Now,' she held her gaze, eyebrows raised, 'are you going to help us or are we on our own?'

'I'd lose my job.'

'Then, stay here in the car. Lie. Say we escaped. Whatever. We'll back you up.'

'We will,' said Rose. 'Stay here. We'll be OK.'

No one spoke for a few moments. Nick looked from Rose to Janice and back again. Then she zipped up her oilskin jacket and wound a scarf around her neck. 'You bastards. You'll need me if you're going to do it properly. Come on.'

The three women headed down the track, the deafening clack-clack-clack of the helicopter over the trees blotting out the sound of their footsteps as they ran. Janice's shoes were the court heels she'd put on that morning in a vague attempt to look presentable for the meeting at her sister's. Completely unsuitable, she had to half hobble along the path trying desperately to keep up with Nick, who wore flat walking boots as if she'd been prepared for this all along. Next to Janice, Rose puffed away, moving like a sturdy carthorse, her hands in the pockets of her neat woollen jacket, her face grim and old. The little pink scarf bobbed around her neck.

They came round the bend in the track and saw the first cordon – a line of tape suspended across the track. Beyond it orange tread-plates on the ground leading into the trees. A loggist stood on duty. Nick didn't stop moving. She turned to face Rose and Janice, trotting backwards in front of them, shouting above the noise of the helicopter. 'Listen. Whatever happens, let me do the talking. 'Kay?'

'Yes,' they shouted. 'Yes.'

They slowed to a fast walk. Nick pulled out her warrant card and held it out at face height. 'DC Hollis, MCIU,' she shouted, as they approached. 'Relatives coming through. Mrs Bradley, Mrs Costello.' The loggist took a step forward, frowned at her card. 'The cordon log, please.' Nick snapped her fingers. 'We're in a hurry.'

He fumbled out the clipboard, unsnapped a pen and held it out to them. 'No one said anything,' he began, as the women gathered round to sign. 'I was told no one past this point. I mean, we don't usually let relatives—'

'DI Caffery's orders.' Nick handed him back the pen and pushed the clipboard at him. 'If I don't get them there in the next five my head's going to be on the block.'

'They definitely won't let you past the inner cordon,' he shouted after them, as they headed off. 'There's been an explosion. You really can't go past that one . . .'

The helicopter banked away, rattling off into the distance,

leaving the woods . . . quiet, the only noise the sound of their footsteps and breathing. They continued down the track, slower now as they tried to balance on the uneven tread-plates. Janice's lungs were sore with the effort. The trail led them straight past the CSI team, who didn't look up from swabbing and taping Skye Stephenson's car to watch the three women pass. As they got further into the wood Janice became aware of black smuts floating down through the trees, like dark fairies. She kept glancing up at them as she walked. An explosion? What sort of explosion?

From far away across the sky the noise of the helicopter grew louder. It was coming back, low over the trees. The women stopped. They put their hands above their eyes to shield them from the light, and watched the dark crow shape blot out the sky above them.

'What does that mean?' Janice shouted. 'Does it mean they've lost him? Is he out here in the woods?'

'No,' Nick yelled. 'It's not the same helicopter. Not air-support craft. It's black and yellow, not blue and yellow.'

'Meaning?'

'Meaning it's probably the HEMS copter from Filton.'

'What's HEMS?' shouted Rose.

'Helicopter Emergency Medical Services. It's a medivac. There's a casualty.'

'Him? Is it *him*?'

'*I don't know.*'

Janice broke into a run, leaving the others behind. Her heart was hammering, and her shoes caught hopelessly in the tread-plates, so she stopped, kicked them off and continued in her stockinged feet. She passed whole new plantations of saplings enclosed in rabbit-guard tubes. She ran through soft orange beds of sawdust until she got to a place where the trees were thinner and patches of sky poked through. There was a clearing ahead. She could see the blue and white splash of police tape. That must be the inner cordon. And now she saw the inner cordon loggist, standing side on to her, squinting up at the helicopter. He was different from the earlier one. Bigger, more serious-looking. He wore riot gear and stood with his feet wide, his arms folded across his chest.

She came to a halt. Breathing hard.

He turned his head and eyed her stonily. 'You shouldn't be here. Who are you?'

'Please,' she began. 'Please—'

He approached. Just as he was almost on her Nick appeared from behind, panting. 'It's OK. I'm MCIU. These are relatives.'

He shook his head. 'Still shouldn't be here. Only authorized personnel in here – and you're not on my very, very short list.'

Rose stepped forward, not scared of him at all. She was bright red, breathing hard, every inch of her skin flushed and shiny. 'I'm Rose Bradley. This is Janice Costello. It's our little girls he took. Please – we won't cause any trouble. We only want to know what's happening.'

The officer gave her a slow, thoughtful look. He took in the stretchy trousers and the little smart scarf at her neck. He took in the piped woollen jacket and the hair damp with sweat and neglect. Then he looked at Janice – carefully, almost warily, as if she might be from a different planet.

'Please,' Rose begged. 'Don't send us back.'

'Don't send them back,' Nick said, a note of pleading in her voice. 'Don't. Please. They don't deserve it with what they've gone through.'

The officer tilted his head and studied the underside of the branches above him. He took slow breaths as if he was doing complicated sums in his head. 'Over there.' After a few moments he dropped his head and held out a hand, indicating a tangle of brambles that had formed a natural hidey-hole. A place a person could crouch and not be spotted. 'You could have walked in there and I wouldn't never have seen you. But,' he held up a finger and fixed Nick's eyes, 'don't take the piss, OK? Don't take the piss or abuse my kindness. Because I'm a better liar than you are, whatever you think. And be quiet. For Christ's sake, be quiet.'

77

The air shafts that fed the tunnel in some places reached well over a hundred feet in depth. Roughly the height of a ten-storey office block. The eighteenth-century engineers had let the waste soil accumulate around the shafts so that they'd come to resemble enormous ant hills – strange funnel shapes jutting out of the ground, holes sunk in the centre of each. Often covered with trees and foliage, they weren't usually very remarkable. This particular air shaft, however, was far from unremarkable.

It was in a natural clearing surrounded by beech and oak trees in the last stages of the autumn drop. Crows cawed from the tops of bare branches and underfoot the ground was deep in coppery brown leaves. At the top of the slight incline the hole gaped secretively, its sides coated with the tarry black evidence of the explosion. The smuts still floated out of it, rising into the air as if on a convection column, reaching to a point above the trees where the air cooled and slowly floated them down again to land in the trees, the grass. They coated everything – even the rope-access team's white Sprinter van.

More than twenty people trampled the frosty grass: plain-clothes officers, some in riot gear, some in caving helmets and complex harnesses. A handler led a German shepherd, still straining on the leash, into the dog van. Caffery noticed that, whatever their duty, no one seemed to want to spend much time near the hole. The two officers who had come with cutters to remove the protective wire around it had worked fast and retreated as soon as the job was over, not meeting anyone's eye. It wasn't just the uneasy knowledge that the shaft plunged straight into the earth, it was the noise coming from it. Now that the HEMS helicopter had landed and switched off its rotors, the sound echoed eerily up from the yawning shaft. Made everyone uncomfortable. A faint hoarse wheezing like a trapped animal. No one seemed inclined to turn their back on the hole.

Caffery approached with five other men: the Bronze commander, a drop-cam operator – who wheeled ahead of him a stainless-steel trolley on which sat a complex tubing camera system – and Acting Sergeant Wellard, who had brought two of his men with him. No one spoke as they crunched through the frozen leaves. Everyone's expression was closed, concentrated. At the edge of the hole they gathered in a line and peered down. The shaft was about ten feet in diameter. Traversing it was a single reinforcing beam, now almost rotted to nothing. An oak tree at the edge of the hole had spread a single root out across the beam, drawing in God only knew what moisture and nourishment from it. Caffery put his hand on the tree and leaned over. He saw a white layer of limestone. Below it, darker rock. And then nothing. Just cold shadows. And that unearthly noise again. Breathing. In and out.

The camera operator reeled out the yellow cable and fed the tiny drop-cam down into the hole. Caffery watched him unwind the electric leads and set up the monitor. It took for ever and Caffery had to stand absolutely still, a tic starting in his eye, wanting to yell at the guy, *Get a fucking move on*. Next to him Wellard had got himself into an abseil harness, had secured himself to another tree, and was kneeling with one hand braced on the oak's root so he could lean out over the hole and carefully lower the gas detector on a cable. On the other side of the shaft Wellard's men were prepping themselves: belaying kernmantle ropes off the surrounding trees and checking safety rigs, buckling harnesses, fixing self-braking descender units to their lines.

The Bronze commander watched the whole thing from a few paces away, a pinched, anxious look on his face. He, too, was unnerved by the noise. No one knew for sure what had caused the blast – whether it was accidental or whether Prody had tried to blow himself up – but no one had even begun to let themselves wonder what the hell it meant for the girls. Or Sergeant Marley. If any of them were in the tunnel too.

'OK.' The operator had got the camera all the way down into the shaft and was powering up the monitor on the trolley. Caffery, Wellard and the Bronze commander all gathered round to watch the image. 'It's a fish-eye lens, so it's distorted. But I'd guess that those shapes you see here are the tunnel wall . . .' He tucked his lip under his teeth in concentration and played with the focus. 'There you are. Is that better?'

Slowly the image became clear. The spot on the camera cast a circle of jerky light illuminating whatever it came near. The first image was of a dripping wall, ancient and moss-covered. Then the camera turned slightly so the spot glinted off dark water in the canal, picking out a few submerged shapes. Everyone was silent. They all expected any of the humps to be Martha or Emily. Minutes passed as the camera trawled the canal. Five. Ten. The sun went behind clouds. A flock of crows left the branches overhead, stretching their black wings like hands across the sky. Eventually the camera operator shook his head.

'Nothing. The place looks empty.'

'*Empty?* Then, where's that fucking noise coming from?'

'Not the canal itself. Nothing on the floor or in the canal. It's empty.'

'It's *not* empty.'

The operator shrugged. He toggled the camera a bit more. Zoomed it to the end of the canal, where the picture grew shadowy.

'Like that,' said Caffery. 'I mean, what's *that*?'

'Dunno.' The operator put his hand over the screen to shade it and peered at the spectral images. 'OK,' he said grudgingly. 'That looks like something.'

'What is it?'

'A . . . I'm not sure. A hull? Of a barge maybe? Christ – look at the way that's peeled apart. That'll be where your explosion was.'

'Can you get inside it?'

He stood. Eyes on the monitor, he dragged the cable spools a few yards along the edge of the shaft. He sat for a moment, his hand on the reel, his eyes locked on the LCD screen. Eventually he spoke. 'I think . . . Yes. I've got something.'

He turned the screen to the men. Caffery and the Bronze commander leaned in to look, hardly breathing. The screen was unintelligible to Caffery: all he could make out was the torn metal of the barge's hull.

The operator zoomed in. 'There.' He pointed at something in the muck and the grime at the bottom of the picture that was moving slightly. 'That's something. See it?'

Caffery strained his eyes. It looked like tarry bubbles wallowing in the canal. There was a flash, the spotlight reflecting off the canal water as whatever it was moved again. Then something in the shape became white for a moment. Darkened. Went white again. It took Caffery a moment to realize what he was looking at. A pair of eyes. Blinking. Those eyes blew straight through him like a hurricane. '*Shit*.'

'*It's her*.' Wellard clipped the karabiner at his waist to the Petzl descender unit, shuffled backwards to the hole and leaned backwards over the lip, testing the rope, his face hard and concentrated. 'It's fucking her and I am going to fucking *kill* her for this.'

'Hey. What the hell do you think you're doing?' The Bronze commander stepped forward. 'You're not going down there yet.'

'The gas test is clean. Whatever exploded it's not there now. And I'm going down.'

'But our target is down there.'

'That's OK.' He patted the pockets of his body armour. 'We've got tasers.'

'And this is my operation and I'm telling you you're not going down. We've got to find out what's making that noise. That's an order.'

Wellard locked his jaw, gave the commander a solid eye. But he took a few steps forward away from the lip of the hole, and stood in silence, unconsciously clenching and unclenching the descender handle.

'Find the noise,' the commander told the camera operator. 'Find what's making that godforsaken noise. It's not her.'

'Yup.' The operator's face was clenched. 'I'm doing my best. I'm just having a . . . Christ!' He leaned into the screen. 'Christ, yes, I think this is it – this is what you wanted.'

Everyone gathered round. They were looking at something inhuman. Something tarred and burned and bloodied. Now they understood why they hadn't seen anything in the water of the canal. Prody wasn't anywhere on the ground. He'd been lifted by the explosion and skewered by a shard of metal high on the canal wall. Like a crucifixion. As the camera came towards him he didn't move. All he could do was stare into the lens and gulp air, his eyes bulging.

'Holy shit,' the Bronze commander whispered, awestruck. 'Holy shit. He is fucked, so fucked.'

Caffery stared at the screen, his heart pounding. He couldn't imagine how Prody could have been so clever. He'd tricked them over and over. He'd tricked them into focusing all their efforts on this tunnel, when the girls, with hours or minutes left, were somewhere else entirely. And the ultimate trick, the ultimate finger in the force's face, would be if he died now. Without telling the police anything.

He straightened. Turned to Wellard. 'Get that team down now,' he muttered. 'And I mean *now*.'

78

The sun had gone and the valley sat still and shocked. The aftermath of the thunder rolled away across the hillsides. Clouds of ash hung low. Birds, made of black oil, gathered on the edges of the horizon.

Dad looked wonderingly at the sky. 'Now that,' he murmured, 'is what I call a *storm.*'

Flea was a few yards away from him. She was bitterly cold. She felt sicker than she ever had in her life. The storm had a stink to it that turned her stomach. It smelt of water and of electricity and of cooked meat. The worms in her intestines that had fed and bloated until they blocked her insides pressed on her lungs, making her chest tight.

In the new silence of the valley she began to hear other noises. A hoarse, gulping breathing. Like something struggling to stay alive. And a more muffled sound. A whimpering? She got to her feet and walked down the slope. The whimpering was coming from a bush at the bottom of the garden. As Flea got nearer she realized it was a child whimpering. Whimpering and crying.

'*Martha?*'

She got nearer to the bush and saw something pale against the scorched earth, sticking out from under it.

'Martha?' she said cautiously. 'Martha? Is that you?'

The crying stopped for a moment. Flea took a step closer. She saw that the white shape against the earth was a child's foot. Wearing Martha's shoe.

'Please?' The voice was sweet. Quiet. 'Please help me.'

Flea slowly parted the bush. A face smiled up at her. She dropped the branch and took a step backwards. It wasn't Martha but Thom, Flea's brother. Adult Thom dressed in a little girl's gingham dress, smiling gnomishly at her. A bow in his hair, a rag doll tucked under his arm. Flea tripped, landed on her back. Tried to kick herself away from the bush, scraping along the grass on her backside.

'Don't go away, Flea.'

Thom pulled his shoe off. His foot came with it. He raised it, readying it to throw.

'*No!*' She scrambled in the earth. 'No!'

'Ever seen a dead body? You ever seen a dead body, Flea? Ever seen one cut up?'

'*Flea?*' She turned. Someone was standing behind her. A shadowy figure that might have been Dad but might have been almost anyone. She reached out for him but as she did she realized she wasn't in the hillside any more. She was in a crowded bar, people jostling for space around her. 'Police,' someone next to her was saying urgently. 'We are the police.' She could feel hands on her, trying to move her. Hanging low above her was a huge pendant lamp on a thick chain, with a blasted glass bowl. Someone wearing climber's crampons and a harness had climbed up on it and was swinging it to and fro. With each oscillation it went a little faster and came a little lower, until it was so close to her face, so blinding, she had to hold out her hand to push it away.

'*Noooooo,*' she heard herself moan. '*Noooo.* Don't.'

'Pupils normal,' someone said, quite close. 'Flea?' Someone was digging something into the lobe of her ear. Nails. Thumb and forefinger. 'Can you hear me?'

'Unnhhh.' She batted at the hand on her ear. The noise of the bar had gone. She was somewhere dark. People breathing fast and echoey. 'Sssshtop it.'

'You're going to be OK. I've got to get a line in you. Here.' She felt someone tap her arm. Lights were flashing in her eyes. And shapes. She dragged in a lungful of air. 'You'll feel it but only for a moment. That's it, just hold still for me. Good girl. You're going to be OK.'

She felt a hand on her head. 'That's good, Boss. You're doing great.' Wellard's voice. Raised as if he was talking to a child. What was Wellard doing here in this bar? She tried to turn to him, but he pressed her back down. 'Stay still now.'

'*No.*' She flinched as the needle went in. Tried to pull her arm away. 'No! It hurshts.'

'Just hold still. Nearly there.'

'Fugging hurts. Don't. Hurting me.'

'There. All over. You'll start to feel better soon.'

She tried groggily to reach for the arm, but a hand stopped her, held her arm down.

'Where's the aluminium blanket?' someone else was saying. 'She's a block of ice.'

Someone clipped something on to her finger. A hand worked its way down her back. Touching her neck. The blanket rustled around her. She felt hands under her neck, moving her. Something hard and warm behind her. She knew what they were doing – putting her on a spine board in case she'd got a back injury. She wanted to comment on it – to crack a joke, but her mouth was soft and slack and wouldn't get the words out.

'Oh, no,' she managed. 'Please don't. Don't pull. It hurts.'

'Just trying to get her through this bit,' a disembodied voice said. 'How the hell did she get herself in here? It's like *Das* bloody *Boot.*'

Someone laughed. Made a jokey *ping-ping* sound. Like a submarine sonar.

'It's not fucking funny. This place could go any time. Look at those cracks.'

'OK, OK. Just give me a bit more room on this side.' A jolt. A shudder. A splash of water. 'There. Good, that's it.'

Then Wellard's voice again: 'You're doing well, Boss. Not long now. Relax. Close your eyes.'

She obeyed. Gratefully letting something sly come up in front of her vision like a third eyelid and slip her away head first into a silver screen of images. Thom, Wellard, Misty Kitson. A little cat she'd had as a child. Then Dad was next to her – holding out his hand and smiling.

'It worked, Flea.'

'What worked?'

'The sweetie. It worked. Went bang, didn't it?'

'Yes. It worked.'

'Last little bit now, Flea. You've done so well.'

She opened her eyes. About a foot away a wall was moving past her. Limestone, with ferns and green slime growing out of it. The light coming from overhead was tremendous, blinding. Her feet were pointing down, her head was up. She tried to put out her hands to steady herself, but they were strapped to her sides. Next to her she could see the face of a man in a caving helmet, lit as if a spotlight was on him, the colours vivid, each pore and line clear and dizzying, the dirt and soot smeared about his mouth. He wasn't looking at her. He was focused down, concentrating on controlling their ascent.

'Basket stretcher,' she slurred. 'I'm in a basket stretcher.'

The man looked up at her in mild surprise. 'I'm sorry?'

'Martha,' she said. 'I know where he buried her. In a pit. Under the ground.'

'What was that?' came a voice from above. 'What's she on about now?'

'Dunno. Feels sick?' The man peered into her face. 'You OK?' He smiled. 'You're doing great. It's OK if you're sick. We've got you.'

She closed her eyes. Gave a weak laugh. 'She's in a *pit*,' she repeated. 'He put her body in a *pit*. But you can't understand what I'm saying. Can you?'

'I know you do,' came the answer. 'Don't you worry about that. We've given you something for it. You'll feel better soon.'

79

'What did she say? What's she talking about?' Caffery had to yell to be heard above the noise of the second HEMS helicopter that was landing a hundred yards away in the clearing at the end of the track. 'Did she say "spit"?'

The paramedic scrambled out of the hole as Wellard and two officers from the top team manhandled the stretcher out of the shaft. 'She says she feels *sick*,' he yelled. 'Sick.'

'Sick? Not *spit*?'

'She's been saying it since they pulled her up. Worried she's going to be sick.' He and Wellard got the stretcher on to an ambulance cot. The HEMS A and E consultant – a small, hard-grained man with dark hair and walnut skin – came forward to examine her. He lifted the portable monitor and checked it, pressed her fingernail between his thumb and forefinger, timing how long it took for the blood to flood back into the tissues. Flea groaned as he did it. Tried to shift on the spine board, reach her hand out. She looked like something that had been hauled out of a Cornwall surf accident, with her ripped blue immersion suit. Her face was clean except for the two blackened smudges under her nostrils where she'd breathed in the aftermath of the explosion. Her hair was thick with muck and leaves, her hands and fingernails caked with blood. Caffery didn't try to get near her. Or put his hand near hers. He let the doctor do his thing.

'You OK?'

Caffery glanced up. The doctor was busy helping the

paramedic lock the stretcher to the cot. But his eyes were on Caffery as he worked.

'I'm sorry?'

'I said you OK?'

'Of course I am. Why?'

'She's going to be fine,' he said. 'You don't need to worry.'

'I'm not worried.'

'Yeah.' The doctor kicked up the brake on the cot. 'Sure you're not.'

Caffery watched them numbly as they trundled her away, down the slope, getting the stretcher on to the track that led back to the clearing where the first helicopter sat, its engines running, the rotors waiting to be engaged. The slow, solid heft of the knowledge came home – that she was going to be OK. 'Thank you,' he said, under his breath, to the backs of the paramedics and the consultant. 'Thank you.'

He'd have liked to sit down now. To sit down and hold that feeling and do nothing more for the rest of the day. But he couldn't stop. A squawk box in the grass near the hole was broadcasting the efforts of the rescue teams still in the tunnel. The helicopter air paramedic – who'd been given a caving helmet and a crash course in rope-access technique – had got into the tunnel, taken one look at the way Prody was skewered to the wall and ordered cutting equipment dropped down the shaft. No way could Prody be simply lifted off the wall – he'd bleed to death in seconds. He had to be cut down with the section of barge hull still embedded in his torso. For the last ten minutes the squawk box had been live with Prody's agonized breathing and the rasp of the hydraulic shear going through the iron. Now the machinery had stopped and a disembodied voice said clearly above the noise Prody was making, '*Prepare to haul.*'

Caffery turned. The Rollgliss pulley system ground to life, the officer at the lip of the air shaft monitoring the spool-up of line. Wellard had already come out of the tunnel and was standing a few feet away, unhooking himself from the harness. Like a demon from hell with his grimy face. There was a line of blood on his face that might be from a scratch on his temple, or might have been someone else's blood.

'What's going on?' Caffery yelled.

'They're bringing him out now,' he shouted back. 'They've worked like bastards.'

'The girls?'

He shook his head. Grim. 'Nothing. We've searched every inch of the place. The barge and through into the next section of tunnel. It's unstable as hell in there – can't keep the team down there a minute longer than we have to.'

'What about Prody? Is he speaking?'

'No. Says he's going to tell you when he comes out. Wants to tell you to your face.'

'Well?' Caffery yelled. 'Do we believe him or is he stalling?'

'I don't know. How long's a piece of string?'

Caffery sucked air through his teeth. Put his hands flat on his stomach to keep the rolling fear still. He looked at the lip of the shaft. At the complex pulley system laboriously cranking away. The lines from the tripod buffeted the shrubs that clung to the side of the shaft, cut gouges into the soft soil at the lip.

'And *haul*,' came the voice from the squawk box. 'Haul.'

Fifty yards away through the trees Flea was being loaded on to the helicopter. The rotors were engaged, picking up speed and the forest was drowned with noise again. The team from the second helicopter was arriving at the edge of the shaft. Two male air paramedics and a woman who, if it hadn't been for the word 'doctor' emblazoned across the back of her green flying suit, could have passed for a gone-to-seed pole-dancer. A short ugly pug of a woman with broken veins on her nose, a scowl and bleached-blonde hair. She carried herself like a centre forward, her solid shoulders set broad and square, her steps slightly wide, as if the muscles on her inner thighs stopped her bringing her feet together.

He came and stood next to her. Quite close. 'Detective Inspector Caffery,' he murmured, holding out his hand.

'Really?' She didn't shake it or look at him. She put her hands on her hips and peered into the shaft, where the first of the access teams' yellow helmets was visible, ascending from the gloom in fits and starts.

'I want to talk to the casualty.'

'You'll be lucky. The moment he comes out of this hole we're getting him into the paraffin parrot over there. His injuries aren't going to let us give him any treatment in the field.'

'Do you know who he is?'

'Doesn't matter who he is.'

'Yes, it does matter. He knows where those two little girls are. He's going to tell me before you get into the HEMS.'

'If we waste any time we're going to lose him. I'll make you that guarantee.'

'He's still breathing.'

She nodded. 'I can hear. He's breathing fast. Tells me he's lost so much blood we're going to be lucky to get him to the hospital at all. The moment he breaks surface he's in that 'copter.'

'Then, I'm coming with you.'

She gave him a long look. Then a smile. Almost pitying. 'Let's see what sort of state he's in when he comes to the surface, shall we?' She lifted her face to the officers. 'When he comes out it's going to be everything on full alert, so this is the protocol. You,' she pointed to two of the men, 'at the top two corners of the stretcher, and the rest of you at the bottom. I'll give you a warning, "prepare to lift", then the order "lift". We go straight to the 'copter. Get it?'

Everyone nodded and peered dubiously into the shaft. The squealing noise of the pulley system reached across the clearing. Caffery yelled at the CSI officer who'd videoed the last twenty minutes next to the air shaft. 'Is that thing recording sound?'

The officer didn't take his eyes off the monitor. He held up a thumb. Nodded.

'You're going to run with me to the helicopter. Get as close as you can – I want to hear every squeak he makes, every fart. Tread on these bastards' toes if you have to.'

'Treat us like professionals,' yelled the doctor, 'and you'll get a lot further.'

Caffery ignored her. He took up position on the edge of the shaft. The ropes were creaking against the tripod. The sound of the heart monitor beeping, and Prody's breathing, were getting louder. The first of the team appeared. Helped by a surface attendant, he scrambled on to the lip of the hole and the two of them turned to help haul the stretcher up. Caffery's palms broke into a sweat. He wiped them on the front of the body armour.

'And *haul*.'

The stretcher came halfway out, pausing at an angle on the lip. 'He's tachycardic.' The accompanying paramedic scrambled out, covered with blood and dirt, holding aloft a drip bag. He was streaming out information to the doctor as he got to his feet. 'Hundred and twenty a minute, respiratory rate is twenty-eight to thirty and the pulse oximeter readings dropped straight out during the ascent – about four minutes ago. No pain relief – not in the state he's in – but I've put up five hundred mils of crystalloids.'

The top team took up the last of the slack and, with one more jerk, the rest of the stretcher was delivered to the hard, cold ground, dislodging a few rocks that bounced and rattled into the echoey dark below. Prody's eyes were closed. His bluish, cyanosed face, sandwiched between the tongues of a neck splint, like a boxer's face guard bulging the flesh on either side of his nose, was expressionless. He was smothered with filth and dried blood. The nylon jogging jacket he'd been wearing had caught fire in the explosion and melted, curling long sections of crisped skin away from his neck and hands. Under the aluminium blanket the stretcher was soaked a dark wet red.

The team got into position at each corner, squatting, ready to lift. As they did Prody began to tremble.

'Wait. He's fitting.' The doctor dropped to a crouch next to the stretcher and studied the portable monitor. 'We're losing that heart rate . . .'

'What?' said Caffery. 'What's happening?' Under the fake tan the doctor's face was hard and concentrated. Caffery's mouth was dry. 'He was fine a second ago. What happened?'

'He was never fine,' the doctor yelled. 'I told you that. He's forty-five beats a minute, forty, yes, he's lost it – he's gone straight to bradycardia now, and before you know it he'll—'

The monitor emitted a long, continuous tone.

'Shit. Cardiac arrest. Chest compressions, someone. I'm going to intubate.'

A paramedic leaned over and began compressions. Caffery inched himself between the two paramedics and got to his knees on the blood-soaked grass. '*Paul*,' he yelled. '*You piece of shit. Paul? You'd better fucking speak to me, that's all. You'd better fucking speak to me.*'

'Out of my way.' The doctor had sweat on her face as she slid the laryngeal mask into Prody's slack mouth, fitted the bag valve to it. 'I said, out of my way. Let me do my job.'

Caffery dropped back on to his heels, pressed his finger and thumb either side of his forehead, squeezed his temples and took long, deep breaths. Fuck fuck fuck. He was going to be beaten. Not by the bitch of a doctor, but by Prody himself. The bastard. The clever bastard couldn't have worked it any better.

The doctor kept squeezing the bag, the paramedic continued the compressions, counting aloud. The line on the monitor stayed steady, the tone echoing around the trees. In the clearing no one moved. Every officer in the place had been turned to stone and was watching, appalled, as the paramedic kept pumping.

'No.' After less than a minute she stopped squeezing the bag and let it rest on Prody's chest. She put her hand on the paramedic's arm to stop him doing the compressions. 'He's in asystole – flatline. His capillary refill's not happening. Really, this is futile. Are we in agreement we stop?'

'You're kidding me.' Caffery couldn't keep still. 'You're just going to let him die?'

'He's dead already. He's never going to make it. He's lost too much blood.'

'I don't fucking believe I'm hearing this. Do something. De-fucking-fibrillate him or something.'

'No point. There's no blood left in him. He's shut down. We can stimulate his heart until the cows come home, but if there's no blood to pump . . .'

'I said fucking *do* something.'

She gave him a long, steady look. Then she shrugged. 'All right.' With a tight, irritated expression, she unzipped her green emergency rucksack and pulled out a set of boxes, shook two foil wrappers out of them. 'Let me show you how futile this is. Adrenalin, one mil to ten thousand. This would jump-start the *Titanic*.' She opened the first wrapper with her teeth and took out a preloaded syringe, which she handed to the paramedic. 'Follow it with this one – three milligrams atropine and run it through with twenty-five-mil saline.'

The paramedic opened the drugs port on the Venflon and pushed in the drugs, flushed it through to make sure it got to the heart. Caffery stared at the monitor. The flatline didn't move. Across the stretcher the doctor wasn't looking at the monitor, she was watching him with steady eyes. 'Well,' she said, 'there's the defibrillator. Do you want me to turn it on, make him jump up and down like a puppet? Or are you satisfied I know what I'm talking about?'

Caffery dropped his hands and sat helplessly in the grass, staring at Prody's slack, yellowing body, the waxy mask of death creeping silently across his face. The steady straight heart-rate line on the monitor. The doctor was checking her watch for time of death and, seeing her do it, Caffery jerked to his feet, turning his back on her as quickly as he could. He put his hands into his pockets and walked twenty yards away, through the crunching frozen grass. He stood at the edge of the clearing, where a pile of felled silver birch blocked the path. He tilted up his chin, tried to concentrate on the sky beyond the branches. On the clouds.

He wished and prayed for something natural and calm to come and lie cool against his thoughts. He could feel Rose and Janice watching all this from the trees. He'd known they were there for the last half an hour, had long felt their eyes boring into the side of his head, but he hadn't acknowledged them or moved them on. They were waiting for him to take the futile, scattered set of facts out of the clearing and bring them down to a calm, measured plan of action. And how the hell was he going to do that now that the only person who could give them a clue about where Martha and Emily were was lying dead on a stretcher in the grass?

80

The men pulling Emily and Martha out of the hole were smiling. They were laughing and shouting at each other, raising their hands in victorious salutes. Both girls had sheets of the purest white tucked around them. Martha was pale, but Emily was pink and happy and completely unmarked, and was sitting up on the stretcher, leaning forward and trying to see Janice among the crowd, craning her neck eagerly. The clearing was full of golden light. Light and laughter and people turning to smile at her, and in Janice's dream no one wore coats or frowns or had to stand with their backs to her to hide their expressions from her. In Janice's dream everyone floated in a summery haze and there were clumps of bluebells under her feet as she crossed to take Emily's hand.

In front of her eyes the mean reality was that the clearing was nearly empty. The helicopters had long gone, the teams had all packed up, harnesses had been removed, equipment returned to vans. The officer in charge had taken the names and contact details of every officer involved and had let them go. In the middle of the clearing, Prody's body was being loaded on a stretcher into the coroner's van. A doctor walked next to it, the sheet lifted so he could scrutinize Prody's face.

Janice was freezing. She had cramps in her legs from crouching and her muscles were weak from the adrenalin constantly flooding through them. Thorns had come through her torn tights and were drawing lines of blood from her knees and feet. The girls weren't in the tunnel, Prody was dead and, judging from the way Caffery and Nick were standing – about twenty feet away among the trees, backs turned, talking in low urgent voices – he hadn't given the police any information at all. But somehow Janice was calm. From somewhere she'd found the strength not to buckle but to stand without moving and simply wait to hear.

Rose, on the other hand, was fragmenting. She was about a yard away, pacing to and fro in a little clearing surrounded by young ash trees that seemed to bend in around her as if they were studying her, or protecting her. Her trousers were muddy, flecked with leaves and the black smudges of the withered blackberries they'd been crouching among; she was shaking her head and muttering into the pink scarf, which she held pressed against her mouth with one hand. Strangely, the madder she seemed, the closer to the edge she got, the calmer and more icily controlled Janice became. When Nick began to cross the clearing towards them, head ominously lowered, Janice was able to stand her ground and wait, while Rose immediately began speaking, clutching at Nick's sleeves. 'What did he say? What's happening?'

'We're doing everything we can. We've got several leads. Prody's wife has given us several—'

'He must have said *something*.' Rose immediately began to weep bitterly. Her hands down at her sides, mouth open in a stiff O, her face naked like a helpless little girl in a playground. 'He must have said where they are. Anything, please, anything.'

'His wife has given us several leads and there are some keys in his pockets, which look like they're from a garage. We're going to search it. And—'

'*No!*' Out of nowhere Rose began to scream, high-pitched, stuttering shrieks that made everyone left in the clearing turn to look. She groped wretchedly at Nick's jacket, trying to shake some different news out of her. 'Search the tunnel again. *Search the tunnel.*'

'Rose! Sssh, now. They've searched the tunnel. It's *empty.*'

But Rose had spun herself round and was yelling at the few officers left in the clearing, her arms jerking up and down. '*Search it again! Search it again!*'

'Rose, listen. *Rose!*' Nick tried to catch the flailing arms. Tried to pin them to Rose's sides. She had to keep her face back, her eyes half closed, to avoid being socked by one of the crazily wheeling hands. 'They can't go back in – it's too dangerous. Rose! *Listen!* They can't go in again – *Rose!*'

Rose threw herself away, still screaming, her hands moving faster, like a wounded bird trying to get some lift. She took a few tottery steps forward, found she'd come to a tree, half turned as if to head off in another direction, turned again, seemed to stagger a little, then, as if she'd been shot in the knees, dropped to the ground. Her whole body folded till her forehead was touching the earth. Her hands came up and she grabbed the back of her neck as if she was trying to force her face into the ground. She rocked back and forth, bellowing into the frozen earth, a long trail of spittle drooping from her mouth and wetting the soil.

Janice came and knelt in the brambles. Her own heart was racing, but the controlled thing inside her was growing. Growing and getting harder. 'Rose.' She put a hand on the older woman's back. 'Listen.'

At her voice Rose stopped rocking and quietened.

'Listen. We've got to move on. We're in the wrong place, but there's somewhere else. His wife's helping us now. We're going to find them.'

Slowly Rose raised her head. Above the little scarf her face was a jumbled knot of red flesh and mucus.

'Really, Rose, I promise. We'll find them. His wife's a good person. She is and she's going to help us.'

Rose rubbed her nose. 'Do you think so?' she whispered, her voice tiny. 'Do you really think so?'

Janice took a breath and looked back at the clearing. The coroner's van was pulling away, the officer in charge was making his way back towards the car park and the last of the teams slammed the door on their van. Something wanted to bubble up through the calm – hard and bitter and desperate – wanted to wrench itself out from the hole that would never be filled. But she swallowed it and nodded. 'I do. Now get up. That's it. Get up and let's move on.'

81

Flea wasn't sure what they'd put in the drip but she knew she'd give half a year's wages for another shot of it. She tried to say that to the paramedic who locked down her trolley in the helicopter, tried to yell it at him as the rotors started. Maybe he'd heard it all before or maybe she still wasn't making any sense when she spoke, because he just smiled, nodded and gestured for her to keep still and lie back. So she stopped trying. She lay and watched the way the webbing inside the helicopter's roof vibrated and merged. Smelt the fresh blue air coming in through the hatch. Aviation fuel and sunlight.

Her eyes closed. She drifted back into the dream. Let it fold itself around her like white wings. She was just a dot in the sky. A pirouetting dandelion seed. Above her the sky was cloudless. Below her the land spread out with its English patchwork of colours. No shadows on it. Just dreamless greens and browns. She saw a forest. Thick and plush. Small clearings with deer grazing in them. She saw people down there. Some picnicking. Some standing in groups. Among the cracked greenish trunks of ash trees that lined a track, she saw three women walking towards a car park: one woman was in oilskin, one in a pink scarf and one in a green coat. The woman in the green coat had no shoes on. She had her arm around the one in the scarf. They both walked with their heads so low they looked as if they might topple over at any minute.

Flea twisted away. She floated across the tops of the trees. She saw the top of the air shaft, cinders floating gently around it. From her vantage-point she could see all the way into the tunnel. Could hear noises. A child crying. And it came back to her. Martha's body. In the pit. It was still there. Something had to be done about it.

She lifted her head. Looked around herself – saw police cars and vehicles leaving the area. Saw the miles and miles of roads stretching away into the distance like a bleached yellow spider's web sprawled out across the winter land. On the lane that snaked away towards the big motorway in the south, bleak sunlight flashed off the roof of a car. Tiny – like a Tonka toy. She fixed her eyes on it and swivelled to face it, waiting for the elemental force to come and take her. It took her by the shoulders and slid her head first across the air, through the clouds. The fields and the trees rushed away beneath her, she saw the road, closed in on it until she could see the fabric of it, its very grain, moving fast. Up ahead she saw the top of the car. The wind was visible like quick-silver, undulating over the car roof as she neared. It was a plain silver Mondeo. The sort some of the specialist units used. She slowed, got level with the car, and drifted down. Hovered next to the passenger window, her hand resting on the wing mirror.

Inside there were two men wearing suits. The one who was driving she recognized vaguely, but it was the man sitting nearest her in the passenger seat – a distant expression on his face – who got her attention. Jack. Jack Caffery. The only man in the world who could burst her heart into pieces with just a look.

'Jack?' She put her face to the window. Knocked on it. He didn't turn. Just sat, staring, his head moving slackly with the motion of the car. 'Jack.'

He didn't respond. His face was so defeated, so lacking in energy or hope, he looked as if he could cry at any moment. He wore body armour over a shirt and tie and there was blood on his sleeves. He must have tried to wipe some of it off, but he'd missed places. Little rusty lines circled his wrists. She pushed her face through the glass. Nuzzled it gently in through the melting milky translucence until she was in the car itself, smelling the thick, overheated air. The combination of aftershave, sweat and exhaustion. She put her lips against his ear. Felt the faint burr of his hair against her nose. 'She's under the tunnel floor,' she whispered. 'He dug down. Put her in a pit. A *pit*, Jack. A pit.'

Caffery put his finger in his ear. Wiggled it.

'A pit, that's what I said. A pit in the floor of the canal.'

Caffery couldn't get rid of the sound of Prody's wheezing. His death rattle. It wouldn't go away. It kept buzzing in his right ear. He poked at his ear, rubbed it. Shook his head. But it was as if someone was sitting close to him, hissing at him.

'Pit.' The word came at him suddenly. 'A pit.'

Turner shot him a sideways look. 'Do what, Boss?'

'A pit. *A pit*. A fucking pit.'

'What about it?'

'I don't know.' He sat forward, looking out of the window at the road markings racing under them. The sun flashed blindingly into his eyes. His head was moving again. Fast this time. Really fast. Pit. He tested the word in his mouth. Wondered why it had appeared completely formed in his head. *Pit*. A hole in the ground. A place to hide things. Search teams were trained to do a 360-degree sweep. He'd been caught out by that before. Looking everywhere except *up*. The way they hadn't looked up to find Prody in the tunnel. But looking *down*. Looking further than the ground beneath your feet, looking *through* it. That was something he'd never thought of.

'Boss?'

Caffery drummed his fingers on the dashboard. 'Clare said her sons were scared to death of the police.'

'Beg pardon?'

'Somehow he'd made them think the police were their enemies. The last people to turn to.'

'What's your point?'

'What's the first thing the team yelled when they went into the tunnel?'

'The first thing they yelled? I dunno. Probably "Police", yeah. That's what they're supposed to do, isn't it?'

'Where was Prody when the teams searched the tunnel?'

Turner gave Caffery a strange look, as if he'd grown an extra head. 'He was in the tunnel, Boss. He was with them.'

'Yeah. And what was he doing all that time?'

'He was . . .' Turner shook his head. 'I dunno. Where's this going? He was dying, I guess.'

'Think about it. He was *breathing*. And loud. You heard it. No one could get away from that sound. It didn't stop from the time of the explosion to the time they came out. You wouldn't have been able to hear anything else down there.'

'They searched the tunnel, Boss. They searched it. The girls weren't there. Whatever you're thinking I don't know how you got to it.'

'I don't know how either, Turner, but it's time you turned this car round.'

82

Janice didn't know how her body would stand this. Her bones and muscles felt like water. She thought her head might explode with the pressure. She stood with her back to the trunk of a silver birch, holding Rose's hand, both of them staring blankly at the clearing. Everything was different. It was no longer the despondent, silent place they'd left half an hour ago. Now the area around the shaft was crawling with people: officers were yelling at each other, equipment that had been packed away was being hastily unpacked. Another medical helicopter had landed and was sitting with its rotors motionless in the clearing. Two pulley tripods had been set up and two men had been lowered into the shaft. Janice knew the burrowing and panicked shouting that must be happening in the darkness a hundred feet below, but what she really couldn't take were the worried expressions on the surface. That awful bloody seriousness. Nick stood a little in front of Rose and Janice, her hands in her pockets, her face grave. It had been Nick who, driving Janice's Audi back along the A419, had noticed cars coming fast in the other direction, sunlight reflecting off their windscreens. She'd recognized them as unmarked unit cars and knew what it meant. She'd swung the Audi into a lay-by, three-point-turned across two lanes of traffic and floored it back up the road after the cars. This time no one had tried to stop the women coming to watch. No one seemed to have the time.

'Stretchers,' Nick said suddenly. 'Two stretchers.'

Janice stiffened. She and Rose jerked their heads forward as four paramedics came across the clearing at a trot. Their faces were flat, focused. They gave nothing away. 'Stretchers?' Her heart began to thump deafeningly. 'Nick? What does that mean? Stretchers? What does it mean?'

'I don't know.'

'Does it mean they're alive? They wouldn't send stretchers in if they were dead. Would they?'

Nick was silent, biting her lip.

'Would they, Nick? Would they?'

'I don't know. I really don't know.'

'Those are more paramedics going into the shaft,' she hissed. 'What does that mean? Tell me what it means.'

'I don't know, Janice – I promise. Please don't get your hopes up. It might be for one of the search team.'

The hard centre that Janice had kept rigid till now gave way with a soft, exhausted slump. 'Oh, God,' she whispered, twisting to Rose, her throat tight, 'Rose, I can't do it.'

It was Rose's turn to be strong. She caught Janice around the waist, taking her weight as she leaned heavily against her.

'I'm sorry, Rose, I'm sorry.'

'It's OK.' Rose got her steady, lifted Janice's arms over her own shoulders. She dropped her forehead so it touched the other woman's. 'It's OK. I've got you. Just keep breathing. That's it. Slowly. Keep breathing.'

Janice did as she was told, feeling the cold air come through her nose and down into her lungs. Tears ran down her face. She didn't try to stop them, just let them trickle off her chin and splash into the dead leaves at her feet. Nick came to stand behind the two women and rested her hands on their backs. 'God, Janice,' she muttered. 'I wish I could do more. Just wish I could do more for you both.'

Janice didn't answer. She could smell Nick's perfume and the rich, woody odour of her oilskin jacket. She could smell Rose's breath and hear her heart thumping. That heart, she thought, feels the same as mine does. Two human hearts pressed one to the other. Each one aching in the same way. There were embroidered flowers on Rose's sweater. Roses. Roses for Rose. There had been roses on the wallpaper in the house at Russell Road. She remembered lying in bed as a child and fixing her eyes on the pattern, willing it to make her sleep. Thank God for you, Rose, she thought. Thank God you exist.

Someone was shouting.

'OK,' said Nick. 'Something's happening.'

Janice's face jolted up, her mouth open. The pulley systems were moving. Caffery was there, about fifty yards away, his back to them. A man wearing a blue headset stood close to him, one earphone lifted, and Caffery was leaning into it, listening to whatever was being said. Everyone else was standing at the hole, peering down into it. They were pulling something up. No doubt about it. Caffery's body tightened – she saw it, even from behind. This was it. It really was happening. Her hands tightened on Rose's shoulders.

Caffery pulled away from the man, his face ashen. He shot a look over his shoulder at the women, saw them watching and turned back hurriedly so they couldn't see his expression. Janice felt her insides crumble, her legs buckle. A rushing sensation flooded her chest, as if she was freefalling, dropping fast out of the blue. This was it. They were dead. She knew it. He was taking a moment or two to straighten his tie. He did up his jacket and smoothed his hands down it, took a deep breath, pulled his shoulders up and turned to them. He walked woodenly, and when he got close to them Janice saw his skin was grey under his eyes.

'Let's sit down.'

They sat in a rough circle, the three women on the trunk of a fallen tree, Caffery on its stump opposite them. Janice sat with her hands in her hair, her teeth chattering. Caffery put his elbows on his knees and leaned forward, looking at the women intently. Nick couldn't take this either – she dropped her eyes to the ground.

'I'm sorry it took us so long to find your girls. I'm sorry you've had such a long wait.'

'Say it,' Janice said. 'Please. Just say it.'

'Yes.' He cleared his throat. 'Prody made a pit. Under the side of the canal. It's quite small, covered with corrugated iron and in it we found a travel trunk. He put them in there, both of them, and they're . . .'

'*Please, God,*' Janice whispered. '*Please, God.*'

He gave her a broken, apologetic look. 'They're very sad. They're very scared and very hungry. And above everything they want their mums.'

Janice leaped up, her heart thumping.

'*Janice*, wait. Let the doctors—'

But she pushed past him, and Nick – who jumped to her feet to stop her – ran into the clearing, her coat flying open. Rose, too, broke free and came running up behind her, crying open-mouthed, heading clumsily up the slope. Someone to their right was laughing. A great, happy, jubilant sound. Three men were clapping each other on the shoulder. Two officers at the shaft saw the women coming and put out their hands to stop them a few feet from the edge, but this time their faces weren't the awful closed-down concentrated masks they had been an hour ago: this time they were almost smiling as the two women came bumping into them, panting and gasping.

'Wait here. You can see everything, just wait here.'

Both pulleys were turning on the tripods. A head in a caving helmet appeared, and a man scrambled out on his knees, holding a drip bag. He turned on the lip of the shaft and waited for the surface team to haul the stretcher on to the ground, settling it a few feet from the hole. It was Martha, swaddled in an aluminium blanket, her face rigid, bewildered by the sights and sounds and the light. A woman in green trousers and a huge waterproof jacket was yelling something and, out of nowhere, paramedics were swarming everywhere. Rose made a loud noise, like a choke, and broke past the two men, ignoring the hands trying to hold her back; she dropped to her knees next to the stretcher and fell across Martha's chest, babbling and crying.

In the shaft someone else was yelling. The second surface crew were leaning down into the hole. Another head in a red caving helmet appeared.

'And *haul*,' someone shouted. 'That's it – *haul*.'

Jerkily the man's head shot up another few feet. Janice couldn't breathe. His face was tilted, concentrating on what was happening below him, sweat dripping down his neck. Another wrench on the pulley and the back of the stretcher appeared, bumping and turning against the edge of the shaft. The pulley attendant reached down to take the weight. As he did the stretcher pivoted slightly and Emily's face was there.

The hard bundle of grief and terror that had been trapped against Janice's heart broke. It flowed around her body. She had to put out a hand to keep her balance and stop herself falling to her knees. Emily's hair was wet, smoothed back against her head, and her face was pale. But her eyes were bright and alive. Darting all over the place, up and down, taking in what was happening, the great drop beneath her, the people gathered on the edge of the shaft. The man next to her on the pulley said something to her, a gentle joke. She turned, looked into his face and smiled.

She smiled. Emily *smiled*.

As Janice stood on the grass, she felt a warmth go up her spine, encase her head in a glow. She felt the warmth unzipping her chest, letting her heart rise up and breathe. Just like in the dream she'd had. Emily looked at her – right into her eyes.

'Mum,' she said simply.

Janice put up her hand and smiled. 'Hey, baby,' she said. 'We missed you.'

83

The pharmaceuticals compound lay in a slight dip on the arid plateau land of south Gloucestershire – a pocket of industrialization dwarfed by the royal hunting estates that haughtily covered much of the county. The police units had used GPR – ground-probing radar – and body dogs brought in all the way from London. All day long they'd worked, gridding the place out, using laser theodolites, then methodically treading every inch, moving machinery, if necessary, working along the wall of the warehouse.

Locally the little huddles of trees that were scattered around the area were known not as copses but by the quaint nineteenth-century name 'covert'. The nearest, slightly elevated one was known as Pine Covert and tonight, lit gold and red by the sunset but unnoticed from the factory, two men stood in the shelter of its trees and watched the progress of the team silently. DI Caffery and the man they called the Walking Man.

'Who do they think they're searching for?' said the Walking Man. 'Not my daughter. They wouldn't be taking this much care if they thought it was my daughter.'

'No. I told them they were looking for Misty Kitson.'

'Ah, yes. The pretty one.'

'The famous one. The biggest monkey on my unit's back.'

All afternoon the sun had crawled obliquely across the sky, lighting but never warming the earth, and now that it was sunset, the team began to break up from the debriefing. They trickled out of the perimeter gate under the great arc lights, back to waiting trucks and cars. Caffery and the Walking Man couldn't hear what they were saying, but they could guess.

'It's empty.' The Walking Man stroked his beard ruminatively. 'She's not in there.'

Caffery stood shoulder to shoulder with him. 'I did my best.'

'I know. I know you did.'

The last of the search teams pulled out of the lane leading to the compound and now it was safe to light the fire. The Walking Man turned away and went a few paces back into the covert where he'd gathered some wood into a pile. He took lighter fuel from under a log and shook it on the branches. Chucked on a match. There was a moment's silence, then a loud whoomph. An orange flame fattened to a ball, thinned and unrolled itself up into the branches, sending a blazing finger of red heat and smoke through them. The Walking Man went to another log and began pulling things out from under it – bedrolls, tins of food, his customary flagon of cider.

Caffery watched him distantly, thinking about the map on his office wall. The Walking Man always had these supplies waiting for him, no matter where he made camp. Somehow this – the gargantuan undertaking, the never-ending search for his daughter – was all planned meticulously. But how could it be otherwise? A search for a child: it would go on for ever. The search that would never end. Caffery thought of the look on Rose and Janice's faces when they saw their lost children come back. It was a look that might never cross his own face. Might never cross the Walking Man's.

'We found that nonce. You know. The one who wrote the letter.'

The Walking Man poured the cider into plastic beakers, handed one to Caffery. 'Yes. I saw you had from your face the moment you walked across that field. But he wasn't as straight-forward as you'd hoped.'

Caffery sighed. He looked across the fields to where the town of Tetbury sent an orange glow up against the clouds. Sapperton tunnel was beyond the town, out in the unlit fields. In his mind's eye he saw the two girls being taken towards the helicopter. Two stretchers, two little girls. And between the stretchers a bridge. A pale, delicate bridge made by the girls' arms as Martha, the eldest, reached across the gap and took Emily's hand in hers. For nearly forty hours they'd been lying together in a storage trunk buried under the floor of the tunnel. Hugging each other like twins in a womb, breathing their fears and secrets into each other's faces. When they'd got to hospital and had been examined they were in better shape than they should have been. Prody hadn't touched them. He'd made Martha remove her underwear and had given her a pair of his eldest son's jogging pants to wear. He'd put cartons of apple juice in the trunk and told them he was the police – that this was a top-secret operation to hide them from the real jacker. Because the *real* jacker was the most dangerous man imaginable. A trickster who would do anything, pretend to be anyone. That under no circumstances should the girls make a sound in the trunk if they didn't want to give themselves away – no matter what guises he took on.

Martha had taken some time to believe him. Emily, who'd been introduced to Prody as a police officer in the safe-house, had swallowed the story. He'd given them sweeties when he told them all this. He'd been kind. He'd been handsome and strong and easy to believe. That was just the way it sometimes went when a child was abducted.

'Sit.' The Walking Man brought out plates from under the log. 'Sit down.'

Caffery sat on a thin bedroll. The ground was freezing. The Walking Man placed the tins and the plates near the fire to start cooking when the fire was ready. He poured his own beaker of cider and settled down.

'And so . . .' He waved his hand at the enclosure the team had searched. 'For this? For doing this for me? What do I give you? Not my anger, that's for sure. Have to take back my anger and swallow it.'

'What can you give me?'

'I can't give you your brother back. I know that's what you're hoping, but I can't tell you anything about him.'

'You can't tell me or you won't?'

The Walking Man laughed. 'I've told you, Jack Caffery, until I'm worn to a shadow with telling it – I'm a human being, not a super-human. Do you believe that an ex-con frittering away his pathetic life on the lanes of the West Country could really know what happened to a boy thirty years ago, more than a hundred miles away in London?'

The Walking Man was right. In the back of Caffery's head he really had believed that somehow this opaque, soft-voiced vagrant might know something about what had happened all those years ago. He held out his hands to the fire. His car was a hundred yards away, just out of sight from the copse. No Myrtle in it: she'd gone back to the Bradleys. Stupid, but he missed the damned dog.

'Tell me about the circle, then. The nice little circle. That me protecting the woman is a nice circle.'

The Walking Man smiled. 'It's against my principles to give you anything for nothing. But this is an exception because you helped me. So I give it to you freely – and I tell you openly that I saw what happened that night.'

Caffery stared at him.

The Walking Man nodded. 'The monkey on the force's back? The pretty one? I saw her die.'

'*How?* How the hell did you . . . ?'

'Easy. I was there.' He waved a gnarly finger in the air to the south, towards Wiltshire. 'Up on a hillside, minding my own business. I told you – all you have to do is open your head: you open it and suddenly it's full of truths you never expected.'

'Truths? Jesus – what are you talking about? What truths?'

'The truth that it wasn't the woman who killed your monkey.' The Walking Man's face was lit red from the fire. His eyes gleamed. 'That it was a man.'

Caffery kept breathing in and out. Slowly. Not giving anything away on his face. A man. Everything in his head began to lower itself, fit itself into what seemed now to be an obvious and a simple pattern that had been waiting a long time for this moment. A man who killed Misty? And Flea had protected him? It would have been her shithead brother. No doubt about it. Caffery got to this knowledge so easily, so unsurprisingly, that it was as if it had been there all along, just waiting to be nudged out from the debris.

'So, Mr Caffery, my friendly policeman,' the Walking Man looked up at the branches, lit in the reds and the oranges of the fire, 'what does this truth give you?' He turned and smiled at him. 'A place to stand? Or a place to start?'

Caffery was silent for a long, long time. He thought about what it meant. Flea's fucking brother all along. He thought about his anger. He thought about all the things he wanted to say to her. He got up, went to the edge of the covert and stood facing the sky. In the distance, near the long-forgotten Wor Well where the ancient river Avon rose, the plateau dipped slightly. The flanks of the hollow were dotted with distant buildings on the edge of Tetbury. Houses and garages and industrial buildings. A hospital. The place Flea Marley had been taken by the helicopter. Most of the buildings had their lights on, illuminating the dark plateau like fireflies in trees. One of them was the room she lay in.

'Well? Is it a place to stand, or a place to start?'

'You know the answer to that.' Caffery felt his foot inch forward. Felt a long, powerful force come through his body. As if he was ready to start running. 'It's a place to start.'

84

The smoke from the Walking Man's fire rose straight and calm into the night sky. It climbed high above the dark trees, unruffled by winds or breeze, just a straight grey finger in the freezing night sky. It was visible for miles around, from the streets of Tetbury, from the farmhouses that lined the sides of the valley, from the agricultural buildings in Long Newnton and the lanes near Wor Well. In a private room in Tetbury hospital, Flea Marley slept. She'd come in with severe concussion, blood loss, creeping hypothermia, dehydration. But the CAT scans were clear. She was going to recover. When they'd got her out of A and E, Wellard had visited, holding a bunch of lilies wrapped in cellophane and purple ribbons. 'I ordered funeral flowers. Because when your real funeral comes around after you've *killed* yourself being an *arse*, I won't be in the church.' He'd sat grumpily on the plastic chair and filled her in about what had happened. He'd told her about Prody dying. He'd told her it hadn't just been Martha down there but Emily Costello too, that both of them were fine and were somewhere in this very hospital, their families bringing in treats and toys and cards. And the unit – well, that was a great song to sing, because Flea was smelling of roses, positively *bathed* in admiration, and she'd better get clean pyjamas from somewhere because the chief constable intended coming over in the morning to see her before she was discharged.

In her dreams now she was at home. The storm clouds had disappeared. Thom had gone and she was younger. Maybe only three or four. She was sitting in the gravel outside the garage, playing with the caving lamp, trying with her pudgy child's fingers to make it ignite. The family cat was still a kitten, and standing next to her, both front paws close to Flea's hands, its tail pushed up in the air, all its energy focused on what she was doing. A few feet away, on the lawn, Dad was digging and raking, scattering grass seed. 'There.' He watered the seeds with an old-fashioned watering-can. 'There you are. It's finished.'

Flea put down the lamp. She got up, came to where he was standing and looked down at the ground. Already some of the seeds had started to grow. Small, emerald shoots. 'Dad? What is it? What am I looking at?'

'At your place. Your place in the world.' He lifted a hand to invite her to take in the view: the tall clouds in the west, the lines of trees that bordered the gardens. An arrow of birds flying overhead. 'This is your place and if you wait here for long enough, if you're patient, something good will come to you. Who knows? Maybe it's on its way. Even now.'

Flea could feel the ground vibrating under her feet. She lifted her chubby toddler's arms and opened them to the horizon, thrilled excitement bubbling up inside. She took a step forward to welcome what was coming, eager for it. She opened her mouth to speak – and woke suddenly in the hospital bed, gulping for air.

The room was silent. The TV was off and the lights in the room were dim. The curtains were open and she could see her own vague outline reflected in the glass. A face, white and imprecise. The blur of a hospital gown. And beyond it the cloudless sky. The stars, the moon – and a thin, almost biblically straight column of smoke.

She stared at the smoke, her head racing, feeling the power of it come across the sky, push through the glass, enter the room and feed itself into her chest. She could almost smell it. Here – as if something was smouldering in the room. Awed, she propped herself on her elbows, eyes wide, the pressure in her chest deep enough to make her open her mouth to breathe. Maybe it was seeing Dad so clearly in the dream, maybe it was the concussion, or the drugs they'd given her, but that smoke seemed to be sending her a message

Something's coming, it said. *Something is on its way to you.*

'Dad?' she whispered. 'What's coming?'

Relax, came the reply. *It won't be long before it's here.*

Acknowledgements

Thank you to everyone who has helped me complete this book: my agent, Jane Gregory, and her wonderful team in Hammersmith, also Selina Walker and everyone else at Transworld publishers, who have been publishing me for ten years now (mad fools). Frank Wood of Elizabeth Francis (Medicall) helped me make the paramedics in the closing chapters approximate reality, and there was a whole army of professionals from the Avon and Somerset force who guided me with the details of police procedures (any mistakes are all mine, and no one is going to claim them for their own): including DI Steven Lawrence, CID trainer, PC Kerry Marsh of the Child Abuse Protection and Investigation Team, PC Andy Hennys of the Dog Section, and PC Steve Marsh of the Underwater Search Unit. Above all, a special thank you to Sergeant Bob Randall, who was as invaluable, insightful and helpful on this book as he has been on the entire series.